The Hunger and the Howling of Killian Lone

WILL STORR

First published in 2013 by
Short Books, 3A Exmouth House, Pine Street, EC1R 0JH

10 9 8 7 6 5 4 3 2 1

Copyright © Will Storr 2013

A CIP catalogue record for this book
is available from the British Library.

Printed in Great Britain by CPI Group (UK) Ltd, Croydon, CR0 4YY

Illustrations © Anna Trench 2013
Cover design: Leo Nickolls
Cover typography: Ami Smithson

Illustrations by Anna Trench

For Craig

"I felt like a boat built of hopeless material, of rotten old wood, launched by the shipbuilder onto the stormy sea of life with the words: 'If you sink it will be your own fault, and you will burn in hell for your failure, burn forever in the eternal flames.'"

Edvard Munch (1883–1944)

"Hoot ffir and smoke makith many an angry cook."

15th-century epigram

There are no ghosts, there are only stories too stubborn to die.

That's all that I am today.

I'm the low ache of sadness long forgotten by the living; the tension of hopes unfulfilled. Always here and always watching, I'm a pressure; a shadow; an uneasy corner.

I am a remains.

It's true, of course, that everyone living is surrounded by the unresolved stories of the dead. But my tale lingers with more weight than most. Indeed, the few visitors that make it here, to Kathryn's lonely cottage in East Sussex, tend to sense my presence the moment they walk through the door.

From the day that she arrived, Kathryn has been surrounded by it. It's seen her every dawn and every sunset; witnessed every moment of rage, sorrow and love. It's stayed with her as she's moved through these rooms with the seasons circling around her.

She's never been able to shut my story out because it's her story too. It tells of blood and splendour, of hope and damage and of the love that grew between us, during those long-gone months.

And now, as the paramedics work in a huddle over her body, they can sense it hovering about them. Lifting her stretcher and manoeuvring it gently out of Dor Cottage, they would surely be amazed to hear of the events that have haunted this pale, reduced woman. Indeed, they are too young even to have heard of Killian Lone.

On the night that I left her, I made Kathryn a promise of loyalty. I meant it to be one final act of goodness; a desperate attempt to erase all the bad. In life, you see, I was a bad man. I did bad things.

And today, here I am – a tale inside whose final scene Kathryn has spent three decades.

A tale that must be told, now, for the last time.

It begins in my boyhood.

In this very kitchen.

1

I was born crying on an early day of frost in October 1965 and the first words that my mother ever said to me were "skin and bone". The nurse who had placed me in her arms gently chided her, "Oh really, Mrs Lone, he's perfectly healthy."

"Well, he is breathing," said my mother, with a reluctant nod. "I suppose that's a start..."

She told this story repeatedly throughout my childhood. I'm not entirely sure why. But I know the thought that lay behind those words. After nine and a half months of pregnancy and thirty-six hours of labour, it wasn't me that she wanted to see at all. It was her best friend Margaret's baby, born nine months before me. Margaret had a swimming pool in her garden and the best extension on our cul-de-sac. Everything she wore, drove in or commented upon was discussed jealously in our home. When Margaret gave birth to Mark, he was commonly described as a "belting, strapping little thing", and that is exactly how he was to grow up. Mark House, with his fair hair and his wide shoulders and his handsome smile that triggered a hundred coos from a hundred envious mothers as he was paraded around the Tonbridge Sainsbury's in his John Lewis pushchair. Mark, with his football playing and his athletics medals and his fighting.

To my mother's endlessly replaying disappointment, it was clear that I would never be Mark, even as a newborn. I

instinctively turned my head when someone peered down at me with their huge grown-up face, and I cried and cried and didn't stop crying for three weeks following my birth. Doctor Feiglen assured my parents that there was nothing wrong with me, insisting to my sceptical mother that I was "just a bit colicky". Nevertheless, my wailing continued. It did so until the day I was taken on my first visit to my great-aunt Dorothy's peculiar old cottage deep in the Sussex Downs. Dorothy had spent the morning baking loaves and the moment the first warm, woody wafts of the bread leaked from her oven and stroked my nose, I finally stopped bawling and broke out into a gigglish grin.

And so it began. As a little boy, I was only happy when I was eating, cooking or shopping for food. When my mother was in one of her rare good moods, she'd spoil me – sometimes to the point of nausea. My most wonderful memory of her, in that period, was the evening she arrived home early from work and confessed that, as a young girl, she had loved Peach Melba Angel Delight. We drove to the shop and bought packets and packets and packets of it, then made it up in huge serving bowls, sprinkled with hundreds and thousands and Jelly Tots and glacé cherries. We gorged until she was sick. Her vomit, as I held her hand in the bathroom, smelled of the acid-sweet Martini she'd been drinking all afternoon. That night, she insisted that I go to bed with her and hug her until she fell asleep. I lay there, rigid, with my arm around her waist, until I heard her snoring, at which point I climbed over my similarly comatose father and hurried to my room.

But those were the rare times, and they grew ever more infrequent as I became older. From toddler-hood and towards double figures, I remained skin and bone, pale and nervous and rarely far from tears. I learned to do my crying in private, during the long grind of the chores which my mother – exhausted from her work as the manager of a large team of social workers – would set me on. I found it particularly hard to hold myself firm during the last twenty minutes or so of every day, when she would conduct her brief tour of the rooms I'd been working on. The bony pad of her finger would be pressed along fridge tops and down toilet bowls and my punishment for its gathering any grime would begin with me having to suck that finger clean.

For the aspiring bullies of suburban Tonbridge, I was a mobile amusement park. I was regularly hounded by a pack of boys that lived up our cul-de-sac, led by Mark House. And at school? Well, there's someone like me at every school. Do you remember me? I was the one with his back to the playground's chainlink fence at break-time. I was the one whose dirty coat the popular boys would dare the skipping girls to touch. I was the one whose hair was a greasy thatch because I couldn't stand to look in the mirror and because Mum never had time. I was the one full of tears and piss who could crumble under the force of an unsympathetic comment.

The only times I felt truly safe were when I was in my favourite place with my favourite person – the kitchen of Dor Cottage with my Great-aunt Dorothy. She was a retired cookery teacher who had long since left her small school in the nearby village of Herstmonceux. Having lost her girls for ever, she had taken to lecturing me instead. I loved her lessons. I loved the food we cooked together. And, more than anything, I loved being in her kitchen. Never before or since have I felt so powerfully that I was in an enchanted bubble, floating above the jags and bumps of real life.

Dor was the subject of an eccentric and rather eerie family legend. I listened to Dorothy recount it as she worked at the table, the flames from the fire burning in her eyes – which were long and lipped with so many folds and bags they seemed like knots in an ancient oak. As she spoke, I could sense something like fear in her, and something like awe as well. It made her stories wonderfully beguiling. It made me love her even more.

"Have I ever told you, Kill, that this place has been in the family since 1676 and it can never be sold?" she asked. "It was built for Mary Dor, your great, great, great – well, a lot of 'greats', believe you me. Mary was the cook for Thomas Lennard, who lived up at the castle. He was the first earl of Sussex." And then she whispered, as if it was all still too dangerous to say, "What a rogue he was! He loved gambling and cricket and eating, of course. Eating more than anything. He loved Mary's food. Declared she was the greatest cook in England. That's why he built this place for her, so near the castle. But it all went wrong, Kill. They began talking about her, down in the village. Saying her broths were so delicious that there must be some sort of devilry involved in it all. They said her recipes could turn anyone who tasted them mad with uncanny desires. The earl didn't listen, not even when his courtiers started whispering. He was too batty about her cooking to care. But then something happened. Something to do with his pretty wife, Anne. Well, you're too young to hear about that part. But anyhow, it was all blamed on poor Mary and they had her burned as a witch. It's still there, in the elm forest – the place where they got her. There's a stone post, about as high as my knee, with strange runes carved all over it. I'll show it to you one day. The tourists who go past that thing, eating their ice creams and walking their dogs, they've got no idea what happened there. No idea about any of it. Anyway," she turned away and said, more quietly still, "just promise to remember what I said. This place cannot leave the family. Under no account. Not ever."

My mother always insisted that Dorothy was crazy, and that the stories about our witch ancestor were ridiculous. And, as in most things, I agreed with Mum. But in a vague and quiet place, I couldn't deny my fears. Even as a very young boy I could sometimes detect an atmosphere of brooding or crowding – a sense of misalignment – in the cottage. And my great-aunt believed the stories, I could tell.

The only room in which you could really feel anything of the power of the building's age was the kitchen. The rest of the cottage was scrupulously neat and dusted. The chairs in the lounge were arranged so that they were all the same distance from the small fire. Pictures on the walls were of hay bales, oast houses and apple orchards. In the bathroom, Dorothy's toothbrush had its own plastic case that sat on the third shelf of the cupboard, next to her unopened packages of Pears soap. The waste bins sat in the dead centre of these sort-of oversized home-knitted doilies. This barren, nursemaid tidiness only heightened the sensation you felt when you first stepped down into the kitchen – shock melting quickly into staggered enchant-ment. You felt as if you were travelling back in time. Suddenly, you were in a place of stone and wood and raw flames; amongst layers of history that had been built up by cooks stretching back for generations until it was this mad, tumbling mess of excite-ment. Hundreds of pots, jars and weird implements gave it a feeling of a madman's hoard or a wizard's bazaar. Every space on every wall was used. There were cupboards of all sizes, each of which looked as if it had been hastily built when the last one had become full.

On one wall there were rows and rows of prongs, spines, blades, strainers, peelers, crushers and corers – the fierce weapons of flavour; on another there were shelves stretching right up to the ceiling, whose contents became more dusty and exotic as you increased in altitude. There were glass jars of pickled ephemera, pots of dried goods, bottles of oddly glis-tening powder. I remember one container in particular that seemed to have some sort of primitive hand in it. It hung in this golden liquid, its reptilian knuckle resting against the brown-stained glass as if it was trying to see out. Although a modern gas oven had been installed, Dorothy still used the range, a fantastic iron contraption of doors and chimneys with a thick window through which you could see the flames.

Whilst the décor in all the other rooms was like a thin, fragile skin on the surface of the cottage, in the kitchen you felt as if you were really in amongst the building's guts; in the workings of its exposed, throbbing heart. When, with a little groan, Aunt Dorothy took the long step down into the room, even she seemed to change, the dark, yellowing shades of age rebounding off the walls onto her face and erasing her paleness, making her seem more alive.

It was on a magical November night in the kitchen, when I was eleven, that Dorothy told me a story that would change me for the rest of my life.

She was roasting beef. She had just lifted the part-cooked meat from the oven and was basting it in its tray, and I could hear the bubbling spray of the liquid and smell its rich, oaken, dark-honey fragrance. When the kitchen at Dor was being worked like this – as if its fires were fuelling a powerful engine rather than a simple range – a kind of spell would come over us. As the scents and the sounds and the heat and the steam built up in that small room, it began to feel as if we'd been transported to a different place; as if all the many sensory detonations of cooking had connected us to something timeless; had tuned us into all the countless happy hours that had been spent there by cooks past.

As she spoke, my wonderful aunty would often disappear into a fascinating monologue, during which her eyes would barely graze over me. I'd sit at the end of the kitchen table, as comforted as it was possible to be by the warmth and safety and the words that sang impatiently from her mouth; the renegade knowledge about food from distant ages and cultures, mixed with stubborn opinion on matters of knotty culinary lore. On that night, I was in my usual place – at the table, facing the range. I can still recall the precise distance between my little feet and the cobbled floor and the quality of the light – golden-brown and secretive – and how the fire threw out a thick pillow of warmth whose limit came abruptly at the always-freezing, always-sinister stairs at the back of the room.

"Did I ever tell you, hundreds of years ago, your descendants used to be employed as spitjacks?" she said, spooning the juices back over the richly sweating beef. "Do you know what spitjacks are, Kill? Well, I'll tell you. They used to work by the fire in the kitchens of knights and kings and so on, turning the spits of meat. That all stopped in the 1500s when some bright spark invented a contraption out of wheels and pulleys which meant the work could be carried out by dogs – dogs that had been bred specially for the job. It was that hard, they had to take it in turns to work – one day on, one day off. Have you heard the phrase 'every dog has its day'? Well, that comes from turnspit dogs.

"Oh, but they were terribly ugly things – all bony with crooked legs and sad eyes. They had an awful time of it. They had to work right next to the fire, and you can only imagine the beating they must've got if they got tired. But," she stopped basting for a moment, her eyes glistening, her spoon raised in the air, "their job could not have been more important. England, back then, was a roast country. On the continent, where the sun was hot, meat would rot in the heat almost straight away. That's why your Italians and your French had to invent all those sauces to mask the smell and why the Spanish cured their pork. None of this was necessary in old England. Here, the rivers would freeze in September and thousands of peasants would have their hearts stopped by the frost every winter. For most of the year, the whole country was one great big living fridge. Can you imagine? All we needed to do to create the most wonderful food was to put an iron pole through a lamb or a pig or a cow and turn it in front of a flame. But that meat was valuable. It had to be done with care, slowly and for hours and hours. And that was the job of the turnspit dogs, those poor little creatures."

I think she meant it to be a kind of horror story, something grim to boggle the eyes of a young boy. But that's not the way I heard it. When Dorothy described those dogs, what I heard was a description of myself. Ugly, bony, crooked legs, sad eyes. Every word she said lit a bulb in my head, and when her tale was over, what I saw in the accumulated light was me.

"Oh, but they were such a special, special breed," she said. "They had to be small enough to fit in the wheel, strong enough to walk it and loyal enough not to eat the meat. They were noble dogs, strong in mind and body. They might have looked a bit unusual, but on the inside – I'm telling you, Kill – they were magnificent. No, I've always thought highly of those turnspit dogs, even though they did our forefathers out of a job. I mean, how could you not? They were so loyal! They were heroes. Heroes of the kitchen."

I moved my arm down by my thigh and pushed my hand into a small fist. I didn't know those concepts could go together. Boniness and strength? Ugliness and loyalty? I hadn't known it was possible.

I was only ever talkative when I was with my aunt Dorothy ,and yet that night, as I pushed my knife through the tenderly roasted silverside, I was silent. Dorothy, with her usual sensitivity, seemed to understand that behind my expression of rough-browed concentration something more important than beef was being chewed over. For once she fell quiet and we went about eating our meal listening only to the music of satisfied cutlery.

I don't think I met her eye at all until – honey-sweetened cocoa drunk – it was finally time for bed. I pushed my chair out, and just before looking to the floor to check how far my feet had to drop, I glanced up, seeking from her a final reassurance.

"Ni'night, Kill," she said, elbows deep in washing-up. "Do you want me to tuck you in?"

"No, thanks."

"Good boy." She turned to look at me again. "You sure you're all right, Kill? Nothing you want to talk about?"

I found myself looking at the latest scar from home, up by my left elbow. "I think I'll just go to bed now."

Outside the warm oasis of the kitchen, Dor could be a rather different place. Although most of the days there were soft, bright and charmed, you always had the sense that this bliss was being conferred on you. It was almost as if you were living inside the thoughts and moods of something else; something that was benevolent only because it had decided to be. At dusk, the walls seemed to embrace the end of the day all too greedily, sucking in more night than their due until the weight of the darkness was such that you'd begin to feel its pressure, pushing you out of the rooms. And of all the hostile, watching spaces that came alive in the ancient building after sundown, those old buckled stairs were the worst. Daylight always vanquished the cottage's strangeness, but even on the sunniest afternoons, a certain trace seemed to linger over those sixteen steps.

I'd feel it as my foot hit the first one. It was as if there was something gathering in the air behind me, something that wanted to push me forward, to make me run, and that was a trick; I knew it was a trick, because the moment I started running, the fear would erupt into the back of my neck, like a great hand trying to grab me, and I'd go faster and faster and I'd get more and more scared and run all the way along the corridor and into my bed with the covers all over me, trying not to let my aunty hear me whimper.

But not tonight. Having taken my fortifying glance at Dorothy, I stood, puffed out my ribby chest and walked those stairs without stopping. One step, two steps, three steps, four. I could feel the fear behind me, bending out of the growling air. I refused to rush. Everyone knew that turnspit dogs weren't afraid of the dark.

When I reached my room and closed the door, I heard a fly buzzing around the light. As soon as I saw its darting motion, it came for me, buzzing in and out, infuriatingly close to my skin. I flapped it away again and again, but still it came. It wasn't quite a phobia, my aversion to flies. I'd feel a sense of panic and revulsion at their presence, but also a kind of murderous fury. It was as if there were something personal in their tormenting; as if their sole, born purpose was to pester me.

That night, though, was different. That fly was a test. I turned off the main light, switched on the wobbly old bedside lamp with the green velvet-tasselled shade and removed all my clothes, carefully folding them in a neat pile on the chest of drawers. Then I lay on top of the woollen blanket, rested my arms by the sides of my body and waited.

It didn't take long. I flinched at the sensation of the fly's legs on my stomach and the grotesque understanding, in its hesitant movements, of the small living thing making judgements and decisions. It took off once more and passed my eyes and I could see that it was sleek and nimble with a silvery body and large red eyes – of the type that I had only ever seen at Dor Cottage.

It landed on my cheek. My hands shook as it walked to the edge of my mouth. I thought about the turnspit dogs that had once worked away downstairs in the kitchen. I thought about Mary Dor and her fraught and magical recipes. I thought about gravy and Eton Mess and Toulouse sausages and fingers of melted cheese-on-toast, made with parmesan and three-year Cheddar and sprinkled with nutmeg and fresh cracked pepper and tangy Worcester sauce.

It lifted off again and came down at the corner of my eye. I lay there as the fuzzy lump on the border of my vision licked and drank. I willed the strength to come, opening my mouth wide to breathe deeply. In and out went the cold, thick air.

In, hold, and out.

In, hold, and out.

The fly whipped away and landed, again, on the edge of my lip. I felt the woollen blanket beneath my damp palms and imagined a lake of melted chocolate and tall flowers with caramel petals and marzipan trees and clouds of still-warm vanilla marshmallows.

Not a movement.

Not a single movement.

The fly crawled, with delicate little pricks on my skin, into my mouth. It buzzed, just once, and walked in further. A muscle in my lip contracted involuntarily and then I closed my tongue over it. The insect was pulled in. I felt its twitching incredulity as it was sucked down into my throat.

Coughing and retching, I sat up and ran to the bathroom to wash my mouth out. When I was done, I caught my reflection in the mirror above the sink. For the first time in my life, I studied my face in detail. I had done it. I would be different from now on. They could hurt me as much as they wanted. They could beat me or pity me or act as if I wasn't there. None of it would matter. I might have looked weak and repulsive but I had strength and loyalty. I was a creature of the kitchen; a controlled, ferocious beast.

I was a turnspit dog.

2

When I was younger, and she was in her better moods, my mother used to dress me up in costumes. Policeman, Red Indian, ladybird, sailor. During nights in which she had friends around, she would wake me in the early hours and force me to dance about in her underwear, which she would make fit using safety pins to take in the slack. "Be our sexy dancer!" she would say, laughing and clapping, and I would jiggle about on the living-room rug, its colours blurring through tears and cigarette smoke. There was a princess dress with a short pink skirt and glittery sleeves that she would make me wear as I cleaned the house, if the previous day's work had been insufficiently thorough. Now and then, she would send me to the shops in it. I would run down the cul-de-sac, my knees feeling as if they might burst open with the effort, in terror of being spotted by Mark. For my seventh birthday, she bought me a king outfit, complete with plastic crown which she would make me wear as I fetched fresh ice from the kitchen and emptied the ashtray of a weekday evening. When things reached a certain point, I would have to stand still as she stared at me. "One day you'll grow up to be my king," she would say. "You'll be my handsome hero. You'll look after me, won't you, darling? Baby darling, tell me, who do you want to marry when you're a big strong man?"

"You, Mummy."

"Who will be your beautiful princess?"

"You, Mummy."

"Such a good boy, you are. Such a good, strong, handsome boy."

And I would stand still and she would stare.

As I entered my adolescence, I grew out of my costumes. She no longer fantasised about me as her king. As time passed, my mother became more likely to remark bitterly that I was turning out to be "mediocre, just like your father". Before the night of the fly, that had made me impossibly sad. After so many safe and wonderful hours at Dor Cottage, I had begun to muster an impossible ambition to one day be a successful cook, just like my hero, the world-famous chef Max Mann. But not now; not any more. I was a dog. And like all good and loyal dogs, I knew my place and was grateful for it. It felt good to finally accept my mother's entirely logical point of view.

Mediocre: it was a release.

At school, I accepted that my level was down in the corner, quiet and obedient, not one of them. When I wasn't daydreaming about food, I'd entertain myself by keeping track of my classmates' internecine battles. It was my own thrilling, real-time soap opera and my love for its latest twists was second only to my obsession with cooking. I'd move about the corridors and locker rooms and hang by the walls pretending to be looking for something in my rucksack when really I was listening. At some point, I acquired the nickname "Eyeballs". Cruel, perhaps, but undoubtedly deserved.

Loyal dog that I was, I came to care about my classmates deeply. And despite the violent attentions of Mark House, I succeeded in training myself to remain mostly invisible and to never cry no matter what the provocation. The only occasion on which I broke occurred when I was fourteen. By then I had grown used to quietly observing the lives of the boys and girls around me, taking pleasure in seeing what happened to people whose days were filled with friends and events. I would watch them and I would think about them and I thought most of them were amazing; funny and clever and alive. But something happened over the early months of that summer term. A kind of tornado swept up all of my thoughts and carried them away in one direction. In her direction. I had accidentally fallen in love.

I don't know what it was about Sophie, but I do know that I wasn't the only one. Not the prettiest girl in the class, no, but she was beautiful all the same. It was her extraordinary kindness that first attracted me, but it wasn't long before her earthly properties – her hair and her eyes and her smile – burned themselves onto the backs of my eyes.

I had a fantasy about her that, over the course of those months, thickened imperceptibly into a plan. It took weeks of saving ingredients, small and dangerous robberies from my mother's purse and so much imagining that I began literally dreaming up new ideas. My work started a week before Sports Day. Every night, at two thirty, I would creep into the dark kitchen and cook by tea-light, always with the dread of what would happen if my mother was woken by the scents. By five a.m., I would be finished, the room immaculate once more. At the end of seven days, I had them, stored carefully in baking-sheet-lined layers in a metal biscuit tin beneath my bed. Twenty chocolates and twenty sugared jellies. Forty different flavours, all for her.

I never really considered what my gift might achieve. It wasn't as if I had imagined her doing anything as terrifying as actually speaking to me. The fact of her eating them, of her joy in my creation, of her taking them in and of my giving her bodily delight. That was enough. That was everything.

I knew that, during Sports Day, I wouldn't be missed. I also knew where Sophie's peg was, in the changing rooms. I stuck some heart-patterned wrapping paper to the tin, and had found some red ribbon, which I abandoned, after thirty frustrating minutes spent trying to tie it into a bow. During the lunch break, I hid in a toilet cubicle with my parcel on my lap. I remained there until I was sure everyone would be down on the fields, leaving me in the safe and echoing quiet.

I crept past the library, past the science lab, past Mr Ariely's English class with its chairs pulled out and the sun on the blackboard, the flowerless pot plant, dusty in the corner of the silent room. The corridors were polished and wide and somehow still rang with the cries of the boys and girls in all their missing hundreds. As I turned into the sports block, I heard talking. I stopped. They were in the boys' changing room. I would go slowly.

"Oy!"

It was Colin, in the doorway.

"Watcha, Eyeballs. What you got there?"

And if Colin was there...

"Oy, Mark!" he called behind him. "It's Eyeballs. He's got us a pressie."

I scrambled away, my pursuers primed with their identical Dunlop trainers and their stinking muscle rub. Out of one block, into another and down towards the third-year lockers, they gained on me. I ran into a toilet, hoping to bolt myself back inside a cubicle, but Mark grabbed me by the shoulders and knocked me off balance, my skull bouncing on the floor, my tin falling on its side. Colin popped open the lid.

"Sweets!" said Mark, placing one in his mouth with his free hand. "Do you want one?"

He took a handful of chocolates and jellies, mushed them into a ball and forced them into my mouth. I spat them out, their sticky warmth crawling down my cheek and chin, and he grabbed my neck and forced my head into the urinal's long gutter. My upper lip hit the blue detergent ball and my face was soaked in the spiky stench of boy-piss. Stephan tipped the tin's contents into the porcelain trough and began urinating on them. Yellow-brown liquid trickled millimetres from my face.

"Here, look," Colin screeched, holding up the lid. "It was for Sophie."

"Do you fancy Sophie?" said Mark. "Do you fancy Sophie?" He turned to address the others. "He's spying on Sophie now. Dirty fucking spy. Stephan, you take him."

Stephan took my neck and Mark disappeared, returning minutes later with a large translucent plastic bottle. The label was white and purple and had an orange square with a black cross over it. Utilitarian letters spelled the words: PAINT THINNER. He unscrewed the cap and yanked down my left eyelid. Reflexively, I pulled away. I felt it tear at the corner. Blood was in my eye.

"Dirty bastard spy," said Mark.

"Don't do too much," said Stephan. "He'll go fucking blind."

"Fuck that," said Mark.

I looked up at them; studied them one by one. Then the burning came. Mark bit his lip in concentration; Stephan's mouth was fish-like. Robert and Andy were standing way above me. Colin had ink smudged on his ear and a scab on his jaw.

The liquid inside my eye felt as if it was boiling. I tried to remain apart from what was happening. I stared hard at the smear of blue biro on Colin's ear. It looked like a raindrop; like Africa; like an upside-down comma.

"He's not even struggling," said Colin.

"I fingered Sophie," said Mark.

It looked like Scandinavia.

"I gave her three fucking fingers."

I swallowed.

"Then I sucked her tits."

I felt the heaviness, then. I felt the upset swell. A sob built defiantly in my throat.

"Then I put my finger up her arsehole and I made her suck it. She loved that. She was moaning."

I stared back at the ceiling. I held myself still as a cold tear slid from the outside corner of my eye, down my temple and then lost itself behind my ear, as if hiding in shame.

"Is he dead?" said Stephan.

I lifted my head, blood and chemical spilling onto my cheek, and said, "I'm fine." For some reason, this seemed to terrify them. With a squeak of rubber heels and a piggery of sniggering, they were gone.

I poured water from a tap into my eye and walked home slowly. The moment my mother saw me, she ordered me to hospital. Three hours later, I returned with a white bandage over a blob of cotton wool for a patch.

"What did they say?" asked my mother. She was sitting in her armchair in front of *Coronation Street*, an iceless Martini in a port glass in her right hand.

"It'll be fine," I said, from the open doorway. "Except that my eyelid might not go back to the same shape it was. But it'll be fine."

The point of her tongue licked slowly along her lower lip.

"Did it hurt?"

"Yes," I said.

"How much?"

"A lot."

"A lot?"

"Yes."

She unfolded her legs, from where she'd been sitting on them. On the television screen, northern actors carried on obliviously.

"Turn that off," she said.

I pushed the heavily springed power button on the bottom of the old Pye set, and took my usual place, standing in front of her. She held her arms out towards me. I walked into them, stiffly, and felt her cold skin wrap around my neck.

"Do you love me, Killian?"

I knew what to say.

"Yes, Mummy, I love you."

"How much?"

I knew exactly how it went.

"I love you more than anything in the whole wide world, Mummy."

I could feel a vein pulsing in her neck; smell the cigarettes and perfume in her skin; feel the pressure around my throat tightening and then releasing as her mind worked on something, over and over and over. Tightening and releasing; tightening and releasing. I wanted her to put me down, but I had to pretend. I knew what happened when I didn't pretend.

"Who did this to you?" she said, eventually.

She released me and I stood there, hands straight down against my sides.

"It was an accident," I said.

"Who did it?" she said.

"Nobody."

"If you loved me, why would you lie to me?"

"Sorry, Mum."

"So why are you lying to me then?"

"Sorry, Mummy."

There was that sense of stirring and strength; the drawing down of trouble.

"If you don't spit it out, so help me God, I'll have you put into a home. Do you *know* what I do for a job? Have you forgotten? One stroke of my pen. Ten seconds' work. You will never see me again. Is that what you want?"

I closed my eyes and whispered, "It was Mark."

"Mark *House*?"

"But I didn't do anything," I said, pleading. "He just *did it*."

I wanted to tell her that her hair looked nice. She had had it coloured, that day. All her greyness had gone away.

"I was just giving this thing to someone in my class and he – " I said.

"What thing?"

"Just some – "

"What?"

"Chocolates and things."

"Chocolates?"

Her nostrils narrowed.

"Who to?"

"This girl."

"*A girl*?"

They had been getting bad, her grey roots. And now they were all gone. All nice. All back to normal.

"God help us. Fourteen years old. Ogling women."

"I'm sorry, Mummy," I said.

"Perving over girls at your age? Pestering them? Disgusting." She leaned forward. "You're as bad as your bloody grandad."

I lowered my head and looked at my socks; my pink toe, the white fringe of its nail poking out of a hole in the material.

"You need to learn something, if you're going to keep living in my house. You don't go bothering women. You don't go treating them like lumps of meat. Do you hear me? *Dirty little boy*. Filthy dirty *rotten*."

She took her tortoiseshell cigarette lighter and clicked up a flame. Placing a long Belair Menthol cigarette between her lips, she sucked the fire into its tip and then laid it carefully on the edge of the blue cut-glass ashtray.

I would trim that toenail later on, with the nail clippers that

I got from the cracker at Aunt Dorothy's on Boxing Day. And then, tomorrow night, I would get the needle and thread and try to darn that hole.

"Come on then, big man..."

She pulled a second cigarette out of the packet and lit that one too, laying it next to the first.

" ...take off your shirt..."

And then my sock would be all mended.

" ...and come here."

All nice and safe and mended.

* * *

The next morning, my mother met Mark's mum at the school gate and slapped her face. I looked on, my heart bursting with love and pride as she raised her finger in the face of a mortified Margaret House and said, "Nobody touches my bloody son." Mr and Mrs House were never invited around for cocktails again.

And then, four years later, my life changed again.

3

West Kent College was a gloomy hustle of 1960s buildings – vandalised, damp and gloweringly concrete – whose catering department had the capacity for fifty-five new students a year. On my first morning, I was one of seventy-nine who gathered in the breeze-block training kitchen underneath the ceiling tiles with the damp, like apple rot, spreading through them. Mr Mayle, our faculty head, told us not to worry too much about the cramped conditions; that the head-count would soon be reduced to a more manageable amount by the inevitable "Malthusian check".

The reason for the course's over-subscription was simple: the rise of Max Mann. During the late seventies I had become intensely fascinated by the ubiquitous chef and his famous London restaurant, King. There were chefs who had more culinary respect in the country – Raymond Blanc, Nico Ladenis, the Roux brothers – but it was Mann who had somehow come to personify the heat and glamour of ultra-fine dining.

They called him "the Gentleman Chef", because of the famously peaceable way in which he managed his kitchen staff. He was known for never shouting at his workers, and was proud of the young juniors he trained into stars and his record of never having fired one – "I'd never give up on an apprentice," he'd often swear on chat show sofas, as if the very idea was heresy.

I knew all the facts about him – lines from the many dozens of press clippings that I would cut out and file carefully into my collection. Like: it was Mann's restaurant in which Elton John and his wife ate Sunday lunch; where Mohamed Al Fayed had celebrated his purchase of Harrods; where the singers went for a free meal following the recording of 'Feed The World'. It was Mann, more than anyone, who had a pioneering appetite for the French food movement, "la Nouvelle Cuisine", and, in part, his celebrity was generated by his reputation for small portions on big plates and the pairing of fruits with meat and fish. All the best comedians would do bits on him. There was this *Two Ronnies* sketch, set in a Wimpy bar, in which Corbett was handed a bowl of chips that came with an unpeeled banana sticking out of them before Barker was given a hamburger that had a slim patty of beef and an entire pineapple jammed between the buns. One Spitting Image joke had a starving Ethiopian bursting into tears when a latex caricature of Mann lifted an enormous silver cloche off a King-style square black plate to reveal a chicken wing and half a grape.

He'd appeared on all the chat shows – Parkinson, Wogan, Russell Harty – and always did variations on the same routine, which the students at college would impersonate. He'd start by taking the presenter's predictable jokes about Nouvelle Cuisine with grace, explain to a disbelieving audience that, honestly, no butter at all was used in his cooking and that the meat and fish really were cooked "*au sec*", by being dipped in cold water and heated in a Teflon pan. This would segue into his dryly sarcastic defence of foie gras and then his anecdote about Michael Jackson's entourage ordering hot dogs. He'd finish by batting away questions about the rumoured OBE and the elusive third Michelin star by laughing and saying "Oh do come on now" in that Etonian accent that was sharper than a January wind.

Whenever you saw photographs in the *Sun* of pop stars or

actors walking into King itself, the flash was always on their faces, blacking out the background. But the background was what I wanted to see. I used to examine those pictures during my lunch breaks, my thumb over the faces of Morten Harket or Liza Minnelli, peering into the dead ink behind them. The most you ever saw was a neatly trimmed rectangular hedge and a canopy over a small door. Somehow, that made the place seem all the more magical. This dull façade, behind which worked Max Mann and his brigade; this unassuming building in a low neighbourhood you'd just walk past if you didn't know better.

It would only be a slight exaggeration to say that, by eighteen, I'd grown to love him. I'd had my head shaved to a grade-four crop, to mimic the hairstyle he demanded of his brigade. I studied how he sat on the TV AM sofa and the particular way he had of crossing his legs with his ankle resting imperiously on his knee. I cut out all the pictures of him I could find – even the postage-stamp-sized ones from the listings pages of the *Radio Times* – and super-glued them onto my bedroom wall.

I ended up on the course at West Kent because my mother was determined that I would go to college. To her shame – and having failed the rest of my exams due to my almost total absence of application – cookery was my only realistic option for study. I soon discovered some unwelcome news about the course. Thanks to Mann's superstardom, Mark House – after toying with rock star, photographer and footballer – had apparently decided that he was destined to become a world-famous chef.

* * *

We'd completed our initial classes in theory, hygiene and basic kitchen mathematics and were about to begin the practical work. With the class gathered before him, Mr Mayle announced that before we moved on to the basics – stocks, mirepoix, concasse, tourne – he wanted to test our basic skills by seeing how good we were at domestic cookery. That coming Monday, he said, we were to present our own preparations of lasagne for tasting by the class. By happy accident of his personality, Mayle always managed to co-opt his students into respectful behaviour by matching their natural teenage instinct for cynicism with his air of gently amused detachment. He spoke with a subtle grin that was so barely detectable as to be tantalising: it danced juicily between one or two tiny muscular twitches at the extreme left side of his mouth. "There's a host of basic skills involved in a simple lasagne," he said. "Let's see if any of you rabble have what it takes to out-cook Signore Birds Eye."

On the morning of lasagne day I was surprised to find that I was the only student who'd arrived in class sufficiently early to begin the process of cooking ragu which, Aunt Dorothy had always taught me, took at least four hours; one for the sautéing of the soffritto and the browning of the meat, three for the softest simmer it's possible to tempt from your hob. This was the kind of thing I'd learn every weekend and school holiday after Mum, usually complaining of my being "under her feet", had driven me to Dor. On birthdays, Dorothy would take me from my home in Tonbridge to some of London's ethnic areas – the Bengalis and Bangladeshis in Brick Lane; the Chinese south of Soho; the West Indians in Brixton – where we'd have lunch for inspiration before spending the afternoon shopping for curious and fantastic ingredients – red gram, white miso, kecap manis, Jamaica flowers, West African giant snails. Then we'd putter back from Hailsham Station in her old Peugeot and she'd go through her collection of stockpots and roasting pans, all of which were so ancient and dented and tarnished by fire that I came to recognise each eccentric one of them as if they were characters in a Gothic children's book. We'd spend the evening cooking an experimental birthday meal on her ancient range.

It was on one such birthday that we had concocted the version of lasagne that I was now so familiar with, I'd almost forgotten it could be made any other way. As I worked in the silence of the West Kent kitchen – my coat hanging alone on the row of hooks outside, my bag of condiments placed reassuringly by my feet like a loyal pet – I added star anise to the soffritto and used ham stock instead of chicken or beef. The candied sweetness of the spice, I knew, worked in gorgeous symphony with the baconiness of the stock and three or four light dashes of Spanish sherry vinegar gave a subtle fizz of acid.

Gradually, my new classmates began to filter into the room and soon they were all frantically working away, the spirit of competition having galvanised them into seriousness. They were as studious as I'd ever seen them, carefully measuring tablespoons of tomato purée and weighing blocks of mince. Many stopped Mayle as he walked the classroom's aisles and asked earnest questions about dried oregano, sunflower oil and tinned versus fresh tomatoes.

I was stirring hard, the steam from the ragu making a patina of sweat glisten on the back of my hand, when Mark House bashed his way through the swing doors.

"Hmmm, Eyeballs," he said, peering into my food. "Bit more salt, maybe?"

He picked up my shaker, unscrewed the top and dumped the contents into the pot.

"That's better," he said. "Now it looks like shit *and* tastes like shit. Consistency, yeah?" And he sauntered off in the direction of his stove.

The salt had fallen in a single iglooish pile that was sinking quickly into the ragu. I grabbed a ladle and tried to remove all the sauce that had had the chance to absorb it. As usual, it was

Mark's casualness that struck me – that ruining my dish wasn't some act of piqued fury but an entirely unremarkable event; a reflexive twitch.

The pressure in the room built as burners burned and lips pursed to taste and arms became sore with stirring. Eyes drifted to Mayle as he strode up and down behind the cooks. Girls smiled up at him, boys feigned professorial concentration. The bolder amongst the students would stop him with a trembling, sauce-filled spoon and say, "Sir, what do you think of this?" or "Sir, enough mixed herbs?" and each time he would politely decline, insisting it was up to them – that it was a test of *their* judgement of flavour, not his. Everyone became aware of their neighbour's desperation to beat them, and that stoked their own insecurities and drew them into trying yet harder. Around and around it went until the designated time, when we lined our plates up along the blue trestle table that had been erected in front of Mayle's demonstration kitchen.

Having managed to rescue my sauce, I watched from the back as everyone picked out a fork from an old water-filled ice-cream tub. As I retreated back to my station to start clearing down, I passed Mark, who was proudly delivering his dish to Mayle. He'd brought in his own special presentation plate, which he was holding with both hands and gazing at with the pride of a new father. His lasagne was a firm, bright brick of red food with a sprig of parsley on the top. In a nod to the fashionable cooking of the time, he'd made a salad of what looked like red grapes and lightly sweated onion. It all looked neat and attractive and completely different from mine, which I now realised was a disaster – a slipped pile of steaming meat, the mornay sauce I'd used instead of béchamel bleeding into the ragu in little landslides of creamy white.

"Sir, please, sir," said Mark, pushing his plate into Mayle's hands. "I don't want it to get cold, sir."

I turned and watched as Mayle surrendered and took a bite. Mark's gaze flicked between the dish and the teacher's lips, his expression one of gelatinous pride, an eyebrow raised in anticipation of the glory.

"Hmm," said Mayle. "Yes. Interesting texture." He closed his eyes and rubbed his tongue along the roof of his mouth. "There's something almost... pre-masticated about it."

It took the boy a good three seconds to realise that what he was hearing wasn't good.

I was about to take another step towards my dirty pots when I noticed, in the long mirror that was suspended above the demonstration kitchen, that a small clot of students had formed at the far end of the trestle table. They were gathering around my plate. I would wash up. That's what I would do. What did it matter if everyone was laughing at my dish? Why would I care? I was mediocre and happy that way. I didn't care *at all*.

As I carried my knives, chopping board and pans towards the sink, I couldn't help but have one final look at what was happening. Mayle was moving towards the group. I turned on the hot tap, squeezed in a spurt of detergent and held my fingers under the scorching water to distract myself with pain. So what if Mark House had made a better dish than me? Why would *anyone* be surprised about *that*?

In the mirror, I watched, with my fingers held under the hot tap, as the teacher cut into my pasta with the edge of his fork and scooped up a mouthful.

In the reflection, Mayle began to chew. The other students were watching the action, many with tight almost-grins. And then it happened. Mayle's eyelids dropped. Aunt Dorothy always said that that, for a cook, is what laughter is to a comedian or what tears are to a storyteller. When he opened them again and tried to seek out the cook responsible for what he'd just eaten, I'll never forget it. He looked as if he'd been provoked.

"Who made this?" he said.

He must have realised who it was by the colour of my face, or the fact of everyone turning towards me. There were giggles and smirks and whispering. I dried my fingers tenderly on my apron and tried to suck some moisture into my mouth. I had never had so many eyes on me before.

"I don't know exactly what you've done here," said Mayle. "But this lasagne is like none I've ever tasted."

Mark House snorted like a hog that had been unexpectedly mounted.

"It's wonderful, just wonderful," he said. "Beautifully, beautifully deep and rich flavour. And so complex! What's your name, young man? How did you *do* this?"

I was incapable of doing anything but shrugging, uselessly. Mayle, to my eternal relief, smiled and gave me the kindest little nod. I got back to my washing-up and tried to tell myself that I didn't care. But, already, it was too late.

It wasn't until I lay down in bed that night that I realised that something essential had changed. All those years I believed that I had removed myself from the competitiveness of the world, I had been fooling myself. I had been competing with almost everyone I'd known and my fight had been harder and more determined than any of theirs. The only difference was, mine had been a race to the bottom. That was the only battle I believed I could win. As I closed my eyes to sleep, I was sure of only one thing.

It wasn't any more.

That night I dreamed of Dor Cottage under months of ceaseless rain; of a long-caged magic in the garden, in the roof and in the mortar.

I dreamed of the sixteen steps that I'd climbed with courage as a boy. I looked up, from the bottom, over the rims of their crooked wooden surfaces. At the top stood a figure, weak and wordless with dread. Her face half hidden in darkness, she stared through me.

I'd not seen her before, but I knew her. She'd been with me always – in my sleep and back in the dead times.

I saw a dying room, tall with windows. Glass murky with the dirt of a thousand rain storms and the black bones of winter trees. And then, a beautiful girl. Long eyelashes and freckles across her face like a fine spray of milky chocolate. A blood mark on her face. Dogs in a circle, their claws slipping on a hard, smooth floor. She was begging them to stop.

And I believed it, then, about the magic and the ancestor. I understood about the hunger and the howling. I understood that it was real and it would come. All of it would come.

I saw fire and flies and turnspit dogs and boiling bones and blood under the fingernails of men.

It was a dream of past and a dream of future.

It was a dream of horror.

4

Around six months after lasagne day, I was summoned, unexpectedly, into Mayle's office. I knocked softly and pushed open the door, which released the usual smell of old books, carpet and Amaretto. An antique-ish standard lamp in the corner cast dull, licentious and yet homely light, of the kind you'd see in an old-fashioned bistro.

"Hullo, Killian," Mayle said. He placed the book he'd been reading, spine down, on his cluttered desk. "Sit down, sit down. I have some good news for you. As you know, in a couple of weeks everyone's going out on their work placements. Trying to place everyone is always a nightmare but we've somehow muddled through as usual. Most of your classmates are off to institutions or big companies. Schools, hospitals, staff kitchens in Safeways – canteen work, in the main. Bean-stirring. Mark House, you might be interested to learn, is spending a fortnight in an oil rig off the north-east coast of Aberdeen."

He paused to let that near-imperceptible smile flicker across his mouth.

"We have had a tiny bit more luck with you, however."

He smiled gently and leaned forward with his hands on his cheeks. The skin on his face bunched around his eyes so that he looked unnaturally delighted.

"But before we go any further, some good news. Your entry

into the 1985 Young Saucier of the Year competition."

"Yes, sir," I said, suddenly alert. This was the award once won by Max Mann himself. Flattered as I had been when Mayle had asked me to take part, I realised that it was only because the college felt it should be represented.

"You, young man, are a finalist."

My jaw slackened.

"You may swear," nodded Mayle.

"Fuck!"

He laughed warmly and swept a bit of imaginary dust off his desk with his fingertips.

"Yes, indeed. Needless to say, this is a first for West Kent. An amazing achievement. A high point of my teaching career and I thank you for it, sincerely. You have a huge talent, Killian. A rough diamond, perhaps, but a diamond certainly. I think you'll go far. But you're going to have to learn to be a bit more of a team player. If you have ambitions to be an executive chef and lead a brigade, you do actually have to *talk* to other people, I'm afraid."

"Yes, sir," I said. "I know, sir."

He held my gaze for a moment.

"Anyhow, because of all this, I have managed to pull a few strings. You'll be pleased to hear that I've arranged your work placement for six weeks, rather than four."

"Thank you, sir."

"You are very, very welcome, young man."

I stood and gave Mr Mayle a grateful bow of the head.

"Goodbye!" he said.

I moved across the room and reached for the handle of his door. Just as my fingers made contact, Mayle spoke again.

"Oh, er – Killian?"

"Yes, sir?"

"Don't you want to know where you'll be apprenticing?"

I turned.

"Yes, sir."

"Well, you'll be working your *stage* up in London."

"London?"

"Yes, you will. London."

London. I wondered where. A bank, maybe. A train station café. A cinema, a theatre, an opera house.

"Okay. Great. London. Thank you, sir."

I turned, once more, to leave.

"At... um... a place called... "

I looked around again. Mayle made a show of carefully examining a sheet of paper on his desk.

"Ah, that's it. You'll be working at... "

He met my eyes and grinned.

"King."

5

London has a grey-blue tinge to it in the hour after dawn. That's what I remember most about my walk, on that first morning, to the restaurant – the grey-blue tinge as I hurried from Charing Cross Station and how it seemed exactly right, somehow. It was the colour of the empty streets; the colour of frozen air; the colour of the thinness of the world as it is at six a.m. before it becomes bloated by life. I wasn't exactly sure how to find the right place. All I knew was that it was somewhere in the tall maze of streets that runs east of Tottenham Court Road. Back then, it was all discount sex shops, broken pubs and nameless outlets with chipboard doors that sold knock-off T-shirts and posters. An unlikely place to find the chicest eating establishment in the country, I thought, naively, as I strode past an open entranceway, behind which was a staircase and a paper notice that announced the presence of a "model" on the first floor. It was a lesson I'd learn soon enough – filth is inherent to glamour; sin its silent promise.

It was the first time that I'd been to London without Aunt Dorothy, and the city seemed dirty and overwhelming without her. I remember its gigantic indifference, as if the huge stone buildings were turning their backs on me as I walked between them. I had in my back pocket the piece of paper Mr Mayle had passed me in his office. There was no need to look at it, as it contained only scant information: the address, 32 Gresse Street, and the time I was expected – seven a.m.

King was almost exactly as I'd imagined, except for the fact it was next to a pub called the Bricklayers Arms and that it smelled. The dustmen hadn't yet done their rounds, and the restaurant was wearing this rotten beard of rubbish bags. It didn't bother me in the slightest. Neither did it matter that I was nearly an hour early. I was content just to stand on the lowest of the five steps that Max Mann and his customers walked up every day and to breathe the same air.

I peered, open-mouthed, through the glass door. As my eyes became used to the light, I could just make out the famous black walls decorated with mirrors, the matching black tablecloths and the orchid centrepieces. I stayed like that for at least five minutes, drinking in all the details, before studying the incredible menu that was displayed in a small illuminated case next to the door: mousseline of quail livers flavoured with port and cognac and served with a trio of fruit jellies; guinea-fowl in a caramel glaze with fresh mangoes; champagne-poached sweetbreads; golden mousse of foie gras topped with diced foie gras and served with supreme of pigeon in a sauce of meat juices with halves of grape...

The previous weekend, Aunt Dorothy had given me a set of packet-fresh chef's whites. She'd even gone to the trouble of stitching my name into the breast in neat blue cotton. I reached into my little backpack and found the toque, which I placed on my head. I looked at my reflection in the small gold plaque on which the name of the restaurant had been engraved in luxurious script. I looked warped and indistinct, my outline fuzzy, my face an empty oval.

On the pavement nearby, one of the bin liners had been left untied. I picked yesterday's edition of *The Times* out of it and flipped through its damp pages. Scargill and Sellafield and

Star Wars and Thatcher enthusiastic about chemical weapons against the Soviets and Israeli jets battering Palestine and one million pounds being spent on fences at Greenham Common. The news was the same as all the other days. None of it held the importance of what was about to happen for me, right here, at 32 Gresse Street.

I sat down on the steps that led to the door. I waited. I spat on my finger and rubbed off a smudge that had appeared on my tunic. A strange temptation began to crawl over me. I found myself going over to one of the bin liners and tearing a small hole in it. A couple of shallot ends and asparagus off-cuts poked out. I took a green, woody stem and rolled it between my fingers. I had this idea, this compulsion, to put it in my mouth and chew down on it – my saliva mixing with this King ingredient, this incredible artefact – it becoming part of me and me part of it.

Just as my teeth were pressing into it, the door opened. I turned to see a chef in his mid-twenties with a black moustache and full, cracked lips, looking at me with all the bewildered fascination I probably deserved. I palmed the stem and dropped my hand down by my side.

"I'm Killian, Chef," I said quietly. "Apprentice. First day."

His expression sagged into one of damp contempt.

"Fuck's sake," he said. "Staff entrance is round the back. Stephen Mews."

With a tilt of his head, he motioned to the alleyway that ran down the side of the restaurant. I thanked the man and ran.

Stephen Mews was a dingy and greasily cobble stoned dead end, surrounded by unpainted four-storey walls. There was an open double fire door, which was framed by a grubby clamour of plastic crates filled with empty bottles of Moët, Perrier and Coca-Cola, a confetti of discarded ring-pulls flattened into the ground around them. A squall of pigeons, perched in the window frames high above me, looked on as I wished myself luck and walked into the golden rectangle of light.

The kitchen was smaller than I was expecting, and fuller. There were twelve chefs, most of whom were busy checking the contents of the morning deliveries. I gawped at the logos and labels on the packages that were stacked on the clean steel surfaces. They were the most thrilling ingredients from all over Europe. There was Valhrona Grand Cru de Terroir chocolate, Xeres vinegar, Beluga caviar, pata negra ham from Iberian pigs who'd been fed purely on acorns, cheese supplied by the lauded Philippe Olivier – even the salt had been imported from the West coast of Sicily. And then, being rushed past me on a large red trolley, I saw something curious. Boxes and boxes and boxes of fresh, delicious, world-renowned Echire butter.

Unloading all of this were the chefs themselves: serious men with careful eyes and conjurers' fingers, awesome in their black clogs and robeish whites. Gods. Dogs.

I stepped deeper into the room and paused to take in the moment. This was it: *his* world; *his* kingdom. This was where Chef Max Mann himself worked every day and made his reputation. These were *his* burners and strainers and sinks and pans and produce.

Directly to the right of the door were four other young apprentices, all lined up along the cold pass, counting out bunches of basil, chervil, parsley and rosemary, trays of mangoes and kiwis and punnets of raspberries, then ticking off the quantities against delivery notes. Their necks were bent at precisely the same angle, their arms and fingers moving in strange synchronicity. I was surprised to find this sight the most beautiful thing of all, even more than the smells and the deliveries of impeccably sourced ingredients. They formed a machine, bent into shape by the will of the kitchen, but they were also something better than that. Because nothing made from cogs or circuit boards, no matter how advanced, could achieve what even those trainees could. It was just as Mayle had once told the class: perfection is out of reach of the automatic. The secret ingredient of unforgettable food is humanity.

The Gentleman Chef wasn't in the kitchen that morning. Perhaps, I thought, he'd arrive closer to lunch service. The *chef de cuisine* appeared to be a man in his thirties, with red hair and acne on his cheeks like gouges made by a peeler. He was busy with something, up amongst the meat, fish and sauce stations where, during service, the chefs would toil at perfection over searing flames, before sending their food to Max Mann at the pass. As I approached him, it registered for the first time how quiet everyone was. I had expected shouts, banter and laughter – those big noises of camaraderie that act as buoyancy aids for packs of men under pressure. But nobody spoke. Nobody even looked at me. "Excuse me? Chef?" I said.

He was leaning over a stove, writing something on a yellow clipboard.

"That's me," he said.

He had nearly-blond eyelashes and the grease in the skin on either side of his nose reflected the light from the ceiling. His chin was a pebble of shininess that marked the base of his head, and it looked as if someone had started there and, with the heel of their hand, pushed upwards. His scarlet ears stuck out of the side of his skull like babies' fists. As I'd observe him over the course of the coming day, I'd be constantly aware of his tongue. It was forever making itself known, whether it was wetting his lower lip or appearing as an arched pillow of slimy muscle as he laughed or coughed. Whenever I stood close to him, I'd get a powerful smell of salami.

Right now, though, my attention was fixed on his arms which were covered in a galaxy of burns, scabs and scars.

"I'm..."

"Late," he said, pushing his biro behind a shrivelled ear.

"Fucking hell, pal, I can tell your tenure's going to be brief. What's that on your head?" He grabbed my toque. "Good God. Take the hat off and he's even uglier."

He looked over at the nearby chefs, clapped twice and said, "All right, chaps, the AIDS delivery's arrived."

I looked at him; at his eyes and mouth, as he raised his colleagues in a giggle. Those eyes had seen Max Mann. That mouth had spoken to him.

"All right, first job of the morning. Fetch me a bucket of steam."

"Where—"

But by then he had turned around, his great hunched back bending towards me as he leaned over the steel pass. I walked past two chefs who were unloading fish that had just been wheeled in, in an unsteady tower of ice-filled polystyrene crates, and began searching for a bucket. I wondered what it was for; what delicate Nouvelle technique I was about to learn. I knew Max Mann preferred to season his food with herbs rather than salt. The steam, I guessed, would be used to very gently blanch some rare and fragile leaf.

I looked in the wash-station at the back of the kitchen, inside the garde manger where the vegetables were stored, in the cloak-room with its broken lockers and its wooden clog-shelves that were now filled with derelict trainers, inside all the cabinets, underneath all the cabinets. I opened a door beneath a sink and pushed my head in.

I would not ask for help, I decided. Self-sufficient and reliable, like when I was cleaning for Mum. That's what I needed to be. A toiler. A *machine*.

"Where's my bloody bucket?" came a shout.

There was an empty space at the end of the cold pass, next to the door that led to Stephen Mews. Beside it, a young woman cut celery into elegant spears with perfect mechanical rhythm.

"Is this my station?" I asked her.

She nodded quickly, unsmiling, concentrating on her work. But as I was walking off, she whispered, "Bucket of steam?"

I stopped and marvelled, momentarily, at her eyes and wrists and hands which worked together, de-stringing, spreading and cutting perfectly identical fingers from these things that started off as ugly, misshapen limbs. She had freckles on her fingers and a small pink lip-shaped burn on her right wrist, its size and position suggesting it had been inflicted by a hot oven shelf. Up the back of her neck, spilling out of her collar, was a pale-red birthmark.

"Are you *actually* this stupid?" she whispered. "Or are you just pretending?"

" ... "

"A bucket. With steam in it," she continued. "A bucket of steam." she said, again, looking at me blankly. "It's a wind-up. Obviously."

"But what should I do?"

She had brown hair, tied in a bun, unusually long eyelashes and freckles across her face like a fine spray of milky chocolate.

"The way I see it, you have three choices," she said. "Option one, get a bucket from over in pastry, hold it over some boiling water and see how long it takes Patrick to stop you scalding your fingers."

"Is Patrick–"

"The one that smells of salami?" She nodded. "Option two, save him a job and just walk out of that door because, let's face it, you'll probably not last the day anyway. Option three, kill Patrick."

"But... "

"I have a knife... " she offered.

I looked at the top of the kitchen in disbelief. When I turned back, the girl had already gone back to her chopping.

"And, by the way – stop bloody talking," she whispered. "We're not supposed to be talking."

6

The bucket was cheap red plastic and I held it upside down above a stock pot filled with water. It was boiling hard, its bubbles rising in an insistent panic. Patrick turned leerily towards me with his hands on his hips, the scars on his ruined arms like gang tattoos.

As my fingers began to burn, I watched him catching the eye of all the other men at the grill, sauté and sauce stations. One by one, they stopped lifting, counting and chopping and began to snigger, each of them checking with Patrick every few moments: checking he knew they were joining in; that they were a part of the gang; that they were all devoted bricks in the wall that was about to collapse on me. Eventually, he approached in a slow, slouching shuffle. He leaned an elbow on the side of the stove.

"Are you a cook?" he said. "Or a cock?"

I felt the wet burn driving deeper into the skin of my fingers and over the backs of my hands. I looked Patrick in the eye.

"A cook, Chef," I said.

He spoke louder this time, and slower, his neck bending towards me like a chicken examining a strange new thing. His blunt, acned head took on an expression of exaggerated confusion.

"But you don't look like a cook," he said. He came closer and swiped some sweat off my forehead with an extended finger.

"And you are leaking piss." The laughter of the brigade burst over me. "So what are you?"

"A cook, Chef," I said.

My hands began to shake with the pain, my fingers becoming redder, my nails feeling as if they were swelling so much that they might pop off. I looked at Patrick's mouth. How much of Max's food had passed through it? Had he eaten the entire menu? It was amazing to think that I was only a couple of feet away from a throat that had swallowed every dish prepared at King. Every dish!

In my hands there was a pure kind of white-blinding agony. I didn't move. As the seconds squeezed past, the smile slowly vanished from Patrick's eyes.

What was the last thing that mouth had said to Max Mann? How many words had it told him? Patrick's face turned paler. I was vaguely aware that the brigade around me had fallen silent. I imagined myself licking his lips. Kissing them. Sucking the Max right out of them.

Patrick shook his head and said, almost under his breath, "Fucking nutcase..."

As he spoke, a fly landed on his upper lip. It was narrow; silvery grey, with rust-red eyes.

"Urgh!" He swiped it away, spitting in disgust. It circled back, returning once more to his lip.

"Argh!" In the confusion, someone took my arm, very softly, from behind. It was the apprentice who'd told me about the wind-up; the girl with the eyelashes and the chocolate freckles.

"You're on stock take in the walk-in," she said, pulling me away.

"Fucking hell," said Patrick. There was a slight catch in his voice. "Here we go – weirdos of a feather, flocking together. That's right, petal. Have fun with the cock. No doubt it's the first one you've handled." As he turned, he chuntered, "Fucking dyke."

The huge, coffin-like freezer door slid open with a smooth crunk. We walked together into the grainy light.

"You know what you're here for, don't you?" she said.

"To cook."

"Oh dear," she said. "Apprentices don't get to go anywhere near the stoves, not unless they're cooking for the staff. We do the grunt work. You do realise that? Everything possible is done by hand in a place like this. Chopping, peeling, squeezing – everything. Believe me, if they could find a fire-breathing boy to lie with a boiling stockpot on his face for ten hours, he'd be out there." She gently kicked a large brown cardboard box with a delivery note on top of it. "Right, first job. There should be 188 bags of frozen peas in there. You need to count them out. When you've done that, do the veal bones, beef bones, rabbit carcasses. Then, stock rotation. Start with the sorbet."

There was an instant of silence that followed her last word, during which she could have left. But she paused unnecessarily. She watched as I pushed my throbbing fingers deep between the large sacks of peas and exhaled silently with the relief of it.

"Thanks," I said. "I'm Killian, by the way."

I felt as if she was studying me, for a moment; making some quiet judgement.

"Kathryn."

The sleeves of her tunic were too long. She had had to fold them over themselves into large, pillowy cuffs. I imagined her having to do it every morning. Pushing her arms in and then neatly rolling up the material, slowly exposing her expert fingers and delicate wrists.

"So who taught you how to cook, anyway?" she asked. "Josef Mengele?"

"My aunt," I said.

"She was tough, was she? Your aunt? Some sort of torturer? You should probably think about looking after your hands a bit better than Aunty Pinochet taught you. There's a chance you might need them."

The merciful numbness was now spreading towards my knuckles.

"Oh, I see..." I began. "No, my aunt taught me to cook, but my mum – she's the one who always taught me to sort of take the pain, if that's what you mean."

Her mouth made a barely distinct movement.

"Ah, the school of hard mums." Her eyes flickered away. "Yes, well. Welcome. You should probably also think about not standing up to Patrick like that. You know, let the Wookie win? They take pride in how quickly they can get shot of apprentices. It's like a game to them. That's what they're like here. Especially Patrick."

"But not Max Mann?" I said.

Max Mann wouldn't countenance this behaviour. I knew that. It's why they called him "the Gentlemen Chef". Because he never shouts.

"He never shouts," I said.

I knew Max. I knew Max better than anybody.

Kathryn smiled, thinly, and agreed. "He never shouts."

7

The room I was working in was eight foot by ten and, according to the thermometer on the wall, minus twenty-four degrees. The shelves were coated in a skin of fine frost and the packing tape on the cardboard boxes had become brittle and dark. Even with the thick orange overcoat and rubber gloves, the pinching air fought its way to my body without difficulty. It scraped the insides of my nostrils and my ears began to sear; so cold they felt hot. I decided to work without gloves to halt the burn in my fingers.

It wouldn't be long now. The first lunch sitting began at midday – less than three hours away – and I'd surely meet Max before then. I didn't know why that girl Kathryn had said what she had about this kitchen, but I knew when he finally arrived things would be all right. He'd want to sit me down, of course, and get to know the new apprentice who'd be cooking with him for the next six weeks – perhaps longer, if he was judged to be sufficiently skilled.

As my mind synched with my body into the rhythm of the counting and my hands began to recover, I relaxed into the daydream I'd been having since the afternoon Mr Mayle passed me the news of my placement. It wasn't a fantasy, exactly – more a hopeful expectation. I'd seen it in my head so often it had come to feel as if there was no other possible sequence of events.

Max would invite me to sit with him on the restaurant floor, at a table near the kitchen. The waiting staff would be polishing silver around us and the chef would be in front of me with his ankle on his knee, his arm draped over the chair next to him, just as it draped over the back of the sofa when he chatted with Parky and Harty and Wogan. He'd ask why I wanted to be a chef and I'd tell him. I'd tell him about the days at Dor Cottage, those weekends and summer holidays when my mum sent me away because she couldn't cope with me always under her feet, always hanging around, and how my great-aunt Dorothy taught me to make a béchamel, and I know, Chef, I know we've gone beyond these heavy, old-fashioned sauces with Nouvelle Cuisine, and that the modern way to dress a dish is with vinegar or lemon juice, but my mum didn't want me under her feet all the time so I was sent away, and I stopped being sad once I became fascinated by the magic of all that, the matching the quantity of butter and flour and how it combined into this greasy roux and how you added those splashes of cold milk and how lumpy it was and ugly and the risk of it all going wrong if you didn't work hard enough, if you didn't whisk and whisk and whisk, and beat the ugliness out of it, with your elbows and forearms burning against the failure of it all, and it didn't matter if you got some sweat in it, that was what my aunt said, it didn't matter that my mum didn't want me under her feet all summer, or that she thought I would only ever be mediocre, what mattered was the work and the fight and the flavour and the silkiness, the thickness, the luxury of it. You could see it, under the light from the bulb in the kitchen, how by sheer will you'd forced the roux and the milk together – they hadn't wanted to go together, but you'd forced them, you'd beaten them, by the fire in your elbow, by the burn in your shoulder – and now, when you stirred, it purred under the light, it ran in slow waves, like the contours of a young body, like hips, it rolled up and down, thickly, smoothly, and I forgot all about home when I saw what I'd created and I grated the nutmeg but also some ground fennel seeds and, one time, some Stilton and some Parmesan and you wouldn't believe how much flavour that sauce could absorb, this sauce that was once so reluctant, so disobedient, so out of my control, swallowing it all until there she was, you couldn't argue with her, this sauce I'd made, this flavour I'd smashed into life, you couldn't deny how it made my great-aunt Dorothy proud and my mum, Chef, the way my mum looked at me when she tasted my food, that sauce wasn't mediocre, she knew it, even though she said I was a typical man and I would only ever be mediocre and that I should want to be something proper that does something good for the world and even though I was always under her feet, there was this moment when she tasted that sauce that her eyelids fell, it was an involuntary reaction, as involuntary as love, if you don't mind me putting it like that, Chef, and I have to tell you about my aunt who would tell me these stories, Chef, these stories about my distant relations. I'll tell you, Max, because then you'll see it's in the blood, you'll see you made a great decision when you chose to hire me, I'm a natural chef, a witch's nephew, and really, as we're talking like this, as we're getting on so well and getting so close, I can tell you that I think you're just like me, and we're going to work together so well because we're the same in lots of ways, just the sa—

"Oy, flid."

It was Patrick.

"Yes, Chef?"

"Le Patron wants to see you," he said. "Upstairs."

8

"You're Killian," said Le Patron. He was reading from a letter that was laid in front of him, which I could see was from West Kent College. The tips of his fingers pressed on the edge of his walnut desk, his nails looking slightly yellow, his square-cut ruby ring looking uncomfortably tight on his thumb. His grey hair was thick – combed and oiled into a side-parting – and he wore his maroon braces over a crisp white shirt that exuded such a powerful simplicity that you could tell it was expensive. A pile of five or six identical shirts, wrapped in dry cleaner's plastic shrouds, had been thrown over the leather club chair in the corner. He appeared to be in his early fifties, his eyes old but his skin tight and relatively unlined.

"Saint Killian," he said. "Irish bishop. Informed the local lord he was in violation of sacred law for marrying his brother's widow. Lord had him beheaded in the town square. Doomed himself in the service of his duty."

He searched my face, as if he was trying to find traces of a decapitated bishop. I hadn't a clue what he was talking about.

"I'm Ambrose Rookwood," he said, eventually. "Le Patron. The proprietor. Your teacher at West Kent college, Robert Mayle. Old friend of mine. Talented cook. Opened my first restaurant with him in 1955. Poor Mayle, couldn't cope. Pace was too much for him. Very sad. He might have told you?"

"No, sir," I said.

"Ah." He peered back down at the letter without focusing on it. "Now, Killian, enlighten me. Tell me what you know about what we do here. What's your take?"

He said the word "take" slowly and loudly, exposing a set of grey teeth. I'd never met anyone like this before and I felt adrift: I couldn't read his cues and unusual tics. My eyes swept across his office, taking in the bare floorboards that became visibly dusty as they neared the walls, the chipped ivory goblet on the mantelpiece, the framed etching of a naked woman riding a sexually excited horse and the ashtray full of the distinctive white butts of Kent cigarettes. I'd always thought of posh people as somehow cleaner than the rest of us; whiter, purer, naturally scrubbed and polished from birth. And even though Ambrose had a grubbiness about him, it felt inherent and perfectly correct. There was something celebratory about it; something expansive and wicked that made me feel intrigued by him, whilst at the same time, utterly terrified.

The problem with giving him my "take" on Nouvelle Cuisine was that Dorothy had taught me classical cooking. I was excited by it and the creativity and the previously unimaginable flavour profiles it promised but I had never actually tasted it. I hadn't even seen it in colour: I'd only looked at the photographs that sometimes appeared in the restaurant reviews in the *Evening Standard* which I'd make a special detour to Tonbridge Station after college to buy. I remember, in particular, a picture of Mann's terrine of vegetables – these blocks of carrot, runner bean and artichoke, surrounded by a velvet ocean of "farce", his red sauce of ham, egg white and arachide oil, famous because all the implements required in its preparation had to be stored in a fridge and used immediately.

I began slowly. "It's definitely revolutionary, Nouvelle Cuisine. You know, everyone goes on about the tiny portions, but it's not about that, it's about lightness, delicacy and taste. Simple ingredients, cooked simply and presented artfully. That classical Escoffier cooking, all those heavy sauces thickened with rouxs, lots of butter, cream, boiled vegetables, overseasoned meats and overcooked fish – we've moved on. There are different techniques, now, like steaming, *au sec* and microwave ovens. The ingredients should taste of themselves, not of butter or sauce."

Ambrose lit a cigarette, sat back and nodded for me to carry on.

"Obviously, it started in France, with Fernand Point at La Pyramide. He'd rebelled against spending days and days preparing loads of stocks and mother sauces, so he said he was going to start with a naked kitchen every morning – nothing stored, nothing pre-prepared, nothing left over, no horrible stodgy floury sauces masking the tastes. It was him, wasn't it, that started thickening sauces by reducing instead of using roux? And he had some amazing apprentices working under him – you know, the Troisgros brothers, Alain Chapel, Paul Bocuse. They all got influenced by him. And then you had Michel Guerard and Roger Verge. The 'Young Bulls', they called them. They had this light, fresh way of cooking – took it even further in their restaurants, swapping ideas, seeing how far they could push it. Then in... uh... " I stalled and looked at the ceiling "...1972 the Gault Millau gave it its name. La Nouvelle Cuisine. But, you know, it's Max Mann that's really brought it to its full potential since then, isn't it? His pan-fried oysters on mango slices with curry sabayon and his deer and tangerine pie are classics and I read in the paper the other day – is it right that he had to take his duck with blackcurrants off the menu because everyone's copied it? Obviously, I've not tasted it yet, but..."

"Cuisine minceur," Ambrose muttered.

He folded his arms across his belly which, now he'd sat back, suddenly popped into existence under his shirt, and looked out of the window. The mid-morning light picked up the smoke from his cigarette and wafted it into his face. He didn't blink.

"Thin cooking," he said. "In more ways than one."

He'd reddened noticeably.

"Fernand Point, the so-called 'Godfather of Nouvelle Cuisine' – he had a little catchphrase. Do you know what it was? 'Butter! Give me butter! Always butter!' Let me tell you, I have had the heavenly pleasure of eating an egg prepared by Monsieur Point. Do you know how he prepared it? He slid a raw egg from a plate into a melted lump of butter, cooked it on an extraordinarily low heat and then melted more butter over the top of it. He then seasoned it. And then? Do you know what he did next? He added *more butter*." He paused, with a sizzle of menace. "And *that*'s your precious godfather of Nouvelle Cuisine! These pop stars and American actors that dine here, they're more interested in their waistlines and being written about in Nigel Dempster than eating a fine meal. They dress for the evening with 'Feed The World' T-shirts beneath their awful Cardin jackets and they can't even feed themselves. Of course, Max is a genius, but –"

He stopped and peered at me curiously, as if I'd just dropped from the sky into the space in front of him. "Oh dear," he said. "I'm getting carried away, aren't I?"

"N–"

"Yes," he said, nudging a space between the butts in the ashtray with his cigarette and extinguishing it with a push of his yellow-stained fingers. "Yes, I am." His face bore the suggestion of a mischievous smile. "Never mind," he continued. "I'm sure you're the soul of discretion. Now, young man, as you're no doubt aware, the apprenticing programme we run here is highly sought after. If, after your six-week *stage*, you're deemed worthy of it, you'll be offered the opportunity of being employed as an ouvrier cuisinier and then, if you survive another year or so, a commis. It sounds like you know all about Max. He's a wonderful, wonderful man to work under." His eyes left me for a moment. "And it is true, what he says about his programme. He has never, in fifteen years, given up on an apprentice. Some may have left of their own accord, of course. Many, in fact. Most. But he has never asked a single man to leave, for any reason, before their six weeks is up – a fact he takes an enormous amount of pride in. That's testament not only to his patience, commitment and faith in the traditional brigade system, but also our selection process. I should tell you that we wouldn't usually take an apprentice from a college such as West Kent, but Robert wrote to tell me you're something special. And, of course, you have reached the finals of the Young Saucier competition."

"Yes," I said. "The same one Max Mann won in –"

"Yes, yes," he said. "As I'm sure you know, the winner will be announced at a luncheon at Grosvenor House later in the month. I have certain contacts on the panel of judges and, of course, it would be imprudent of me to reveal the outcome early. Perhaps I'll just tell you we don't hire losers, here at King, and leave it at that. So. I'd like you to prepare my lunch. Steak, mashed potatoes and some of this award-winning sauce."

9

I arrived back downstairs from Ambrose's office weightless with the news. In the previous twenty years, there hadn't been a winner of the Young Saucier of the Year competition that hadn't gone on to be starred in the Michelin Guide and receive at least a 14/20 in the Gault Millau. There had certainly never been one that had come from a low, municipal college like mine. It was Max Mann's win in 1972 that had given him his first small taste of national fame. You'd sometimes read about it in interviews with him; how news of the Young Saucier rarely breached the mainstream press, but how that year the papers ran cartoons alongside stories about the prize that were thickly marinated in irony. Max's father was Brian Mann, this notoriously nouveau-riche millionaire. He owned the roadside café chain Speedy Sam's which, even back then, had a reputation for serving unreasonably priced food that, once plated, seemed to have a miraculous capacity to generate its own flood of water and grease, rendering what was already barely edible so soggy that it usually ended up being scraped into an overflowing bin. But Speedy Sam's thrived regardless, probably due to his monopoly over all the A-roads. Those same interviews would also note the suicide of his mother, and how Max was supposedly ashamed of both his culinary and familial roots and how the Gentleman Chef became uncharacteristically prickly when they were mentioned.

I stood by the kitchen door for a time, watching. I had learned at school that if I placed myself in just the right shadow and didn't move, I could remain unnoticed for a length of time that would astonish a normal person. When I'd been there long enough to roughly work out where the necessary pans could be found, I collected them together and returned to my station.

Next to me was that girl, Kathryn. She was julienning mangoes, carefully transferring the matchstick slices into a small steel bowl nesting in a Tupperware container filled with ice.

"I need some ingredients," I said to her, quietly. She flinched at my voice, and ignored me.

"I have to cook Le Patron his lunch," I said.

"On your first day?"

She looked astonished.

"Is that good?"

"Jesus, impressing Ambrose is the best way to get a job here," she whispered. "That's how Patrick started. But don't screw it up. If Ambrose doesn't like your food, you're fucked."

She lowered her head as Patrick walked down the line, in conversation with a rangy cook with a brown food smear on his tunic and biro all over his left hand. I pretended to be busy and, after they'd passed, Kathryn made no effort to speak again. Her eyes had darkened, her lower lip was pushed downwards in a look of blank concentration. Her fingertips, with their gnawed edges, pressed gently into the firm mango flesh. A little crease between her unplucked eyebrows told me that she was annoyed. I wondered if it was because we'd almost been caught talking.

Hers was a very English prettiness. The cream skin, the freckles, the hair that was simultaneously modest and conspicuously beautiful in its gentle curls and lustre. Her irises were startling – green with crumbs of black and dark gold. Her lips held themselves in an arrangement that told of a tough and perhaps dangerous humour and she had that busy, active alertness about her presence that speaks of intelligence; a mind constantly running. The quality of her culinary technique was also evident. She worked with confidence and tenderness; concentration and economy; delicacy and power; not a movement wasted. And her birthmark, it was –

"Can I help you with something?" she whispered. "You appear to be staring at my face. Is my birthmark fascinating you? Pass me some oil and a pan and I can make you one just like it, if you want."

I looked down, my cheeks heating with shame.

"I need some Worcester sauce and some paprika, port and ground fennel," I whispered. "Do we have any ground fennel?"

She looked at me with an expression of apparently genuine confusion and said, "You must stop now. Stop looking at me. Stop speaking to me. Whatever you're thinking, when you're thinking about me, please stop thinking it. Unless it's hatred. Your hatred I can cope with. In fact, I welcome it. I think we'll get on best of all if you hate me. And if you can't manage that, try pretending. Can you cope with that? Do you think?"

"I'm sorry," I said. "But I *have* to make this sauce."

She sighed, deeply, as she carefully lifted the last of the mango sticks with the blade of her knife and pushed them into the tub. "Fuck's sake," she said. "There's no paprika. And definitely no Worcester sauce."

"You're joking," I said, accidentally back to normal speaking volume. Kathryn winced.

"I've got to go to the shop. If Patrick asks, could you tell him I'm still upstairs?"

She closed her eyes and, shaking her head, said: "Be quick."

10

I already knew it, as I sprinted out of Stephen Mews, my chef's clogs slipping on the cobbles: I didn't have enough money. I had dropped 15p into my pocket that morning – enough for a sausage roll in the event that lunch wasn't provided. And yet to prepare the sauce I'd created, I'd need extra ingredients that would cost me... one pound? Two?

Even as I ran past the newsagent's on Charlotte Street, I knew what I was going to do. I ran into a branch of Mace and hunted out the paprika and the Worcester sauce. The decision to do what I did next had arrived, predetermined, the moment Kathryn told me there was none in the kitchen. Once it came, I had a vague sensation of ordering myself not to think about it any more, just to go into automatic, to keep any conscious processing to an absolute minimum, lest it trigger doubt or fear or conscience. I hid at the end of an aisle, holding the ingredients down by my side. Checking in the large security mirrors that noone was watching, I slipped them into my pocket. It was easier than I had imagined. I was almost shocked, as I exited the shop, that nothing happened. The world didn't jump; sirens didn't flash; my reflection didn't change.

Kathryn was preparing the staff lunch when I arrived back in the kitchen. I fired up the burner next to her, fried off some shallots and crushed garlic, added beef stock and port, brought it to a simmer, reduced the heat and stirred in four tablespoons of tomato purée, some Worcester sauce, ground fennel, paprika and began to reduce it down. Soon, it began to release its sweet, rich and aniseed aroma.

Kathryn and I didn't speak as we worked. I had just started to peel and chop the potatoes for the mash, when I heard her whisper, "No!"

I paused with my knife and frowned in her direction. "Fuck, Killian. You need to boil the potatoes with the skins on and peel them afterwards. Otherwise they'll take on too much water and won't absorb enough butter. Ambrose – if you give him watery mash, you might as well start making enquiries at Garfunkel's right now."

"Hello?"

It was Patrick. A flutter of alarm moved through Kathryn's face and body.

"Sorry, Chef," she said.

He walked towards us with a steaming ladle.

"We've got time to stand around and gossip, have we?"

"*Non*, Chef," she said. "Sorry, Chef."

Patrick mimicked Kathryn. "'*Non*, chef'," he said, pecking at her forehead with the hot ladle. He peered into the bubbling pot of basil and tomato sauce she was preparing for the staff lunch.

"Is this the family meal?"

"*Oui*, Chef," she said.

He stood upright and called, "Brigade!"

Slowly, one chef after another stopped what they were doing and shuffled towards us. They hung back from the scene with their pale, greasy faces and their smiles of anticipatory pleasure. Patrick picked up a spoon, took some sauce, tipped a drop between his teeth and pressed it to the roof of his mouth. A crusted ball of matter hung from a net of little black hairs in his right nostril. It wobbled there, as he considered the flavour.

Finally, he gobbed Kathryn's sauce out through a curled tongue. It fell to the floor with a distant splat.

"Fucking disgusting."

He passed the spoon to a lanky chef next to him. "Perhaps Chris can give us a second opinion."

Chris spat his taste at Kathryn's feet and shook his head with an exaggerated grimace. As every cook in the gang tasted and spat, the whites of Kathryn's eyes shattered with red.

"You," said Patrick, addressing me. "AIDS." He nodded towards the pan. "Why don't you have a go?"

I took the spoon, dipped it in the pot and tipped a few drops in my mouth, just as the others had. It was a roasted tomato and basil sauce, with some chicken stock reducing in it and, I thought, a small amount of honey. How could it not be delicious? I glanced over the faces of the cooks who were watching me, impatient for my verdict. In their pallor and in their burns and scabs and cuts I could sense their dedication; their talent. They were the men of King. *Max's* men. They were here. With me. Waiting for me to join them.

Kathryn moved her gaze from the floor to my face. One of her cuffs had slipped down, unrolled. It was covering a part of her hand. She'd need to roll that back up, I thought. She'd need to sort that out, if she was going to cook any more today.

I met Patrick's eyes and took a steadying breath.

"It's fine," I muttered. "It's good."

I swallowed dryly. Patrick blinked. Immediately, his attention shifted to the stitching on my whites that Dorothy had carefully completed at the weekend.

"What does that say?" he said.

"Killian, Chef," I said. "My name."

As he pushed his nose up to mine. I could smell his faecal coffee breath and the overwhelming damp salami stench of his skin.

"You," he said, "do not have your name on your jacket. You're just a fucking apprentice."

He picked up a cleaver, pinched the blue cotton stitching between two nubby fingers and pulled it towards him. With a sawing motion, he sliced it off, the red tomato juice soaking from the blade into the white fabric. It dropped into a small foamy puddle on the floor.

"Max has a rule. You probably know it. Never sack an apprentice. It's a bit of a shame that Max isn't here this morning, isn't it?"

He gave a leery sniff and rubbed the hanging matter from his nostril with the back of his hand.

"Go on, you little weirdo. Piss off. I don't want to see you in this kitchen again."

Every emotion and every sensation left me.

"Go on, then! Let's have one last demonstration of your award-winning skills," he said. "Show me how to fuck off in under thirty seconds."

I turned slowly and walked down the room, past the rows of apprentices in their clogs and whites, past the empty stations where Kathryn and I had worked so briefly together and out towards the flat grey light of Stephen Mews with its pigeons and cobblestones and high walls, their stoic magnificence humbled by a hundred-year layer of dirt. The door closed behind me with an underwhelming clunk. I was gazing at it in shocked silence when it opened again with a rattle.

"Killian?" Kathryn looked smaller outside the kitchen; tender and hesitant and pale. "I just wanted – thank you." She'd sorted her sleeve out now. She'd rolled it back up. Ready to carry on cooking for Max. Ready for the rest of her life. "I have to get back in," she said. "But... you know. Thanks."

She'd be fine now, with her sleeves all rolled up properly. She'd be fine going back in there and cooking with Max Mann.

A cold wind blew through the hole in my tunic.

"I have to go back to Tonbridge," I said.

"Yeah, that's what I'm saying. I'm saying sorry."

"I never even got to meet him." I heard myself whimper. She put her hand out to touch my arm and I threw it back.

"Don't touch me," I said.

Her elbow hit the door. It clattered angrily with the impact.

"Fucking *twat*," she replied. And without pausing to look back, she disappeared into the kitchen.

11

I allowed myself to be pulled by the current of the crowd as it drained towards Charing Cross Station. As I drifted past the Hippodrome and the eastern fringe of Chinatown, I made the decision to leave it as long as possible before telling anyone of my dismissal. I imagined standing in front of everyone, absorbing their reactions: my aunt's sadness, my teacher's disappointment, my mother's sour amusement. And then what? Back to Tonbridge, back to college, back to a life of routine smallness.

Arriving at Bridgewater Close, I walked past the near-identical buildings, past the Houses' place with their large extension, and turned into the path that ran up my front garden – an unremarkable rectangle bordered with pretty flowers and shrubs that rang, somehow, with an almighty sense of emptiness. My door key slipped into place with its familiar run of clicks and bumps, I walked through to the kitchen and, for the first time in my life, suddenly understood father.

There it was, right in front of me: defeat in the form of a forty-seven-year-old margarine factory worker. He was looking down in concentrated silence at the salad cream sandwich he was preparing, wearing a tight blue V-neck jumper with a Bell's whisky logo above the heart. There were grease-gummed crumbs of dandruff glued into the hem of the V and the skin between it and where his hair started was a dull waxen yellow. Everything was forever drawn down with my father – his mouth, his chin, his shoulders, even his flat feet gave the impression that the gravity of life was too much for his narrow bones. I stood there looking at him with the surreal sensation that my emotional self had somehow leaped from my physical body and decided to spread salad cream on some bread with the back of a teaspoon.

From where I was standing, I could hear the television in the lounge next door.

"Been at college?" said Dad, his Irish accent hardly having weakened at all in spite of his thirty-one years in Kent.

"Work experience today," I said. "In the best restaurant in the world."

"That's nice."

He squinted as he worked the unctuous spread into the very corners of his Mighty White.

"Make us a sandwich, Killian," came a shout from the lounge. "Hellmann's and turkey."

"Okay, Mum."

I prepared it carefully, with the halved cherry tomatoes and the pile of salt and vinegar crisps on the side, just as she liked it, and took it to the lounge, on the way quickly rearranging the telephone receiver into a position where it wouldn't ring – I didn't want any awkward calls from college asking what had happened. Mum hadn't turned the light on, and was sitting in her armchair in the dark awaiting the beginning of *Grange Hill*.

I laid the plate on the arm of her chair and, without looking at me, she said, "You're not in London on Saturday night are you? I told Felicity you'd baby-sit."

"I was going to visit Aunt Dorothy on Saturday," I said.

"That's fine, then. Visiting's five to six," she said. "You'll be back by seven o'clock."

"Visiting?"

She tutted and rolled her eyes.

"Bloody hell, Killian – hospital. Visiting's over by six. You'll be at Felicity's for seven, easily."

The words she was saying bumped around in my head, trying to make sense of each other. As they did – slowly – my mother became visibly delighted. She had that aggressively teasing look; the expression that overtook her when the world proved, yet again, to be crueller and much funnier than she had given it credit for.

"Didn't anyone tell you? She had a fall, a couple of days ago. She's broken her hip."

She was beaming.

"Look at you!" she laughed. "Oh, what a picture!" She sighed contentedly, tutted and went back to the screen. "You and that bloody woman."

"How is she?" I asked.

She shuffled her bony legs, irritably.

"She'll be fine." A pause. A grip in her blood. "She's ninety-two, for God's sake! She should've been put into a home years ago. The stairs in that cottage. Let's be honest, she had it bloody coming."

12

I ran to the station and took the next train to Tunbridge Wells. When it pulled in, ten minutes later, I tore across the lonely triangle of common, under the imperious glare of the Victorian hotels that lined Mount Ephraim like so many bankrupt yet still-haughty duchesses, and then paced, breathless, along London Road towards the Kent and Sussex Hospital.

My day looked to be getting even worse when the receptionist informed me, with a kind smile, that I was two minutes late for visiting. I put my hands on the counter and decided to have a try at pleading.

"Please," I said. "I've only just found out what's happened to her."

The receptionist thought for a second.

"I don't know. No harm in seeing," he said, quietly. He adjusted the telephone with the tips of two fingers so it was in perfect symmetry with his desk-pad, before dialling a four-digit number and having a short conversation, the receiver shielded by a tightly cupped hand.

"Thought so," he said, placing the phone softly on its cradle. "Your aunt's on Bev Cowan's ward. Bev's one of the nice ones. She said you can go up as long as you're quiet."

It took me another ten minutes to find Ward 10; running through high corridors and up and down empty stairs that twisted around lift-shafts, only to find myself back where I'd started. When I eventually found the place, I entered silently.

The ward's brick walls were painted a puce white. Pipes ran in all directions. Tall windows, their glass murky with the dirt of a thousand rain storms, looked out onto the black bones of winter trees and a sky erased by cloud. A feeling of déjà vu lowered itself darkly into the room. Rows and rows of strangers lay in steel beds, in all the mess of their vulnerability. I tried not to look. I was aware, though, of clear tubes up noses and ancient lips quivering like a young bird's and a man with what looked to be some sort of yellow discharge or ointment around his ears.

"You all right?"

The nurse appeared from behind a screen holding her hands in front of her, her fingers stretched out as if they were wet.

"Miss Moran," I said, and was about to explain that I had permission to be there when she interrupted me. "Down at the end. She's a little sleepy. Painkillers. She's had quite a nasty break."

"It'll mend okay, though?" I asked.

She moved her head from side to side, unsurely.

"Well, the doctor says it either needs pinning or replacing and she's very old. It's very invasive, that kind of operation. If you ask me, though, she'll be fine. She's been complaining about the food, and that's a good sign. It was spag bol last night and she suggested that we might want to try cooking the spaghetti for ten minutes less. She was very nice about it. Has she got much family?"

"Never married," I said, and I was about to add, "She never had much of a personal life," but a memory stopped me: my mother saying with an almost proud sneer, "Don't let Dorothy fool you. She might look like a sweet old dear, but that doesn't mean she doesn't have secrets."

"Well, try not to be too long with her," said the nurse. She hurried away, presumably to wash her arms. I watched as she disappeared, long before the echo of her footsteps.

The lights appeared dimmed. It was that gloomy, early-dusk time, when there's not yet enough darkness for the bulbs to shine against. I found Dorothy in the bed at the end of the room, the glow from a green fire escape sign not doing her complexion any favours. It was only later that I considered it notable that she wasn't doing anything when I saw her. She wasn't reading one of her large-print Jeffrey Archer books, she wasn't doing a crossword, she wasn't sleeping, she wasn't listening to the radio or one of her cassettes. She was just lying there, gazing out at the ward.

I sat on the chair beside her bed and waited for her eyes to connect and for her smile, but it took a long time for her life to find her body; as if the levers and dials were some distance away and she had to struggle to get there.

"Hello, Kill," she said, at last. "What a lovely surprise. You really shouldn't have come, you know."

I was taken by how little space her legs took up under the sheets. And her face: it looked different – diminished in a way that I couldn't quite decipher. It somehow wasn't the explosion of meaning a healthy face is. Her arms were laid gently upon herself, one frail hand on top of the other, a tissue scrunched lightly between two fingers. Her left arm, I noticed, appeared to be shaking.

"It was my own silly fault, Kill," she said. "My doctor, Dr Sanjeev, he always says I shouldn't be using the stairs in the cottage. He's been telling me for years and I've not listened. You know me, Kill, I just can't bear to leave that bedroom. It's the sun in the morning. It's so lovely." She looked down towards her hands, but without her glasses I wasn't sure she could actually see that far. "The doctor here, he's not so nice. A Dr Graham, or something. Says I'll have to walk with an aid of some sort. No more stairs for me. It's my own silly fault. But no matter. I'm just happy to see you." She pulled her chin back and rallied a little, relieved to be pushing the attention away from herself. "So, come on! Tell me how it went at King. They let you out early, then? Not on my account, I hope."

I moved my chair forward in an attempt to squeeze as much hospital out of it as possible.

"I'm just on lunch service in my first week," I lied. "They like to start apprentices off slowly."

"Well," she said, with a satisfied nod, "they sound like very nice people."

"They are," I said.

The lift of her smile finally became evident in the thick creases around her eyes.

"Here, do you think they'll keep you on once the apprentice-ship is over?"

"I reckon," I said. "Guess what? I've won the Young Saucier of the Year award. They told me today."

And that's when she came fully alive; became my wonderful great-aunt Dorothy. She rolled her eyes in the mock-crazy fashion she always used to and opened her mouth in a comic exaggeration of awe.

"Oh marvellous, Kill," she said. "Oh, that's bloody marvellous, that really is. Well done you. And did they like your outfit?"

"They were all very jealous."

She studied me closely. Her pencilled-on eyebrows took a small dive.

"So what's the matter then? Why are you sad?"

"Oh, it's just Mum," I said. "She didn't tell me you were in hospital. She did it on purpose, I think."

Her jaw muscles mashed as she thought something over.

"You know I don't like to speak badly of family," she said, eventually. "But I know how she treats you, Kill. Well, you're a grown-up now, that's what I say. You've got a job of your own, near as dammit, and the sooner you can move out of there, the better."

"She's only doing her best," I said. "Even if I did get a full-time job, I doubt I could afford to live by myself. The money would be awful, to start with."

"Well," she said. There was an almost imperceptible nod, as if she was measuring a thought. Around me, I became aware of the sounds of shuffling and coughing breaking against the hard, high walls. The busybody striding of a passing nurse added to that almost cruel taint you can feel in hospitals, where bureaucracy meets agony and work meets death. When she turned towards me again, I noticed her pupils were dancing all over my face: my mouth; my eyes; my cheeks; my hair; my nose. It was as if she was trying to recall something. When she spoke again her voice had the tiniest thread of hardness running through it.

"You'll be fine, Killian. You will. Trust a wise old buzzard. You're going to be a big hit in London. Already are, by the sounds of things. All you need now is to get out of that house. I know you don't tell me the half of it. All these excuses you make for her."

"She doesn't mean it," I said.

She reached over and closed a shaking hand over mine. Her skin looked shiny and hard, like vinyl. I could see the muscles and mechanisms inside it; rods and hinges and thick blue pipes. I could see everything moving about.

"Can I ask you a funny question, Kill?" she asked, carefully. "Do you have dreams sometimes? About the cottage?"

I saw her heartbeat throb inside a vein. I saw the push of the pulse, defiant in the face of her decay.

"No," I said, still looking at her hand. "I don't know. I don't really remember what happens in them."

"You know you're a special lad, don't you, Kill?" she said. "You've got the Dor blood. You've got Mary in you."

With a miniature groan, she sat herself up, just a little.

"I want you to listen to me now. The next year or two – you might find them to be a little testing. What I mean is, you'll probably *be* tested, in ways you can't possibly begin to imagine. Now, I know you think I'm a dotty old thing, with my funny stories about the cottage and all that. But you must understand. There's more to this world than you might think. When it comes, when it happens, you have to be strong enough to be good. And I know you will, my dear."

She looked settled enough, in her bed. Content. I wondered about the painkillers. It was probably the drugs, making her confused.

"Okay, Aunty," I said. "I understand."

"But first things first," she said. "You need to be allowed to grow up. You need to strike out on your own."

"But I'm never going to be able to move out of Mum's house," I said, pulling my hand up from under hers. "Even if they keep me on, I won't be able to afford it."

I had a sudden doubt about her smile.

"Trust a wise old buzzard," she said. "You'll be all right."

And my room was flooded with golden light. The air was simmering, and I was elevated inside it, lifted by the most wonderful of fragrances. Feathers of flavour were stroking the weight from my body, now the scent of strawberry, now thyme, now roasted chicken, now frying shallots, now lemongrass, now tomato, now satsumas, now chocolate, the air blushing with oranges, greens and pinks. It was as if I were dreaming, not with my mind, but with my nose, mouth and tongue. In that moment, as I floated in the ecstasy, I felt in total command of all of nature's gifts.

13

Having lied to Mum, I realised that my only option was to take the 06.52 to London as if I hadn't been dismissed at all. I walked around for an hour or two and eventually ended up outside King. There was a post office on the opposite side of the road whose window faced the restaurant. It had a counter running beneath it, upon which customers were supposed to stick stamps and write addresses. I spent a long time leaning there, pretending to read pamphlets about the dole and housing benefit. I filled in four passport applications and applied for road tax twice. But what I was really doing was the thing I did best: watching in the silence. I wanted to see them – Ambrose and Patrick and Chef Max Mann. I wanted to see Kathryn.

During lunch service, I walked some more. I went to Billingsgate, Smithfield and Borough Market. I made pilgrimages to Le Gavroche, Tante Claire and Chez Nico. I peered at the menus in Inigo Jones, Le Caprice and Langan's Brasserie. Halfway through the afternoon, I took the train to Tunbridge Wells. Aunt Dorothy was missing.

"Is she still in Ward 10?" I asked the receptionist when I arrived at the Kent and Sussex. I had been looking forward to her sympathetic company and felt pleased that, this time, I could have a full two hours. The hospital was busy. The people moved with a curious slowness; the tired slouch of cleaners, weary invalids, harassed visitors and doctors wired on 5p machine coffee.

"Do you know when they were operating?" he said, picking up the phone with the same friendly smile he'd greeted me with the day before.

"No," I said. "Not yet, though."

He mumbled into the receiver, then placed his hand over it. There was a pause as he listened to something, then span around in his chair. My legs ached from the day's walking and I leaned my weight against the counter, running my thumbs impatiently along its edge, which was coming away to reveal the chipboard beneath. I glanced about at the plastic signs, plastic chairs and the dusty plastic light fitting that was hanging dangerously above me from the suspended ceiling.

"Is she still in Ward 10?" I asked, again, when he was off the phone.

"Sorry, sir, could you excuse me for a second?" he got up from his seat. "I've just got to check something..."

He went into the back office, through a door marked "Staff Only", and I could just see him talking to someone through the window, which was louvred with mirrors. He glanced at me, fearfully.

I walked as fast as I could without looking conspicuous. I went around the corner and ran – up the stairs, left down the corridor, radiology, Ward 8, Ward 7, hang on, hang on, I'm going in the wrong direction, back past radiology and upstairs and right and straight down the corridor, neonatal, coronary care, intensive care, no, no, no, maybe downstairs, two flights this time, where are the signs, where are the signs, steps, steps, steps, down past the lift, I remember these murals, I remember that cartoon tiger, it was somewhere around here, I know it was definitely somewhere around here, physical therapy, Ward 5, Ward 6, oh no, how could this be?, down there, right down there to the end, more stairs, I'll go up this time, oh God, not Ward 8 again, hang on, hang on, I remember endocrinology, it was here, it was around here, Ward 9, no, no, no, got to be down here, there, there, those green doors, there they are, those green bloody doors – and I ran; I ran as fast as I could.

"Can I help you?" said the nurse. She was standing over the bed of a man with remarkable eyebrows who looked as if he was concentrating very hard on sitting up.

"Dorothy Moran," I said. "Is she down there?"

The nurse moved into the centre of the corridor. She spoke low and tentatively.

"I'm so sorry," she said. "Somebody downstairs should have told you. She went at about half three this morning."

"Went?"

"I'm so sorry, sir. We had your mum down as next of kin but – has your phone been disconnected? It doesn't seem to be working. We've been trying all day."

The nurse took a tiny step away from me and her hips moved towards the nearby door.

"I'm really, really sorry," she said.

I stood there, surrounded by the moment.

"That's okay," I said, trying to look calm. "But she was fine. I saw her. I spoke to her." I glanced towards the bed Dorothy had been in. A single fly circled over the space where her head had lain.

"Actually," she said, "I think she was a little distressed about the operation and about not being able to walk without assistance. I mean, the doctor told her yesterday morning she might not walk again." She took a little step back towards me and allowed her voice to become softer. "I know it sounds weird, but sometimes – when they get to that age – sometimes you just get the feeling they're ready to go. They just decide it's time, you know? You see it a lot on this ward. Sometimes, they just decide."

I didn't cry when I left the hospital and I didn't cry when I got home and I didn't cry when I was alone on my bed trying not to think about anything at all.

14

For the first part of the week that followed, I continued to sustain the fiction that I was working the lunch service at King. I'd spend the days watching in the post office or sitting on a bench in Soho Square, before making it home in time to heat up a Findus dinner with chips for my parents.

That Thursday, I walked into the lounge to meet the sharp silence of a conversation abruptly halted. The television was on, but Dad was standing in front of it in his gold-buttoned suit, his navy-blue tie in a wide shiny knot. Mum was in her armchair, having made her usual move of changing out of whatever it was she'd been wearing in the day and putting on her pink Harrods slippers and a thin cotton 'CHOOSE SLEEP' nightdress that went to her knees. Her small round face hung like a failed sun beneath the horizon of her heavy black fringe that was shot through with lightning strikes of grey. A half-smoked Belair Menthol sat glowing in the heavy glass ashtray – a souvenir from a Mediterranean cruise that she had been on with Dad.

She sprang from her throne as I entered – her spine, her upper lip, her finger poking towards me – all curled up and nasty; one great human-sized jab.

"Joy," said Dad, holding his arm out to stop her. His suit was too short and his gold bracelet clashed with his orange skin and hairs.

"What did you say to her?" she said. "What did you say to her?"

She turned to my father. "It's not right. It's not right." And to me, "You greedy little bastard, what have you been scheming?"

"What's going on?" I said.

"We've come from the solicitor's," said my father.

"Congratulations," Mum said. "Greedy bastard. I hope you're satisfied. You've got what you wanted."

"What do you mean?" I said.

Mum broke free and slapped me around the face.

"Not now, Joy," said Dad.

"You're not too big for an old-fashioned hiding, you know," she said. "I'll get the fucking kettle boiling."

"That's not..." began Dad. "This is not the way to solve this situation."

I looked back at my father, squinting in confusion; surprised by the calm strength he was exhibiting.

"The house," he explained. "The cottage."

"Okay," I said. "Just tell me what's going on."

"As if he doesn't know," said Mum. "Acting the bloody innocent. This is how I get treated, after everything. This is how I'm repaid."

"Sit down, Joy," said Dad. "Let me try."

He lowered himself onto the sofa with a stiff grunt, his slow movement somehow having a calming effect on the room. "Now," he said, looking up through reasonable eyebrows. "At some point, your aunt Dotty changed her will to make it so you got the cottage." He patted the arm of the chair. "You're just a boy, Killian. She didn't know what she was doing."

The only way I could hold myself together was to lean back on the sofa to stare at the ceiling – at the bottle-green tasselled lampshade, the long cracks in the plaster, like spider's legs, and the remains of the twilight leaking through the net curtains.

"It's not right," said Mum with sorry, pleading eyes. "It's not right."

"We've been relying on getting that house," said Dad. "It's supposed to go to us – next of kin. We need the money, son. We've got to sell it. I'll be retiring soon. We've got loans."

I couldn't remember seeing them this *combined* before.

"Come on, son," said Dad. "There are times in life when you've just got to do what's right. For the family. We've brought you up. This is the least you can do for us. You owe it, really."

When Mum spoke again it was with a careful mix of affection and softly spun hurt.

"All those years I raised you," she said. "I've given you everything I've got. You should see some of the cases that come across my desk. You don't know how lucky you are. This is your chance to help us for a change. To help your mother. To show me how much you love me." Her eyes raked me up and down. "If you still do, that is. All grown up now. Big man. Don't need your mum any more."

My eyes flicked back to the ceiling. I remembered Dorothy, lying there. *Trust a wise old buzzard.*

"You can have it," I said. "I don't want it."

I avoided looking at either of them as I stood. I didn't know where I was going. It didn't matter: the only important thing was to leave. I'd just see where my feet wanted to take me. Maybe to the park. Maybe to a pub. Maybe I'd do as my father always did and poison the discomfort with whisky.

"You're a good boy, Killian," said Mum as I passed by. "It's only right, after everything we've done for Dorothy. We loved her. You know we did. She was family."

She was stroking the arm of the chair with the pad of her thumb and peering down at it in a detached sort of gaze. It was a caring, gentle motion. She was watching herself in the act of it. Being caring. Being gentle. I observed her for just a second.

For some reason, I lost control.

"Well, that's bullshit," I said.

Her neck twisted towards me. I could see the sinew in it and I could see something pulsing.

"What did you say to me?"

A U-turn, right round to the front of her and I was there, crouching to the height of her face. I was conscious of the pressure in my thighs; the torque in the muscles as I held myself steady. Her legs poked from beneath her black skirt like pistons.

"You wouldn't even let her come for Christmas," I said. "She looked forward to Christmas dinner all year and you wouldn't let her come. Do you know what she ate on Christmas Day, whilst we were eating turkey? I know, because I saw it in her bin. She ate a can of Campbell's tomato soup."

I stuck my face into hers just as Patrick had done to me.

"Campbell's. Fucking. Tomato. Soup."

I stood up to my full height.

"I don't want to be here any more," I said. "I don't want to live here. I want to live on my own. I really think that's best." Silence. "That's what I want. And that's what Aunt Dorothy wanted. What she didn't want was you lot selling the cottage."

"And what have I got?" Mum shouted, rising from her chair. "Who's going to look after me when I get old? Not him. Not that bloody useless sack of a man." She gestured to the sofa behind me, where Dad confirmed her prediction by doing absolutely nothing at all. "We need the house, Killian. We need the money. I need it."

"It's supposed to be mine, Mum, and I'm sorry but I promise, *I'll* look after you," I said. "*Of course* I will. I promise."

She slapped me, aiming her long nails, as was her habit, at my injured left eye. Her nipples hardened beneath her nightshirt. I lurched back and sunk towards the carpet, covering my head. In the background, I could hear a baked beans commercial showing on the lounge television: *"My brother's been really kind to me lately. He's given me all his comics..."*

"Look at me when I'm talking to you, you ungrateful little bastard."

"His magnifying glass, his favourite poster. He's even given me his share of Heinz baked beans."

She kept it coming and coming and coming, shouting, "After everything I've done for you."

"Genuine too! All of them covered in lovely thick tomato sauce."

"You don't give a shit about me. Typical fucking man – "

"Heinz beans are the business! And me? I gave him the – "

"– cunt."

It would be over soon. She would be sorry and she would hold me again just like she used to. It was going to be fine. It was going to be fine.

* * *

When I got home from drinking in Tonbridge Park that night, I found her in the armchair, asleep with a half-drunk bottle of Martini at her feet. I helped her upstairs and put her to bed. I made sure she was warm and comfortable, the quilt tucked up to her chin and the night-light on, her face cast gently in its safe orange glow.

And I felt the caged magic in Dor Cottage. I felt it breathing; moving towards me as I slept. I reached out and touched it with my fingers, sliced with blood, pushed through dreadful undergrowth. They tore at plants as a great fire burned around me.

In the kitchen, the woman I had always known turned to look at me. Gently, she took my hand and pushed my finger into a pot of hot broth. She held it in the thick and roiling red, until my skin peeled off. She said to me, "And now you've come, so. From the land of Uz, all perfect and upright."

Outside, the elms were filled with night and the voices of children. I could hear them chanting, "Earl's heart and earl's leafs and earl's lusts abounding. Earl's fires and earl's grace and earl's witch is burning."

And dogs surrounded the king of all cooks. He pushed them back with his bleeding fingers. "Who's going to stop them barking?"

And I was king of the dogs, dog of the kitchen, dog of the lost.

I was dog of the kitchen, dog of the lost.

15

West Kent's catering department was deserted. I walked through the training kitchen, amongst the cold ovens and the unclattered pots and pans. All the students were on their work placements. I would have imagined that Mr Mayle wasn't there either, if it hadn't been for the message I found by the telephone at home that said he wanted to see me in his office.

I knocked on his door and when, upon his cheery "Hello", I pushed it open, I couldn't work out what he'd actually been doing in there. With his blinds pulled down and his standard lamp on, he blinked at me from behind his desk, looking like a startled mole. If I had had to guess, I would have said he'd just been sitting by himself, quite happily.

"You'd better sit down," he said.

He took off his glasses and leaned on his elbows with a sympathetic downward smile.

"Where have you been?" he said. "We've been trying to get hold of you. I heard from Ambrose..."

I pulled the plastic seat back and sat down. Mayle's office was completely unlike that of any other teacher's room I'd been in. It wasn't just the paperbacks or the biscuit tin or the dusty, tassel-fringed standard lamp; the room's aura was such that it could only have come from his long years of treating it, not as a place of work, but as an extension of his home.

"We've had a few family problems," I said. "My aunt. She passed away."

The words felt too big for my throat.

"Sounds like you've had a rough time," he said.

There had always been something reassuring about Mr Mayle; something that made you want to confide all your most secret frailties. He had these masculine, hairy wrists poking out from his cuffs, small sideburns and his hair was a rich biscuity brown. He'd wear smart mock-tweed suits and tan brogues and yet there was always a comfortably scruffy air about him – an unironed wrinkle in a collar; a reminder scrawled in biro on his hand; his consistently odd socks – that loosened any implied rigidity.

"Pretty rough," I said.

"Overdue for the boils, eh?" His smile became broad and warm, like an arm around my shoulder.

"Sorry, sir?" I said.

"Job," he said. "Book of Job. Did you do any RE at school? 'There was a man in the land of Uz and his name was Job and that man was perfect and upright'?"

I felt suddenly unpleasant, as if a cloud had passed over the room.

"It rings a weird kind of bell," I said.

"You should have a read. I think it's your kind of book. Anyhow, Mr Lone, I need to talk to you about a very important decision you have to make."

He folded the arms of his glasses and placed them neatly on the desk in front of him. Meeting my eyes in a sustained way for the first time, he said, "Is this really what you want? To spend the rest of your life in a professional five-star kitchen? I think you can hack it, Killian, I really do. You're tough, there's no doubt about it. It'll take a lot of perseverance and hard work but I think you'll get there. It's not the talent I'm worried about." He gave a small, reluctant sigh. "You know, Killian, personalities are quite infectious. Do you know what I mean by that? We think our characters are fixed – that we are who we are and that's it. But it's not true. We're porous. We absorb the world around us. The company we keep, the people we look up to – eventually, it becomes us. You know, fine dining, it's... it's not a kind world. And if there's anyone I've ever met that could benefit from a spot of kindness, it would probably be you."

"I can hack it," I said.

Mayle drummed the fingers of his left hand once along the tabletop.

"You're a decent guy, Killian," he said. "You're very bright and you're probably the most naturally talented young cook I've ever come across. But to get to the level of someone like Max Mann, there'll be sacrifices. The long hours and low pay, I'm sure you'll be fine with. The work is the easiest part. It's the other sacrifices. If you want to be in the top one per cent... Well, it's rather like serving on the front lines in a war. Nobody survives with their hearts in one piece. Believe me, I've been around. I'm not convinced it's worth it. You might be surprised to hear this, but I could have been in that one per cent. I decided I didn't want it. I know it's not always obvious, but I'm very happy teaching. I enjoy it. And I like the fact I get to go home at night and spend time with my wife and daughter. We cook, me and my family. We're happy. If I'd pursued all my youthful dreams, I'd be up there, executive chef of somewhere like King. But I'd have none of what I've now got, which may seem very dull and pedestrian to a hungry young man like you. But when you get to my age, believe me Killian, it's everything."

"I'm going to win the Young Saucier," I said. "Did Ambrose tell you? I'm going to win the Young Saucier of the Year."

He smiled, flatly, and picked up his glasses again, opening one of the arms and staring at the hinge. "He did tell me," he said. "And I'm delighted for you. I couldn't be more delighted. I'm delighted for me too. I never thought, in all my years, I'd watch one of my students accepting an award like that. It'll be the proudest moment of my teaching career, it really will, when I accompany you to the ceremony. You've got that under your belt, no matter what you decide."

"I want it," I said. "I really do. It's the only thing I've got. I don't have anything else but this."

He turned his telephone around and pushed it towards me.

"Very well," he said. "In that case you should call Ambrose."

I watched him flick through his notebook to find the number. My right foot tapped violently as I dialled. One ring, two rings, "Ambrose Rookwood."

"Hello," I said. "It's Killian Lone. The apprentice. I –"

"Yes," he said. "I'd like you to come and see me."

"When?"

"Well..." He sounded rather insulted. "Now."

16

I rushed through the machine, with its blue, white and steel shades and its pots, smells and blades, hoping that nobody would notice me. The chefs were as silent as the job demanded, and as focused. Lifting, chopping, boiling, peeling, never looking up unless necessary, never talking, only communicating – an essential distinction, as I was to discover. As I passed through, I thought I glimpsed something bizarre over by the fish station. A slightly overweight cook, working over lighted burners, who appeared to be naked from the waist up. Convinced I must have been mistaken, I looked away and, as I did I caught sight of her working with her usual intensity. She turned in my direction and, I swear, as soon as she saw it was me, she stopped what she was doing for just a moment, and stared.

Upstairs, outside Ambrose's office, I tried to get comfortable on the springs that were straining beneath the papery leather of the aged chair, whilst watching the passing waitresses, who were arriving in preparation for service. They were famous, these women. Max was oft-quoted as saying he wanted his wait-staff to be "terrifyingly beautiful" and to achieve this effect he clothed them identically in skin-tight black dresses that ended high at the thigh. They wore their hair stretched back into pony-tails, their eyeshadow black and heavy, their lips full, red and glistening under the restaurant's smartly recessed spotlights.

There had been grumbles about these uniforms by feminists in the *Evening Standard*, but as I sat there, I couldn't make sense of their logic. These were the least subservient-looking waitresses I'd ever seen. They radiated a kind of alien power, taller than was human and almost insectoid, the sheer dark fabric like an exoskeleton, the eyes swollen huge in the inky kohl, the lips glowing a warning colour. Yes, they were terrifyingly beautiful, but to this young man, they were mostly terrifying.

"Sit down, sit down," Ambrose said when I was finally summoned. As I approached his mahogany desk, I almost slipped on the worn rug that lay loose on the floorboards. I wondered, fleetingly, if it might be some sort of test for the apprentices who brought up his meals, and this, in turn, made me wonder what he'd ended up eating for lunch on the day that I disappeared.

"You've been admiring the parade," he said as I sat. He didn't pose it as a question but announced it as fact. The thing his eyebrows were doing made me wonder if I might be missing something about the waitresses: perhaps the feminists had a point after all. I smiled meekly in response and sat forward in my chair. Ambrose was in a bow tie today, his red braces tight over one of his perfect white shirts. His ashtray was perilously full, a recently discarded butt still glowing orange at the edges. There were no paperbacks in this room, I noticed, or homely standard lamps or biscuit tins. In fact, the whole feel of this office was completely unlike that of his old business partner Robert Mayle. I was sure Ambrose felt just as comfortable in this space as Mayle did in his, but with its chandelier resembling a petrified spider's web, its shelf of awards, its sexual etchings and its framed photos of the occupant himself with powerful businessmen (I recognised two from the newspapers as Robert Maxwell and Tiny Rowland), it wasn't a room that was much concerned with making visitors feel safe.

He sat back and folded his hands beneath his chin, the red ruby in his ring dulled and waxy on his thumb.

"Following your dismissal on Monday," he began, "another apprentice – that girl – finished your sauce." The light slid across his thickly lacquered hair as he dipped his head to look down his nose at me. "It was very good indeed. Contemporary, imaginative, really very promising, for a cook your age."

I lowered my head and bit my cheeks until the urge to smile faded.

"I heard about your incident with Chef Patrick. It is unfortunate, I have to say – your decision to leave so quickly. But I assume by your presence here now you that would like a second chance. Well, I have been informed as to what happened and I have to tell you, we simply do not accept that sort of behaviour here."

As he'd said the word "behaviour", he appeared disgusted, as if he could detect a faint odour of vomit in the air.

"You do not undermine your superiors. This isn't some Derbyshire colliery. This is a two-Michelin-starred fine-dining establishment in the centre of one of the greatest cities in the world. We abide by certain rules here. We have a way of doing things that has operated since the time of Escoffier."

He didn't move, as he spoke. In fact, the only movement in the entire room was that of his jaw beneath his pale skin which, in the light that was coming through the sash window behind him, looked dry and withered, as if it had been hung for years in a forgotten smoke-house.

"One might feel, when one works in the brigade's lower orders, that things aren't fair. But if one excels, one very quickly comes to appreciate the absolute necessity of the way we work. A great many lesser kitchens may concern themselves with rights and wrongs and romantic notions of fair play and so on. But you won't be surprised to learn that here at King we don't regard ourselves as a lesser kitchen. Our goal is not merely filling stomachs and cash registers. We're going to earn our third star when *L'Inspecteur* return this year. We have achieved this pre-eminent standard by eliminating all traces of this sort of thing from the kitchen. We've inhibited our own petty and irrelevant needs and wants in service of what we're here for. The pursuit of perfection."

A thin, paternal smile.

"*L'amour du travail bien fait,*" he said. "The love of perfect work. At King, this is our minimum requirement."

"Yes," I said. "I understand."

"If you want to concern yourself with rights and wrongs may I suggest you join the social services where your needs will be richly served every moment you spend tramping around the sink estates of Lambeth and Wandsworth, attending to the needs of the illegitimate children of Negroes and the lesbians?"

He leaned forward and spoke in a hush.

"But we know better than that, don't we, Killian?" he said. "So this is your opportunity to tell me. Are you with us? Or the lesbians?"

"I'm with you, sir," I said.

His smile dropped and all warmth left the room.

"Good," he said. "Then let's have you back in tomorrow, first thing."

"Tomorrow?" I said. "It's my aunty's funeral tomorrow, sir. In the morning."

His expression didn't alter. It was as if I hadn't said anything at all.

"I'll let Chef Max know to expect you at seven a.m. sharp."

17

A meaty arm blocked my exit through the corridor.

"No, it's okay," I told its owner. "I've just seen Ambrose."

He looked at my shoes, at their ragged laces and scuffs and the place where the sole had split from the leather. When his head raised up again, there was that leering, tonguey smile on his tiny pink mouth.

"He said I can start again tomorrow," I told him. "He said it was fine."

"We don't do second chances here, pal," he said. "This isn't Space Invaders. You don't get three lives."

"But he said because of the—"

His smell was still there.

"Your award? Yeah, I know about that," said Patrick. "Doesn't mean shit in here. Mate, you're not coming back in my kitchen and that's that."

Salami.

"No, my sauce. I think that's why. He liked my sauce. He said it was imaginative and contemporary and I think, well, I could make it for you if you like, I think you'll – "

He scowled me into silence.

"No one comes back. Once you've walked, you've walked."

"But you—"

He spoke over me, "I'll be watching that door tomorrow and if I see you in it, I'll push you right back out of it, into the fucking road, do you understand me?"

A shape filled the doorway at the end of the corridor. I stared over Patrick's arm, which was still preventing me from moving. There was light and noise from the kitchen and this great black silhouette. I knew it. I knew the curve of the skull. I knew the line of the neck.

"Do you understand me?" said Patrick, with increasing insistence. "Don't worry about what Ambrose said. You're not coming in tomorrow. You've gone. You walked. You've lost."

It was him! How could he have been present in the building without me sensing it? How could the ceiling not grow taller or the light burn brighter or the walls not bend out with the force of his extraordinary presence? How could the laws of nature treat him as if he was human, when he was Chef Max Mann?

He turned and he walked towards us. It would be fine, now, all this misunderstanding. Everything would go back to normal.

"Patrick?" he said.

And he was there, just there, talking to Patrick about a cod delivery. So close that I felt I could lick his breath right out of the air. I was shocked at how lifelike he looked. Exactly the same as he did on television, except somehow more compact and concentrated; drawn in startling detail. He had his name stitched onto the chest of his whites and the effect, perhaps perverse, was to imply humility; as if anyone needed to be told. His eyes appeared to have been planted right at the sides of his head, as if keeping out of the way of the great oaken nose that sprouted down the centre of his face, this magnificent organ that gave the impression of having such a history of extraordinary scents drawn up it that it had reacted by bolstering itself with layers of regrowth like new skin on a worn heel. As large as his eyes seemed to be, they had no particularly distinguishable colour; they just seemed watery, glassy and in a vaguely fish-like state of constantly searching for something; on the hunt for danger in the tiniest of details. His mouth was small, thin, and vertical creases lined both of his lips, as if he'd spent too many years sucking everything in his path onto that world-famous palate.

But there was one discomfiting way in which his real image varied from his famous one – the bags beneath his eyes, so leaden and swollen it was as if they were struggling to contain all the shadows that were seeping out of him. Taken in combi-nation with his grey stubble and cropped hair, they gave his presence a crackle of dark instability that I wasn't expecting. Strangely, however, this didn't alter the central fact of Chef Max Mann. He seemed to have achieved that ultimate level of self-confidence in which every look, thought and movement is possessed of a perfect singularity of intent. There was no doubt, question or confusion in anything he did and that, of course, is as rare a quality in a man as it is attractive.

I couldn't suppress the loony grin that spread across my face. It didn't matter. I was with him now.

"I'm so pleased to meet you, Chef," I said, when they had finished.

He addressed Patrick.

"Who's that?" he said.

"An ex-apprentice," said Patrick. "He was here for about half an hour before service last week."

"Half an hour?" said Max.

"Forty minutes, tops. Then he walked."

Max grinned.

"A record!" he said.

"But I didn't walk," I said, being sure to smile. "That's okay, though. It doesn't matter. Ambrose said I can have another go. I can come in tomorrow, he said – " Max's face darkened. "He said I could come back."

Max blinked. He looked at me. He blinked again.

"Come back?"

"Not because of my award, because of the Young Saucier which I think you already know I'm going to win, it's because of the sauce that he tasted and I wanted you to know that I'm a hard worker and that you'll be pleased with me." My jaw was shaking. "I'm not disloyal. I'm probably the most loyal cook you'll ever work with, I can absolutely promise you that, Chef, all my life I have prided myself on being loyal and I've always wanted to be a cook, I've always felt most at home in a kitchen, actually I feel more at home in a kitchen than anywhere else and if there's one thing I am more than anything it's obedient, I've been training myself to be obedient all my life, Chef, and I know we'll work well together and I know, it's funny to say, but I've always thought we're a bit the same, you and me – "

"The same?" he said.

Patrick's lips rose over his yellow teeth.

"What I mean is, with your background, with your dad and everything with Speedy Sam's, well, it must have been hard for you to be taken seriously with all that, and you had to fight for it, and I have too, with my mum, you see, she never wanted me to be a chef, she wanted me to get a proper job–"

"You think we're the same?" he said.

I stopped.

"And we've both won the Young Saucier."

Nothing happened.

"I can cook," I said. "I can cook really well."

"He thinks he's an undiscovered genius," said Patrick. "He thinks he's doing us a favour."

They exchanged a look.

"Not a genius," I said. "But, I come from... my ancestors... I should tell you about my great-aunt Dorothy, in fact, that's what I wanted to ask you. I was just wondering if I might be able come in in the afternoon tomorrow. It's my aunt's funeral in the morning – her cremation – and my aunt – she's the one who taught me to cook so – "

"Stop," he said, softly. He held his hand up, and his smile took on a form that I'd never seen on the television.

"If Le Patron has really given you another chance, then so be it," he said. "*Bon.* I sense that Patrick and I will have a bit of fun, training you up."

"Thank you, Chef," I said.

Patrick snorted lightly.

"You're very welcome," he said. "But allow me to offer a little advice before it all begins. The trick of being a successful apprentice is to be unflappable, exactingly precise, consistent, hard-working and to never, ever make a mistake. And do you know what the catch is?"

"No, Chef."

"*Non.* You say '*non*, Chef'."

"*Non*, Chef."

"The catch is, there is no trick."

He looked me up and down.

"*Bon*," he said, evidently pleased with his little speech. When he turned his back to walk away, I thought I heard Patrick say, "Let the games begin..."

18

I'd never known noise could have an effect like that; I was actually breathless. There was chopping, boiling, scraping, searing, doors slamming, crates dropping, clogs hammering, pots clattering, washing-up splashing and thudding and more and more and more chopping – a thousand blades hammering on a thousand surfaces. And then there were the voices: instructions, blunted syllables thrown like rabbit-punches and the constant calling of "*chaud*". I knew that was French for hot, of course, but the chefs let out the warning cry no matter what they were carrying as they passed behind you – plates, pans, produce. Having no windows didn't help – that feeling of being removed from time and the ordinary order of things. Nor did the continual heat and pressure, nor the smells.

By the time the lunch service was at full power, Max had been in the kitchen for two hours. He had begun the shift in the manner I would soon become accustomed to: emerging silently yet with vast resonance from the passageway at the top of the kitchen, glowing celestially in his starkly laundered whites. He would stand there for a moment, framed by the doorway, hands behind his back, before taking a deep sniff, as if he could detect, with his nose alone, everything that was happening before him.

The most senior staff would greet him respectfully with

"Chef" and, if this was to be a good day, he would nod almost imperceptibly. Then came his tour, walking up and down the kitchen, peering over shoulders, picking up bits of produce and sending his inscrutable gaze deep into each piece.

Max's dominance was such that the kitchen effectively became a part of him; his consciousness extending from his skull and crawling out to encompass the whole space. The power of his presence was so strong that even if you couldn't see him you'd know when he was there.

We apprentices didn't move unless we had to. Not an inch out of place. We'd run to the toilet, having held it past the point of pain. Although a simple pasta lunch was prepared for the full-time chefs, for the apprentices food was nibbled on the job. Kathryn quietly let me know that there was a camping shop in nearby Covent Garden where Danno, the washing-up man, would stock up on Kendal Mint Cake and make a small profit dishing it out to the rest of us on the quiet.

That morning, I decided that basil was the answer. I would use it to take my mind off what was happening in that dismal crematorium in Kent. In front of me was a dewy mountain of bunches, each one composed of fifty-odd stems fastened with a red elastic band. My job was to remove each leaf by resting the top of the stem against the pad of my forefinger and cutting through it with a firm push of the thumbnail. The good, large leaves were to be used in a dish – I hadn't been told which and knew better than to ask – whilst the small and the bruised were to be turned into pesto.

I found myself rocking back and forth very slightly against the countertop. I was soothed in a small way by the knowledge that, despite everything, my parents were going to attend the short service at the Kent and Sussex Crematorium up at Benmall Hill Road. I thought back to the last time I had been there – when my grandmother died. I was about seven years old and I remembered feeling horrified at myself for not being more upset. My Nan was dead and I knew that the required emotion was devastation. But I felt nothing but a faraway calm when my mum yelped in distress as the coffin disappeared behind the curtain. And then that sensation of feeling utterly baffled by grown-ups: the sight of my mum and Uncle Paul sharing a joke in the car park at the very moment their mother's body was burning. They were laughing about something under that terrifying black finger of smoke and I wondered, then, if we might all be monsters.

As I chopped, I felt an urge to run to the toilet and let the tears out, like some shameful act of defecation. But I hadn't cried for almost a decade and I certainly wasn't about to start today. I looked around for a hot spoon or anything that I could press onto my skin to shock me out of the hurt.

I jumped as Patrick moved in behind me, so close we were almost touching. He pulled at the plastic tub that contained the rejected basil leaves; the ones I'd decided were good only for being crushed for pesto.

"Good enough, good enough, good enough," he said, stacking the leaves into a precarious little pile. "Do you have any idea how much basil's costing us at the moment? Are you trying to bankrupt us?"

I couldn't understand what he meant; couldn't believe that some of the leaves he was rescuing were good enough for King. There was what appeared to be a small semi-circular slug-munch out of one of them and a dark, wet bruise on another.

"*Non*, Chef," I said. "These I didn't think were perfect..."

He was so near that I could smell his reply as it came out of his mouth, meaty, rotting and sour.

"If this happens again, I'm marching you down the TSB and you can draw out the cash to cover the wastage. Do you know there are kids dying in Ethiopia? There are millions of bloated little fuckers who would claw your fucking eyes out for a lovely bit of basil. Don't waste it, you wasteful fucking racist."

"*Oui*, Chef," I said. "Sorry, Chef."

He walked off and I began gathering the leaves back up. Then, he stopped, waited and walked towards me again.

"Are you a racist?"

"*Non*, Chef," I said.

Shaking his head, he turned towards the grill station.

I dropped Patrick's basil in the "keep" box and tried to concentrate hard on the difficult logic of this new selection criterion. Ten minutes later, I felt the presence of Max as he moved in beside me. I watched his perfect fingernails sifting through the leaves. I couldn't believe it. He was helping me. *He* was helping *me*.

He tipped up the "keep" box and began to slowly, deliberately place all the leaves side-by-side on the steel surface.

"Tell me," he said, eventually. "Which culinary school have you joined us from?" He had made four rows by now, each one ten leaves in length.

"It's not really a culinary school, Chef," I said. "It's a college. West Kent. In Tonbridge."

He placed another leaf down.

"Your father. Employed?"

"*Oui*, Chef," I said.

And another leaf down.

"Has he always been in work?"

And another.

"*Oui*, Chef."

And another.

"Mother?"

And another.

"*Oui*, Chef. She's a social worker. My dad works in a factory. Margarine."

A pause.

"Money's tight?"

"Sometimes, Chef."

And another.

"I'm attempting to fathom your motives," he said. "What I'm wondering is, is he jealous? Is that why he's trying to sabotage my food? Perhaps he's jealous of the people who can afford to eat here?"

My hands were shaking, the black-green juice from the herbs staining my nails.

"*Non*, Chef," I said.

Silence again. He began straightening the leaves with his manicured fingers, so that all their stalks were at a perfect ninety degrees to the edge of my work surface.

"You know, you mustn't envy successful people for the lives they're able to lead. That's the way nature works, whether you approve of it or not. Some people just happen to possess admirable qualities. Some are born bright, brave and resilient. Others are born stupid, useless and poor." He paused. "As you well know. We all get what we deserve in life. It's no accident that the wealthy are the wealthy and the poor are the poor, no matter how much you or I may wish it otherwise."

I watched him pick up a damaged leaf – the one from earlier, with the slug munch in it – and put in the "reject" tub, where it had been in the first place, before Patrick had intervened. He lowered his voice to a menacing hiss.

"You are going to make my basil, grape and sweetbread salad look and taste disgusting," he said. He leaned forward and whispered in my ear, "You're going to make my food taste like filthy, dirty, cremated old women. Is that what you want?"

"*Non*, Chef," I said.

He left. When he reached the pass, I heard Patrick let out a single laugh, like an auditory punch. Fifteen minutes after that, the *chef de cuisine* was back again. He tipped over my "reject" tub and picked out a leaf.

"The nasty little racist, I don't believe it: he's still trying to fucking bankrupt us."

And so it went. On and on and on. First Max then Patrick, then Max again. And as the kitchen worked harder and harder around me, as everyone else moved from job to job to job, they had me sorting and resorting basil, their threats and abuse becoming more pungent with every round.

Four hours into it, Max walked up to me and stood there, staring coldly as the silence slipped out of his mouth and wrapped around my throat. He slammed his fist, first into one pot and then into the other. I jumped both times, the noise so loud it cracked right through the racket that permeated the room. He stared some more, his thin lips lightly quivering with all the rage. It was then that I realised why Kathryn wore such a curious smile when she'd agreed with me that he never shouts. He didn't need to. Max Mann was an expert with silence. He used it like a master torturer, to create squirming, sweating, groaning discomfort; to generate the unique agony of the mind turned against itself: all the insecurities and monsters contained within it suddenly animated and growing with every empty second that passes. I felt like taking up the paring knife and drawing it across my arm, just to prove to him that I could take it. Behind him, Patrick's face was that of a six-year-old watching the climax of a magnificent firework display.

"If you don't get this right the next time," he said, "I will have you in the yard, polishing the cobblestones all night and back in here to start again first thing in the morning. Do you hear me?"

"*Oui*, Chef."

I turned and picked up the leaves which, by now, I knew intimately. I felt dizzy as I worked; faint. Speckles of yellow and red and blue flashed up before my eyes. I hadn't eaten in eight hours and hadn't drunk any water in three and the noise was like a waterfall of concrete blocks. I wanted to go home. I wanted my aunty.

My eyes darted to the water-filled pot in front of me in which there was a collection of knives. An idea presented itself to me. I could do it, too. I'd done it before, in times of far less distress than this. I had never seen it as "self-harm" – as an act of weakness. Rather, I'd got the idea during an RE lesson in which we were taught about a Catholic priest called Father Jean Vianney who used to fortify himself against temptation by wearing a belt of spikes and whipping himself with a metal scourge. My teacher, Sister Maria, proudly told us that Vianney's housekeeper would have to take a step ladder and mop the walls every single morning as they were splattered high with fresh spurts of blood. He was the strongest man I'd ever heard of. How could I not be impressed?

Nobody was looking. Nobody would notice. I picked out a paring knife and laid it casually on my chopping board. I pretended to trim a few stalks with it. Then, holding the tip of the blade between thumb and forefinger, swiped it into my arm. I felt my skin part and the sting as the tip touched into the flesh beneath it. Pulling my sleeve back over the cut, I dropped the knife back into the pot.

Half an hour later, Patrick came up with a fresh stock of basil and asked Kathryn to pick and sort it.

"Pathetic," he said to me as Kathryn started working through the new leaves, quickly and surely. "First day, easiest job, and you've set the whole kitchen back. The worst apprentice I've seen in five years, easily."

I looked at the pile of sorry herbs on the chopping board in front of me.

"What should I do next, Chef?" I asked.

"Sort your fucking leaves! Sort them and sort them again until you've worked out how to do it, you ugly fucking racist."

"*Oui*, Chef," I said.

He strode back towards Max at the pass, his words disappearing into the noise. "He's truly, properly useless this one, Chef. Maybe we should test him. Palate test."

So I began all over again. Soon I began to feel so faint that I wasn't sure I could carry on. Kathryn moved an inch closer and slowly, gently placed her pale, freckled hand on the back of mine. She squeezed just once, before pulling it back again. She didn't look up or give any other clue to anyone that she was comforting me.

I had to stop, momentarily, to gather myself.

* * *

At the end of service, when almost everyone else had cleaned down and dragged their wilting bodies home, Kathryn and Patrick remained, him finishing off some paperwork and her mopping down the floor over by the grill. As soon as Patrick had slunk towards the changing room, I stopped what I was doing and leaned against the countertop, rubbing the pain from my wrists. Kathryn left her mop and bucket where they were and approached. My focus hardened so that it was rigid on the floor.

"Is there something you wanted to say to me?" she said, leaning back, next to me, on the pass.

There were about a million things I wanted to say to her.

"Sorry," I said.

She put her hands behind her, onto the steel edge, and looked out into the dark, empty kitchen.

"Sorry?" she said.

"About hurting your elbow the other day. I didn't mean to."

"I was thinking more about how I finished your sauce and served it to Ambrose. He thought it was all right, you know."

"All right?" I said.

She touched her bottom lip with her tongue and looked away.

"That's what he told me."

"Thanks," I said. "Thank you for doing that."

I looked at my clogs; at how narrow my ankles looked inside them. *Skin and bone.*

"I wish I could say he thought you were a culinary genius and wanted to drive you down to Michelin HQ to insist on immediate delivery of three stars and a little badge with your name on it," said Kathryn. "But, you know, 'all right' for Ambrose is pretty good. You should be pleased."

I had been watching Kathryn. As far as I could tell, she never talked to anyone, not even when Max and Patrick weren't about and you could get away with it. Nobody really talked to her either.

"What's he like? Ambrose?" I asked.

"He's like a schizophrenic ghost, haunting himself."

"..."

"No?" she said, for once looking a little vulnerable. "He's obsessed with his own youth, that's what they say. Can't leave it alone. He grew up in France, after the war. That's how he got into his Grande Cuisine – the full Escoffier. Got a taste for it in Lyon, then made it fashionable in London in the fifties – late fifties. He was quite famous. Bit of a playboy. Everyone says he's a snake, but he seems decent enough to me. I heard he's been a bit grumpy about that new place in Charlotte Street. Rue St Jacques. It's all classic Parisian and it's looking like it's going to get starred. Andy, the pastry chef – he told me that Ambrose is planning something new along those lines. More traditional. Read into that what you will. If you ask me, it's not a bistro he's trying to build, it's a bloody time machine."

A tide of fatigue passed through me and I gave a deep arcing yawn. She watched me with a kind smile.

"Don't take it personally, what happened today," she said.

I remembered her hand on mine. It didn't seem possible.

"I couldn't work out what I was doing wrong," I said. "I tried. I tried so hard."

Maybe it wasn't. Maybe I had imagined it.

"But you weren't doing anything wrong, Killian. It's just what they do here. It's like I told you – it's a sport for them. They love to bully apprentices into quitting. That thing they say about never sacking any of us – it's like an in-joke. They don't sack us because they don't need to. I just – don't take what they do personally, okay? You seem like a nice guy and they appreciate 'nice' around here about as much as they appreciate Hawaiian pizza."

"But Max Mann." I said. "He wouldn't do it if it wasn't for a reason."

She gave me a look of baffled concern. "You think?"

"But everybody – " I began, and then stopped at an unwelcome memory – Patrick walking down the corridor. *Let the games begin.*

She turned and began clearing away my basil leaves which, by now, were torn and blackening. "Thanks, but Patrick said I had to finish them," I said.

She ignored me, scrunching the herbs into a damp ball.

"Fuck Patrick. He'll have forgotten all about this in the morning."

"But he's the boss."

"Well, the boss has left me with the keys and I have stuff to do for my mum and if I don't – "

She trailed off as she threw the leaves into an empty bin liner and the pots into the sink, ready for cleaning tomorrow.

She walked off, leaving me alone, and I followed her into the changing room.

"Your mum," I said, as I let myself into my locker. "Does she live nearby?"

Kathryn lifted her home clothes into her arms and held them there in a slipping bundle.

"My mum?" Kathryn said. "Yeah, well, if you take a left out of here, keep going for about a hundred yards, then take a right, follow that through the city, take a left there, and you'll arrive at Number 3, None-of-your-Fucking-Business Avenue."

She disappeared into the toilet and closed the door behind her. The lock bolted. She said, "Let yourself out, will you?"

And as I slept, I heard the flies in all their gathering. I felt the Hunger rising. I heard the howling of the dogs.

And I saw him, from my place in the grass outside Dor. I saw the wise man, the finder man. He turned to look towards the garden. I pulled my head down and closed my eyes. I could feel it. The air was filthy with it. The old trouble. The held trouble. The trouble in the ground and in the attic and in the mortar. All of it stirred as I slept. All of it moved towards me.

And the finder man looked in my direction.

His eyes searched the grass with great Hunger.

19

Early one morning a week or so into my time at King, a photographer from *The Face* magazine arrived to take pictures of the brigade, which would accompany an article about Max. When the chefs gathered for the shoot, I took the opportunity to study them closely and became transfixed. Their hair and faces were coated in a uniform layer of dimly shining grease; their chins and eye-sockets grew in unnatural directions; their noses were red and asymmetrical; their skin had turned the same lifeless green as the fluorescent lighting strips which they spent almost their entire waking lives beneath; and there were nicks and cuts and leery, random outcrops of beard-hair, the result of shaving hung-over at five a.m. every morning. They looked as if they'd just staggered in from some nuclear wilderness; a band of outlaws arrived to commit dark acts upon the trembling villagers.

Their appearance spoke of their utter commitment; they were giving everything for their calling. Their sacrifices were so deep that they had come to define the architecture of their appearance. The photographer was a lanky New Romantic with a pirate-costume jacket who couldn't pronounce his w's. He was visibly terrified and soon lost the nerve to actually direct his subjects, leaving them to lean threateningly against the counter and insult him in ways he could barely understand.

As he blushed and snapped and quivered, all he knew was that these were swaggering bastards of the like he had not previously encountered, and he would never be allowed into the warm prison of their comradeship.

I knew this because it was precisely how all of us apprentices felt, every single day.

The brigade was more relaxed in the hours before Max arrived – there would be manly banter and occasional horseplay. But that all changed the moment Max appeared at the pass, as if we were trapped inside a held breath that would only be released at the end of the double shift – an unimaginably distant time in the future.

I'm sure that the chefs feared him equally, but he seemed to truly value their friendship. I noticed that, when a particularly brutal round of punishment had been meted out to one of us, he'd return to the pass with a whip-like smile and he'd sort of bounce around his strip of ground for a minute or two, enjoying the approval he'd glean from them all.

On my fourth shift, Max appeared looking five years older than he had the day before; paler, thinner, and yet more concentrated; honed somehow by the darkness. We didn't yet know it, but the *Evening Standard*'s weekly gossip column had run a piece that day about a "posh chef, famous for his gentlemanly nature, who doesn't welcome mention of his mother's tragic suicide. Rumours abound that her naturally gloomy demeanour was compounded by a secret addiction to barbiturates".

I wasn't aware of Max speaking at all until the tickets started coming in at the beginning of service. In the preceding hours, you could tell by the behaviour of the others that a new set of rules had silently clicked into place. Patrick kept a wide circle around him, assuming all of Max's usual responsibilities. Max himself seemed to just hang there, staring at the same page in a folder, then at the fingers of Carlo in the fish station (Carlo losing several shades of colour as he did so). You immediately thought, "That man should be in bed," but, of course, you knew that the best place for him was the kitchen.

But then came service. That was when he plugged himself in. Everything was double speed on Max's bad days and everything was worse. If some pastry was too dry, some sauce underseasoned, some timing out by even a few seconds, it would start. First, of course, came the silence that always made you feel as if you had fallen through a hole in time. Then the climax, as he tried to remain composed, the muscles in his face tensed, and he began to stutter "N-n-n-n-n-n-no!", his lips tense and blueish; syrupy white balls of spittle in the corners of his mouth; veins in the backs of his hands like throbbing worms. You'd be desperate for him to erupt – just to explode and get it all over with – but he'd suck it all back inside himself. It was awful, like watching a balloon being inflated long past its popping point. And when it did come – that was when we were most at risk from getting hurt. Whilst he'd always leave the physical abuse to Patrick, his verbal attacks could inflict a violence that was far worse. Sometimes he'd hiss and whisper things that seemed designed to break you from the inside. On other occasions, he'd simply stare at you, assaulting you with his grotesque silence, the only clue to the rages within him his unyielding stare and a pale, sinewy look about his eyes, as if they'd been glued open.

Of course, even on his good days, Max actually cooked nothing. His role was to stand at the pass at the top of the kitchen, calling orders in this strange squeaky voice, operating the machine that clanked and hissed and steamed beneath him. Patrick would plate up and Max would stand there, inspecting everything, perhaps adjusting a flower petal here or wiping at finger marks with his torchon. He'd prowl around the same square metre, sipping peppermint tea from his personal silver pot, continually running a comb through his sweat-sopping

hair and issuing newly delivered orders to the brigade's "*Oui,
Chef*" before inspecting the food whose constituent parts had
made their way from disparate corners of the kitchen to their
final triumphal coming-together on the plate in front of him.
He'd also insist on seeing what came back from the dining
room – each waitress would stand at the top of the pass with
the dirty crockery, and if anything substantial had been left,
he'd send her away with a disgusted flick of the arm. Not that
his fury would ever be taken out on the girls or the maître d'.
Even when he did become cross with them, he was never intimidating, merely resorting to an "Oh come on, come on, come on,
you can do better than this...". The glutinous fondness he had
for his "girls" was undisguised. Indeed, the only time he ever
seemed distracted was when his eyes followed one of his "terrifyingly beautiful" waitresses as she glided from the kitchen.

But if he didn't prepare any actual food, Max did cook one
thing with the skill of a grand master: loyalty. I saw it happen
on the first night. It was incredible; a kind of elemental magic.
Unusually, there was a separate station for the cooking of fish,
and the *chef de partie* who worked it was, aside from Max, the
oldest worker in the kitchen. Carlo was a melancholy Italian
divorcee – still heartbroken after the discovery of his ex-wife's
various infidelities – who walked around as if he was still bent
over his stove. His head was the shape of an upturned light bulb;
his face bulging out from where his hat stopped, as if he'd been
wearing it so long it had dictated the growth of his bones. From
my place at the bottom of the kitchen, I could just about see
Max admonishing him for overcooking four pieces of salmon.

"Are you trying to test me?" he said.

"*Non*, Chef."

"Are you trying to see whether I'm worth three stars?"

"*Non*, Chef."

"Don't you think I'm worth three stars?"

"*Oui*, Chef."

"I don't think you do. You think I'm lucky to have two."

"*Non*, Chef."

"Do you know what happens to cooks I dismiss from here?"

"*Oui*, Chef."

He moved in closer, his voice becoming quieter.

"*Oui* Chef, *oui* Chef, they end up working in hotel restaurants in Redcar making prawn cocktails for slum landlords. They become nothing. Do you know why? Because I make sure they become nothing. Do you really think you'll be able to stroll out of here and into the arms of Nico or Albert? It won't happen. I won't allow it. Do you want me to prove it, you amateur? You moron can't-cook-a-fucking-piece-of-f-f-fucking-salmon-fucking-schoolboy?"

"*Non*, Chef."

He smiled emptily. The corners of his eyes twitched with rage.

"No wonder Jacqueline took your boy. No wonder she tried to f-fuck every chef in here. You didn't know that, did you? She wanted a man who could take care of her, who could cook a simple piece of fish and she got lumbered with you, you Italian streak of piss, you fucking limp dick. You're pathetic, do you know that?"

"*Oui*, Chef."

I wasn't in a position to get a clear view of Carlo's face when all this was happening, but I saw it the next morning when Max gathered his men for their usual conference. Overnight, everything had changed. He put a hand on Carlo's shoulder and announced with a grin that crackled, hearth-like, with warmth and brotherhood, "And Carlo's given me his personal guarantee that he'll treat today's salmon with the precision for which he's so justly admired, haven't you, old boy?" And in that moment an alchemy took place that was as miraculous as anything that occurred in any pot, pan or oven. Carlo might have been up all night, cursing Max for his ingratitude, disloyalty and for stamping so hard on his already ruined heart. He might have sworn to himself he wouldn't tolerate the vile bastard for a second longer and that, as soon as the sun was up, he'd begin making enquiries about positions in Nico's kitchen. Every mote of pride in him – every small achievement he'd accrued in his three decades of kitchen work – might have collapsed under the impossible weight of Max's disapproval. And yet in that instant, as the king of King welcomed him back inside the cocoon of the brigade, you could tell that Carlo had done more than merely forgive him. Max had saved the banished Italian from everything he feared and you knew his gratitude felt endless.

Nothing like this happened with the apprentices. During one shift, I watched the trainee on the other side of Kathryn have perhaps the worst day of his life. At twenty-seven, Gregory was the oldest of all of us and it showed in all the good ways. He was more than six feet tall with long and delicate watchmaker's fingers. He was easily the best amongst us, his powerful, expressive hands working the blades and fragile ingredients seemingly of their own volition.

One of Gregory's responsibilities was cutting the fat from veal sweetbreads. As Max was passing behind him that afternoon, Gregory accidentally cut himself.

"Ach!" he said. "Shit."

Max stopped. He squinted over Gregory's shoulder.

"What have you done?"

"*Pardon*, Chef."

In the steel tub in front of him, two or three little drips of red were visible on the shining glands.

"You're bleeding on my sweetbreads." Max stared down the apprentice in all his wintery silence. Gregory pushed a thick squeeze of blood from his finger. Max didn't move.

"Give me your tunic," he said eventually.

"You want my... ?"

"Take it off. Give it to me. You will work the rest of this shift with your chest bare. During service you will assist Patrick on the sauté station. There's a lot of hot fat over there. There's a lot of fire. You will learn to be careful. You will *learn*. And if you make any more mistakes, I will have the rest of your uniform. Now give it to me."

Gregory glanced down the line, to see who was watching. Guiltily, I looked away. I could hear his poppers undoing and the small commotion of his disrobing. As he handed his top to Max, I could see the humiliation of his spotty back, his thick armpit hair and the domey paunch that sat above his trousers.

He worked like that all morning, before disappearing into the fires of Patrick's domain. At the start of evening service, we heard Max hiss at him again.

"You," Max squealed.

We all turned around to see him staring directly at Gregory. "Here."

The apprentice, his shoulders filmy with sweat, put his knife down, ran his beautiful hands down his torchon and walked to the pass. He was blinking madly with the tension as Max glowered coldly at him.

"Can you see this?" he said eventually.

Patrick was beside him, holding the nugget of offal.

"*Oui*, Chef." said Gregory, with an efficient nod.

"Can you see what's wrong with it?"

"*Oui*, Chef."

"Are you absolutely sure?" he said.

"*Oui*, Chef."

Patrick held it up to his eye, causing Gregory to pull his head back slightly.

"I'm not sure that you can," he said. "Because if you can see it now, why couldn't you see it earlier, when you were supposed to be trimming it?"

"*Oui*, Chef, I can see it, Chef."

"Chef Patrick, will you allow him to see it more clearly?"

He punched the hot ball of offal into Gregory's eye. The apprentice, trying not to make a cry, gasped horribly – it was an animal sound, more like a grunt – and slipped on the wet floor, banging his head on the counter with such force that the metal spoons on it clanked. I glanced at Kathryn to gauge her reaction. She looked as if she was very cold.

"Get up," said Max.

Gregory fumbled for the side of the counter and pulled himself back up, his clogs slipping on the wet floor as they struggled for purchase.

"How long have you been cooking?" he asked.

"Ten years, Chef," Gregory said, trying desperately not to cry.

Once he was up, the young chef rubbed the injured side of his head and, as he did so, his arm apparently roused Max's curiosity.

"Show me your arms," he said.

He held them dumbly in front of him.

"You don't have enough burns to work in this kitchen," he said, with a withering sigh. He turned to Patrick. "Make him presentable, will you?"

"Certainly, Chef."

Using his torchon, Patrick picked up a set of metal tongs that had been resting in a hot pan and walked, grinning, towards Gregory, who now had terrible patches of drained white skin extending down from his eyes into his cheeks. It didn't take much. Patrick only had to tap the scorching metal onto his arm for all six foot-plus of him to collapse back to the floor in a mess of snivelling and crying. He began wailing, "I don't care what you do. I don't care any more. Do what you like. I don't care, I don't care, I don't care."

Max stood over him.

"This," he said, "is a defining moment. Now stand up. And *cook*."

Gregory didn't reply. He didn't even look at Max. He just scrabbled up again and walked back to his station, his still-terrified face running with tears and snot.

The next morning, something had changed in Gregory. There was no passion; no urgency; no life. The day after that, he didn't come in at all. Nobody commented upon his absence.

20

After my first day, I was assigned yet again to basil duties. The moment Patrick handed me the crate, I felt an acute urge to run out of the door and back to my bedroom. But the work I did was unremarked upon and soon I was de-crusting bread and cutting it into squares for croutons; squeezing limes and lemons; peeling freshly boiled broad beans and then nicking-out the little cords that connected their two halves; filling *beurriers* for the tables and so on.

At the same time, I was busy going through the ancient retinue of pain that kitchen apprentices have known since the eighteenth century, when the first restaurants were opened after the French Revolution and the Reign of Terror, which drove all the aristocrats from the country, leaving their newly discharged cooks to wonder how to go about making a living. The bending down and the hours of tiny repetitive movements cause a very specific pain, like a knuckle pressing into your vertebrae at a single concentrated spot between the shoulder blades. Slowly, it ripples out into two great angel's wings of agony, spreading laterally and then down, down, as you go into your ninth hour, when it collects at the coccyx. It stays there, growing in pressure, as it begins to leak its leaden soreness into your legs. Soon, the hurt encompasses your entire frame.

Only once, during those first two weeks, was I asked to

prepare Ambrose's lunch again. As I was doing so, I became aware of Max observing me from a distance. Those great watery eyes examined me in a coolly fascinated way as I chopped my onions and leaned into the steam of my pan. My sauce was still five minutes away from being properly reduced when he finally approached and dipped a teaspoon into it.

"You're thickening with tomato purée?" he said, taking a step back so that I could continue cooking.

"*Oui,* Chef," I said. "And reducing. No roux."

I watched him taste it, his tongue slapping twice against the roof of his mouth and his throat moving with his swallow.

"*Bon, bon,*" he said. "So you have been learning something here. *Bon.*"

I glanced back into the pan, at the simmering, savoury red pool.

"Actually, Chef," I said. "I designed this sauce about a year ago."

There was a fleeting muscular twitch around his eyes. "Obviously, I think what you do here is amazing, though," I added quickly. "You and the Troisgros brothers and everyone. You revolutionised food back in the seventies."

He gave a smiling, quizzical expression.

"So – what?" he said. "What are you saying? It's dated, is it? What we do here?"

I was aware of his height beside me; the grandeur of the physical container which held his genius. He was wanted around the world, this man: legendary; famous; brilliant and brilliantly beside me; focused so intently on *me*. I had *so much* to tell him.

"No!" I said. "Not dated. Of course not. But, you know, nothing stays still, does it? I mean, do you ever think of what all this will turn into in the future? I mean, I love the freshness and the lightness that you do here and everything, but my aunt – well, I was brought up on rich French stews, Italian ragus – you know, fat and alcohol and wine. Have you ever thought about if you melded the two? The old and the new? I mean, it's like this sauce – it's not exactly healthy. It has butter and port in it. But it doesn't fill you up like an old-fashioned roux sauce and the flavour – the flavour's massive."

I could feel his breathing.

"You're going to teach me something about flavour?"

I could see all the colours of his stubble and I could see his skin, pale pink and pale yellow.

"*Non*, Chef," I said. "Definitely not. Absolutely not."

"You want me to believe that you came here, from your pitiful little college, already with all these skills?"

"But I did, Chef."

He gave a small, bitter snort and looked dismissively at my bubbling sauce.

"Go," he said. "Serve Le Patron. You've far more important things to be getting on with than making his lunch."

Five more minutes, and this sauce would be beautiful. But not now. It was too thin.

"It's not ready, Chef."

He leaned down so that his face met mine.

"Go. Now."

It wasn't even a sauce, yet. It was soup. Under-seasoned, under-cooked, useless watery broth. It was impossible to serve this to Ambrose. If this was presented to him as my best work, I would be–

"*Go.*"

– finished.

And I was at one end of a tunnel, looking down into a hot pan that was very far away. Way down there, I put my finger in the sauce as if to taste it. And I left it there, stopped in the heat. Stay, stay, stay.

Stop.

Stop.

Stop.

From my great distance, I could tell there was pain. But it was okay because I was in a different place. Miles and miles and miles away, the scalding, the burning, the agony building in the bone.

"Oh! Are you having some sort of tantrum?" Max smiled. "Oh, how utterly gripping. Do carry on."

He watched impassively. A silvery fly buzzed across his eye-line and settled on his tunic, right where he had his name stitched in cotton. He didn't move. My jaw began to shake. I whipped my finger out of the sauce and pushed it deep into my mouth.

"Now get upstairs."

When I came to collect Ambrose's dishes after lunch, he didn't even look up to greet me. As I picked up the plate, my thumb squelched into a great puckering slick of thin, leftover sauce.

* * *

It is probably hard to understand for someone who has not experienced kitchen life, but despite the vivid disappointment of having to serve Ambrose such a foul version of my sauce and despite the hunger, thirst, weakness and dread, there was also much to love.

Feeling so inextricably part of a team conjured a sense of power and family that proved quickly addictive. My first seduction was by raw ingredients. Standing at my station with the morning air around me bursting with sizzles and blooming with wonderful scents heightened my awareness of the role I had to play in transforming these unprocessed lumps of this and that into dishes that would elevate some of the most cynical and celebrated diners on the planet into ecstasy. Leaves, roots and carcasses ceased being gently decomposing artefacts of nature and took on enchanted forms. The basil I worked with was no longer a wilting plant, but the greatest fragrance I'd known. I would breathe it in and let it play grand with my imagination – fresh, playful and innocent, it was a warm wind over summer fields; a pink Sicilian dawn; sunshine through the dress of the most beautiful girl in the village. Those leaves became precious things. And my job – our job – wasn't to slog repetitively for hours over a chopping board. It was to perform a kind of sorcery.

The second seduction was the struggle. The beauty of that struggle is something no culinary college can ever teach; the sense of service being like a malevolent force that exists as a humming, swelling mass on the other side of the umbilical corridor that connects kitchen to restaurant floor. As we worked through the night, we had no experience of individual diners, only the early jets of adrenaline that accompanied the first orders just after seven and then the urgency – always on the very edge of panic – as Max called more and more, the pressure building and building, and the brigade rising up and fighting back as the orders kept coming, the mind and the ears and the fingers working faster and faster, always concentrating, always watching yourself, always with your attention stretching tentacle-like to the others in the kitchen, pushing harder, pushing harder; and when we were winning, when the kitchen was communicating and the machine was fully powered, something happened. The machine became conscious; a sort of hive mind was generated. This is why it hurt so genuinely when you made a mistake. It was worse than letting your boss down. It was worse than letting your brigade down. You had sabotaged a part of yourself that you'd come to value more than anything else; the part that had become God. And when the final order was closed and service had gone well, we would look at each other – it would never be mentioned, what we'd just been through; it was all too strange and precious for that – we'd look at each other and we'd know.

Then there was the third seduction – the one I was to endure for the length of my life. When I recall how it grew, it seems to have come on both quickly and by infinitesimal degrees; with every shift, every service, every task, every minute and every breath it grew stronger, the feeling I had for that girl whose presence I had come to sense by instinct, as if it was fire.

21

It was about nine and a half hours after Max had sent me upstairs, to Ambrose, with the watery sauce. He'd actually been in a decent mood since Thursday – he'd sat for an interview with *The Times* that had apparently gone well – but by ten p.m. any residual levity had deserted him. He pushed past me, causing me to slip with a tray of crabmeat, a small amount of which had spilled onto the floor. I crouched to pick it up and he hissed, "Idiot!" As I was down there, a heavy pan fell off the side and hit me on the back. It could only have been knocked onto me by Max. I collapsed into the mess, stunned and partially winded, and he bent down and whispered, "How do you like that for some old-fashioned, 1970s kitchen craft?"

Come the end of service, I was taking my frustrations out on my cleaning when Kathryn approached.

"What you doing tonight?" she said, leaning back on the counter.

"Going home," I said, pausing in the punishment that I was meting out on the world via my cloth. She'd taken off her cap and looked bright yet nervous, in a way that I had never seen before. But she looked beautiful too, in all the ways that I kept on finding myself remembering and imagining.

"Some of us are going for a Chinese, if you fancy it."

"I can't," I said. "I've got to get to the station. Last train."

Her smile broke down. She looked anxiously towards the approaching figure of a man – the chef with the chapped lips who had opened the door to me on the first day.

"Is he coming, then?" asked the man.

"Has to get the last train," said Kathryn.

"Why don't you stay at ours?" he said, wiping his hands down his flour-strewn whites. "You can kip on our sofa."

"But don't put yourself out," said Kathryn. "You know, get your train. Whatever you want." And then – I wasn't exactly sure – but she added something like, "Don't imagine that I give a fuck."

It wasn't until we were out of Gresse Street that I began to loosen up a little. I'd come to love stepping into the London night after service. The air in the kitchen was as hot and thick as tomato soup and the post-midnight city was the perfect antidote. And then there was everything else: the clubs, the stilettos, the preying minicabs, the mysterious open doorways that you only noticed after dark; the drunks, the punks, the city slicks, the ageing ska-boys, the red-laced Oi! boys and the odd stray New Romantic looking pale and vaguely terrified and in danger of tripping over his lacy cuffs. And above all this mess and mad theatre, the street lamps that cloaked everything in their dangerous, unreal light whispered in unison that the daytime world had gone away and under their watch you could try anything. Night-cast London was a constellation of a million sins and there was a thrill in walking amongst them; you could feel those sins bubbling into being around you, as sure as you could see the walls and windows and the orange-black sky. As a member of the team at King, I felt authentically part of it all; truly one of the city's people.

As we walked in the direction of Oxford Street, I made a decision to be cautious of Andy. He was walking alone, three paces ahead of us. I could guess what was going on: he was Kathryn's boyfriend, he had guessed how I'd begun to feel about her and he thought it was hysterical.

"I've been offered a job," Kathryn said, as we dodged some bin liners that were being tossed from the door of a Pizzaland. "Ambrose asked me today. It's my last day as an apprentice tomorrow. From Monday I'm an ouvrier."

She was wrapping her arms around herself, hugging out the cold. I had never seen her in her civvies before: she was in stonewashed jeans and, underneath her green and pink ski jacket, had on a plain white woollen turtleneck jumper.

"That's great," I said. "Fantastic."

"Cheers," she said, with a dismissive shrug. "I never thought they'd let me stay. I just thought Max was a sexist prick who thinks women are only good for carrying trays and sticking your fingers in. But when he told me, he actually smiled. He said, 'We have detected some trace of latent talent in you'."

"That's amazing," I said. "I hope I get asked."

Kathryn surprised me by looking thoughtfully concerned.

"I saw him laying into you today," she said.

I pushed my mouth into the shape of a smile.

"Well, it's all part of it, isn't it?"

"They gave me a hard time when I started," she said. "I cut into a tureen of chicken liver pâté before it was properly cooked and Max told me to eat the whole thing. And, actually, it was delicious," she said. "I did have to take a couple of cheeky vomit breaks afterwards, though, but credit where it's due – Max's food tastes pretty good even when it's coming out again."

"Urgh," I said, with a laugh. "Has Patrick ever hit you or anything?"

She shook her head. "I'm a girl, you see," she said. "For some reason, they seem to believe that it's fine to torture female cooks in a million different ways, just so long as they're never struck by fist, foot or flying cutlery. Chivalrous of them, don't you think?"

We walked on in silence for a few moments, me frowning at the pavement and Kathryn pushing her hands ever deeper into the nestling blood-warmth of her coat. Even if she was telling the truth about the pâté, I thought, it goes to show that when Max gives you a hard time, it doesn't necessarily mean you won't make it through the six weeks. As long as Ambrose was happy, you had a chance. I wondered about my chance for a moment. I wondered what I'd do if I didn't make it.

"How often have you made Ambrose's lunches?" I asked.

"Oooh," she said. "Six or seven times now?"

"Shit, really?" I said. "I've only been asked twice. Didn't go very well the last time."

"I'm sure you'll get another chance. You deserve to." She looked at me. "You're quite talented."

Quite?

"Quite?"

"Quite."

Ten minutes later, we were all sitting down to duck pancakes and jasmine tea in an upstairs room at a Chinese restaurant which, I noted with a resonant pang of sadness, was next to the Asian grocer I'd once visited with Aunt Dorothy to buy Thai fish sauce and dried bonito flakes for a partially successful meatball experiment. The place was decorated with pictures of the Great Wall, stalking jungle tigers and Samantha Fox that had obviously been chopped out of used calendars. There was a locked door backed with a cracked mirror, a spread of damp in a ceiling corner and the musky-brown scents of hot oil, cigarette smoke and old, spilled beer. An elderly Asian man in a blue blazer, sitting by himself in the corner, kept sucking on barbecued ribs, licking his fingers then reaching under the table to scratch his crotch.

"Did you hear George Michael and his girlfriend were in tonight?" Andy said. He was pouring himself some tea and the pot was dribbling, a trickle of liquid running invisibly down the outside of the spout and re-emerging at its base, where it coalesced and fell, spreading into a translucent spill on the disposable paper tablecloth. I was attracted to the carefreeness of Andy's mess-making; the fact that here, in fantastic contrast to the place we spent so much of our time, it really didn't matter.

Kathryn tilted her head towards me. "Andy gets all the gossip. He's worked everywhere."

"Really?"

She was resting her left hand on the table, five or six inches closer to me than seemed strictly comfortable.

"He's trained in some of the best kitchens in London and Paris, with the best chefs." She looked at him. "You're working your way through the stations, aren't you?"

"Just learning pastry now." He waved his hands in front of me, like a stage magician casting a spell. "Mastering it."

I watched Andy bite into his pancake. A stray curl of spring onion shot from the end. I hadn't realised he had so much experience. I found myself sitting up, a little, in my seat. There were so many questions I wanted to ask him.

"Anyway. George Michael, if you're interested, ordered a deer and tangerine," he said, his mouth half full. "Apparently he paid more attention to his food than to his blonde. Max was delighted, naturally. He was out there like a shot, bidding him bon appetit. He's such a star-fucker. Well, he would be given half a chance. When it comes to fucking, Max mostly just concentrates on the wait staff."

I looked at Kathryn to gauge her reaction to this unlikely allegation. She raised her eyebrows in amused confirmation. Andy began trying to peel another papery pancake off the small stack with the tine of one of the forks that had been provided alongside the chopsticks. He turned to me. "Have you heard about his little accident? You know he's got one of them pregnant?"

"Really?" I said.

"This Russian girl," nodded Kathryn. "Wannabe actress or something. She had to quit work because she started to show. Max has paid for it to be 'dealt with'."

"That's good of him," I said.

"Oh yeah, very good," said Andy. "Paid her a fortune, apparently." He mimed someone picking up a telephone and spoke in an exaggerated Russian accent. "Hello? Is that Nigel Dempster? I got a leeeettle story for you... God, Nige would kill for a story like that."

What was he talking about?

"I wouldn't look so shocked, Killian," Kathryn said. "Max is a right terror. It's common knowledge. Did you know the waitresses aren't allowed to wear underwear? Unwritten rule. You should see them on the restaurant floor, bouncing around inside their tight little dresses. I can see why he does it. It's good for business. We could put six varieties of corned beef on the menu and we'd still be booked solid for the next year."

Andy leaned forward with a grin, savouring the delicious evil of what he was about to tell me.

"He has them round for parties over at Ambrose's," he said. "I went to one of them when I was working with Nico. They're bloody hideous. It's basically Max, the wait staff and all Ambrose's rich mates every Saturday night snorting coke and shagging. They'll be at it now, I guarantee it. Ambrose will be boring them shitless, reminiscing about his glory days in the 1950s – those faraway times when he could still get a hard-on. And Max? Well." He leaned in even closer. "Did you know he tries to whore the waitresses out to his powerful mates? I'm not joking. He tells them which fat millionaire is after them and makes it very clear he considers extra services to be part of their official duty. There was this gorgeous Lancashire girl, a couple of years ago, engaged to some fella or other. Tara – she was about nineteen. Some pissed-up old tycoon took a shine to her, and Max makes it clear what's expected. But she wouldn't have it. She told him she was getting married in a fortnight, so he tells her the only reason the waitresses work at King was because it gave them the chance to 'fuck themselves rich'. Tara was out of a job within the week. Bit of a dampener on the old wedding. Plenty of them have gone through with it though. Lots of them with him. I bet he's inching towards Ambrose's spare room with a new recruit as we speak."

As he'd been talking, I had been thinking about all the years I'd loved Max. The piles of interviews I'd kept in neat shoe-boxes under my bed; the pictures from the *Radio Times* and the *Sun* that I'd glued to my wall; the video tapes of his television appearances. I remembered how I'd tried to mimic the way he sat and smiled and held himself about the shoulders.

"I don't think it's good, to be honest," I said, quietly. "To be talking about Max like this."

Andy looked comically alarmed. Kathryn peered down at her plate and, with her fingernails, tried to separate some strands of spring onion that hadn't been properly chopped through. The old Asian man was now drilling into his mouth with a toothpick with one hand and into the Stygian mines of his crotch with the other. Kathryn remained fiddling with her food, examining it intently.

"Here," said Andy, breaking the silence. "Look what I've got."

He waved an early copy of the next day's *Times* that he'd picked up from a seller outside Tottenham Court Road tube as he'd walked ahead of us. "Should've got a *Sun* as well," he said, clearing a space on the table, so he could flick through the paper. "They've got a story about some mystery business leader who was caught in an S&M club. Wouldn't it be amazing if it was Ambrose?" He looked up with another rascally grin. "You know they have to have a secret code word, those lot? That they say when the pain gets too much? I bet Ambrose's is 'Nouvelle Cuisine'. I'll tell you what mine would be: 'Shipham's Meat Paste'. That'd ruin the mood."

We laughed, more out of politeness than anything. Kathryn was blushing. It was odd – almost as if she felt as uncomfortable in the backwash of Andy's yabbering confidence as I did.

"Hey, what happened to that apprentice? The big one?" he continued, still turning pages.

"Gregory?" said Kathryn.

"Yeah, Max had his cunt helmet on for him this week, didn't he?"

"He left," Kathryn said, not meeting Andy's eye.

"He was a nice bloke," I said, "but he couldn't hack it."

Kathryn put her fork down.

"The poor man was in tears," she said. "Didn't you see him? He was like a cornered animal. But I suppose, yes, you're right – he couldn't hack it. Like the Yorkshire Ripper's victims couldn't hack having their brains caved in with a claw-hammer."

"But that's what it's like in fine-dining kitchens," I said. "They have to be like that, don't they? You know – drill out the weak ones."

"God, you sound like bloody *Max*," she said.

"Not all kitchens are like this, actually," said Andy. "King is easily the most brutal one in the country. Everyone knows it. Worst-kept secret in the business." He looked at Kathryn with an implied wink. "You've only got away with it because Max so clearly wants to fuck you."

"Piss off, Andy," she muttered.

She turned to me, unsmiling. "Max is an absolute *bastard*. I don't understand how you can defend him. If he didn't have so many mates in the press, I swear he'd have been exposed. He'd never have got away with all that 'gentleman chef' bollocks that Ambrose came up with."

"But it's because everyone's so loyal so him," I said. "The brigade would do anything for him."

Kathryn reared away from me just a fraction.

"It's sick. It's a disease these chefs have. It's an infectious mental illness."

"You don't get three Michelin stars by letting your standards slip," I said. "Max wants the best chefs. The toughest ones. The ones who are the most loyal. It might not be nice, but I don't expect many people who are obsessed with excellence are worried too much about nice. Doesn't mean they're not good people. They're exceptional and they have to make sure everyone who works for them is exceptional too."

"Gregory was the best apprentice in there," she said. "He's twice as good as me. The reason he's now saying he's going to quit cooking *for ever* is because of their vile game of knock-down-the-new-boy. Michelin stars are nothing to do with toughness; they're to do with talent and experience, and thanks to Patrick and your hero Max, that man is never going near a professional kitchen again. And don't give me that bullshit about loyalty. Loyalty's a con. It's a bloody trick of the devil. Loyalty's the real root of evil, not money. My dad was just like you," she said, her tone softening slightly. "He was a soldier. He was loyal to the queen, the country and the army. He was loyal to everyone. And look where loyalty got him."

I looked at Andy for help.

"Northern Ireland," he whispered.

"Oh," I said. I shifted in my seat; sat up. "Sorry. I'm sorry. But, what I'm saying is, everyone knows Max is nice. Everyone knows. I mean, it's just..." I trailed off as the logic of my argument evaporated from my mouth. Kathryn closed her eyes. Andy reached out across the table and patted my hand.

"Killian, dear," he said. "Learn when to shut up. We'll wait and see if you're so loyal to the big man by the end of your apprenticeship."

Kathryn placed her fingers over mine.

"Killian, listen, look at me."

I did as she asked and, even in the dimness, I could make out those crumbs of green and gold.

"Do you not see, in any of the tiniest parts of your naive, star-struck brain, that Max is just a bully?"

"But – "

"Think about it now. Don't speak for a moment. Think about it, then tell me the truth."

"He has to get – "

"Whatever you say next, don't you *dare* use the words 'stand-ards', 'loyalty' or 'stars'."

I felt as if something critical, in my neck or eyes or head, was going to rupture.

"It's just, his kitchen," I swallowed. "I suppose it's true to say that it's not exactly what I was expecting. It's not what you think of, is it, when you think of Max Mann?"

To my alarm, my eyes had begun to feel dangerously heavy, my throat swollen and dry.

Andy picked up the steel pot and grinned into the weird-ness. "Tea anyone?" He began to pour. "Max wants his third star, that's what's driving him insane. He wants that more than anybody has wanted anything in the history of bloody history. He's tormented by it. He's getting madder and madder by the day. He can't get through half the services without P-p-p-p-patrick." He put the pot down and continued flicking through his newspaper. Nobody spoke. "Here you go," he said finally. "Found it."

I listened as Andy read out excerpts that he thought were espe-cially amusing, such as Max waxing lyrical about the personal philosophy that's earned him the nickname 'Gentleman'. "Most chefs believe you simply can't get the results if you mollycoddle staff. But I don't call it mollycoddling. It's more like support or nurture."

"He's campaigning for his OBE," said Kathryn. "Or his next date with Wogan."

"Oh, Jesus," Andy continued, "listen to this – 'and Mann's famously benevolent management skills look as if they're paying off: although he refuses to be drawn as to whether he thinks he'll finally win his third Michelin star when the next guide is published in January, his face tells you what most in the industry already seem sure of: it's in the bag. Nevertheless, the chef is not without his detractors. Many agree that Nouvelle Cuisine, the style of cooking to which he's so firmly attached his name, is in its final throes, with predictions of its culinary death coming as soon as the end of 1986. Mann has always been a vocal critic of what he describes as traditional "fat cooking". Some say to keep up with the vagaries of gustatory fashion, he'll have to completely reinvent himself. Does the Gentleman Chef have what it takes?"

"I'm hearing that more and more, you know," Kathryn said. "Nouvelle Cuisine is becoming a bit of a joke. Even George Perry-Smith's got oxtail with grapes on his menu now."

Andy scratched the corner of his mouth thoughtfully.

"Maybe that's why Ambrose is planning on opening this 'Glamis' or whatever it's going to be called."

"Glamis?" I said to Kathryn.

"The new place. The bistro. That's what it's going to be called. Glamis."

Andy spoke over her: "Max has got to be a shoo-in for a third star this year. It'll be us and the Waterside Inn. Nico, probably not, poor fucker. God, I dread to think what it'll be like in the kitchen if Max doesn't get it. Most of the decent chefs I know reckon he doesn't deserve it and none of them in France would even dirty their mouths with his name. That's what he can't bloody stand."

Andy began gossiping about Alain Senderens buying the Lucas Carton, the incoming ("British!") senior chef at Le Gavroche and Bruno Loubet's Gastronome One on the New Kings Road. But I was only half concentrating. I was aware, simply, that I'd made a mess of things. It was the first time I'd been invited anywhere. And yet I had the sense that I had ruined it. All I wanted to do, as Andy gassed happily, was disappear into a bathroom stall and busy myself with one of those knives.

And then something unexpected happened. Kathryn went to the toilet and Andy gave me the fully unrolled version of his mischievous smile.

"Who's a lucky boy then?" he said.

I didn't understand.

"Kathryn," he said. "You know, I've been living with that girl for eighteen months and this is the first time I have ever known her do anything even vaguely sociable."

"Oh," I said, uselessly.

"Well, it can't be *me,* can it?" he said. "The reason for this sudden interest in acting like an ordinary, friendly, functional human being? And if it's not me..."

22

Kathryn and Andy lived in an upstairs flat in an old terrace in Brixton, nearly an hour's journey from the West End on the Number 3 bus. The walk from the stop was at once exhilarating and intimidating, with the drunks and the dealers and the pale faces hanging in doorways and corners, eyes skittering with dangerous intrigue over the landscape of tungsten and black. We passed a homeless man, camped out by a lamp post. He appeared to have an easel erected beneath a grimy bin-liner awning. "He's always here," said Kathryn, as an aside, once we'd passed him. "I'd love to know what he's painting."

Her front door was white and featureless – more like a fridge door – behind which a gloomy wooden staircase, cluttered with piles of telephone directories and old shoeboxes, led squeakily up two dark floors. We sat in a small lounge, on a sofa that was covered with a small Indian-looking throw. By my elbow was a brown monopedal ashtray with a retractable silver lid. There were no curtains, just lopsided office-style blinds, and a Van Gogh print with an Athena logo in the bottom corner, Blu-tacked straight onto the wall above the long-dead fireplace.

"Night-night you two," Andy said, after re-emerging from the kitchen with some tap water in a pint glass. He had that disreputable look again and I noticed a kiss of reddish pink appear faintly on each of Kathryn's cheeks. And then we were alone. A moment passed. Then another. I tried to think of something to say that wasn't to do with Max or the kitchen or her new job.

"Do you ever wonder," I asked, "what any of those extinct things might have tasted like?"

"Like a dinosaur?" she said.

"Exactly," I said. "I keep a list of things I have to eat before I die, and it makes me sad that there are all these, you know, *meats*, that are lost."

"You have a list?" she asked suspiciously.

"I do."

Her eyes brightened.

"I have a list too," she said.

"*You* have a list?"

"What, you thought you were the only one who had a list? The arrogance! At number one on mine is a giant tortoise."

"Aren't they extinct?" I said, laughing.

"Not sure."

"I want to try elvers," I said. "Have you heard of them?"

"Baby eels! What about ambergris? The most expensive food in the world. Charles II ate it on his eggs. It's whale snot or vomit or something. I prefer the sound of this Asian dish, have you heard of it? Son-in-Law Eggs?"

"Son-in-Law Eggs?" I replied, almost coming off my seat. "I can't believe you know about Son-in-Law Eggs. My aunt told me about them once. I'm *desperate* to try them. It's Thai, isn't it?"

"Whole eggs deep-fried in light batter and when you break into them–"

"– the warm yolk! Do you know they got their name because they're supposed to be so good that if a woman makes them for her son-in-law–"

"– he'll never leave her daughter."

By now I was so thrilled that I was on my feet.

"Let's get some now," I said. "Where can we get some?"

"Bangkok," she giggled. "But not London. Believe me, I've looked everywhere. And I've tried to make them. They're impossible."

"One day," I said, sitting back down, closer this time, my knee almost touching hers. "One day, let's cook them together."

"Okay," she said. "It's a plan."

When Kathryn got up to use the bathroom, I used the opportunity to examine the damage to my finger. As we'd been talking, I'd become increasingly conscious of the pain from when I'd placed it in the pan of hot sauce earlier. I gently unwrapped the bandage and winced at the sight of the white blister, pregnant with fluid, that was stuck on the end of it. I was blowing on the end of it when Kathryn returned.

"Oh my God, how did you do that?"

"Accident," I said. "I put it in a pan that had sauce in it."

"Bloody hell, how long for?" she said.

"I don't know," I said. I looked up at her. "I was annoyed. At Max. He said my sauce for Ambrose was finished and it wasn't. I kind of lost it a bit."

She sat down beside me. The room was lit only by a weak standard lamp in the corner, and its caramel light lay gently on her face.

"So, hang on," she said. "You did that *on purpose*?"

"No," I said. "God, no!" I laughed, and thought, I'm saying "no" too much. "No, I'm not *mad*. No, no. I was using my finger to taste it. No, I think I was just so annoyed that I wasn't really feeling the pain. That's how it is when you get angry, isn't it?"

"Not really," said Kathryn, frowning quizzically.

She fetched an old grease-stained first-aid kit from a drawer in the kitchen and began to wrap a bandage around my finger. So that she could see what she was doing, she took a bobble from her pocket and tied her hair into a ponytail. I could see the full stretch of her high, almost Nordic cheekbones. She had exposed, too, more of her birthmark than I had seen before. I looked at it. I wanted to touch it.

Holding my hand over her lap, she pulled the thin white material over the burn with the same purposeful delicacy with which she julienned mangoes. The stretching of my arm pulled my sleeve up a little, exposing a thrill of thin, crumbling needle-ish scabs from cuts on my wrist. I moved closer, so that my shirt covered them over. Our thighs, on the sofa, were touching.

"I'm sorry if I said the wrong thing about Max earlier," I said.

"You can say what you like about him. Your little crush on Max is nothing to do with me."

I took a moment to gather the courage to continue.

"I don't understand why he made me serve my sauce when he knew it wasn't ready," I said, carefully. "It seemed like... I mean, why would he do that?"

She smiled as she opened up a small safety pin and, with great care, leaned in and pierced the material. "You're an odd boy." She paused and smiled again. "You'll get it, though."

I looked at her neck, at the way the hem of her T-shirt lay over her collarbone and the dark canyons of shadow that fell down beneath it. As she held the end of the bandage in place in preparation for pinning it down, I tried to think of something else to say.

"I had a good time tonight," I said. She was nibbling the edge of her lip in concentration. "I can't remember the last time I went out for a meal. I never go out much."

She closed the pin and held my finger in hers for a moment.

"Billy-no-mates, are you?" she said.

I put my hand in my lap, curled my bandaged digit back into my palm and squeezed it as hard as I could.

"Me too," she said. "I think it's kitchens. They attract people like us. Things make sense when you're cooking, don't they? If you're good at your job, everyone likes you. If you're not, they don't. It's straightforward. Understandable. Not like out there." She waved dismissively towards the window.

"Were you moving about all those army bases when you were young?" I asked. "With your dad and everything? Is that why you didn't have many mates?"

"It wasn't to do with that, really," she said. "It was... I don't know."

It didn't seem possible that everything that was Kathryn was taking up the small space in front of me. The idea of her seemed so vast, and yet there she was. Just there.

"I don't usually talk to anyone either," I continued. "I find it hard, people. I don't know what to say to them so I mostly just don't say anything. Then they think I'm being arrogant or aloof or something." I braced myself. "For some reason," I said, "it's not so difficult with you."

She looked down at her lap. She was smiling. It was a good smile, I think. Self-conscious, definitely, but happy. A strange quiet fell over the room.

"You and Andy..." I said.

"This is his flat," she said. "And there's another girl here too. Jenny. She's a barmaid. Australian. We don't see much of her. She's still operating on Toowoomba time. Do you want a drink or something? Jenny's got some beers in the fridge."

Kathryn left to organise the drinks and I stood and browsed absent-mindedly through the pine bookshelves. I pulled out a tattered travel guide to Britain belonging, presumably, to the Australian. I'd just looked up Herstmonceux Castle when Kathryn returned with two cans of Hoffmeister, which she put down on the coffee table.

"I've got a house here," I said. I sat down beside her, and pointed to a black-and-white illustration of Herstmonceux. "A cottage. Well, sort of here. It used to be part of the grounds of the castle. Been in the family for hundreds of years and it's been left to me. It's a weird place. Dor Cottage, it's called. There was a witch lived there, once, they reckon. I'm going on Sunday – I'm moving in. It belonged to my aunt. My parents are pretty angry about me getting the place. My mum – at this rate, I don't think she's ever going to speak to me again." I turned so I could watch her closely. "Can I ask you something? You mentioned your mum, the other day..."

Kathryn sighed in such a way that I instantly regretted asking.

"Sorry–", I began.

"She's not well," she said.

"She's sick?"

"She's in a home. A kind of hostel."

She gazed at the dully shining top of an aluminium beer can. For a long moment, I was scared that she might cry.

"Are you okay?" I asked.

She shrugged, smally, without replying. Then, she said, "The place that she's in – I want to get her out of it. It's a shit-hole. That's kind of why I'm working so hard at the restaurant. It's..." She looked up at me. "I think, the people in that place, they don't treat her properly."

I wondered what would happen if I placed my hand on hers, just as she had done to me the other day. I could do that. Couldn't I?

Her skin felt cold. I let my hand lie there, my arm stretched uncomfortably, damp soaking out on my fingertips. There was that kiss of reddish pink on her cheeks again and even though she was a year older than me, our proximity made me aware of her youth; of the simple clarity it afforded her skin and hair and neck; how her face could have been formed from a single, fresh drop of wax. I could feel the baying darkness outside and my heart beating inside and the seconds thumping past. She didn't mind, you see. She liked it. I looked at Kathryn's mouth. I shifted closer. I wasn't a child any more. I was here, in her flat. She had invited me here. We were touching. Not a boy, not any more. A *dog*, I leaned in towards her.

"What are you doing?" she said, rearing back. "For fuck's *sake*!"

"Sorry," I said. "Sorrysorrysorry. I'm sorry, I–"

She stood up and took a few steps back. "Forget it," she said. "You're just a stupid, silly man. You can't help it. Forget it. It's fine. Do you know what, though? I'm knackered. I'll get you a blanket and pillow and stuff."

There was a branding on my arm. A hot butcher's stink as my skin bubbled and melted.

Then I was outside in the grass of Dor, amongst the rain and dark soil. I felt the earth shift beneath me. It moved with all the trouble in all the surrounds.

I heard footsteps up by the cottage. I watched from the grass, through filthy air, as the finder man led the earl's man along the narrow path. He spoke quietly: "They say that she boils Feathers and Blood together using devilish Speeches and strange Gestures. She hath an Evil thing within her and the Devil attends her in the form of a Fly. She hath been heard to say that in her visions she sees four colours, red, yellow, green and black and that black is always Death."

The wet wind whipped his voice away.

There was something about a black book.

Something about mischief.

Something about devilish plants.

23

I was straining in alert silence in the kitchen the next morning, when I finally heard it – a movement on the staircase. I dropped my basil leaves and went quickly, pushing my wet hands down my torchon and hurrying through the washing-up area towards the open door. By the time I got there, Ambrose had almost got away. He was high up, nearly at the well where the stairs turned ninety degrees. I could see his shiny brown shoes, his scarlet socks, the back of his trousers and his surprisingly plump bottom under the tail of his jacket.

"Um, Mr Rookwood," I said.

He stopped and peered back at me, over his shoulder, his hand gripping the banister, his white face floating in the gloom.

"I was just wondering if you wanted me to make your lunch today?"

"Not today, thank you," he said cheerily, and began moving again.

"Was it all right last week?"

"Not as good as I remembered, since you ask," he said, now just a voice disappearing into a lofty, dark echo.

Two hours later, I was cutting lemons into wedges; carefully removing the pith and pips with my paring knife – correcting all the ugly inconveniences of nature – when in my peripheral vision I noticed Carlo on his way to the fish station, delivering an eldorado of the very same butter that Max habitually promised millions never featured in his kitchens. I'd watched Carlo use it for his salmon, which was cooked *rosé à l'arête* – fried on one side before a hand-grenade of French butter was thrown into the pan and a lid put on, which allowed it to steam in a hot mist of yellow fat. If anything could have given me cause to doubt Max, it was this incredible deceit. Although he did use Nouvelle Cuisine principles, the idea that he merely used water and 'Teflon pans' to achieve his two-starred version of perfection was a fiction that had been sustained so long it was never even remarked upon in the kitchen.

By now, Kathryn, who had been working all morning in the walk-in freezer, was back next to me. I tried to catch her eye. All I wanted was one small, true smile, to tell me that I was forgiven.

"I can't believe how much butter Max uses," I said to her, trying to grin as naturally as I could. "I wonder what Nigel Dempster would have to say?" I made a telephone with my hand. "Hello? Is that Nigel Dempster? I have a story concerning Max Mann and four tonnes of French butter."

A cold swipe of air on the back of my neck. Somebody was behind me. God, no: *Max*. I braced myself for the assault. But he just walked past, as silently as he'd approached.

"Idiot!" whispered Kathryn, when he was safely gone. "Do you know what he'd have done if he'd heard you?"

I looked at her blankly. She said, "Keep your head down for the rest of service," and shook her head contemptuously. "God..."

It soon became apparent that Max was having one of his stuttering days. I was aware of him shuffling around at the pass, his apron tied tight around his waist. The bags beneath his eyes were like dead bat wings. He looked as if he hadn't slept and his gaze was snuffling around the place. But he wasn't looking at our hands to see what we were doing; instead he was inspecting our faces.

Later, Patrick told me that I would be helping to prepare one of Max's signature desserts, a light passionfruit and lychee mousse that had a topping similar to that which you'd find on a crème caramel. My job was to sprinkle sugar over it, use a blow-torch to heat up a brand that had been moulded into the shape of a King logo and push it down, so the name of the restaurant was rendered in crisp, bubbling caramel. It wasn't easy. The brand was precisely the same size as the ramekins that the desserts were set in, and Max didn't want any excess sugar crystals visible on the surface. So how did you get them out? You couldn't tip the mousse. You couldn't blow on it. You couldn't fish them out with a spoon without disturbing the surface. The only way, I decided, was to sprinkle on the exact amount of sugar in the right places so that not a single crumb remained un-caramelised. The branding had to be done just before the dish was sent out, so it was still warm on the tongue.

The first desserts were usually plated at just after nine p.m. and immediately I had three to prepare. I began heating the brand with the blowtorch. Constantly aware of the sucking presence of Max at the pass, I dipped a tablespoon into the sugar and distributed it over the mousse surface in a thin drift. When I was sure the brand was sufficiently hot, I pushed it onto the sugar and watched carefully, my head no more than two inches away from the pudding. Pulling it up, I raised the brand just in time. Perfect.

For the next mousse I sprinkled on a touch more sugar – I thought it could take it and I was right. The logo came up even better than before. I sprinkled yet more on the final dessert. In my mind, I saw Kathryn. I was beaming, telling her, "My mousses were great. You should've *seen* them."

And then I realised – too much sugar. I could tell that it was too much sugar.

"Where are my mousses?" Max was calling, his voice piercing through the noisy kitchen.

"Coming, Chef," I shouted.

I desperately tried to spoon off the excess without damaging the fragile surface of the pudding.

"Mousses, mousses, mousses! *Speeder!*"

I had another two desserts to prepare immediately and another five for three minutes after this. I pushed the brand in and it sizzled greedily. Perhaps if I held the heat there for a second longer, more of the stuff would melt. I smelled something rich, sharp, acid. A thin line of steaming black bubbles squeezed out from beneath the hot metal. I pulled the brand back.

It was burned – and fringed with excess sugar crystals. Ruined.

"Where are my mousses?" he called. "*Speeder! Speeder! N-now!*"

I placed them on a tray, lifted it carefully and made my way to the pass, the kitchen turning into a blur, the hellish noise seeming increasingly as if it was directed at me. I paced back to my station and sprinkled perfect dustings of sugar into the next two ramekins and began heating up the brand, holding it into the flame of the blowtorch until the dark steel lightened. I saw him through the hot, rising air. I saw him: his whole height, his whole fame, his whole majesty, walking towards my station with one of my desserts in his hand.

It was as if the air chilled as he stood in front of me, holding up a ramekin, his great nose rising in fury. He had a row of black hairs in each nostril, sprouting from a bed of broken blood vessels where, uncharacteristically, he'd failed to trim them.

"What do you call this, you fuck-eyed mudlark?" he asked,

showing me the burned, crusted mess. "What do you c-call this? I'll tell you what I call it. A f-fucking cremation. What are you trying to do, you wretched pikey – send your dead aunt an offering?"

Underneath the scorched sugar, the mousse looked like Peach Melba Angel Delight. That had been one of my mum's favourites when she was a girl. Peach Melba Angel Delight with chocolate hundreds and thousands sprinkled on top of it.

"*Oui*, Chef," I said.

I wondered if Max Mann had ever eaten Peach Melba Angel Delight with chocolate hundreds and thousands sprinkled on top of it.

"Mistakes," he said. "I hate mistakes."

I imagined myself feeding it to him. Spooning it between his teeth; his lips closing over it. Gently cleaning away a smudge that had fallen onto his chin.

"Show me your arms."

I knew what was coming. I'd seen this before.

I pulled my sleeves up, bunching the material of my tunic securely into my elbows. I remembered the last time I'd eaten Peach Melba Angel Delight.

"You don't have enough burns to work in this kitchen."

I picked up the brand from where I had left it on the pass. The edges were still whitened with heat; the dark steel of the word "KING" a light, wispy grey. I gripped my fingers around the plastic handle and brought it towards me, feeling the hotness of the metal as it approached my skin. Max's eyes followed what I was doing. They tracked my movements as I tracked his.

I imagined Max and my mother seated around a picnic table in a sunny garden, and me carrying in a vast dish of Angel Delight to them, pale and sculpted and wobbling and decorated in chocolate hundreds and thousands and Jelly Tots and chopped glacé cherries and popping candy. I would cut into it and there would be real peaches inside, peaches that had been macerated in Armagnac and Max would give a little clap and Mum a gasp of joy and I'd spoon it out onto silver plates.

For just the tiniest moment, the brand's contact against me felt cold. I pushed it in, hard, and then the agony and then nothing but pure white floating peace and the battlefield stench of scorching hair and skin.

There would be peaches inside that had been macerated in Armagnac and I would spoon it onto silver plates and give a little bow and Max would grimace and wretch and mock and my mum would say she didn't even like Peach Melba Angel Delight, it was disgusting, awful, baby food, full of chemicals and sugar and rot and those foul, soggy *peaches*...

I swallowed as a jolt of pain ran up my spine and made my upper lip twitch again and again and again. Max took a step back. He was even paler than before. A fly started turning noisy circles around his head. A single drop of sweat fell from his brow and onto the end of his nose.

He hit the brand out of my hand. It clattered to the floor.

"No more mistakes," he said, his voice shaking slightly.

"*Oui*, Chef," I said, bowing my head in deference at his retreating form.

On my arm, the word "KING" was tattooed in a grotesque scarlet logo, the edges of the letters bunched up and livid, a blister quickly forming. Andy, having seen what had happened, filled a bucket with cold water from the fish sink and forced my arm into it, whispering, "That was amazing. You nutter! I have never, ever seen anyone shut Max up like that. Are you totally bloody insane?"

I didn't reply. I just wanted to get back to my desserts.

24

It was after one a.m. by the time I arrived at Dor Cottage, my eyes wired with exhaustion, my left arm in a loosening amateur bandage. I unlocked the heavy wooden door that opened straight into the lounge. Turning on the light, something caused me to pause. I had the strange experience of being alarmed by the scene, but for no obvious reason. The room felt as if it had been brooding in the darkness. There was Dorothy's green armchair and her little coffee table and the cat-print curtain that went across the TV cabinet. And there on the mantelpiece, a framed picture of me as a boy with raspberries on my fingers, oblivious to the loving gaze that she was sending towards me. It was a stage set for yet more magical lunches and warm, cloistered evenings with fennel-caramels and vanilla ice cream with salt and peanut butter and my great-aunt – all the props were poised expectantly, unaware of the disappearance of the essential actor.

Aware of my pulse and breathing, I paced through the shadows, straight to the kitchen. It seemed active, somehow, in its mad, toppling stillness. On the side, there was an open box of 40 PG Tips, a half-filled kettle, an old Sicilian cookbook and a Collins English-Italian pocket dictionary. I refilled the kettle and leaned against the counter, my eyes nervously tracking about the room. My forefinger tapped on the surface as the sound of the water roared into a boil. Mug of sugared black tea prepared, I carried it – slowly, defiantly – into the lounge and sat myself in the armchair. This is my house now, I thought to myself. Then I said it. "My house."

It wasn't long before the day caught up with me. My eyes became heavy and I welcomed it. As focus became harder to maintain, I lowered my still-full cup onto the carpet and rested my head against the worn, comfortable upholstery. I don't know how long I slept for – it may have been only minutes but it ended with a jolt. I lurched forward, letting out a small cry. I had no notion of any sound or movement – no evidence of the thing that had disturbed me so abruptly.

The sudden interruption from dreaming meant that I could still remember the contents of a kind of confused swirl of colliding nightmares. A mess of images and sounds: the night sky outside Dor, long ago, and a strange and frightening man whispering, walking up the path. I could recall, with all the substancelessness of a rapidly vanishing scent, dogs' mouths barking – white teeth and livid gums. And there was the voice of Dorothy, "Don't you ever go over that wall."

I rubbed my eyes. On the end of the arm of the chair there were two silver-grey flies. In the slithery light, I was revolted to see that they were mating. I stared at them for a drowsy moment. Still wreathed in the ghouls of my unconscious, I reached forward – quietly, gently, semi-awake – and I crushed the insects between my thumb and forefinger.

25

Something changed while I slept that night. As I'd taken myself upstairs the previous evening, I'd hesitated before going to bed in Aunt Dorothy's room at the front of the house. I had stood there on the buckled floorboards for some time, my hand stilled on the door handle. Why did the idea of it feel so much like a betrayal? I looked up and down the landing, the silence by now feeling so utter as to be deliberate. I wondered why the flaws of age always seem to give inanimate things human qualities; sagging walls becoming sagging cheeks, cracks becoming wrinkles.

I was being stupid. Weak. I stepped inside, turned on the light and set about clearing her things with a forced casualness. I took away the teacups and the Teasmaid; the tray with its dried fruits and its half-sized packet of dark chocolate McVities. The bed-sheets were stained with urine.

I slept as if unplugged and awoke filled with a reckless excitement, longing for the day to begin. I gathered some apple crates and some old newspapers from out the back and began to fill them with all the possessions, scattered about on shelves, hooks and cabinets, that made the place not mine: coats; shoes; a brass-handled walking stick; a collection of glass dogs and cats; a small pink-tinged photograph of Mum on a pebble beach – Hastings, probably. She looked so different, sitting there, grinning under the precarious English sun. I studied it for a while, before placing it back on the mantelpiece.

By half past ten, I had six full bin liners, the skins of which were beginning to stretch to a dangerous translucent grey. Without bothering to put my shoes on, I carried them carefully to the dustbin by the side of the house – the quickest route to which was via the front door. On my way back in, I stopped to admire the place, the warmth of the path's bricks soaking through my socks.

In a way, it was perfect, with its little white portico and satisfyingly fat chimney; ivy swarming up the walls and around the stumpy, nobly weathered front door. It was a reassuring scene; something about the harmony of the man-made and the natural managed to suggest that the world was ordered and rational and safe. If you were forced to name a single thing that was less appealing about the cottage, you'd probably pick out the small, deep-set windows that gave the building a defensive, furtive aspect. And then, of course, there was the garden.

Dorothy never seemed to relish spending time in the surprisingly mean patch of green that lay on Dor's eastern fringe. As a child, I'd long since given up asking her if we could play outside, as she'd unfailingly have "a much better idea" which would tend to involve desiccated coconut or chocolate drops or vanilla pods or, more likely, all three. It was a narrow and shaded space bordered, on the castle side, by a crudely built wall and was entirely empty bar the scrubby grass, some holly and rhododendron bushes and the shed that I used to spend entire afternoons in when I was young. Its walls unshaven with a million splinters, its uneven roof like a tinker's hat, it sat in a distant corner of the lawn like some banished relative, and I loved it. That shed had been my spaceship, my boat and, of course, my restaurant kitchen. I'll never forget the afternoon I discovered some dirty postcards wedged under a rickety work surface that someone had built in there, using dowelling for legs and a thin plank of eternally damp plywood.

It was out here that I had, for the first and only time, seen dread in Aunt Dorothy. She had been having some sort of baking crisis in the kitchen. Time had escaped her, and she'd forgotten to monitor my whereabouts. When she emerged out of the back door, drying her hands on a tea towel, I was scaling the brick garden wall, trying to see what was behind it. I had an odd memory of there being some strange statue over there – some stone monster or bird of prey bawling in a violent, retching pose.

"Get down!" she had shouted.

Seeing such terror on Dorothy's face had made me freeze. She ordered me down, then pulled me over her lap and proceeded to spank me with the full might of her strength.

"Never, never, never, never do that," she said. "Never, never, never go near this wall again."

She hit me so hard that she rocked back and forth, using the momentum of her body to give her strikes extra force. There was her face and the blue summer sky behind it and a rim of wet gathering in her left eye and then her right and then it spilled from the left, a tear that ran a faltering course, down past the creases and wrinkles in her skin.

I stood, remembering all this, with my hands on my hips and my feet square. I was about to go inside when I noticed something I'd never seen before. There was a small, dark window in the roof, peering out towards the clouds like a single, hooded eye. My arms collapsed by my sides. What was up there? An attic? How could I have never noticed it before? It didn't seem possible. Perhaps, because it was mine now, I was seeing the property with a kind of fresh proprietorial view. Whatever it was, I was certain I had always been completely unaware that... or had I? Although I had no recollection of the physical sight of this thing, the fact of its existence seemed somehow familiar in my memory's undercurrents. It was like recalling a childhood event, and being unsure whether it was something that had happened to me, or a scene from a television programme or perhaps even a dream. The attic in the cottage. Yes, of *course* there was an attic in the cottage.

I quickly gave up trying to understand it all. Besides, if it really was an attic, there was only one place the entrance could be. I strode up the path, flattening the weeds that were sprouting beneath the flagstones, and pushed open the back door. Just as I entered the kitchen, a cloud must have covered the sun as there was a sudden dip in the light. I ran up the stairs noisily and turned into the corridor, my neck craning upwards, waving away a couple of flies that were turning in circles at the end, just outside the sunny bedroom and – yes, my God, there it was – a recessed wooden square. A door in the ceiling like a sucked-back laugh. I wondered how long it had been since Dorothy had been able to get up there. Had she *ever* been up there?

I heaved the creaking apple crates filled with Dorothy's things up the stairs and left them in a pile on the floor beneath the entrance, ready to carry upwards. Then, wiping the hairlets of blond wood from my hands, I rushed to the shed to fetch a foldaway ladder.

The ladder's steps meowed irritably as I climbed towards the attic entrance. Once at the top, I gave each corner a firm thud with my fist and it opened surprisingly easily. I was so startled by what came out that I almost fell backwards onto the floor. The light! It was that time of day when the sun roared into the front bedroom, and as perfect as the windows in there were for capturing its rays, the attic was obviously even better placed. The light fell from the hole, as if a great store of it had been trapped up in the roof, building in weight for decades. It was a torrent of white and pale gold that broke apart as I squinted back at it, bursting into stars of red, blue and green.

Protecting my eyes with the back of my arm, I climbed up. As I sat myself down, I realised that the ground was covered with small, brittle balls that were crunching beneath my weight. When I looked at my palms, there was nothing left of the things but dust, with the odd fine little rod or thread amongst the grey smudge on my skin. Brushing it off, I waited, with my legs dangling towards the corridor below, until I became used to the brightness.

At first, it was impossible to make out anything at all. The attic seemed to be filled with large misshapen black forms that were lined up in a sulky parade. I realised that these were thick cloths that had probably been draped over whatever was underneath them in an effort to defend them against the sun's daily assault. Pushing myself to my feet, I saw there were more of the crispy balls on the ground. The place was blanketed in them. I leaned down to see what they were.

Flies. Fly carcasses. Thousands of them. So old that when any pressure was put on them they'd burst into a small puff of powder. Covering my nose with my sleeve, I crunched across them gingerly. In the eves, I could just make out the dried body of a bird and a couple of spiderwebs so thick they looked like nests. I sniffed uncomfortably, my nostrils suddenly blocked, and pulled back the cloth that was directly in front of me, and a clatter of ancient insects hit the floor.

Recipe books. Some with glossy spines and titles such as *Sauces of Italy, Ancient and Modern*. But many more old enough that their leather bindings had taken on deeply marinated shades of brown and red – the colours, suitably enough, of earth and blood. On each of the wooden shelves were handwritten labels saying "Italy". I tried to make out some titles in the earlier volumes: *De Re Coquinaria*; *Liber de Coquina*; *De Honesta Voluptate et Valitudine*. I pulled a book towards me and it struggled for a moment before finally giving way with sticky "tk". It was heavy and embossed with a golden spoon whose handle was the head of a serpent. It opened with a sound that was midway between a crack and a tut and its rough pages weren't laid out like any recipe book I'd seen before – no ingredients list or step-by-step method. Just dense paragraphs of arcane script in a language I couldn't understand.

It was only then that I grasped the proportions of the room I was standing in. It was a low space – my neck wasn't quite able to straighten at the ceiling's highest point – but the corridor of shelves had a surprising depth. I pushed the Italian book back into its space and removed more of the heavy cloths to reveal shelves labelled "France", "Spain", "Prussia & Scandinavia", "The Orient", "England", "The Americas". I peered into the "England" section and selected something entitled *The Forme of Cury*.

"For to make a formenty on a fichssday, tak the mylk of the hasel notis, boyl the wete wyth the aftermelk, til it be dryyd and take and colour yt wyth safron and the ferst mylk cast ther'to and boyle wel and serve yt forth."

"Serve yt forth," I muttered with a small shake of the head.

I gave *The Forme of Cury* back to its slot and removed the shroud from the neighbouring unit. On the wood, where previously there had been written the names of various culinary continents, was the word "Dor". The volumes on this shelf seemed to be homemade: some hard-bound notebooks that looked perhaps a hundred years old, some stapled and relatively modern, but others merely dishevelled piles of ancient rough-edged paper tied together with brittle yarn.

At the dark end of the corridor of books was a pile of boxes. The largest was a wooden trunk – oak, it looked like, with brass hinges that had dulled to the colour of moss. I bent down, brushed off a layer of petrified insects and pushed up on the lid, which yielded with an indignant groan. There was hay, and amongst that some heavy glass bottles – some brown, some greenish-clear, most with a moustache of dried earth around the thread at the top. They'd been labelled, each in a different hand, in fading watery ink, "Witch Bottle, discovered Aug 12th 1876, two ft beneath rosemary patch"; "Witch Bottle, March 31st 1845, 18" in earth beneath entrance gate, Dor Cottage"; "Witch Bottle, excavated March 10th 1869, 'neath thyme". I carefully lifted one from its bristly bed but it must have been already cracked because the top came away, soundlessly from its base. I let the pale, powdery soil empty on the floorboard. The was a knock, and then another – hard objects falling from the dirt. I picked one of them up and, in a horrible reflexive movement, threw it across the room with a "fuck!" that almost made me jump again, its sudden volume in the swaddling silence reminding me quite how alone I was. It was hair. Human, by the looks of it. Auburn curls tied in the middle and attached to something waxy.

The area where I'd thrown the thing was black and indistinct, and I stared into it, rubbing my fingertips on the denim of my jeans until they became reassuringly sore.

"Time for lunch," I muttered. But by now my eyes had warmed to the darkness and I could see an incongruously modern shoebox that had been stowed in the corner. Creeping over to it, and pulling it towards me, I opened the lid. It was full of... pictures... letters... newspaper clippings. On the top was a wedding portrait in a creamy card frame – black and white with the photographer's name embossed in partially flaked-off gold in the corner. I didn't recognise the groom, although he looked both kind and actually thrilled to be getting married, which is something, when I came to think about it, which you usually don't see in these sorts of photos. And next to him, humble bouquet in hand, beneath the Norman arch of an English country church...

Dorothy?

26

I decided that the best thing would be to leave Aunt Dorothy's secrets where they were; to keep forgotten what was quite obviously intended to be forgotten. And yet I couldn't help noticing that I'd brought the shoebox down into the kitchen. I eyed it as I drank my tea, before announcing my surrender with those two words that precede untold millions of regrettable acts every day.

"Fuck it."

Lifting the wedding photograph out, I found a carefully folded newspaper cutting: an article from the *Sussex Messenger*. The headline read, "Popular Local Baker Announces Early Retirement". They'd pulled out a quote in bold in the middle of the text: "'A terrible shame,' Rosemary Pope, Castle Bakers."

"Popular local baker Dorothy Drake of Dor Cottage, Herstmonceux, announced last week that she will no longer supply the village bakery with her popular homemade cakes that are affectionately known to locals as 'Dotty Cakes'. Rosemary Pope, proprietor of Castle Bakers who sold the iced fancies, told a reporter from the *Sussex Messenger* that the news was, "A terrible shame".

"'We sell 300 Dotties every week and could easily do double that if only Mrs Drake had the time to bake them,' said Mrs Pope. 'We always find a little queue for them at 7 a.m. on Friday mornings when she makes her deliveries. We've no idea what she puts in them, but they're no ordinary fancies, I can tell you that. They're quite addictive. I've always told Mrs Drake she'd be a millionaire if she decided to sell the recipe to Mr Kipling.' When contacted by the *Sussex Messenger*, Mrs Drake declined to comment."

Beneath the article was a certificate of marriage to a Bryan Stanley Drake dated July 5th 1956. Next to that, divorce papers, filed eight and a bit years later. And then, in an immaculately opened envelope, a letter.

25th Nov, 1964

My Darling Dorothy,

I don't need to tell you again how deeply sorry I am for the way I have behaved. I have brought great shame upon you and I know you will find it impossible to ever forgive me. I cannot blame you for this, Dorothy, and find myself unable to say much in my defence. You know now that I did use that blasted herb for my own ends, reprehensible as they were.

I am currently staying with Mother in Portsmouth. As you can imagine, she was terribly sad to learn that our marriage has come to an end. When I confessed that it was down to my own adultery she was crushed.

My darling Dorothy, I am writing to you to make an appeal. I promise this will be the last you shall hear from me. I beg of you to remember the man I was before all this. I hope you remember that I was upstanding, moral and am still churchgoing.

We've had much fun (and made much profit) turning out Dotty Cakes for the past six years or so. I beg you to stop now. In fact, I go further. I propose that you allow me to build a wall that will extend the length of the garden and block out the Physic Garden completely. I know you could never bring yourself to destroy the garden itself. I ask only that you grant permission for me to build a high wall that is completely inaccessible to anyone.

I must furthermore confront a subject that we always failed to speak about properly. You might consider my addressing it now to be a fair measure of my desperation. Dorothy, you told me yourself that your relative was burned as a witch. I know that you noticed the change that seemed to come over the house when we started to harvest that herb. After long reflection, I have come to accept that, entirely by accident, we might have set off something evil in the place. Please understand that I am entirely sober-minded when I tell you that, in using those plants, I believe we invited into our home, in some form or guise, the Devil. I can only recommend the services of a local priest. Perhaps Father Demick could be trusted to act with the necessary discretion.

Please consider what I ask seriously. I await your reply.

Yours with all my love and tenderness,

Bryan.

27

It was the mortar that gave it away. It looked lumpy and unfinished; you could see thumb-smears and casual licks that had petrified in the shapes they had been in on the day it had been built, presumably by this newly discovered uncle. The bricks weren't quite straight, the edges sticking out uncomfortably here and there. It was tall, though – the ladder was just about able to lift me to a clear view. Even though I was high up, I felt cowed by the elm forest whose blind distances stretched on towards the castle. I squinted into the velvet murk beneath. *Oh my God.* There were walls down there, almost as tall as this one, enclosing what appeared to be an abandoned garden about the size of the cottage again. They'd been built with the same ochre bricks as Dor, yet these were glum with damp and sickly with moss and lichen. Directly in front of me was an entrance – a wooden gate between stone pillars that were crowned by the screaming stone gargoyles that I remembered. The garden itself was strangely breathtaking; an ocean, moving slowly but with extreme violence. Silent crowds of nettles in the corners looked out onto a torment of weeds, thorns and tangles; vast clumps of dead-looking vegetation with dried stalks like ribcages a few leafy stems poking bravely through here and there. They looked like herbs, although not a variety I could remember seeing before.

"What the bloody hell are you up to?"

I turned towards the voice and, when I saw who it was, I climbed down the ladder so quickly I nearly twisted an ankle.

"Christ!" I said.

Kathryn seemed nervous, standing there at the garden gate, not sure whether to open it or not.

"Sorry," I said, brushing the dirt and brick crumbs from my hands. "I was just having a look – there seems to be an old garden back there."

"A garden? What sort of garden?"

"An overgrown one," I said, opening the gate. "Herbs, it looks like. What are you doing here?"

She shrugged in a way that suggested she was giving herself a little hug.

"I don't know. I was bored. Sitting around in that craphole of a flat with Andy in his pants, stinking of Babycham and Marlboro. Jenny brought some bloke back last night and he was in his pants too. I couldn't move for hairy thighs and ball bags. I thought, 'Sod this, I'll get in the car and go to the country'."

She managed to look me in the eye for the first time. I didn't know what to say. She glanced over her shoulder, towards Wartling Road.

"I just wanted to see the castle, really," she said. "I love castles. I think it's the military. It's in my blood." She turned back towards me. "I can piss off if you like."

"No!" I said. "Come in."

I led her through the gate. She paused to take in the house. "God, it's gorgeous, Killian."

"We can walk to the castle, if you like," I said. "It's ten minutes that way."

"What, right now?" she said, with an excited grin. "Cool. Go on then."

Wartling Road crept through the ancient fields of Sussex under a dim tunnel of trees, the sun just managing to sprinkle itself through the leaves above, attacking the shade with tiny arrows of pale light. We hadn't been walking down its crumbling tarmac edges for long before Kathryn gave me an uncertain look.

"I'm sorry if I was awful to you yesterday," she said.

"You weren't."

"I shouldn't have been so cross with you. I should've realised – men are kind of automatic, aren't they? Like moths, except it's not light bulbs, it's tits. You're all the same, really."

I smelled the smell of menthol cigarettes, back when I was young. I saw red fingernails pressing into the white filter and ash bunching up on my skin, then softly falling, like snowflakes, towards the carpet.

Kathryn looked at me: at my silence and colour.

"It's just – I have had bad experiences with men," she said. "To be frank about it, I've probably got a chip on my shoulder. So it's me that should be saying sorry, not you." She breathed out. "So I'm sorry. I'm trying really hard, Killian."

We continued in silence for what felt like too long.

"So anyway, I was worried about you," she said eventually. "After yesterday? You dashed off after work – your arm."

"I just wanted to get down here." I shrugged and lifted my bandage towards her. "It's fine now. Got some Savlon on it. It's just throbbing a bit. I quite like it when it throbs."

She glanced into the distance. "Why did you do it?"

"I don't know," I said. "I just wanted Max–"

"I don't know why you're so in thrall to him."

"Because he's the best."

"Is that what you think?"

When I thought of the Max that I used to love, and the Max I had known in recent weeks, I saw separate people. My image of him was like a double exposure, two not-quite-there men, neither fully resolving.

"I just want him to know I've got what it takes," I said.

"But, Killian, you don't need to … It's like you don't think you deserve your place in the kitchen. But you wouldn't be there if you didn't. You know, in this industry, you don't get anything unless you deserve it – jobs or customers or good reviews or stars. Whatever you get, you deserve."

"I know."

"I don't think you do."

She stopped and stood in front of me.

"You're going to be a huge success, Killian. You'll get a job, even if it's not at King, you'll get one and you'll become a head chef. What you did yesterday –" She began walking again. "Have you ever done anything like that before?"

"Not really."

"What about your finger that time? Was that on purpose? When you put it in the sauce?"

My mind felt crowded with answers, and yet it presented me with no answer at all. I wondered if we'd reached it now; if this was it, actually happening right as we were walking: the moment Kathryn realised that I was some sort of freak and stopped liking me.

"You don't need to impress anyone, you daft bastard," she said, eventually. "We can all tell you're talented. You've got the knife skills, the speed and it's… oh, you know, it's just the way you *are* around food, the way you touch it, the way you look at it, the way you talk about it, the way you pile those basil leaves so bloody perfectly in their bowls, the way you talk to those blackcurrants under your breath when they're not behaving. It's obvious. Anyway, you should be pleased. Max is giving you extra attention."

I felt a sudden lightness in my knees.

"Do you think so?" I said.

She started laughing.

"No," she said. "Not really. You're probably fucked."

We turned right onto the long castle drive, past the green domes of the observatory and on towards the magnificent pomp and portliness of Herstmonceux Castle. We talked about food – how, like me, she adored creamy sauces and four-hour stews prepared with whole bottles of red wine. It was the cooking of the ages that we loved: fat, alcohol and blood.

We meandered through the formal gardens and on towards the visitors' centre, on the outside wall of which was a mural that listed Herstmonceux's previous owners. I stopped and silently read down it: Idonea de Herst; Ingelram de Monceux; Maud de Monceux; Sir John Fiennes; Joan Dacre; Sir Richard Fiennes; Margaret Fiennes.

"You interested in all this?" Kathryn asked, her feet pointing in the opposite direction.

"Not really," I said. "My great-aunt – the one who died – she had this story about how the cottage was built hundreds of years ago for the cook of the castle's owner." I squinted at the list. "I'm not sure if I ever believed it. I can't remember what she said his name was, but it wasn't any of these. She might have been mistaken. My mum doesn't even think the cottage is that old. It's made of brick, you see."

"But so is the castle," said Kathryn.

"Yeah, and the castle was rebuilt in 1910. It *feels* old, the cottage. It definitely has that feeling about it. But maybe it isn't. I don't know."

Kathryn looked back at the castle, her nose squished with disappointment. I followed her into the small visitors' room where we browsed the photos and information in a half-bored silence.

"Here, Killian, look at this," she said, shortly.

I followed her nod to a small typed notice, on the green baize board in the corner.

"It was not until the middle of the 15th Century that a large building constructed wholly of brick appeared in Sussex: Herstmonceux Castle. Its sheer size necessitated making the bricks on the spot."

"Jesus," I said. "It *is* old."

Nearby, a typewritten list on white A4: "Owners of the manor of Herstmonceux".

I leaned into the small black type, scanned it carefully and stopped when I felt a thud, like something trying to break out of my chest.

"There he is," I said, pushing my finger against the line: "'1662: His son, Thomas Lennard, Lord Dacre, Earl of Sussex, 1654 – 1715'. That's the one my aunt told me about. Thomas Lennard. He had my ancestor burned as a witch."

It felt, suddenly, as if there was something prickly in the room with us. I looked over my shoulder and straightened up.

"Shall we go back and have some tea?" I said.

We spent the afternoon baking and half-watching videos – *Trading Places*, *Kramer vs Kramer*, some Kenny Everett rubbish. That night, I prepared one of my favourite ragus: the one Dorothy claimed was Catherine de Medici's preferred preparation: beef, pork and soffritto browned until it's all crackling angrily, then cooked until nearly scorched with a couple of tablespoons of tomato puree, then the milk, which the parched sauce always drank down with desperation, and then white wine, lemon juice and then another hour or two in a lazy oven with cinnamon, coriander, nutmeg and cloves. We ate in bleary silence and drank through three bottles of wine.

After the pasta, I plated some freshly baked rock cakes and sprinkled icing sugar over their golden, still-warm tops.

"I can't believe how beautiful this place is," said Kathryn, taking a bite of the cake and gazing at the beams on the ceiling. "I'd love to live somewhere like this. You're so lucky."

"I know," I said. "I feel a bit bad. My mum was pissed off that she didn't get it. I wonder if I shouldn't just let her have it, sometimes."

"But it was left to you..?"

Something distracted me. I looked down at my rock cake. Beneath the snow-like layer of icing sugar, something was twitching, lazily. I dismissed it. It must be nothing.

"My aunt had a thing about this place," I said. "She was convinced there are all these family secrets here. Things to do with the witch stuff. Dangerous stuff. I'm not sure what she was going on about. But this is definitely a weird place. You do get the feeling there are... sort of... I don't know. You probably think this is all nonsense, though? You don't believe in anything like that?"

Perhaps unconsciously, she touched the small silver crucifix around her neck.

"Well, I do pray, if that counts," Kathryn was saying. "I pray every night. You're not allowed to laugh at that, by the way. Laughing is not okay when I'm telling you things like that."

The surface of my cake shifted again. Peering down, I brushed the jerking powder away. There was a raisin there, beneath the icing sugar. It was moving. I pulled the cake apart, a little, with the edges of my thumbs. It had red eyes and a silver body. A fly. It was there, in my cake, sliding its front legs against each other in a grotesque knitting motion.

"You're a Christian?" I asked.

"I don't know," said Kathryn. "I suppose so. My mum, a long time ago, studied theology. She taught me a lot of stuff that helped me understand it. Religion's not all it's cracked up to be. Organised religion, I mean. The Church – it has an amazing history. In a bad way. Horrible. Murder, genocide – the kind of stuff they don't really go into on *Songs of Praise*. But that's not to say I don't believe." She paused and shook her head dismiss-ively, as if throwing the subject clear of her mind. "Anyway," she said. "These witch secrets or whatever they are. Why do they mean your mum didn't get the house?"

Gingerly, I put the cake back on the plate.

"She wanted to sell it and my aunt wouldn't let that happen. My mum was brought up in a pretty wealthy family but she married a working-class guy and I don't think she's ever got used to living on less. I think she only married him to piss my grandad off. Bit of rough, you know. But now they've run up debts, so they need money. But Dorothy seemed to think that selling Dor would be dangerous or something. I don't know why. To be honest, I think she was going a bit senile for a while there."

"What's she like, your mum?"

Kathryn had the most beautiful mouth; thin at the sides, her top lip gathering gently into a lovely, heavy, pink cushion of flesh. I wondered what my mum's mouth looked like when she was young. Had it been as pretty as Kathryn's?

"She's," I smiled uncertainly. "She's a social worker. You know, kind. Kind-hearted. Given-up-her-life-to-help-other-people sort of thing. She can be very, very loving, but she doesn't take a lot of shit from me or Dad. She's a bit like Max, in a weird way. She can get pretty angry."

"How angry?"

Memories flashed through my mind. Stills. Images.

"Oh," I shrugged.

I saw the backs of my mother's hands; the tips of her finger-nails. With a mock-dismissive shake of the head, Kathryn asked, "She doesn't ever *hit* you or anything?"

I saw my mother's ankles as she walked away, their thin framework of muscle and sinew and vein.

"She doesn't mean it. She can be nice – she used to be nice, when I was a boy. And she always says sorry. Always. And I know why she does it – her dad used to beat her mum around and what with that and all the shit she sees in her job, it means she just doesn't like men very much and you can kind of understand her point. I mean, I don't want you to think – she's a good mum. She used to stick up for me when I got bullied. You know, she's so loyal, she'd do anything for her family. She just finds it hard to cope, that's all. And she's right about my dad – he's useless. When I was growing up, I had to take the slack with housework and everything, because my mum was always working and – I'd get things wrong and I'd be punished a bit sometimes. But it's done me good, in the long run. I'd never be able to cope with working at King if I hadn't been toughened up a bit."

I'd become so absorbed in what I was saying that I hadn't noticed that Kathryn's eyes had gone elsewhere. I'd lost her. But it was more than that. I could sense, in the tiny combinations of her muscles and mouth and breathing, that a kind of sadness had come into her. And then I remembered.

"Sorry," I said. I put my hand out to comfort her. I was deciding whether to touch her knee or arm or shoulder, but I just placed it down again, on my lap. "Your mum..."

She closed her eyes.

"I just miss her," she said. "She had a kind of a breakdown after my dad died and now she's sick with this fucking *thing*. She can't do anything. She can't go out. I try to see her when I can, but the hours – since I've been at King, I've hardly been able to visit her at all. She has bruises, sometimes. They say she falls and I know, sometimes, she gets violent with them. But you should see it – it's awful. She has to share a room with four other people and it stinks. It's filthy. I can't bear it. I asked Max if I could visit her, one time, when there was a problem, and he went crazy. Gave me this big fucking speech."

I put my hand out, tentatively, towards her. She took it,

squeezed my fingers and placed it on her leg and then laughed bitterly. "I can't believe I'm letting you see me like this. I'm sorry if it's boring or anything, it's just–"

"Once, years ago, when I got upset, my aunt Dorothy told me I should close my eyes and paint a picture of heaven," I said. "It's obviously kind of childish, cheesy. But it works. I still do it sometimes. For years I imagined myself running a restaurant. Running King, actually."

"I still do," she smiled.

"You want to run King?" I asked.

She said. "Somewhere like that. Somewhere starred, at least. I can't think of any other way I can get Mum out of that place. To go private, it's hundreds of pounds a month."

"But you'll make it," I said. "Some day you'll be able to afford it."

"It's going to be years before I'm the executive chef of anywhere. And by then..."

Carefully at first, I put my arms around her. I felt her tears crush between our cheeks. "Do you know what upsets me most of all?" she said. "I can tell my mum thinks cooking is this shitty, nothing job. She'll never get to see where I'm working – how amazing it is. She'll never get to taste my food. And you should see the dirty *shit* they feed her on." She broke into soft sobbing and I held her as still as I could manage. She tightened her grip around my waist and I could smell her neck. I moved my nose towards it, towards the little mole that sat in the dusk of her creamy, shadowed shoulder and the lines in her skin, so fine that even Kathryn had surely never seen them, never been this close, never studied the curve of the back of her neck and that birthmark, so strange and sad, that disappeared down beneath the hem of her shirt and I was closer and closer –

She pulled away from me and said something that made this a moment for the stars.

"You're very special to me. And that's all I'm going to say."

I led her to the spare room and I left her to sleep, happily, alone.

28

Behind my station, underneath the butchery block, was a row of four grouchy-looking polished-steel fridges. The door on the second fridge was broken. In order to close it properly, you had to pull it up on its hinges before pushing it to. In all the motion and ferocity of the kitchen, the chefs and apprentices frequently forgot about this uppity little eccentricity and simply dealt with this door as they did all the others – with a light heel-kick, at which point it would hit the frame with a thunk rather than a click.

The next morning, I was cutting the stalks off the blackcurrants when, deep beneath the layers of the chopping, clanking and sizzling, this dull clunk sounded. Without thinking or even moving my neck, I said, "Fridge door."

I heard the chef in question mutter, "He's got eyes in the back of his bloody head."

It was the apprentice Malcolm. He was standing there, with a tray of butter, looking at the door which was slowly gliding open as if compelled by a mischievous ghost. For a moment, I had no idea how I knew Malcolm hadn't shut it. But as my fingers and blade worked accurately and automatically on a blackcurrant, I realised that the cacophony that had made me so breathless on the first day had slowly come to make sense.

The menu might have looked like nothing more than a

solemn list, but each one of those dishes had its own unique and violent song that had been filling the ears of the brigade for hours. Those songs combined to create a symphony; a secret music that every kitchen has its own version of, but which is possible to decipher only by total immersion. I could hear it now. There was the scrape and knock of the lamb racks being French-trimmed; there was the shik-shik-shik of the trout being de-scaled; there was the splash and clatter of Danno the pots man washing the bread tins in the sink. All in order; all in time; all correct and comforting. I'd developed the ability to hear the song of the kitchen using all my senses. I could smell the sweet herby richness of the rabbit stock reaching its simmer; feel the increase in heat as the grill station was fired up; sense the texture of the pressure in my gut and so read the mood of the kitchen. Now, after nearly six weeks of apprenticeship, my nose could tell me the time of day, almost to the nearest minute.

It wasn't long after this that I became aware of a silence that was overwhelming the top of the kitchen. Peering between the shelves, I could only see Max's back bending down to meet the face of one of his brigade.

"You've burned your finger?" I heard him say. "What am I supposed to do with a cook whose fingers don't work? What use is that to me? Do you think, when I pulled you out of that trough of mediocrity that is our apprentice brigade, that I did so because you were clumsy?"

I put my knife down and walked around the corner for a better view.

"Clearly, you need some supplementary training. *Bon. Bon.* You will have some. Let's have your tunic."

I could still only see his back. But Patrick – Patrick was looking down at the target of Max's ire and leering greedily, that spitty, pointed tongue resting on the inside edge of his lip.

"I'm sure you don't believe that I'll treat you differently

because you're a girl," said Max. "This is, after all, the age of sexual equality."

I pushed past the apprentices and walked up behind Max, aware that the music of the kitchen – now slowed and loosened – was on the verge of collapsing since the conductor had become distracted. In the gap, between Max's arm and the tall steel wall, I glimpsed Kathryn slowly, defiantly, unbuttoning her tunic. Behind her, Patrick's tongue worked in little pumps, pushing out at his lower lip. The brigade threw excited glances between their work and the action.

She was doing it with the edge of her thumb, popping one white button out and then the next. I wondered which finger was burned. I wondered if she was in pain. The blue flames hissed and the hair on the back of Max's head was thin and wiry. Little white crumbs of dead skin hung inside it, here and there.

Max would stop her in a moment. I knew he would. Max wouldn't allow this to happen. He was testing her.

Then the bottom button was released, and Kathryn, chin down, cheeks blood-red, opened up her tunic. Patrick's tongue was free, half an inch of it poking from his mouth, his cigarette-stained teeth pushing down on it; his slimy taste buds like fur, like wet, grey velvet. The tunic hung from the end of Kathryn's fingers.

I'd never seen her stomach before. Her beautiful shoulders; the prominent mole on her right arm. I'd never seen the shape of her collarbone; her belly button, the soft curve of the peak of her hipbone. And now Patrick and Carlo and Simon and Chef Max Mann, they were all seeing my own Kathryn, standing there in her smallness and her secret perfection and her white, wash-dulled bra and the smooth weight of the tops of her breasts.

I found myself pushing past Max. There wasn't much room between Kathryn and him, but I got into the space and I stood there in front of her and now nobody could see her.

"Are you lost?" he said. "You belong in the cold pass, not here with the g-grown ups. I suggest you get back there, *tout de suite*."

I could feel the warmth of Kathryn behind me; the sound of her folding her arms over her chest. Her breath was on the back of my neck, wet and fast. Max didn't realise that he'd gone too far. He would realise, though, when he was in a better mood. I undid my top button.

"If you want to test the limit of my patience," he said, "please do carry on."

And then the next one. And then the next.

"But let me warn you, young man, there will be consequences."

I pulled my tunic down, feeling the cotton run and bump over my arms, and handed it to Kathryn. By the time I turned back to face him, all the power had left Max's face. His eyes were sinking down the skin of my torso. They took in the scars on my chest; the scalds from the kettle; the cigarette burns on my nipples; the raised furrows of tissue from the whip-slashes of buckles and belts. In that instant, Max saw two decades of motherly discipline cut into the flesh of my body. And then, my own work, on my arms and the soft sides of my stomach. From pencil sharpener blades and razor blades and kitchen blades and the broken glass of bottles of wine and whisky and gin.

He took it all in, the Gentleman Chef, his eyes stuttering all over me, unable to disguise the horror, and for one beautiful moment the silence in his kitchen was mine. His jaw moved inside his skin, as if it was loose in there, this great slab of hinged bone all slack inside his face. I plucked Kathryn's tunic from his fingers.

"I don't have time for this childishness now," he said. "Once more, allow me to suggest that you go back to your station and get on with your work whilst I decide what to do with you. I'd do it now, if I were you."

I bowed my head before him.

"*Oui*, Chef. Sorry, Chef."

As Kathryn composed herself once more, Max turned to face the onlookers.

"Work," he hissed. "*Now*."

* * *

Ten minutes later I found myself in Stephen Mews, alone with her. She had rushed up to me, urgently, with the news that Max and Patrick had left the kitchen for the back office – the rumour amongst the chefs was that something concerning Max had been spotted in the *Evening Standard* and it wasn't good.

"Come with me," she'd whispered. "Quick. Before they come back."

The kitchen door closed with a rattle over the sound of traffic and fussing pigeons and a stray newspaper page that was being blown across the ground. A day of sun was trying to lighten the courtyard's great grey walls. A tiny grain of heat and sparkle was reflected from each of the little cobblestones.

"Your chest," said Kathryn. Her head was cocked a little to the right and her face was pinched with something like anger. "My God, Killian."

And then I realised. Of course, she had seen me now. She had seen my skin and my bone and the indelible tracks of my ugliness.

"It's disgusting," I said.

"Oh *no*, Killian."

With that, her expression fell open and she came towards me and took both my hands. There was a moment of hesitant tension. I could see her swallow; a fleeting glimpse of fear darted across her eyes. Then she put her arms around me. I yielded, gratefully, and she tightened her grip until I was held fast against her, my chin over her shoulder. She was pressing into me, her breasts against my ribs and her hot cheek into mine. Then she whispered, "It's not disgusting. Killian, I'm telling you, it's not disgusting *at all*."

I let my chin rest upon her shoulder and she said, "What you did in there, with Max – I can't believe you'd do something like that for me. And I just wanted to say, before I get too scared again, that I like you and I wanted to tell you, just in case you were interested or anything, and if you aren't, then can we just pretend this never happened? Please."

I moved my head back from where she'd been whispering. I would never have believed, when I met her on that first morning, that I would ever see her like this. All traces of sarcasm gone; nothing to her expression but openness and hoping.

"It's okay, Kathryn," I said. "It's fine, because I love you."

And with that, everything became automatic. Her lips came to mine and there began a kiss that dropped the floor, lifted the heavens and unmasked the universe. The courtyard, the kitchen, the city, the world – the whole of creation revealed itself to be nothing more than an elaborate stage set whose entire purpose had only ever been to guide the two of us into this moment.

"In that case... uh," she said, when it was over. "It's ridiculous. We've only known each other for... " She swallowed. "Anyway, sod it. I love you too."

Before I'd had the chance to absorb what she had said, she grabbed my hand tightly and led me towards the door. "Come on, before Max gets back."

We were lucky. Just a minute after I returned to my station, Max called down towards me.

"Er, Killian, do you have a moment?"

I followed him in struck silence into the dining room. There

187

was a waitress, not yet changed, vacuuming in the corner by the window. Glasses were being polished and fresh orchids being placed in tall black vases. Even out here, everyone worked quietly; the hush a mixture of reverence, fear and self-importance.

Max nodded for me to sit at the table nearest the kitchen – Ambrose's favourite dining spot. He pulled out the chair opposite and sat, crossing his legs in that TV-AM way I had once so admired. I could see the place where his sock met his leg. I could see how thin his limbs were. Little spirals of dark hair curled on skin the colour of tripe.

"I was just a little concerned about your display earlier on," he said.

His tone was calm. He wasn't staring. In the dry melody of his voice, I was sure I could even detect the soft lift of a note of concern. Over his shoulder, the sommelier shot me an envious glance. I sat up bolt-straight.

"Sorry, Chef. I know discipline is important, Chef. And you do these things for a good reason. But that thing in particular..." I swallowed. My pulse lurched. "Maybe it's different with a woman."

His upper lip stiffened as he interrupted me.

"I am enquiring about the marks on your skin. Are you having problems at home?"

My colour rose as I decided to tell him what I'd once told Mr Callum, the PE teacher. "I was in a car accident when I was young. I was pretty cut up."

"And those fresh scabs on your arms? They are from a child-hood incident too?"

"Just an accident at home, Chef. Nothing important."

"*Bon*," he smiled. "Good."

He stretched his left arm out on the table and stared at his manicured thumbnail for a moment.

"After my apprentices have been with me for some time, I like to take them to one side just to find out how they're getting on."

His grey eyes tracked up and down my face.

"Not finding it too tough?" he said.

"It's fine, Chef," I said. "I love it."

"Well, you must stop these petulant little displays of defiance. I run my kitchen as I do for a good reason. A less patient man than I would have fired you some time ago. But, as you know, we don't do that here."

"*Oui*, Chef."

A waitress I hadn't seen before walked by. I only saw her back as she glided past in regulation model fashion, one foot in front of the other, but that didn't prevent her leaving an impression. It held itself in the air for a tantalising moment, her static carnival – her shape, her movement, her posture, her sway, the way her wrists hung loose by her hips. And there was a scent: colourful and sherberty, its lovely fizziness fading very slowly beside us.

Max asked the maître d', "Is that one new?"

"*Oui*, Chef?" she replied.

"She's wearing perfume."

"*Oui*, Chef", said the maître d', before scurrying off obediently.

Perfume, I was to learn, wasn't permitted at King lest it interfere with the smell of the food. Max sat back in his seat and draped his hand over the chair next to him.

"That waitress," he said. "She looks a little like my first girlfriend, Grace."

He smiled and took a deep breath, filling himself with the memory.

"I'll let you into a secret. I used to be a very jealous boyfriend. Passionate, I used to tell myself, but that was a rather silly excuse. It was jealousy, pure and simple. Grace had had a boyfriend prior to me. I can't remember his name. I was – well, let me see – nineteen? Nineteen or twenty. Grace a little older. I'd somehow got it in my head that this ex-boyfriend had had the best of her. I think I'd seen a picture of her when she was sixteen, seventeen and... well, I realised that when a woman is fourteen or so she's too young to be really attractive. They can still look like an uncomfortable amalgam of Mum and Dad at that age, can't they? And by the time they're over thirty, say, they're past their best. Which means, logically speaking, there must be a point between those two ages when a woman is at her peak. There must be one afternoon, say, when her body and face are at their most sublime and everything else – her mood, her dress, the quality of the sun – coincides to make these few hours the ones in which she's at her most perfect. She'd never believe it, because to her it would have been the most wonderful day, but the truth is she'll never be as beautiful again as she has just been. It's terribly sad. It all drips away, doesn't it? I know it's not a very modish thing to say, but a woman's beauty is always her most prized possession, and for any female unfortunate enough to be born without it – well, that's a loss from which she never recovers."

By now the maître d', without being asked, had delivered two espressos. Max took a sip of his, pushing his upper lip into his teeth and sucking it back as if to extract every last molecule of flavour from it.

"But anyhow, I became convinced, for some strange reason, that Grace had been at her most perfect when she was with her ex-boyfriend. And I just couldn't live with it. That was the first time I became obsessed with the idea of perfection. Luckily, nowadays, all that passion is directed at my food. Is that mango at its moment of perfect ripeness? Is that jus reduced to the exact point where any longer on the heat and it'll start to become syrupy? It's a much healthier way of expressing perfectionism, don't you think?"

I tried to think of something to say that wasn't "*Oui*, Chef".

"You could say the same about our job."

Underneath his top lip, Max slowly licked his teeth.

"How so?"

"Well," I said. "Is there a point where a chef is at his most talented? Is there one afternoon when he's cooking his best and he'd never believe it if you told him, because he thinks he's on fire, but he'll never be as good again?"

Max looked into the little cup that he was holding daintily in his thumb and forefinger.

"No, I wouldn't say so. Not at all," he said. "That's quite different. Quite, quite different."

There was a strange silence.

"Now why don't you tell me something about *your*self?" said Max. "Are you courting? Getting along nicely with young Kathryn?"

"Well, I... I hope to."

He smiled back at me and a helpless grin broke out across my face.

"Good luck with that one," he said. "She's a fair cook. Pretty too. Bit straight-laced, though, it's always seemed to me. A bit sullen."

"I don't know," I said. "Maybe."

"Your mother must be pleased you're doing so well."

"Not really. She says that male cooks are just a bunch of Larry's."

He didn't respond.

"You know, Larry Graysons. Gays. She thinks I should be doing some good in the world. She thinks all the evil in the world is the fault of men. I think she expects me to do something about it."

His gaze had wandered above my head and seemed to settle on the front window of the restaurant. "Yes, of course," he said, unsmiling.

He sat forward abruptly, and his large eyes fixed onto mine.

"So, Killian. Now that we're friends again, why don't tell me what you know about the item on page 9 of today's *Evening Standard*."

I cleared my throat.

"Nothing," I replied. "I haven't seen it."

He moved closer; spoke more insistently.

"The report," he said, "apparently concerning me. My personal life. Information that must have come from this kitchen."

I shook my head.

"Come on, come on," he said, his voice thinning. "Don't be like that. You can talk to me. You can tell me. After all, I know full well who you socialise with. I've heard you myself, threatening to leak information to Nigel Dempster."

His mouth was smiling, but his eyes looked like holes in tarmac.

"It wasn't me," I said. "Honestly, Chef I wouldn't, I would never..."

Max stared at me for a long time. Two or three people walked past, not acknowledging us. And then, suddenly, he broke the spell.

"Very well," he said. "*Bon*. If it wasn't you, then I know what to do."

"Right," I said. "Good."

As we both moved to stand, our faces naturally broke contact. But, partly so I could remember the scene, I glanced back at him earlier than I otherwise might have done. He was wearing an expression so devoid of meaning, so utterly empty, it was startling.

* * *

A couple of hours later, Patrick called my name. He was holding the kitchen phone in his hand. "You're wanted in the office. Be quick."

I ran up the stairs with my head down. I knew which day this was and even though I had planned exactly what I was going to do, I could still feel a hot clamour rising in my chest and throat. I just wanted to be left alone to get on with my blackcurrants.

I knocked on the door and was summoned immediately.

"Well, look at the chef! Wonderful! Every inch the award winner." It was Mr Mayle, in a new-looking tan trench coat, paisley scarf and Oxford brogues that had been polished to a varnished mahogany. He'd dressed up, more smartly than I had ever seen him, in order to take me to the Young Saucier of the Year awards. The words evaporated from my tongue as he stood to greet me. Ambrose was sitting back in his chair, his usual red braces stretched over the foie-fed hillock above his hips, looking ostentatiously relaxed, as if keen to impress on his old friend that he was so much the king of his kingdom that its rule didn't even require him to sit up straight.

"I'm not going," I said. "I'm needed here. I'm sorry, sir. I'd forgotten you were coming. If you could collect my award…"

Mayle's hands squashed themselves in front of him. He looked crushed. Ambrose pulled himself up in his leather chair.

"Nonsense, Killian," he said. "This is a proud day for you and Robert. I'm sure the kitchen won't miss you."

"The kitchen will miss me, I think," I said. "We're an apprentice down now that Kathryn's been promoted."

Mayle took a step towards me and said, with beseeching eyes, "But please, Killian. Come on. I'm sure…"

"I'm sorry, sir. I've got to get back. Have a good time."

29

By twelve o'clock that night, the brigade was beginning its final clean-down. All the steel units were being pulled from the walls and washed and tides of soapy water were pushed around our feet as the floor tiles were scraped, scrubbed, mopped and dried. It was the only part of the day in which we were allowed to chat, although it was mostly abusive banter which acted as both bonding glue and mettle-tester, with any crack in composure caused by the insults watched for and feasted upon. Still not fully used to the eighteen-hour shifts, it was easy to allow my exhaustion to overcome me. The others, I could tell, felt energised and victorious, having beaten back the forces of another double service.

That night, though, I was scrubbing my unit with even more determination than usual. I became aware of Ambrose coming into the kitchen, nose pinked and smile hardened by a night spent, presumably, entertaining friends and generally celebrating himself at his usual table.

"Attention!" he clapped. "Please, *mesdames, messieurs et gamins*. Don't stop what you're doing, but I'd appreciate it if you could give me as much attention as you can spare."

Everyone did as Le Patron had asked and popped their heads up. I paused, on my way back to the cleaning cupboard with a bucket, and noticed that someone was with him – Mr Mayle. He was holding a white presentation plate.

"Whilst you were all busy, Grosvenor House were doing their usual no doubt profoundly mediocre job of hosting the annual Young Saucier of the Year competition, a title that one or two of the wonderfully talented chefs present here have been short-listed for in the past *and*, of course, the award our very own Max won years ago at the start of his long journey to international repute..."

The entire brigade had stopped. They could tell by the direction in which Ambrose kept looking that I was the winner. Carlo was smiling and nodding his head; the other apprentices spread their faces in expressions of simple astonishment. I dried my hands on my torchon and took a tentative step in the direction of Le Patron.

"It gives me great pleasure to announce the 1985 Young Saucier of the Year is our very own Killian Lone."

As I made my way towards Ambrose, the rest of the brigade began to clap. I watched my clogs slapping on the damp floor tiles and kept my head bowed, in an attempt at hiding the daft grin that had erupted across my face. As I got nearer, the appreciation of these marvellous men grew in strength and I began to feel as if I could hear every individual palm slapping another and I tried to hold the sound in my head, so that I could keep it for later and replay it again and again. Even Patrick was striking his muttony hands together. Everyone was doing so, except Max, who was leaning against the wall with the air of someone awaiting a late-running bus.

I shook Ambrose's cold right hand and took my plate from him, which was heavy and silly and brilliant. I tucked it under my arm and made a brief attempt at meeting the faces of the cooks, before dipping my chin again and grinning at my toes.

Beside Ambrose, Mayle stepped forward, flush-faced and wobbly on his heels. He had a Victorian-style pocket watch in his jacket. Its gold chain dangled as he spoke.

"I'd just like to say a few words to you all, if I may," he said. "I, like you, used to be a chef in a fine-dining restaurant. I was rather good at it, actually. I worked many long shifts for Ambrose, my business partner. And I have to tell you that I feel right at home being back. I could just dive right in there, right now, and grill off some beautiful filet mignon, sauté some gorgeous carrots in fine French butter, whip on a fresh rabbit stock, get a cassoulet bubbling or a fine lobster bisque."

Patrick sniggered. The smile vanished from my face.

"I suppose, looking at me now, it's probably hard to believe that the rather podgy old man that stands before you–"

To my left, Carlos muttered, "Can we go home now?" I tightened my grip on the plate and closed my eyes.

"–could have been a fine-dining chef in a restaurant of world repute. Even though I have been many years out of the kitchen, it still only feels like yesterday that I was doing double shifts, six days a week in clogs that were two sizes too big for me–"

Max shifted his weight against the wall and sighed.

"–not far from here, as a matter of fact, in a little side street just off Piccadilly. Anyhow, I digress. When young Killian here first walked through the door of my teaching kitchen, I must admit, I barely noticed him–"

I glanced at Max again. He looked back at me. A dark flurry of shame washed down the bones of my back.

"Great!" I said, placing my award beneath my knees. "Thank you, Mr Mayle!" I started clapping my hands. He stopped talking. Patrick stood upright, a magnificent smile drawing his large, tired face upwards.

Mayle looked in my direction, as if to say, "What are you *doing?*" Patrick nodded his encouragement at me. I felt myself swell and rise and puff like a fast-baking loaf. "This is me," I said, still clapping, "saying, 'Shut the fuck up'."

The brigade ignited into laughter. It echoed off the tiles on the walls and off the suspended lights and the pots and the pans and the sinks and the ovens. Patrick let out a huge, spasmic guffaw and clapped his hands three times over his head. Mayle's jowls sagged. His fringe sat limp and damp and thinning on top of his sweaty head. His eyes sank to the floor.

"I also have a few words to say in gratitude to our young winner here."

The noise was killed instantly. It was Max.

"As you know," he began, his eyes moving around all the chefs, meeting them in turn. He looked thinner than ever, his hands rubbing warmth into themselves in front of him, all bony and crickety and slow. "I do not tolerate disloyalty in my kitchen. I expect, by now, you've all heard about the item in t-today's newspaper. Having conducted a thorough investigation this morning, and having been ably assisted by our talented young apprentice here, I have, this afternoon, dismissed Kathryn Riding for gross misconduct with immediate effect. Moreover, I will do my u-utmost," he twitched, with force, and stuttered, "t-to ensure she does not find meaningful employment in any serious kitchen again. That's all I have to say on the matter, apart from congratulations, Killian, for your prize, but more importantly for your brave show of loyalty today."

As one, the faces of the cooks in front of me took on a long, hollow quality. For a moment, there was no sound at all. A drip of water bulged from a tap over an empty steel sink; a patina of blue light reflected off the plastic surface of a safety notice; a decapitated duck's head stared out from the top of an un-emptied waste bin. Someone at the back of the room blinked. For a second, we all just existed. And then, as if there had been a silent signal – bustle; the brigade operating without looking at me; without acknowledging that I even existed.

I strode down the length of the room and around the corner,

into the pastry section. Andy was wiping down the sides of his sink.

"It wasn't me, Andy," I said.

He turned on the hot tap and the sound of water beating against metal filled the space. I watched as he slowly squeezed out his cloth beneath the stream. His knuckles bulged with the force of it.

"Did she go home?" I said. "Is she at the flat?"

He twisted the wet material into a tight spiral. A number of clear, bright trickles burst onto the draining board.

"She doesn't want to speak to you," he said. "Nor do I."

"It wasn't me, Andy," I said, suddenly wishing that I wasn't holding an award. "I didn't say anything. Tell Kathryn. Could you please tell Kathryn? I didn't say *anything*."

"Yeah, of course you didn't, mate," he laughed and, finally turned to face me. "I warned her about you. What is this thing you've got about Max? Have you got a crush on him or something?"

"I just want you to tell Kathryn," I said.

"She doesn't want to see you," he said. "Do yourself a favour. Piss off back to college. Nobody's going to want you here any more."

30

I drove as fast as I could in Aunt Dorothy's old Peugeot, back to Dor. When I reached the cottage, I took the sledgehammer from the shed and tried to exorcise my rage by throwing it with furious strikes against my uncle's garden wall. I had a suspicion that what lay behind it was the "secret" Dorothy had warned me about.

It was more resilient than it appeared and the sharp knuckle of pain between my shoulder blades that I'd felt during my first shifts rose again, before spreading out and dropping to my lower spine. My neck stiffened, my arms throbbed, my fingers blistered. As the moon arced over my head and the elms gossiped in the forest around me, I relived all the aches of my six weeks at King, except this time I enjoyed them. Just before five, when the first rumours of dawn were becoming apparent behind the trees, the wall finally gave.

I stepped over the three-high lip of bricks that were too low to easily knock through. The space between the busted wall and the ancient gate was boggy and filled with a pointy kind of grass that was sticking up in spiny crowns. I pushed at the herb garden door. It was unpainted and of the same design as the one in the cottage, with its square-headed nails and heavy hinges, except these were so rusted they looked as if they were dissolving into the fabric of the wood. I shoved it with my shoulder, which just served to wedge it further into the earth behind it. It took almost ten minutes and all my remaining strength before I was able to squeeze myself inside.

By now, a blue haze was coming through the trees and the birds had begun their wild chorus. I trod slowly, careful not to let the brambles swallow my foot, and I tried to survey the garden. There was little contrast between the grey light and the thin dawn fog and it wasn't easy to see much detail. Perhaps it was just the angle I was viewing it at, but everything looked different from how it did before. The dead vegetation was all the same but there seemed to be more of the green shoots, with thick stems and fresh leaves, like flattened teardrops, every one a persuasive, plump green.

Flies buzzed over the garden, travelling in complex, busy directions. They seemed to inhabit an invisible airborne metropolis, all en route to some essential destination and then turning, immediately, to find another. They seemed convinced of their logic and yet there was a madness about their movements; a randomness and fervour that reminded me how much, as a child, I used to fear them. Waving them away, I rubbed a leaf from one of the plants and sniffed the pad of my thumb. I could only detect a faint earthy smell. Not one you'd necessarily associate with a herb, more a fungus or root. An early lick of dawn wind hit my cheeks as I picked a large leaf and put it in my mouth.

Immediately, my eyes dropped and I allowed the flavour to sink into my palate – that was the sensation, of it *sinking in*, soaking down into the roots of my taste buds, taking over my entire tongue and then gathering strength as it washed with a palpable kiss of pleasure down my throat.

There was a top note that carried a vague herby sweetness, not dissimilar to marjoram. But the booming, resonant flavours had more in common, in an obscure way, with some of the exotic foods I'd tried with Dorothy, like oysters, truffles and abalone. It was strangely organic, musky, intimate. A secret, adult taste.

And it was delightful. Incredible. Blissful. Like nothing I'd ever experienced before. Each morsel of leaf contained a complex symphony of pointillist glories that all coalesced into this heavenly whole. The deliciousness was so extreme that your instincts warned you off. It was as if some rogue God had taken the entire palette of gustatory pleasures and combined them for the purposes of mischief. It was a flavour that took ordinary beauty and violently challenged it; that took perfection and humiliated it.

My tongue, I realised, had actually begun to tingle. My palms were wet. I felt a gluey lurch of nausea and the dew of sweat on my forehead. Just as I was trying not to panic, the sickness in my belly lifted to be replaced by an effervescent heat that began to gather itself about my hips and pelvis.

And that's when it happened; this terrible sexual craving. I had never felt the pull so suddenly or so overpoweringly. There was very little I could do to satiate myself. I ran to the house and bolted the front door. Finding the bathroom, I did everything I could to relieve the maddening urge that had came over me.

I was eight again, at the foot of the stairs. Mary Dor was at the top. On the third step, in the centre, a clean, cold cup of milk. I reached for it. There was something in it; silvery, alive. I watched it for a moment. Struggling, whirring in circles, dancing its own death. I put the cup to my lips and drank. Mary watched. I felt the silvery thing crawling and buzzing as it went down.

Mary spoke. "Now it is done, so. Now you will no longer know the difference between God's miracles and the Devil's."

And she showed me her hands and her wrists were bound, tightly, with rope.

Up in the roof, I saw all the parts, the yellow, the red, the green and the black. Out amongst the elms, I could hear the children singing: "Earl's heart and earl's leafs and earl's lusts abounding. Earl's fires and earl's grace and earl's witch is burning."

And I knew that I was King of the Wastelands, King of the Hunger, King of the More and I knew that I could never stop them barking.

The old trouble, the quiet trouble, louder now, big and terrible and close.

31

As I drove up the A21 towards London that morning, the fatigue and the strange night combined to make the world seem two-dimensional, as if it was all a projection that was running both too fast and too slow. As I drifted dazedly onto the M25, I couldn't stop thinking about the unbelievable flavour of that odd herb. If there was any way to harness it, to remove it from its goblinish effects, just imagine. I could make the most incredible sauce. And as for Dorothy – well, perhaps the long years in the cottage surrounded by all that sensed history had made her grow overly superstitious. The plant had some carnal, aphrodisiacal effect, some active component – that was obvious. But it wasn't magic. It was a product – and one which I would be fascinated to experiment with. First, though, I had to push through another day.

I walked into the locker room to find it choked full of silence. Everyone gave the impression they were concentrating extremely hard on what their fingers were doing: untying laces, fastening buttons, zipping up bags, sliding clogs onto feet. I dropped my rucksack onto the floor as Patrick passed by. "You're back, are you?" he said.

I didn't quite now how to respond.

"Still haven't had enough?" he continued.

"Of course not, Chef," I said.

"You've got a pair of bollocks, I'll give you that. You're hardly Mr Popular round here at the moment, you realise. Not after what happened with Kathryn."

"That was nothing to do with me," I said.

He gave a quick, powerless snort and walked away.

The previous week, I'd been charged with a new job: preparing the citrus for Max's signature dish, his deer and tangerine pie. Every morning, a new bag of thirty tangerines was delivered, twenty of which had to be juiced, the other ten segmented, deseeded and peeled for use in the garnish. Before they were squeezed, each piece of fruit had to be rolled with pressure on the chopping board, in order to loosen the summery liquid inside.

I'd just begun this process when Max walked up to me, the lid of his daily brand-new biro sticking like a medieval knight from the breast pocket of his dry-cleaned tunic. I instinctively looked at my hands to make sure there wasn't anything I could possibly be doing better.

"You," he said. "Stock rotation."

All the warmth from the previous day had evaporated. I placed the tangerine firmly on the chopping board so it wouldn't roll off and headed for the heavy, storm-coloured freezer door, where I found the protective coat and gloves to be missing from their hook.

"Does anyone know where the coat and the gloves for the freezer are?" I shouted into the kitchen.

I didn't see Patrick when he responded. I could only hear him.

"Fucking get on with it, dipshit."

I pulled down the steel lever and slid the door open. The shelves were filled with sacks of ice which was to be crushed and served in a bowl beneath the chilled melon soup. Above those were frozen peas and the steel tubs of sorbet and ice cream

204

that I'd have to sort through and rotate, so the freshest was at the back. The light had a hollow, metallic quality and the place smelled of cold beef and rubber. The air in front of the recessed light was thick with cold. How could I possibly do this without gloves?

I crouched and began to pull the tubs onto the floor with my bare hands. There were glaces of nougat and walnut, Armagnac ice, sorbets of prickly pear, blackcurrant, acacia blossom, three types of apple and citrus – which was served in a halved and hollowed-out lemon.

The pain wasn't long in coming. It began as balls of low hurt deep inside my knuckles before spreading through the bones of my hands. My fingers started to sting as they stuck onto the icy metal containers; there was a constriction in my nostrils and a hardening in my sinuses that began to swell as if something was trying to break out of them.

The job took nearly twenty agonising minutes. All I wanted to do as I walked back into the kitchen was curl up in the toilet and push my hands between my legs for warmth, but I was desperate to know if someone had covered me on the tangerines, which should have been done by now. When I arrived back at my station, what I saw was Patrick stirring a small copper pan with his usual bullish intensity, wearing the thick orange freezer coat and black workman's gloves.

A crumble of laughter went through brigade and apprentices.

"You've got them…" I said. "You fucking…"

Patrick turned and pointed at me with his hot teaspoon which bled a quick trickle of sauce onto his clogs. His nose had reddened in the heat whilst the rest of his face remained the colour of beef dripping. His eyes looked tiny, as if they'd been shrinking away from the heat of the flames.

"Something you wanted to say, grass?"

I retreated back to my tangerines and picked up my knife from where I'd left it on the board. Something wasn't right. It was the quantity. There were supposed to be thirty pieces of fruit and... I made a quick count. Twenty-eight. I looked back towards Patrick. He'd gone – probably to take off the coat. I was aware of members of the brigade glancing at me; I could feel their flickers of attention like intermittent sparks of light.

Lunch service went by in a swimmy slick of time, the loss of Kathryn in my vicinity feeling ever more boundless with each hour. I managed to remain invisible until just after two p.m.

"You there," said Max.

I turned to see him standing at the top of the kitchen, the yellow glow from the pass casting cruelly over his cheekbones and sunken temples. He was holding up a large square black plate with the King logo on the side of it. It was smeared with a drying crust of reddy-brown sauce and there was something else on there as well: a dark nugget in the corner.

Max beckoned me with his manicured finger.

As I loped towards him, I could see it was a pip. A fresh, nearly-white tangerine pip.

"You have ruined my signature dish."

His tongue ran over his lower lip.

"Do you know who this plate belongs to?"

"*Non*, Chef."

He growled with bitter menace.

"Zsa Zsa fucking Gabor."

He jabbed a finger into my chest.

"Do you think you've made it, now that you've won that ridiculous prize? Do you think you can do what you like now?"

His fury generated a kind of electric field; a livid haze of energy through which his ugliest features became yet more grotesque.

"*Non*, Chef."

"*Non*, Chef, *non*, Chef..."

I stared back at him. I fixed all my muscles in place.

"Why did you sack Kathryn?" I said, quietly, my breaths becoming rapid and shallow. "Why did you do it?"

They were listening, the other chefs. They were pretending that they weren't, but they were.

"She was disloyal." His nostrils thinned. "Just as you told me."

"I didn't–"

He threw the plate at my feet and it smashed against my right ankle. I couldn't remember seeing him this furious before. His upper lip was quivering and lifting at the sides. He was actually baring teeth. When he spoke again it was in a whisper.

"You disgust me, do you know that? You make me feel unnerved." And then he left.

* * *

Two hours later I was cleaning celery in the between-service lull when Max approached in that severe, mincing way that I had learned to dread.

"Come," he said.

The corridor filled with the dull thump of clogs on antique carpet as I followed him. There was a boil on the back of his neck, nestling in the creases of yellowing skin, and his manicured nails appeared chewed. He opened the door to a large broom cupboard and nodded for me to enter. It was illuminated by a bare low-powered bulb and there were buckets and gloves and mousetraps and cockroach bait and white plastic bottles filled with cleaning chemicals. The light swung on its wire in response to the sharply closing door; the shadows of the mops and pots around us moving across the walls in an excitable, jeering dance.

In the middle, there was a wooden chair and a pile of sealed Tupperware boxes with a filthy torchon draped over them. Patrick was there, comfortable amongst the darkness and poisons, his smug smile pulled over his nibblish little teeth.

"Sit," said Max.

I did as I was told.

"Don't look so worried," he smiled. "It's the last day of your *stage* tomorrow, and this is just something we like to do with apprentices when they reach the end. A bit of fun. A tasting session. A palate test. You should consider yourself lucky, not everyone gets this treatment. Only special apprentices."

I gripped the seat, feeling the gritty dust on its underside.

"*Merci*, Chef."

"Special," he said, lightly. "And you *are* special, aren't you?"

I swallowed, my tongue dry, my throat tightening.

"*Non*, Chef," I said.

"Award winner!" he said, loudly. "Very confident young man. Confidence is good. But sometimes confidence can go too far. Tell me, what makes you think you can question me? What makes you think you can defy me in front of my brigade?"

"I'm sorry, Chef. I didn't –"

Max opened his hands up. The lines that ran across his palms were deep and red and purple against translucent skin.

"Don't panic," he said. "Don't worry. You poor thing, perhaps you misunderstand me when I say that I have never sacked an apprentice. Perhaps you took that to mean that you are somehow trapped here. But you must know – this is not a prison. You can leave at any time you want."

He looked enormous, looming over me like that. It is how I'd always imagined him – huge and all-powerful. Awesome in his height and presence.

"Do you understand?" he repeated.

"*Oui*, Chef."

"Now, I realise that you consider yourself a three-star apprentice and here at King we have cruelly made you wallow in the squalor of two, but still…"

"No, Chef– "

"Shut up," he said, his words popping out in a sudden punch of uncontrolled temper. "Now, sit back and concentrate. If you pass this test, Chef Patrick and I will not hesitate to congratulate you. But if you decide that you can't do it, if you want to leave, that's just fine. There's no shame in it. You can finish it at any time. Stand up and go. It really is that simple. Go. But if you do happen to decide to leave, you must not stop until you reach wherever it is you came from. Okay. *Bon*. So, Patrick's going to blindfold you."

I closed my eyes, my fingers gripping my seat ever harder, as the grimy torchon was knotted around my head.

"Tongue out," he said.

I heard Patrick move to my left. There was the brush of material, the popping of a lid, a chink of cutlery. I flinched as something tipped onto my tongue. It was lukewarm. Waxy. I bit down and felt fat separate from flesh. The flavour was sweaty, salty and hollow and it was so greasy that my teeth slid about on it.

"Bacon," I said. "Raw."

Trying not to gag, I used my tongue to push the semi-masticated mush into a ball before forcing it into the back of my mouth and down.

"Streaky," I said. Then, remembering the style that was used at King. "Oak-smoked."

"Oak-smoked!" said Max, with a sarcastic laugh in his voice. "Oh, bravo."

I heard Patrick snigger.

"*Bon*. Very good. Next."

Despite the fact that my mouth was coated in a layer of thick slime, I could tell what the next ingredient was the moment it landed on my tongue.

"Chilli," I said. "Piri-piri."

There was a silence.

"He's very specific isn't he?" said Max, irritably.

I spent a moment trying to generate enough spit so that I could wash some of the intensity of the heat away. I heard the rustle of a packet as a film of feverish sweat soaked onto my brow and the water in my eyes threatened to well.

"No, don't cut it," I heard Max say. "Put it all in."

This one was even easier. These were my dad's favourites. Patrick was pushing it in quicker than I was able to chew. I was on the verge of choking, but luckily my saliva glands had been prompted to fire a wash of pre-vomit spit. I pumped my teeth on it as quickly as I could manage and smushy clags began to spill from the corners of my mouth and fall to my lap. The texture was the worst thing, like something verminous that had decomposed to the consistency of mash. There was an undeniable farty note in the background, which hung beneath the dominant flavours of fat, offal and old grey meat.

"Sausage," I said as soon as I was able. "Pork. Wall's."

It was the act of saying the name out loud rather than swallowing the thing that finally induced a gag as wide as a lion's roar. Strings of gastric phlegm hurled out and fell, splatting coldly down my chin.

I could do this. I had to.

"Ten out of ten so far," said Max.

If I could pull this off and just speak to Max; just make him understand; sit him down and explain how much I had loved him; tell him about the pictures on my bedroom wall. We could talk about what's happened, forget it all, reset it all...

"Next!"

I smelled the next one coming. The fact that my sinuses had

been cleared out by the piri-piri meant that the savage bang of the old fish entrails entered my nostrils in a wave that was almost overwhelming. Patrick shovelled a heaped dessertspoon full into my mouth and they squished out into my cheeks, each slippery node, tube and lump picked out in vile detail by my tongue. It felt as if the tastes and textures were filling my head and I had to clamp my hand over my lips to force my system not to reject them and their flavours of stale blood and gut rot.

I wretched, twice. A layer of chilled sweat formed just below my eyes.

"Entrails," I said. "Herring."

"A little something to wash it down with?" said Max. "Purse your lips."

At first I thought it was olive oil. Then I felt the layer of carbon, tiny particles of black, and the flavours of scorch, fat and grime hit the back of my tongue.

"From the extractor fan," I said.

There was a silence.

"The extractor fan above the meat station."

Neither of them responded for a moment.

"Is that blindfold on properly?" Max asked.

Patrick gave the knot a sudden tug that threw my head back painfully.

"Looks like it."

"Hm," said Max. "Well, I suppose if you've been raised feeding from the trough, you are going to be familiar with the tastes of its fruits."

Patrick smirked. I became aware of more activity by the Tupperware near my feet.

"Don't bother with all that other stuff," Max said to Patrick. "Go straight to that one. No, not that. No. Right. Did you get some?"

"Yeah," said Patrick.

My stomach lurched as Max addressed me again.

"Tongue out, flat," he said. "No – flat. Flatter. Flat like a tray."

Somebody's fingers clamped my nostrils shut with a sharp pinch.

"Oh, God that's revolting," Max muttered. "Oh, you didn't..."

There was a hesitation.

"Go on," said Max.

"Yeah?" said Patrick.

"Go on."

I gagged once, twice, three times.

"No," I said, trying to block it by waving my hands to and fro.

"*Oui*," said Max, gripping the sides of my jaw with his thumb and forefinger. "Oh, *oui, oui, oui*. Tongue out."

A cheese biscuit was laid on my tongue. I pulled it in and crunched, barely believing this was happening. There it was, this gritty paste. Warm; the temperature of blood. My nose was released. I chewed. It stuck on my teeth. It was the particles that tipped me over. I felt a seed-like nugget, then something – a kernel of something – burst open.

The sounds that came from me then were not of my voicebox but from my gut. It was primal.

My nostrils were released. I heard them move out of the way. Cold, fizzing spasms ran up my cheeks and down my neck and I could feel sweat on my wrists. The vomit, when it came, was wetter than I expected and hot from the chilli.

"Uhh, the dirty fucking animal," said Patrick. "He's got it all over himself."

"Have you quite finished?" Max asked.

"It's shit," I said. "On a Ritz cracker." I took a guess. "Chef Patrick's shit." There was a surprisingly strong additional flavour, separate from that of the cracker. "And he's been eating cheese. Blue cheese. Roquefort?"

There was another silence.

"How the fuck did he know?" said Patrick.

Nothing seemed to happen for some time. There was a sound of movement, then material being moved about. It hit my chest first. Then Patrick adjusted himself and the hot, salty tasteless spray of urine hit me. I squeezed my mouth shut and closed my eyes hard behind the torchon. When it died down, after maybe ten seconds, I sensed that only Patrick was in the room.

"We can't have you in the kitchen in that state," he said. There was a hesitation. And when he spoke again, an undeniable tremor of concern in his voice. "Piss off home. Sort yourself out."

Having changed and washed my face, I took the bus to Brixton and knocked on Kathryn's door. Nobody answered. I might have been freezing and filthy with cloying vomit and urine, but I wouldn't give up. I sat there on the step, my bony knees raised up to the level of my chin, and watched the people coming to and from the nearby market as the train rattled angrily across the bridge above us all. That peculiar man, the homeless painter, was busy beneath the lamp post just outside her door. I began to rock gently back and forth, my teeth clenching and releasing painfully on my tongue and my right heel bouncing up and down. I sat there, getting up every now and then to knock, for more than an hour.

Finally, the door opened an inch.

"Go away," said Kathryn.

I pushed and the chain scraped against the wood, the brass bolt clanking in its housing.

"I have to speak to you."

A ribbon of dull light fell on her nose. Her eyes were in darkness. I wanted to put my hand through the gap. I wanted to feel her.

"Why don't you go and sit on Max's doorstep?" she said. "You seem the stalkerish type. He lives in Chelsea, I think."

I moved my head about in an attempt to get a clearer view of her. "Kathryn, I didn't say anything. He's lying."

"No, it's my fault. I knew your career would always be more important than me. That's fine, you know, you go and be a good, loyal, successful boy. Just leave me the *fuck* alone whilst you're doing it."

She would see that I understood her, and that she understood me and the accident of us finding each other was something like a miracle. I had to make her know.

"But listen to me, we both want to be great as much as each other," I said. "We both want to be executive chefs at King or somewhere. We'd both do anything for it. It's like, you know..." I tried to think of an example. "Like when you work a double shift instead of seeing your mum. I understand it, I get it."

"Cunt!"

The door slammed.

"No!" I kicked it. The sole of my shoe left a scuff of black rubber on the paintwork. "No! Kathryn!" I kicked it again and again. "Kathryn!"

I waited for another hour or so. There was nothing much to do, except to watch the homeless man. He was oddly dressed for a vagrant, in a mangy tweed suit with a bow tie over an old white shirt. I began to wonder what he was up to. He was sitting in a picnic chair, leaning forward under the homemade awning that he'd fashioned from some opened-out bin liners he'd taped together. Whatever he was working on, under there, he was evidently doing it with considerable care.

I examined him, from my place in the shadows. Suddenly, he looked directly at me.

"Sorry," I said. "I was just – "

"Drawing," he said.

The whites of his eyes had a yellow tint. There were three teeth missing from his lower jaw.

"I've seen you here before," I said.

"Every day, oh yes, indeed."

He looked proud; delighted to be in conversation.

"What do you draw?"

"Precious stuff. W-where we met," he said. "My wife and I."

"That's what you draw? Every day?"

He smiled wide and it was wet and foul – greys and browns and blacks and livid swells of red. More like an infected wound than a mouth.

"Oh yes, indeed I do," he said. "Oh yes, indeed, very much I do, oh yes. Every day and every night. Always here, yes, indeed. Keep trying. Keep drawing. Never give up. Never never give up. Please," he gestured to what I now understood to be a covered easel. "Look."

I stood and peered carefully under the awning, and squinted at his pad. It was in pencil, and it was immediately clear that he had sketched the same scene countless times, one version over the top of the other. You could just about see two people in the middle of it all, in some sort of embrace. He'd drawn the lovers so often that they had become monstrous, dark lines scored onto dark lines, their eyes a torment of black layers. In several places, the pencil had gone right through the thick paper, leaving great gashes and rents.

"Oh yes, you see," he said, putting his head close to mine. "Perfect, you see. I do it again, all again and again and all over again. I have to make it perfect. Perfect, you see? Always and never, nothing else than perfect."

32

I returned to Dor to find storm clouds boiling darkly, stretching in all directions over the elm forest. The whole place cowered under an atmosphere of bluster and hectoring. I couldn't remember ever seeing rain before in Dorothy's little sun-trap, and as I stepped over the lip in the wall and squeezed into the herb garden, I felt the first fat tears of what promised to be a dramatically wet few hours.

"*Christ,*" I whispered to myself when I realised what had happened.

The cloud of flies had thickened and maddened. Their movements were too fast for the eye to follow and they seemed to have been attracted to and excited by the herbs. Hundreds more leaves had grown over night. Tribes of plants pushed themselves up through the spaces between the darkness. They rose with proud, keen and wobbling heads. I entered the humming zone of insects and began to pick. Flies hit my face repeatedly. After perhaps fifteen minutes, I felt a gust of warm air and the weather broke. I ran into the kitchen and, without stopping to remove my sodden coat, reached under the sink for some red onions and began chopping. As I was unscrewing the cap on the tawny port, the telephone rang.

"Killian?"

"Mr Mayle?"

Could it be him? The voice shared my teacher's biscuity timbre, but it seemed so graspless, so removed.

"I'm having to call now, because you haven't had the courtesy to get in touch," he said.

"Okay?"

"Well, it's your final day at King tomorrow and I don't yet know whether or not you'll be back at college on Monday. I contacted Ambrose but he wasn't much help. He had yet to speak with Max about it so was unsure. But I can only assume, as you're not there at the moment, that we will be seeing you?"

"I'm in," I said.

"You *are*?"

I gripped the receiver. "Of course," I said, with a lightly insulted laugh. "Max just gave me the afternoon off as a reward. A treat for all my hard work."

There was a moment of quiet.

"Well, congratulations," he said. Some of his warmth returned. I heard it and I felt it, too, lifting through my body. "I'll be sure to tell the class the good news. They'll be delighted for you."

I experienced a sudden and almost overwhelming fondness for him.

"Thanks for all your help, sir," I said. "It's all because of you."

I wished he was there with me now. I wished he could help me.

"Yes, well... Killian. Be careful. Don't..."

The drenched wind swiped at the roof above me. Glass shook in the panes. I stood there, alone.

"Yes," I interrupted him. "I know."

I finished preparing my sauce. This time, though, I added just half of the small, teardrop-shaped leaf. At the moment it reached the correct consistency, I dipped my teaspoon in the sauce and blew on it. I was in such a state of urgency that extra space seemed to have been pushed between the seconds. I was actually aware of the time passing between the stuff hitting my tongue and the taste being detected.

My eyes were the first to go and then the back of my throat – a feeling of release as the pleasure of it caused muscles to involuntarily relax throughout my body. I groaned and grabbed onto the kitchen worktop as if to support myself. The most curious thing about it was that if you weren't looking for the herb, you wouldn't know it was there – this earthy, corrupt hum which was somehow redolent of young, intimate, sweated skin. It rang through all the sauce's extant layers, drawing out in each previously unknown depths of flavour. The port sang new hymns of cherries and strawberries; the tomatoes became prouder and juicier, the Worcester sauce took on a cavernous spice and tang. The whole thing become three-dimensional. It seemed to drench the palate and the lust it generated for more was thrilling; magical. But then, disaster: the heat and then the brutally gathering sexual urge.

I woke up twelve hours later in the place where I'd dropped off, on the bathroom floor. The alarm was sounding down the corridor in the bedroom.

I knew, as I scrubbed my skin in a madly steaming shower, that if I was to get this right, I had to think like a grown-up; separate the personal from the professional. This was *business*. Max had been as good as his promise: he had not dismissed me, given up on me, even when I had erred. Surely I had proved myself. I had survived the worst of his apprentice tests. I had done enough now. I had played their game and passed it. Surely I would be offered a job as full-time ouvrier.

Leaving the house for work, I tried not to notice what I was doing as I pushed the small, quietly dying leaf deep into my back pocket.

* * *

As I worked at my basil that morning, I tried to concentrate, but found it impossible to expel Kathryn from my mind. I wondered how it would look to her if, later on that day, I was told I hadn't proved worthy of a paid position in this kitchen. What would she think of me then? *Would* she think of me then?

I kept my eye on the station at which Ambrose's lunch was usually prepared at eleven thirty each day. The moment I saw Malcolm bending into the fridge beneath it, I walked purposefully up to him.

"Change of plan," I said. "Ambrose wants me to do his lunch today."

For all Malcolm's youth, he still managed to look five years younger than he actually was, with his silky blond hair on his upper lip and jaws.

"Says who?"

"Says Patrick," I said.

"Bollocks." He stood for a moment, holding a full steel milk jug. "Really?"

"You'll probably get a go tomorrow," I shrugged.

He hesitated.

"I don't think so."

What would Mr Mayle say if I was dismissed? What about Mark House? My mum? I grabbed Malcolm's wrist, circling its skin with my thumb and forefinger.

"*What are...?*" said Malcolm, looking down, half irritated, half confused. I squeezed.

Flashes. Cigarette smoke, menthol. Steam.

"*Argh!*"

"Not today," I said.

Just like your father.

"Get off!"

219

I squeezed it harder, pushing my nails in.

"Tomorrow," I said.

When it comes, when it happens, you have to be strong enough to be good.

I gave Malcolm's arm a final jerk. His milk jug dropped, clanged on the tiles and bounced once, its contents flying from its mouth in a small eruption of white and wet.

"Fuck!" he said. "You fuckin' freak." He rubbed at his skin. "That *hurt*."

"Sorry, Malcolm, it's just what I've been told." I nodded towards my *mise-en-place*. "Could you give us a hand with that basil?"

As he loped off, I reached into the back of the fridge for my supplies. With them all laid before me, it was with a sense of sudden vertigo that I realised that *everything* depended on these modest ingredients. Everything, that onion. Everything, that bottle of sauce. Everything, that half-spent, crusty-lidded tube of tomato purée. I couldn't risk it. I had to use the herb in my sauce, just to make sure. I *had* to. It was obvious.

And then, as I began to chop, it wasn't.

I could feel her around me. There was Dorothy, as I sweated off the onions and I added the port and the tomatoes and everything else. There was Dorothy, as I felt for the herb that I had put into my pocket that morning. There was Dorothy, as I hesitated over the pan and the steel and the fire. There was Dorothy as I left the herb undisturbed and decided, finally, to be good.

33

"Oh," said Ambrose when I arrived with his heavy silver tray. "No Malcolm?"

"To be honest," I said, being careful not to slip on the loose, frayed rug. "It's my last day. I just wanted to see how you thought I'd got on."

Ambrose was leaning forward, holding a pair of half-moon spectacles between his thumb and forefinger.

"Oh, of course. Silly me," he said. "How could I forget that it's *you* who's in charge of what I eat for my lunch?"

I noticed the size of his desk. There were little carved elephant heads on its corners and its feet were fat and swollen like an old woman's ankles. I lowered the tray slowly and removed the cloche. Ambrose's eyes fell disappointedly to his lunch. He sighed and put his glasses down beside it.

"Reports on your *stage* have been less than satisfactory," he said. "I'm told there's a certain sloppiness. Tangerine pips left in pies and so on. That's not the end of the world in itself." He shrugged. "Could be nerves, youth... Sloppiness can sometimes be trained out of a cook your age. But, overall, Max describes you as mediocre."

"I'm not mediocre," I said, quietly.

"You did very well to win the Young Saucier and, I have to say, when you manage to make it properly, this sauce is good.

But – " His face took on a cold seriousness. "Chef Max tells me that there are certain questions as to its provenance."

"What?" I said.

"He says you purloined the recipe. Stole it."

"But *I* came up with this, at my aunt's house," I said, breathing heavily.

Ambrose gave an impatient shake of the head.

"If your thieving of the recipe wasn't enough of a mark against your name, Max tells me you have a poor palate. Palate, I'm afraid, is like character. It's just one of those things you're born with. You either have it or you don't and, it must be said, it would be highly unusual for a chap like you to have the sort of refined sensibilities that we insist upon here at King. Someone like you can have a very nice career in hotels, golf resorts, Trusthouse Fortes, that sort of thing. So," he glanced again at his cooling plate. "Cheer up and Godspeed. And by the way, if there are any reports in the *Evening Standard* that arouse our suspicions over the next six months, we'll know exactly where to direct our solicitors."

Over the endless moments during which Ambrose had been speaking, the two images of Max that I held in my head finally corresponded. Everything Kathryn had said about him was true. And, worse than that, he hated me. *Hated* me. Of course he did. An ominous weight gathered in my face. I remembered that afternoon at Sports Day, when Mark House pinned me to the floor and said what he had said about the person I'd loved. I could feel it again, the swelling in my throat. The choking.

"So I'm afraid that's that," said Ambrose.

I touched the corner of my eye. My finger came back wet.

"Are you okay?"

I nodded.

"Well, there's no use standing there looking sorry for yourself, I'm afraid," he said. "There's nothing you can do."

Max hated me. Of *course* he did.

"It's for the best, really. Stealing recipes, calling them your own. It's the kind of professional dishonesty that's usually an indicator of deeper troubles. Working at this level would only make them worse. Now go on, then. That's right. Goodbye."

I couldn't speak. I turned to leave.

"Don't think me cruel," he said. "It's just this business we're in. You understand, we can't have B-players like you and that girl at a place like King."

I stopped, midway down the carpet.

"What – Kathryn?" I said. "But she was good. You gave her a job."

"Her priorities were all wrong," he said, adding with a mutter, "Constantly blithering on about her bloody mother."

He picked up his knife and fork. I walked back to his desk and leaned over it to retrieve his plate.

"What *are* you doing?"

"Sorry, Ambrose," I said. "I'm really very sorry. I forgot to season your sauce."

He shrugged, his expression drenching me in contempt.

I could see my hand shaking as I placed the cloche back over his food. I ran carefully with the tray back to the kitchen. At the stove, I picked out the oval of fillet steak with my fingers and put it aside, before spooning as much of the sauce as possible back into a pan.

Unable to bare it any longer, I grabbed for a paring knife, pulled up my sleeve and enjoyed the tender resistance of my skin in the moments before it split. But it was too late to stop what was coming. I hadn't cried for so long and as I stood there, with the kitchen dancing obliviously behind me, a warm snake-head of wet made its tentative way down my left cheek as generous reserves of tears gathered beneath both eyes. I continued working, adding a splash more port, half a teaspoon of purée and subtle doses of all the necessary herbs, spices and condiments in order to inflate it back to its almost-cooked state so I could bring it all back down again to the point where its disparate flavours perfectly coincided.

I reached into my back pocket for the herb and tore off the tiniest crumb, flicking it from the pad of my thumb into the pan. It was greedily taken under and, in the strange state that had overcome me, I could almost detect something about the sauce change. My vision had taken on a zoomed-in quality: I could see the entire landscape of the sauce, the cool wet peaks and the hot valleys of its shifting topography. Under the flat white kitchen light it took on an unusual luminous quality. Eddies of steam appeared to arrange themselves as gaping mouths.

As I worked, my mind rebelled. Dorothy. That was it, now. I had defied her. It was done. Clearly I was not the good boy that she had believed in. But probably, you know, she was being over-protective. I was the grown-up now. Dor was mine. These herbs were mine. I would use them just this once, just to nudge me past this difficulty. They would secure me the job, which should have been mine anyway. Then, somehow, I could act to get Kathryn rehired. I would use the herbs only to do what *should* have been done in the first place. They would be a correction, a making-good. Yes, an act of justice.

Once the sauce was ready, I splashed water on my face to hide my crying and mounted the steps for what I realised might well be the last time.

"Here," I said to Le Patron on my return. "Sorry about that. All done now. Just perfect."

I turned to leave and, over my shoulder, said, "Goodbye, then. Thanks for giving me a go."

Ambrose peered irritably down at his plate. "Fine. Fine. Yes. Okay." He waved me away.

I closed the door behind me and waited at the top of the

stairs; the music of the kitchen building exquisitely to its lunch-time crescendo without me coming from below. Nothing. I began walking down and stopped on the third step. I thought I had heard some chinking or knocking or... no.

Back at my station, I picked up my chopping board and took it to the corner sink with the pans where, despondently, I began blasting them with the hose. I thought, again, about West Kent. I wondered whether Kathryn would ever let me speak to her and, even if I could convince her of my innocence, whether she'd want to see me when I was nothing more than another shit student in a shit town in shit England.

With the noise of the water, I have no idea how I became aware that someone had walked up behind me.

"Ambrose?" I said, as I turned.

On the wall behind him was a large blue electric fly-killer. Its dense blue light fell over his neck and shoulders in a humming coating of ghostly material. Long shadows were thrown beneath his eyes, nose and chin. His parting had collapsed over his fore-head. His hands hung limp by his sides, his mouth half open, his jaw moving slightly as if trembling. His chest rose and fell beneath his shirt.

"How did you make that sauce?" he said eventually.

I shrugged and glanced over at the station where I'd prepared it, as if to wake the snoozing memory.

"Just the usual way," I said. "Port, tomatoes, paprika, Worcester, fennel. I didn't get the seasoning quite right the last two times I made it for you. Actually, the last time, Max made me serve it to you ten minutes before it was ready so it was a bit sloppy."

Amrbose glanced at his shoes and frowned. The insect-killer flickered and buzzed as it sent its killing charge into a stray fly.

"Did he really?"

"Was it okay?" I asked. "Your lunch?"

All the life inside him was concentrated in his eyes. They pulsed with electricity and greed and possibility. But he didn't say anything at all. He just stood there in his red braces and his priceless white shirt. He just stood there by the sink and stared at me.

34

Up in Ambrose's office, there was only the plate. I mean, there was everything else, of course – the obscene pictures, the stentorian desk, the mob of awards on the shelf – but the moment I walked through the door, my eyes focused exclusively on that black square of fine bone china. All that was left of his lunch was a faint ghostly brown hardness painted onto the plate's surface with finger smears, and a steak rind that had been sucked so clean it seemed stripped naked, lying prone and trembling and ravished on the rim.

Ambrose was in silhouette, standing by the window.

"Talk me through this sauce again," he said.

His hands were behind his back and his gaze was cast towards the roofs of central London. His legs, meanwhile, were jiggling.

"It's just a case of treating the ingredients correctly," I said. "Not just bunging them in at a rough temperature. Sauces, it's more like pastry cooking. You need to be absolutely precise about your quantities, timings and temperatures. You have to know at exactly what level of heat each ingredient will yield its absolute best flavour – that's the secret. It's like science." I paused, worried that I was overcooking it a bit myself. "But I have practised a lot with that sauce, obviously. It's mostly practice."

Ambrose turned towards me, rubbing the tip of his tongue repeatedly over his lower lip, as if in an attempt to dig out some leftover flavour from beneath the surface of his skin. As he spoke, he kept losing control of his eyes, which would bounce between me and the plate before he could reassert his will and point them back out towards the window.

"And you could make it again, just like that?" he said. "You could do it again and again and again? It's consistency that marks the professional, you know. My chief concern is that you've made this for me two or three times now and it's ranged from very good to horrible... and now..."

"Of course," I said. "Of course I could. This sauce... " I shrugged "... this is nothing, really."

He glanced at his plate and blinked three times in quick succession. I noticed he had begun moving his lips almost invisibly against each other, like a man in the early stages of possession.

"Well, let's see, shall we?" he said eventually. "Let's go downstairs and make another. Come on, we'll do it together."

"Sure. Fine."

In the four seconds it took me to walk to the door I must have imagined and rejected at least half a dozen ways of extracting myself from this potentially disastrous situation.

"Damn," I said, stopping at the base of the stairs. I could see the shapes through the open kitchen door: the churn of dogs moving this way and that; the dance that accompanies the song. "I've used the last of the Worcester sauce. It's not a standard kitchen supply – I brought it in especially and it's all gone. I'll dash out and pick some up. I'll give you a knock when I'm back."

Ambrose moved to speak, his face darkening with questions.

"I just have to go to Mace," I smiled. "You're not going to

come with me to Mace?"

"No," he said, snapping out of it. He waved me off with a fey flick of the hand. "Yes, you go."

I waited in a corner of Stephen Mews until I was sure he'd be back in his office, before sliding back through the kitchen to begin the sauce without him. It was all bubbling heartily, just a minute or so away from being at that quiltish consistency – so essential for a good sauce – that summons up the sense memories of being cosseted and caressed and soothed on cold evenings. I reached into my pocket for the leaf.

"Fuck it," I muttered.

I dropped in a double quantity, gave it a stir, poured the lot into a porcelain ramekin and finished it off with a couple of pinches of freshly ground black pepper. Perfect.

"I thought we were going to do that together?" said Ambrose when I walked into his office with my fragrant gift.

I held it forward, giving the scent a chance to take him.

"Have a taste," I said. "See what you think."

There was something of the obedient schoolboy about how perfectly he was sitting upright. I could see him as a nine-year-old, in his cap and shorts and mittens. He took a spoonful of the sauce and sniffed it. Shadows moved across the ceiling, cast by the traffic below. He moved in his seat. Silently, he swallowed another spoonful. Then another. He groaned.

"Is it okay?"

He looked as if he was going to cry with pleasure.

"I'm not entirely convinced it's the same as the last one," he began. "It's different somehow."

"It *is* the same," I said. "It's exactly the same."

He smiled again and moved his hand distractedly towards his crotch.

"Perhaps you'll give me five minutes whilst I finish some things. Then we can do it again. I'm just curious to know how you've made this, that's all. I'm sure you understand. My friend at the Young Saucier did tell me your concoction was good, but..." a greasy, grey toothed smile lashed out across his face. "You'll indulge a curious old gourmand?"

I couldn't understand it. I felt a sudden heat in my throat.

"You know, I've made this for you four times, Ambrose," I said. "Either you like it or you don't."

He looked up at me, his eyes lizardy and fierce.

"What I mean is," I said, "I don't want to be rude, but I don't work for you any more. If you give me a job, I'll make this sauce for you as often as you like. You can serve it on the menu. It's all yours. You can have it. I'm bored of it anyway. I've got much better sauces than this."

His antique wooden chair squealed as he crossed his legs. He glanced into the ramekin and pulled it just a little way towards him.

"You'll need to work on your consistency."

"I'll work on whatever you tell me to."

"And then there's Max. I'll be frank, if I may. Max's reaction to you was..." He swallowed. "The truth is, he doesn't want you anywhere near him. I mean, I don't know, exactly, what you did–"

I felt as if something hot and invisible was trying to push me over. My eyes lost focus momentarily.

"I don't care about Max," I said. "I won't work with him."

My legs began to fizz with weakness. Ambrose's gaze followed me as I pulled out a chair and sat down.

"Well then, what on earth are you suggesting then?" he said.

"Is it true you're opening a French place? Glamis?"

He reared back slightly.

"Dear me, you *are* well informed, aren't you?" There was a silence. He picked up a fat black fountain pen and put it down again. "Well, Glamis might work actually. Although I *am* concerned as to how you came to find out about it." He leaned forward, towards the ramekin which seemed to distract him. "May I ask who told you?"

I ignored him as he took another spoonful and gave a soft, involuntary groan. Behind him was a shelf of small silver statuettes of women: a naked adolescent with breasts like tender kisses; an adult woman weeping into her own arms; another with her hands in the air screaming at the gods. I surveyed them, emptily, my mind filled with thoughts that I'd never had before. New thoughts of Max.

"I'd want a senior position," I said.

"Don't be bloody ridiculous," he yelped. "You're an apprentice! You'd be lucky to be on the *line* in one of my kitchens!"

"I'm the best saucier you'll get."

"You're too young," he said. "You don't have the experience."

"What about Alain Ducasse? Two stars by twenty-seven."

"It's impossible, Killian. Absolutely impossible. I'm terribly sorry. I admire your ambition. You're more like Max than you probably realise, but I think this time you're letting your hunger for success cloud your powers of reason. But do not worry. You will have your moment. I'm certain I can find a place for you at the bistro."

"I want to be head chef."

He rose a little from his chair.

"You *can't* be head chef!" he said.

"Then I'll take my sauce to Nico."

"Oh fuck off," he shouted.

The rage sent him to his feet.

"How dare you?" he demanded. "Who in the name of God do you think you are?"

I leaned forward over his desk, picked up his fountain pen and scratched the phone number for Dor Cottage on his notepad.

"That's my number," I said.

Standing up, I reached over, intending to retrieve the ramekin, but the moment my fingers touched it, I changed my mind. I marched across the room, for the first time not intimidated in the slightest by his ridiculous slippery carpet, and just before I left, turned to deliver my final demand.

"And I want Kathryn to be my second."

35

As I drove home, the sun was shining high over London. It was so hot in the city that you could smell the pavement, whilst out in the countryside the scent of trees and wildflowers was released into the air as if the whole of nature was being cooked on a low simmer. But as I neared Herstmonceux the weather changed dramatically. The further I travelled up the long track into the woodland clearing in which Dor nestled, the worse the storm became, my car wheels slipping in the mud and the rain forming a sheet of exploding water on my windscreen.

Turning off the ignition, I rubbed the mist from the window and surveyed my uncle's wall, now half destroyed and looking like a great, gaping smash-toothed mouth. I couldn't wait to finally obliterate the thing. Running through the rain, I decided it was too wet to launch my final attack on it and so determined instead to pay another visit to the attic.

The small door pushed open easily and I climbed the ladder into the loft. It was freezing and the storm was coming down onto the old roof like an assault. There was no wind; the only thing you could hear was the barrage, the relentless grey fall of rain. It must have been all over Kent and Sussex by now.

I spent perhaps an hour in the French section, hunting for dishes that might impress Ambrose if he did decide to give me a chance. After a time, I went to the section labelled "Dor". There were piles of old notebooks – some left by Dorothy, others by what must have been previous occupants. On the top shelf, in the furthest corner, I spotted the most gorgeous book of all. Black leather and with no decipherable title on the spine. I felt my narrow biceps strain as I took it down. Brushing the veil of dust and fly remains away with my sleeve, I read the words, *Index plantarum officinalium, quas ad materiae medicae scientiam promovendam, in horto, Dor Cotagium, Herstmonceux'*.

I opened it slowly. Every beautiful age-dried page was composed of hand-drawn illustrations of plants, each one crowded by closely rendered inky text. Page by page I turned and recognised, in amongst the etchings, many ordinary herbs. Marjoram, rosemary, meadowsweet, purslane – each was accompanied by descriptions that seemed to describe not their flavour, but their supposed medicinal properties. But the further I got into the book, the stranger its contents became. I stopped recognising many and then most of the plants, all of which were apparently once grown right here at Dor. Gradually, the sentences took on their own strange form, as if becoming affected, somehow, by the item they described. Eventually they ceased even to be written in straight lines. Instead they bulged and spread, sometimes following the contours of the particular herb they accompanied, sometimes following a logic all of their own. The result was a wonderful maelstrom of words that spoke of awe and magic and barely controlled terror.

I sat against the shelf and took my time with the index. Above my head, the rain crashed down ever harder as, beneath me, the cottage settled into its dark and favoured state. As the day fell away into night, I reached one of the final pages of the book. I felt myself gasp, a cloud of cold breath billowing visibly from my mouth. The picture in front of me – unmistakably, it was *my* herb, the one shaped like a teardrop. It was called 'Earl's Leaf'.

The text was close and difficult to read. I strained to make out the words:

"*... must thereby be Warned that a Triumvirate of Plantes does grow in the Physic Garden of Dor Cottage that hold much Perille and Danger, causing vile Fites and Madnesses in each of man's distinct planes, Libido, Body and Spirite. If Takene together, these Plantes will cause Great Agonies and Death in Full Grown Men. Local Men and Women have been Bewitched by these same Herbes and Mary Dor Burned as a Witch on the Groundes of Herstmonceux Castle for the sin of Formenting same...*"

A sensation came over me, of being tiny in that attic; swallowed. I tracked down the text, fascinated by what I could make out of its discussion of my precious Earl's Leaf which, it said, causes "madness of libido" and "*...inflicts the Eater with a wicked and terrible desire to commit Foul Venereal Acts...*".

Turning the page, I came across a drawing of something called Cauter which was erect on a thick stem and had a tiny ball of thin thorns hanging from it. This would apparently cause a "madness of the body". The final of this "deadly triumvirate" of herbs, labelled Hindeling, had a stiff, five-petalled flower with a curling, tongue-like stamen which triggered a "madness of the mind". From what I could decipher, each one caused a different effect and, if taken together – according to the increasingly hysterical author of the book – they would kill.

Downstairs, I fetched my raincoat and the sledgehammer from outside the back door. My boots were sucked into the mud as I made my way towards the hole in the wall. I stopped and peered in. In the torch's beam – it didn't seem possible. The Earl's Leaf was thick, leery and wild, almost reaching out towards me. I moved my torch around and saw other shapes in amongst the Earl's Leaf. There it was, thicker, shinier, with its white spikes and hanging head – the Cauter. And there in the distance – the purple, serpentine stamen of the Hindeling. I heard a sharp wooden groan from deep in the elm forest. It was thrilling to be amongst these plants that hadn't been seen for centuries. I stood there, in the rain, and laughed. The 350-year-old physic garden was *alive*.

I picked up the hammer and hurled it against the remaining bricks, which cracked and fell with satisfying ease. I soon got into a rhythm, my arms, legs and the rough wood-handled tool working in harmony. When the wall was finally down, I harvested an armful of Earl's Leaf. Trimming each tumescent stalk, I laid half the crop out in the kitchen and the other in the airing cupboard on sheets of newspaper to dry.

* * *

I was in the midst of some kind of nightmare when I was awoken by the telephone ringing.

"Good morning," said the voice in the receiver.

"Oh, Ambrose," I said. "Hi. Hello."

I looked at my watch. It was late – eight thirty a.m. I still had that peculiar sensation that accompanies nightmares: the inescapable feeling that you've been violated, somehow, by outside forces. I had the name "Mary" in my head and a memory of clawing, howling dogs.

"I've been considering our discussion and I have a proposal to put to you. You should consider this to be a final offer, do you understand?"

"Yes," I said, still groggy.

"If this conversation comes to a close with anything other than you answering in the unqualified affirmative, the offer will be withdrawn immediately. Am I making myself clear?"

"Absolutely," I said.

"I have had a long conversation with a good friend of mine,

a *patron* back in France. Claude tells me he made a young man about your age *chef d'cuisine* at a wonderful little restaurant, La Barriere de Clichy, a while back – Bernard Louiseau. You'll be pleased to hear it was a great success. Louiseau's down in Saulieu now and is thriving. So that is the position I am offering you. *Chef d'cuisine.*"

"Great…"

"However," he said, pausing for a moment, "you will be seconded by Chef Andrew Silverwood. It is Chef Andrew who will take ultimately responsibility for *all* aspects of the kitchen and the food. Unofficially, he will be your *chef de file*. For the avoidance of any potential unpleasantness down the road, I wish to also make it clear that your wage will be half that of Andrew's. Until he judges you to be sufficiently competent to take charge of the kitchen, you will not be carrying out the full duties of a head chef. You'll make your sauces and work on running the pass. If it emerges that you have the ability to call tickets and lead the brigade, and when you have learned to do it well, then of course we can renegotiate. Now then, Killian. All I want to hear from you is a single syllable. What's it to be?"

"So it will look like I'm in charge, but really it will be Andy?" I said.

"One syllable."

I made myself a promise. I would use the Earl's Leaf only when it was strictly necessary. I would honour Dorothy, as much as I reasonably could. I would be responsible. *Good.*

"Are you there?" said Ambrose.

"Yes."

"Yes you're there or yes you accept my offer?"

"Yes to both."

"Ah, the gratifying sound of a good man making the right decision. Excellent. Right. We need to discuss menus. It will be traditional bistro food, but tweaked in order to show off your sauces. You have more, I assume, than the one you prepared for me?"

"I do," I said. "And I have little twists on the French classics that I think you'll like. They'll be perfect for Glamis."

"I'll talk with Andy and we'll go over everything on Thursday afternoon. We'll meet at Glamis where you can prepare all your sauces for tasting. Don't let me down, Killian."

"Could I also have Kathryn?" I said. "I want Kathryn there."

"I thought I'd made myself clear. No conditions."

"Not as my second," I said. "Just on fish or meat. Please. She's brilliant and I'll work fantastically with her and Andy. She should never have been fired. You know that."

I listened to the humming telephone quiet.

"Oh, fine, fine," he said. "But if she gives any indication that her mind is with her damned mother, rather than with her work, then she's gone."

"And tell her that it was nothing to do with me. Please, Ambrose. Can you tell her what happened? Tell her it was Max, being a cunt."

There was a silence. When Ambrose spoke again, there was a world-weary note in his voice.

"The address is 11 Charlotte Street. Not far from King. I'll see you on Thursday."

I could see Mary in the kitchen, her rough cloth shawl and her hair, wet with steam and sweat, and her plum-blushed cheeks, and she was strong and young and handsome.

On the oaken table, she was laying out the Earl's herbs. Sheafs of freshly harvested stems with leaves like flattened teardrops. She squeezed one between her thumb and forefinger and breathed in the scent. Her tongue, pink and wet, pushed over her bottom lip and she smelled again. With a ball of twine, she began tying them together for drying.

Then footsteps up the path.

She stopped, her right ear angled up into the filthy air. To listen. To wait. To feel her heart in her chest.

Whispering outside: "They say she has an Evil thing within her and that the Devil attends her in the form of a Fly."

A hammering on the door. It shakes the Fly from where it was watching. It lifts and dances its spirals and circles. It's all around her as she listens through the filth.

A hammering again.

She drops the leaves and hurries up the stairs.

What about the fear? What about the burning? What about the trouble that's been breeding between the cracks in the beams and the cracks in the mortar and the cracks in the floor? What about the mischief

239

that's been buried in the ground and is stirring? The old trouble, the family trouble, that old mischief come to find me.

36

The first dish ever made at Glamis was grilled quail with sauce Bois Boudran – a herby, tangy French concoction, made with tomato compote, vinegar, chervil, chives and tarragon. I prepared it in the newly installed kitchen.

Andy was at the butcher's block, working on the quail. He barely lifted his head to greet me. He just motioned at the blue A4 folder that included the method for Bois Boudran, which I only took for the sake of appearances. I was already familiar with the recipe and I was thrilled: it would be perfect.

Over the previous three and a half weeks, I had been working through the nights, practising a variety of sauces without using Earl's Leaf. Although I had been pleased with how they had all tasted – and convinced that they would be entirely adequate for the purposes of an upmarket bistro – they were never quite enough. If I was to prove that Max had treated me unjustly then I would need dishes that were far beyond adequate. Beyond perfect was an absolute necessity. Moreover, if I wanted Kathryn to earn enough money to move her mother into humane accommodation, I realised that for me to take undue risks would be immoral. So I decided that, just for the time being, I would use a whisper of Earl's Leaf in each sauce.

Over those anxious days and heavy-lidded nights, I began to wonder if I might have exaggerated the herb's effect to myself – really, in a sense, it wasn't much more than a kind of seasoning. It lifted the flavours a little, that was all. When truly I thought about it, I decided that an untrained palate, in all likelihood, would barely be able to tell the difference – at least, not at the quantities I was using.

As I worked, I was surprised to find that I was thinking about Max as much as ever. I remembered finding a photograph, tucked into the cover of one of Aunt Dorothy's recipe books, of my parents enjoying a picnic in the grounds of Tonbridge Castle. They looked to be in their very early twenties and my dad had obviously said something that amused Mum – her laughter was such that she was leaning backwards, her gaze so worshipful it felt almost improper. How could such evidently powerful love transmute so cleanly into hate? As I held that picture, years ago, I couldn't understand it. But now I had experienced something of that nature myself. Where there had been wild adoration for Max, there was now a rage of equal force. I wondered if it was all made of the same essential material, if hate was just love in shadow. And I felt ashamed at how thoroughly my devotion to Max had spun its illusion around me. I couldn't rid myself of the thought that he had developed such a vigorous dislike of me. Of *me!* The one who had loved him more than anyone!

The mood in Dor seemed to alter itself as well. I couldn't work out the extent to which I was imagining things, but the upstairs room that had once been Dorothy's favourite had become, in some indistinct way, unwelcoming. I would go to sleep with the door and windows closed and still wake up to find flies buzzing over the bed.

I found myself more and more adept at reading the different kinds of silence that were present in the house, as if they constituted a private language that was known only to me and the walls. Each version of quiet had its own pitch, texture and density. It was the density that I feared the most – that sense of crowding. I felt this, most commonly, in the kitchen and, of course, over the stairs.

* * *

As I worked in the Glamis kitchen that morning, I listened to the radio. The blank voice announced all the things that were going on out there: Neil Kinnock trying to isolate the far left of the Labour Party; Moscow warning Reagan against arming the Afghans; the Pentagon stepping up the use of lie detectors to determine employees' patriotism; Iraq bombing border villages in Iran; the Chinese leader Deng Xiaoping planning to make his country an "economic powerhouse" in the twenty-first century; George Bush meeting Thatcher to agree ideas on combating terrorism. There was something strange about it. It wasn't the same old news any more. It seemed different. It felt like the future.

When the moment came to drop the Earl's Leaf in, Andy was concentrating hard on cooking the quail, tongs in hand, bottom lip between his teeth, peering into the hazy heat. I retrieved an Old Holborn pouch which I'd cleaned out and filled with fresh Earl's Leaf. I watched the smallest pinch fall into the pan in front of me and disappear amongst the rest of the fragrantly glistening greenery. That would be enough. Just a breath of it.

"Quail'll be there in thirty seconds," Andy called. "Give it five minutes to rest."

"Yes, Chef."

When it was ready, Andy arranged the quail on one of the new white plates with some steamed vegetables that he'd finished in a little butter. I watched him taking charge of putting the dish together with his usual purring craftsmanship. Without meeting my eye, he held out his hand for me to pass him my pan of sauce. I ignored the gesture, and deliberately defying the Nouvelle Cuisine practice of saucing beneath the protein, I spooned it over the still-steaming bird.

Lifting the quail to one side, I made a kind of platform with the carrot spears and baby potatoes and put the meat back down on top it and drizzled another spoonful of sauce to repair the messy damage. It looked ridiculous, but that wasn't the point. I had made the dish mine.

"Okay?" I said.

Andy looked at the plate.

"If you want," he shrugged irritably.

I picked up the dish.

"Let's do this," I said, and led the way out onto the restaurant floor.

As it was a bistro, the dining space was larger than King's and the walls had been hung with dark-framed mirrors, decorated in gold leaf. The workmen were halfway through painting the ceiling a faux tobacco colour – Ambrose had given them the afternoon off, lest the fumes interfere with our tasting session – and there was a row of antique hat stands in the small corridor on which coats were to be hung. An exciting touch was the addition of an ostentatious "top table" that was constructed on a small platform and would be discreetly spotlit. There would be a twenty-per-cent surcharge for its use and, Ambrose predicted, would be highly in demand by newly minted City folk.

Still, all the decorators' best endeavours couldn't block out the deadening unromance of London that poured in through the windows that morning – the dreary dishwater light; the combustion farts of taxis and buses; the seagullish calls of a nearby newspaper seller. It was gloomy in the interior, too, as the bulbs hadn't yet been fitted. I could only make out the silhouette of Ambrose with his sleeves rolled up, leather-bound notebook on the table and cigarette on the go. And – he was with someone. Her hair, I noticed, was in a ponytail that had been tied low, from the base of her head. For some reason, it hurt me that she was wearing it in a style that I'd not seen before.

"Kathryn!" I said. "Great! How are you? You're here!"

She was leaning forward, her shoulders in a slump, her eyes cast down. She looked at me briefly before readjusting, quickly, to meet the eyes of Andy behind me.

"Yes, I am," she said.

I placed the plate down carefully in the middle of the table and grinned at her again.

"Presentation's a little off," Ambrose said, as I pulled out the chair next to Kathryn. "Why is it piled high like a tower? Nobody wants high food. They want it flat on the plate. They want to see what they're eating. And let's be more generous with this sauce please. This isn't King – we don't want too much china showing. We're supposed to be giving the impression of plenty. Right, come on ladies and gentlemen. The big moment is upon us. Who's going to say grace?"

I tried to coax Kathryn into smiling at Ambrose's joke. She sat there awkwardly, staring at the dish, her lips pushed together in a sad, swollen pucker as Ambrose tipped the beautifully browned bird off its platform and sliced into the breast. He pushed a piece of carrot onto his fork and then, with his knife, spread a generous layer of the green-flecked sauce over it. My heart made its presence felt on the inside of my ribs as I followed the parcel through the air, trailing a faint pall of steam, to be placed on the proprietor's much-feared tongue. He pulled the fork from his mouth. There was a moment, suspended. And then it happened. His eyes dropped. There was a single chew and silence. Then he chewed and chewed and finally swallowed. His unhealthy skin gave life to a fine drop of sweat, like blood from a pinprick, above his left eyebrow. He put his fork down gently, sat back in his chair, stared at the ceiling and spoke quietly.

"Good God."

Clearly bemused, Andy leaned forward and took a bite. As his jaws worked, a frown of intense concentration came over him, his eyes cast seriously towards his mouth.

"Fucking hell," he said, before he'd even swallowed. "Wow. How have you... ?"

I shifted uncomfortably. He pushed the plate towards Kathryn, dipping his little finger helplessly back into the unctuous green slick and tasting it again. Ambrose gave a little loinish "uh" and relaxed his neck completely, so that his head hung limply back.

"Try that," Andy told her. "It's unbelievable. Oh my God, Jesus Christ. It's amazing."

Feverish now, Andy stood up and put his hands on his hips, staring down at the plate with a ridiculous smile on his face, his black moustache crushed up between his lip and his nose. Ambrose's throat released another deeply satisfied post-coital grunt.

The change that came over Kathryn was something I will never forget. It was like watching a flower bloom into life. All the dour suspicion left her, her cheeks pinked and her eyes became alive and danced with admiration and pleasure and that intimate, thrilled, quasi-sexual shock that all cooks covet, that look that said I had touched her, I had given her pleasure and she couldn't help but crave for more.

"Mmmm," she said, modestly holding her hand to her mouth. "God, *mmmmm!*"

She took another bite. I noticed, with another small lurch of alarm, that her lips had pinked and swelled. I looked at the other two. The effect was less noticeable on them, but it was undeniably there.

Taking another dose of sauce, Ambrose chewed slowly and held it in his mouth for a time before reluctantly swallowing. He sat back and gazed adoringly in my direction.

"You have a first-class talent, Killian," he said. "Absolutely first class."

I shook my head and puffed out my cheeks, dismissively.

"Not really," I said.

"Oh, but you do. You have a way with flavour... You, you, you... as you say, you know just how to extract layers of flavour that I have never, in all my years in this silly business... It's like you can read the mind of the ingredients. It's like a second sight."

"Not really," I said again, sitting up. "Can you really...? I mean, it's not... It's just seasoning, really."

"What rot!" said Ambrose. Suddenly energised, he leaped to his feet and clapped his hands together, his expertly concealed kettle-drum belly bouncing like a bald extra head above his belt. "And this is just the first dish of the day! Ladies and gentlemen, I think we're going to have a success! A huge bloody success!"

"They'll be queuing round the block," said Andy, his mouth full again.

"Rubbish!" shouted Ambrose. "They'll be queuing round the block to get to the block where the fucking queue starts. They'll be rioting in the streets. Bravo, Killian! Bravo!"

* * *

That afternoon we ate our way through the entire menu. By the time we were done, no one seemed in any doubt about the sure success of Glamis.

"You've done really well," said Kathryn.

Ambrose and Andy had disappeared into the kitchen. Kathryn had lifted her ski jacket from the back of her chair and, looking towards the door, was pulling it on.

"Are you going?" I said.

I put my hands on my hips and tried to looked relaxed about things. Breezy.

"Stuff to do," she said. "Mum."

"You know – what Max said," I began. "It's not true, Kathryn." Relaxed and breezy. "He's a fucking liar." I could feel a vein pumping in my forehead. "I know you think I worship him, and you probably had a point, back then. But he lied about you and he lied about my sauce. And, you know, the whole reason I want to do this – the whole reason I asked Ambrose to hire you – is because I want us, me and you together, to show him how it's done. Nouvelle Cuisine is over. We'll prove it to him, and to everyone."

Relaxed and breezy and carefree. That's the way to do it.

"Blimey, you're keen," she said. "You've never even run a pass before."

A light above us began flickering. A yellowish pall blinked on and off over Kathryn's nose and cheeks and shoulders. Yellow and black, yellow and black, yellow and black, like wasps.

"Well, if you don't think I can do it..."

"I didn't say that."

"...why are you here?"

"Because I need a fucking *job*."

Relaxed and breezy and I could feel this sensation of *density* expanding behind my eyes and this restless, flapping urge in the joints of my fingers and the bones of my knees. The bulb flickered all over the white tablecloth. I sat back down and put my head in my hands. A passing motorbike rattled the window and I felt its vibrations in my elbows. I heard the chair next to me being pulled back and the sound of Kathryn sitting into it. She took my wrist and pulled it away from my face. For the first time since we were at King together, I saw the beginning of her vulnerable smile.

"Sorry, Killian," she said. "I'm sure you can do it."

I ignored her. She let me go and smoothed down the front of her jacket, which had puffed up with the action of her sitting.

"Max lied, you know," I said. "I didn't tell him anything."

"I know. Ambrose told me."

The bulb stopped flickering.

"So why are you being like this?" I said. "Why is it still weird between us?"

"I'm just nervous about it," she said. "You know, my life has been all over the place." A silver fly landed on the back of my hand. I watched its legs bend, its proboscis lower into one of my scabs. "I just want a piece of calm. A bit of peace. I don't know if us, being together – maybe it's not a good idea."

It started again, the maddening strobe, flashing on the walls and our skin and the marks on the tablecloth. It was enough to trigger a migraine. One of the cuts on my wrists began to itch. I scratched. As the fly zoomed off, small crumbles of dried blood fell onto a white napkin.

"But I didn't do anything wrong," I said, squinting.

"Breaking up with you made me realise how much..." She looked away, briefly losing her thread. "I feel a lot for you, Killian. *A lot.* I can't go through anything like that again. It was too much." She hid her face in her hands. "You're too damaged, Killian. You're a fuck-up."

I reached out and touched her chin with my finger. Her skin felt smooth and cold and soft and she didn't move away. The corners of her mouth trembled slightly.

"Yes but, Kathryn, you're a fuck-up, too," I said, smiling. "We'll be fuck-ups together."

Nothing happened for a moment. I looked at her sitting there, utterly unable to fathom what she was thinking.

"I love you," I said.

"Don't make me cry," she said.

I took her hands in mine and squeezed them, rubbing my

thumbs over the surface of her palms. I felt removed, as if I was looking down on us, huddled together under the failing bulb. I would have to remember this; to store the sensory information of what it felt like to touch her skin; to feel her narrow wrists; to breathe her out-breaths; to be so near to her face and body without her flinching. I'd have to save it, carefully and accurately, just in case.

"I promise, Kathryn," I said. "It will be worth it. I know it sounds a bit crazy, but I really believe in my sauces. I really think I can make Glamis a massive success. Then you can earn proper money and get your mum out of that awful home. Get her somewhere where they'll look after her properly."

She peered up at me.

"It's like you told me," I continued. "You don't get anything in the restaurant business unless you earn it. And I deserve this. So do you." I paused. "That's what I think, anyway. Maybe you don't. But can't we give it a go, just in case?"

She looked down again, still unresponsive. I whispered, "Max is over. We're going to make sure he is. We're going to fucking *destroy* him."

As she leaned over and put her arms around me, the bulb started going again. "Our success should be for our sake, not just to get back at him," she said.

"So...?"

She smiled. "But if I ever find myself having to put a Max mask on just to get your attention, there'll be trouble."

As soon as she was safely gone, I would climb onto the table, remove my shoe and, holding the chandelier with one hand, smash the flickering fucking lightbulb with the heel. I would savour the small calamity of sound and the sensation of hot glass falling all over me.

"I swear," I said. "There's nothing to worry about any more. Everything's going to be perfect."

37

The media greeted the opening of Glamis with a level of expectation that the British restaurant world had never witnessed before. In the kitchen, we couldn't see the cameras and the lights and the crowd of more than two hundred that had amassed on the street to glimpse the arrival of the various celebrities that the *Sun*, the *Mirror*, the *Evening Standard*, the *Daily Mail* and even the *Guardian* and the *Daily Telegraph* had listed as attending. We could feel the excitement, though. We were all experiencing everything in sharper focus. Colours and smells and tastes became richer and time ticked by with a swagger that was palpable, as if the seconds themselves knew they were a part of history.

During the weeks in which the decorators had been finishing and Andy and I had perfected the menu, Ambrose had been squeezing all but the last drips of goodness out of his contacts book. He arranged for us to give confidential tastings to newspaper editors and food critics and other powerful entities on the strict condition that they wouldn't formally review the restaurant until it opened. It was a masterful plan. On a series of afternoons and evenings we cooked for everyone in London that mattered. Encouraged by the scent of exclusivity and secrecy that surrounded it, word bounced from critics to journalists to their influential friends.

Our most nerve-wracking night was a blustery Tuesday, when Barry Gruenfeld came for a meal. Gruenfeld, who was celebrated in the nation's kitchens for the gripping drama of his ugliness – his nose like a stamped frog, his lower lip sitting above his top one and his foul-smelling, rot-toothed smile – wrote a weekly column for the *Sunday Telegraph* and was easily the most feared critic in the country. Two years previously, Max Mann had had him evicted from King and – rumour has it – subsequently threatened him after he poked fun at the Gentleman Chef's appearance on the cover of the *Radio Times* with two fried eggs placed over his eyes. Ambrose was forced to hush the incident up with some senior publishing figure – a straightforward enough task, given that the executive happened to be a regular at his debauched Saturday parties. Aware of these behind-the-scenes machinations and livid at his neutering, Gruenfeld had never forgiven Ambrose or Max. For more than two years, he'd used every excuse he could to snipe at King in print.

Initially, he refused to even take Ambrose's calls. But after several days, in which he suffered wave upon wave of thrilled gossip from his friends and colleagues, he finally relented. Of course, we fully expected Gruenfeld to feign disgust or lack of interest when he got here. What he did, on the night, was clear his throat, adjust his tie and, with a wide-eyed nervous politeness, ask for second helpings.

The rest of Ambrose's formidable business talents had been directed towards his network of kitchen informers. He tapped them all in an attempt to locate the most skilled young chefs in the country and then tempt them with the promise of long hours, low wages and a possible scintilla of reflected glory, all the while making it sound like the most astonishing deal imaginable. I blamed the fact he was only partly successful on Max working against us. The result was that we ended up with what must have been the youngest brigade in the country – only two were over twenty-six. I found myself in charge of my own apprentices, the best of which was a shy boy from Leeds named Marco who'd trained previously at the Box Tree in Ilkley and with the Rouxs. He was oddly attractive, with his long curly hair and the grave bags beneath his eyes that gave him a look of power and wisdom. He had an urgency and an instinct for graft that reminded me of myself. I liked Marco a lot. I believed he'd go far.

By the time opening night came around, we were already booked up for three weeks. Due in the restaurant for that first service were Phil Collins, Moira Stewart, Ian Botham, Nik Kershaw with his wife Sheri, Steve Davis, Keith Floyd, and three of Five Star along with a few actors from the new BBC TV show called *EastEnders*. And so, on the insistence of Ambrose, was Chef Max Mann.

As the hands on the large clock on the wall shifted thrillingly towards six p.m., I stood at the pass with Kathryn to my left and Andy to my right, and gathered the brigade around me. Everything in the kitchen was clean and perfect, including my chefs, their eyes direct, their hands folded obediently by their waists.

"Chefs," I said. "We have a lot to prove tonight. As most of you know, Glamis started out as nothing more than a side project for Ambrose – somewhere he could relive his wild Parisian days. As you can tell by all the noise outside, we're already punching considerably above our weight. It's not every 'local' bistro that gets three out of Five Star in on their opening night."

I paused to let this fact sink in.

"We've done this by creating a brilliant menu. But make no mistake, not everyone sitting out there in the restaurant wants us to succeed. Some actively want us to fail. You know who I'm talking about. Some of you have worked for him. One or two of you may still feel a little bit of loyalty to him. If so, you can take off your apron and walk out of that door right now, because I don't want you here."

Nobody moved.

"It's not just his silly 1970s food that has no place in this restaurant; it's his outdated way of running a kitchen. I'm going to make a promise to all of you right now. There will be no place in here for the kind of bullying that happens at King. Disrespect will not be tolerated in my kitchen, not from anyone. We will prove to Max Mann that you don't need to torment people to achieve the highest standards. I expect every cook here to want it badly enough to be their own drill sergeant. You should want it enough that you stop thinking about yourself, your well-being, your wants, when you're in here. You should walk in at seven every morning, slip into your clogs and become a part of Glamis. Everything you do should be for the restaurant. Because your career – everything that you work for – lives and dies by the restaurant. We need to prove to Max Mann that the days of Nouvelle Cuisine are over. The days of *Max Mann* are over! We're delivering to the people what they've always wanted – the luxury, the sensation, the richness, the *flavours*. We're taking the best of the past and the best of the present and, by doing so, we will become the future. And that future begins *right now!* So let's get him," I shouted. "Let's prove to Max that we can do it. Let's make a booking for the mad cunt's funeral–"

Kathryn squeezed my hand and glanced at me as if to say, "enough". Exchanging looks amongst themselves, the cooks scattered back to their stations. Minutes later, the maître d' came in with the first orders.

"Okay, listen up," I shouted. "Two St Jacques, two foie, one bouillabaisse."

"Yes, Chef," came the response, gruff, stolid and resolute.

They snapped to it, necks bent and perfect.

"Is everyone with me?" I shouted.
"Yes, Chef!"

*   *   *

As much as I would have loved to have rejected every aspect of la Nouvelle Cuisine, it was obvious to me that this would have been foolish. I knew that if we were going to make a dent on the world culinary scene, we would have to be reasonably sparing with our butter and our cream (unlike Max who, no doubt, had begun cooking "the new style" – deglazing with water and thickening with carrot and onion purée and so on – but had clearly secretly reneged on that promise as part of his flagellating crawl towards his three-star dream). At Glamis, we would throw off the obvious pretensions, the gigantic plates, the meat-and-fruit combos, whilst keeping the essential architecture of the style – the freshness, the lightness, the reverence for the sanctity of the ingredient in its natural state. But we would bring to it the velvet luxury of Old Europe: truffles, foie gras and portions whose size verged on intimidating and which I insisted, mainly for reasons of stubbornness, upon arranging high on the plate as I had on the day of the tasting.

I also knew that we wouldn't be taken seriously if we didn't prepare everything in the modern way – to order, and from a standing, naked kitchen. And that had to include sauces. As well as running the pass (I had convinced Andy to let me try and, to my surprise, he relented with only a hint of complaint), it was my job to prepare them. I insisted that Kathryn hand me the pans in which she'd cooked plump 300-gram cuts of beef, lamb or veal and equally generous portions of Bresse chicken and woodcock, so that I could deglaze them and create the jus that would anoint the final dish at my own special sauce station. Even if I hadn't had that old tobacco pouch filled with Earl's

Leaf secreted in my tunic, I would have insisted upon working this way.

I had no doubts about my wait staff, who had been mercilessly drilled by my stern and decidedly un-French maître d', Ms Drusilla Langton-Grey – a bony, fifty-something spinster with aristocratic roots, alarming green eyeshadow and a seemingly endless appetite for fatty offcuts, which she'd scrounge by appearing abruptly at Kathryn's side at the sauté station, clicking her long fingernails like a hungry cricket and asking, in her deep, dry, upper-class tone, "Any trimmings, darling?"

When the *coup de feu* finally arrived, it was with a warm bloom of satisfaction that I found that the first table ordered two entrecôte with sauce Glamis – my award-winning sauce, which Ambrose had christened after the restaurant. As I took that pristine white ticket, I wondered, yet again, was using the Earl's Leaf somehow cheating? Did it count as such because it was unfair? What about all those customers at King who are celebrated by the world for their beauty or talent? We elevate them as if they've earned it. But you don't earn what you're born with; you steal it from God. If they were worthy of the gifts that had been passed down to them, then why wasn't I? Kathryn had been right. I deserved this.

And there it began, for the first time, the brand-new music of my kitchen. Following the first ticket there were two more orders for steak Glamis. Then three more – a run – and two for *tournedos Rossini* and two for *poularde à la vapeur*, then three chicken stuffed with truffles, foie gras and boned pigs' feet and then six *turbot à l'amiral*, which came with both a white wine sauce and a red, and then another steak Glamis and then the music reached a dangerous pitch, a kind of gnawing quiet broken by shouts of "behind" and shouts of "how long for..." and shouts of "fucking talk to me" and shouts of "where is it?" and then two turbot and a *poularde* and a cod for Table 12 and more pans go on and my wrist is burned, and then one Glamis, two cod and a Rossini and then have Table 9 had their starters yet and who's this plate for and the waiters, the waiters in their black trousers and their white aprons, they wait, they wait for me in a small queue and they try not to look at me and a woodcock à Glamis and a cod for Table 5 and is this the Glamis for Table 9 yes yes I think so and has 9 got their order yet then where's their fucking ticket and they try not to look at me but they stand there waiting for their food glancing at each other with raised eyes and whispering and ouch fuck my hand and is that over-reduced taste it taste it a little bit but fuck it and what do you want now can't you see I'm doing it I'm doing it just be patient fuck hang on where's that cod have we had the cod yet the cod the cod and there's Andy here's Andy what does Andy want it's not that bad –

"Come on!" I shouted to the brigade. "This isn't good enough, guys. Please! Come on!"

"We're fucked," Andy whispered. "We're completely fucked."

"We're not fucked," I said. "They'll just have to wait. It's good food. It's worth it."

As the minutes went by, and the trouble mounted, I forgot to worry quite so much about hiding the fact of the secret pouch in my apron. I only realised my mistake when I noticed Kathryn staring at me in bemusement.

"What?" I asked.

"Why are you sprinkling pocket fluff into your sauces?"

The world froze around me.

"That's a fucking stupid thing to say," I snapped.

And then the moment was broken, by, "I'm sorry, Chef." It was one of the waiters, his fringe fashionably wavy and extending from his hairline down to his left eyebrow, fingering a tray that had two plates of entrecôte on it, the deep crusted-brown trackmarks of its cooking still visible between the chubby red slides of sauce that I'd poured over it. "Is this for Table 7?"

"Yes, yes, yes," I said. "Just take it. Please."

"Wait," said Andy, approaching behind me. He pulled the tray back by its silver handles, the plates slipping a little on the purple paper liner, with its elaborate Glamis logo in gold art deco script.

"Fingerprints," he said, examining the china under the golden glow of the heat lamps. He pressed the back of his thumb down on the meat before closing his eyes. "It's cold." He checked the ticket. "And are you seriously telling me these are well done? They're still fucking farting."

"Fuck it," I said. "Damn."

Not wanting to lift my concentration from my pans, I quickly turned to Kathryn who was balancing a worryingly high pile of glistening meat on a metal sitting plate.

"It's under done, Kathryn. For fuck's sake!"

Fuck! I stirred one pan. I tasted another. I kicked the steel wall of the unit by my feet so hard that my clogs rammed into my toes. Andy softened his face and placed his hands behind his back. What *was* he still doing here?

"Listen," he said. "Why don't I take over on sauces? You can concentrate on the pass, calling the orders. That's what you want to do, really, isn't it? Call the orders? That way you can keep on top of things and I can keep things moving along here."

In my peripheral vision, I could see a torchon, dangerously near to a burner.

"I can manage."

Was it smoking?

"Do you want me to call the orders then?" he said. "And you can concentrate on this?"

I glanced at it again. Andy followed my gaze, spotted the

cloth and immediately lifted it away from the flame.

"I can manage, Andy," I said.

He leaned further in and whispered so closely that I felt a fleck of spit on my ear: "*Fucked.*"

By nine thirty p.m., no plate had left the kitchen for twenty minutes. I looked up from my station to see Ambrose in his checked suit, his purple lining flashing as he paced past the line of fractious waiters.

"What the fuck is going on?" he said, his eyes bouncing around the piles of pans and meat and the wet floor and the endless row of tickets that were hanging down in front of me.

"We're on it, Ambrose," I said. "Sorry. We're on it."

He took my arm and pulled me into the empty corridor that led to the changing rooms.

"Don't fuck this up, little boy," he said, his breath sour with wine and dry with tobacco. "I've put all my faith in you. I have risked my reputation telling the whole world and his mistress what a prodigy you are. There are people sitting within fifty feet of you right now who could break your career a thousand times over. And they will, believe me, if they don't get fed soon." He observed me over his pale nose and horsey nostrils. "Maybe this little factoid will help motivate you. There is only one person out there who is enjoying himself right now, and his name is Max Mann."

By the time I had slunk back, Andy was at the pass. He was calling out tickets, his voice magnificent with order and consequence. The brigade were answering him in kind. A fierce element had been introduced into the kitchen and everyone sounded, for the first time in more than an hour, hopeful. I bowed my head over my stove and tried to catch up, working for the rest of service in as much silence as was possible, avoiding the attentions of the brigade as best as I could. I made the sauces, for the rare and complex dishes that reached the heat lamps, most of which I didn't have the skill to cook myself, and watched Andy ride that pass like a cowboy on a bucking bull.

* * *

"Come, come," said Ambrose, sometime after eleven p.m., when all the diners had finished eating. I followed him down the short passageway and into the soothing dimness of the restaurant. After hours in the shadowless white of the kitchen, my eyes weren't yet used to the grainy light and I didn't have time to make out any individual faces in the crowd before Ambrose clapped three times and said, "Ladies and gentlemen, the best new chef in Britain, please welcome Mr Killian Lone."

They stood and cheered so loudly that the chandeliers began rocking on the ceiling. Their clapping was a million tiny cracks breaking the air; a dark rumble of stamping began rolling out from beneath it. There was something unnerving about the bedlam. Something desperate. They were a mob of maddened, straining people, palms hot, eyeballs wide, necks stretched and nostrils flaring. On and on and on it went. This wasn't a collection of men, women and dignitaries who'd just enjoyed a pleasant dinner. This was unnatural. They were *wild*. What had I done?

"Thank you all for coming," Ambrose shouted in an attempt to calm them down. But they continued, their stamping now synchronised, the cheers looping and colliding against whoops and whistles.

"Okay, okay, okay!" Ambrose shouted eventually. "Thank you, thank you, thank you. As I'm sure you all agree, the food here tonight was of an utterly sensational standard. And that is all thanks to this awesomely talented young man."

Where was he? Where was Max? The silhouette of the crowd was a great black monster in the gloom, spotted here and there with the fiery trails of cigarettes and cigars. It was impossible to pick him out. I stood there as Ambrose finished his speech. When it was over, and at the end of another, only marginally less ravenous applause, the beastly crowd came for me, and I was in it, swallowed inside its walls, surrounded by its arms and legs and wide, wet, licking mouths as they whispered and thanked and pushed napkins and menus and matchbooks on me to sign with my name.

"I'll leave you to it," Ambrose said as he escaped, unscathed through the middle of the thing.

"Where's Max?" I called after him.

"Gone."

I turned into the beautifully dressed mob and stared, entranced. For the first time it seemed so insanely possible: that I might, someday, have King, Dor, Glamis and all.

38

The reviews that came in over the next couple of weeks were considerably better than spectacular. They listed the many wonders of Glamis in paragraph after adjective-choked paragraph. It was curious how the pleasure they'd clearly experienced from my sauces caused them to judge everything else with unfailing sympathy. The delays on the opening night and the mistakes I knew had gone out in every service – the sometimes sloppy presentation, the over-reduced sauces, the under-rested meat – were absent, forgotten entirely after the critics had tasted the magic of the crucial element. One even hailed our "confidence" in having only three desserts, when that paltry list was actually due to the fact that we hadn't, yet, found a full-time pastry chef. Admittedly, my lack of enthusiasm for that project was because I hadn't yet worked out the technicalities of successfully inveigling Earl's Leaf into puddings.

Ambrose would come in at eight thirty every morning, fattened with clucking pride and with an armful of newspapers, which he'd already pored through for references to Glamis. At first, he wanted me to read them out during my daily team talks, but I refused. I gathered my chefs around me for one specific purpose – to impress upon them that, although Andy was running the pass, I was in charge. And, of course, to motivate them with my speeches about Max Mann. I'd work on these every day – ideas for the next morning's address would scrap messily for precedence in my head as I cooked.

Increasingly, I'd find my mind running helplessly with thoughts of him – hostile memories, strange fantasies and imagined conversations that, when I was alone in my small office, I'd sometimes speak out loud. When preparing a sauce for a dish I was particularly proud of, I'd picture him eating it and being so overcome with pleasure that he'd smile and shake me by the hand and then pull me to his breast in recognition of this connection between fellow journeymen.

At other times, I'd see him crumpled in humiliation at the flavour of my sauce Glamis. He'd throw his torchon to the ground, knowing he was beaten, knowing he'd made a mistake when he lied about me and made me eat shit, and then he'd fall to his knees and weep at this final failure and I'd comfort him, I'd stroke the back of his head and then, too late, too late, too late, old cunt, I'd take his head and throw it repeatedly to the floor, until I was healed completely by the blood and the silence.

One morning, before my team talk began, Ambrose read out a particularly mucilaginous review from Evan Parker-Scott in the *Daily Mail*. He ladled praise on this "prodigy of British cuisine" whose "incomparable gifts" would "finally put to rest the claims by our ancient enemy across the Channel that England is not a cooking nation", even going so far as to suggest I be awarded an OBE. When he had finally left, I addressed the brigade.

"We've had some great write-ups and I know you're all very pleased with yourselves," I said. "But I don't want us to be obsessing over the media. That's the trap our friend Max has fallen into and look where it's got him. Self-obsessed, scared, fucking fried eggs on his eyeballs. And anyway, those reviews are of last week's dinners. Forget about them. That's why I've asked that all the framed cuttings be taken down from the walls of the corridor out there. I want every night's meals to be better than the ones before."

There was a silence as I tried to gather up their direct attention. There were eyes to the floor, eyes to the side, eyes to each other, eyes to folded hands. But no eyes on me. None.

"Okay?" I said.

"Yes, Chef," said one or two voices.

From behind me, Andy stepped forward.

"Thanks, Chef. That was great. All right, guys, great work this week but as Chef says, I know you can do better. Let's get to it."

"Yes, Chef!" they cried.

In those first few weeks, Michael Heseltine, Jonathan King and Mike Yarwood all made lucrative offers for me to cook in their homes. Barbara Windsor booked a table of eight to celebrate her divorce from Ronnie Knight. On one midweek evening, Princess Diana ate with some relative or other – at least we assumed it was a relative, as she was being generously affectionate with her guest and he definitely wasn't Prince Charles. I declined invitations to appear on *Pebble Mill at One*, *TV-AM* and *Food and Drink*. Our customers, meanwhile, became increasingly ravenous for our food, some trying to book themselves in every night for a week or more. We became fashionable with the young executives from the Manufacturers Hanover Trust or "Manny Hanny" – a glamorous bunch who some in Ambrose's circles had witheringly christened "young aspirational professionals" or "yaps". They all seemed to carry leather Filofaxes, drive BMWs and live in Stoke Newington. Before Glamis opened, Le Caprice, Garroway's and the Bombay Brasserie had all the lunchtime expense account business, but now they begged for space at our tables. Eventually they would become widely known as "yuppies", but to me, in those early weeks, they were a fascinating, beautiful and repellent new race.

But we couldn't feed them all. At one point, Ambrose had to step in to stop a black-market auction for tables. During the third week, our reservations book was stolen, and everyone listed in it was phoned up and offered thousands of pounds for their seat. Rumours of the strangely aphrodisiacal nature of our meals spread, too, with male yaps bringing beautiful dates in the evening and hoping for a bit of "Glamis luck", which rarely failed them. The *Daily Mail* ran a story about an expected generation of "Glamis babies" in nine months' time. It became ordinary for us to find young couples having sex up against the wall in Percy Passage, which ran near the building. We'd frequently find discarded lingerie on the dirty brick floor and, once, a pair of red braces that looked suspiciously similar to those worn by Le Patron.

Ambrose added fifty per cent to the prices and then another fifteen and it didn't make any difference. Despite my not working at the pass, he raised my wages from £2750 a year to £5500, the same level as Andy's. Beautiful girls began waiting for me at the kitchen door, but I was blind to them all. Kathryn and I were so busy, we barely had time to appreciate the brilliant love which had come to surround us. We would escape after service and kiss in the dark, my hands moving under her clothes as our forms moved anonymously in the passageway, next to whichever diners hadn't managed to make it home.

The success of Glamis and the success of my relationship with Kathryn seemed so intertwined as to be impossible to separate. But perhaps the greatest joy for me was seeing how it changed her. If Kathryn hadn't shown me that shard of compassion on my first day at King, in all likelihood, I would have only ever known the person that all the other chefs saw – a cold, sarcastic and tough young woman; just another wounded soldier of the kitchen. Working next to each other and fighting through the lunch and evening service as if we were battling our way through terrible gales, rapidly built foundations between us that felt grand and permanent. And all the time we had the awareness that our restaurant was growing, that with each of the day's twin victories Glamis was becoming more famous throughout the country and the security of our future was surer.

Whenever we weren't cooking, we'd huddle in my small office and talk. I'd sit on the already-broken Argos swivel chair and she'd perch on a cushion on top of the huge green iron safe and we'd gossip about customers and the brigade and rehearse the war stories that we imagined we'd one day be telling Wogan and Harty and maybe, if things carried on being this perfect, our children and grandchildren.

More than once, Andy caught us kissing. Whilst he feigned comic disgust at this, Kathryn appeared genuinely shamed. It was in front of Andy that she seemed to cling hardest to the old version of herself. But she was changing. I'd notice her smiling more and more in public; she even occasionally engaged other chefs in small talk in the lunch room. Although they were still slightly wary of her, I could tell they admired her. One or two of them even came to know her as *nice*.

Things soon became so frantic that, inevitably, tensions arose between us. I worried that she just wanted this less than me. Once she was earning enough for her mum to be taken care of properly, would her ambition slump? I became perhaps overly attentive to signs that she might not be truly committed. She complained, also, that I would regularly disappear back to Dor without her, the moment service finished. She didn't know it, of course, but I had no choice. It was vital that I tend the herb garden and gather and prepare a fresh batch of Earl's Leaf for the next day. So, naturally, Kathryn couldn't come with me. I could never risk her finding out my secret. If she or anyone else discovered it, I could only expect to be ruined.

39

Kathryn had barely spoken a word since she'd arrived in the kitchen, eleven hours earlier. She was angry with me. It was her mother's birthday and I'd told her that, this being a Saturday, she couldn't take the time off to visit her. Actually, this was a half-lie. I had put into action a plan that I hoped might cheer her up.

Ambrose's fine idea of having a "Top Table" on a platform under discreet spotlights had, since the restaurant's opening, ended up mostly benefiting Ambrose. On the majority of weekend nights, he would reserve it for himself, and entertain notorious business leaders or celebrities or influential editors and critics. The other diners would ogle them enviously as they sat, elevated on their illuminated dais, wisps and trails of cigar smoke surrounding them like the traces of angels.

But I had made it clear that Ambrose was not to have the top table tonight. When he arrived, at getting on for our peak time, with a party of three and insisting that he have it, despite my pre-existing reservation, I knew that I had trouble.

"I'm sorry, Chef," said Drusilla, having joined me at the pass. "I'm not sure what to do. You know what Mr Rookwood's like. He's very insistent when he's insisting on things."

I looked up at the clock.

"Oh, Jesus," I muttered. "Perfect timing."

I pulled my various pans off the burners and called over to Kathryn. "I might need your help with this one."

"What? *Now?*"

"Yeah, it's Ambrose."

She threw a basting spoon towards a tub of water. It missed, clattering against a steel butter pot.

"Oh, that's fine then, if it's Ambrose," she said.

"Look, I know you're pissed off with me today," I said. "But Ambrose is being unreasonable. There are diners booked on the top table already. I can't have him feeling humiliated. I think it'll help – a woman's touch."

"I can offer a woman's touch on his bloody jaw. Would that be helpful?"

As I walked onto the restaurant floor, Drusilla quietly explained the details of the issue. As I'd planned, the top table was empty and Ambrose was standing at the base of the steps that led to it. Three men in tuxedos loitered in the shadows behind him. I thought one of them looked like James Goldsmith, but I couldn't be sure. To my discomfort, when they realised it was me, they started peering nosily over his shoulder in my direction.

"Ah, Chef!" said Ambrose, running his thumb down one of his red braces. "You really shouldn't have been bothered with all this. There really is not a problem. For some unfathomable reason, Drusilla is telling me that there *is* a problem. But there's not a problem, is there?" He smiled his very particular smile that said "I'm not smiling".

"Sorry, Ambrose, but there's a reservation already for the top table," I said. "The thing is, Drusilla tells me these guests have already arrived. And it's quite important that they have this table. In fact, look, they're over there, by the door."

Kathryn, who was standing at my arm, looked towards the podium where Drusilla usually stood with her reservations book.

There was a taxi driver there, the one that I'd hired. And there was a frail woman with her hair in a damp ponytail. She looked nervous, doubtful, overwhelmed, as if she couldn't believe she was in the right place.

"Mum?" Kathryn whispered. She clamped her hand over her mouth.

"Do you want to sit down?" I said to Kathryn, motioning towards the table. "One of those places is for you."

She looked up at me, a thick film of wet covering the surfaces of her eyes as she realised what was happening. Grabbing my arm, she whispered, "Thank you, Killian. *Thank you.*"

"I'm sure we can find your guests somewhere to sit," I said to Ambrose. "You understand, I know you do. It's Kathryn's mum's birthday today and she's here as my guest."

"Right," he said, and I saw the muscles in his jaw pump. "Of course. Yes."

Kathryn's mum was being led up the central isle which was specifically spotlit so that guests could be seen – especially the ones destined for the top table who, in order to reach it, had to walk its entire length. Except this time, with this diner, the effect appeared to be backfiring. A waiter was leading the way as Kathryn's mother, in her dirty coat and tracksuit trousers, shuffled towards us. In one hand she clutched an inhaler and a half-used pack of pocket tissues, in the other, a Swatch watch with a broken strap. As she inched painstakingly towards us, the chinkle of cutlery quietened, as did the chatter. I could see chins rise and mocking eyes pivot towards her. From a corner table, four yaps, with crisp shirts and mousse-sculpted hair, burst into laughter. Kathryn's mother dipped her head in shame. The effort she made, keeping the smile on her weak and yellowish face, was palpable.

I stepped forward, so that I was directly beneath a spotlight, and held my arms out towards her. An audible murmur moved through the darkness of the room. The diners, in their hushed luminous pools, gazed towards me and I could hear their whispers, *Killian, Killian, Killian,* the middle letters of my name jutting from the low, rolling sound like a thousand tiny legs.

"Mrs Riding," I said, loudly. "My very, *very* special guest. Happy birthday and welcome to Glamis. The best table in the house is ready for you, as is your extremely talented daughter."

As Kathryn stood and embraced her mum, I retreated back into the safety of the kitchen. Barely ten minutes had passed, but already the disappearance of Kathryn and I had had an effect. A dangerously long queue of tickets had built up and I was met by an ugly collage of irritated faces, all silently asking of me, "*What the fuck?*"

"Andy, can you take over the sauté station?" I said.

I had to work triple quick and, immediately, the wings of a terrible fluster began beating on my back. I had arranged my station in such a way that only Kathryn had a clear view of my cooking. But now Andy was beside me. Moreover, I had been in the job for long enough that most of what I did had become automatic. So what happened next was almost inevitable.

"What's that in your apron?" asked Andy.

He was staring at me. His tongs were held over a spitting veal fillet, the blue flame running hard beneath the blackened metal. I froze completely, my fingers in a damning sprinkle position directly over the top of a pan.

"What?" I said.

"You keep doing it," said Andy. "Taking something out of your pocket and putting it in the food."

A commis chef called Leon had moved in behind us, holding a tureen containing half set mousse. He was standing there, watching it all; listening.

"It's where I keep my pepper," I said. "I keep my pepper in here."

"But I can see your pepper," said Andy. "You've been adding pepper from the pot that's right there. So what's that in your apron?"

"It's pepper with a bit of ground clove in it. I put it in every-thing. For fuck's sake Andy, what's the matter with you?" I turned around. "Leon!" I shouted. "Fuck off before I boot you out of the fucking window."

I bent over my stove. Andy, in my peripheral vision, glanced back towards me, amused and bewildered and suspicious. He splashed some brandy into a veal pan, which he tipped into the flame to ignite into a whooshing cloud of pink and purple and ruby.

40

"Have you seen the *News of the World*? I wouldn't worry about it too much, but it is a little concerning. Never nice to feel there's disloyalty in the ranks."

It was Ambrose, calling from his home, eight days after the incident with Andy. I was alone in my office planning the motivational brigade talk about Max that I was to hold in half an hour's time. I pulled my chair closer to the desk.

"What's in it?"

"Oh, it's nothing really," he said. "Why don't you have a look? But don't overreact please. Call me back straight away if you want to discuss it."

I headed for the door, my walk turning into a run. Without stopping for my coat, I bolted out into the deserted Sunday morning streets which couldn't have been emptier if the Soviets had finally dropped the warhead we were forever being warned about. I bought a *News of the World* and began flicking as I walked back to the restaurant. It was right there, on page 4, a large photograph of me and the headline: "TEARS, RIVALRY AND SEXY INGREDIENTS: SECRETS OF GLAMIS REVEALED. Exclusive report by Bill Hastings."

I stood still on the pavement, only vaguely aware of the early buses and the colours of concrete and morning and the tarry city smell that was blowing over my face and fingers and

272

through the cotton of my tunic.

"In stunning allegations that can be exclusively revealed today – which come from a source close to Killian Lone – the young London chef, who is the talk of the nation's gourmands, has been adding a sexy secret ingredient to his pricey dinners. Since the opening of his glitzy London restaurant, the so-called 'Glamis Effect' has become notorious amongst his well-to-do-diners, who include many of Britain's best-known stars of stage and screen, including Marc Almond, *Dr Who*'s Colin Baker and Stephen 'Tin Tin' Duffy. It's always been said that Lone's luxurious menu is so delicious that it gives anyone who eats it a raunchy aphrodisiac effect. But someone close to Lone has finally revealed his naughty habit. 'It's no secret that the punters who love Glamis food tend to get certain, shall we say, physical reactions,' says our source. 'Lone would have you believe it's all down to his genius. At his age? Come on, he must think we were born yesterday. Everyone in his kitchen is convinced there's some sort of trickery involved, possibly involving chemical pheromones bought from Soho sex shops.'

"In further claims that will rock the glamorous London restaurant scene, we can also reveal that Lone's famed skills as a top cook don't quite match his ability at the head of a professional brigade, a role that demands years of experience. 'The opening night was a disaster,' reveals our source. 'Killian got a big telling-off from the proprietor, Ambrose Rookwood and he was in tears. He had to give up running the kitchen completely and pass control to his second-in-command Andrew Silverwood. It's been like that ever since. Lone may be executive chef in name but he doesn't do much more than the sauces. He's lapping up all the glory, but everyone knows Andy's the one with the real talent.'

"Silverwood, 32, has trained at the altars of some of Europe's most celebrated chefs, most recently the legendary Max Mann, of the restaurant King – also part of the exclusive Rookwood Group of celebrity eateries. Our source reveals that it was Mann who taught Lone how to make the sauces, which, in the six weeks since the opening of Glamis, have already caused an international sensation, with reservations coming from as far away as Los Angeles, Cape Town and Tokyo and tables in the bistro being booked eight months in advance. It is also alleged that Chef Mann has confirmed to his staff his suspicions about Lone, calling his deadly Glamis rival a 'fraud'. 'Max told his brigade that Lone is 'Paul Daniels posing as Paul Bocuse', our source alleges, citing a world-famous French chef. 'His staff lapped it up'."

By the time I had run back to my office and picked up the phone, my throat felt as if it was blocked with wire wool.

"Bastards!" I shouted when Ambrose picked up.

"Calm down," he said. I looked around the room – at the files, the paperwork and the recipe books. I wanted to burn the whole lot of it. I wanted to go home. "Honestly, Killian, it doesn't matter. It's not going to affect the bottom line, I guarantee it. If one or two gullible readers stop coming, there are one or two thousand more waiting to replace them. Besides, the *News of the World* is not our market. Do you think the sort of idle rubbish that reads it would ever darken the doors of one of my restaurants?"

"It's not true," I said. "It's lies, all of it."

"Killian, my dear, of course it is," laughed Ambrose. "Drugs in the food. Even by the standards of the *News of the World* that's preposterous. You really don't need to deny it. I mean, pheromones?"

"And the thing about the tears! I wasn't crying. I can't have people – God! It's just bullshit. I'm going to sue them. I'm going to sue this fucker, Bill Hastings and I'm going to sue Max. Who is Bill Hastings, anyway? Do you know him?"

"Now, now, hang on there, young man" he said. "I can absolutely assure you that Max had nothing to do with this and I resent the implication. Max has been a close friend and colleague of mine for more than a decade and I know him to be an honourable man who always plays with a straight hand. He wishes you only the best."

I kicked the waste-paper bin, its contents spilling across the carpet.

"Bollocks," I said. "Why are you lying to me? Why are you *lying*?"

"Killian, you must calm down," he said. "Far more likely it's someone in your own brigade. It reeks of petty jealousy, the whole thing. The stink of envy fair rises off the page. It's probably one of the juniors trying to make an easy buck. Think about it – calmly. But in the meantime, you must trust me. I will look after you. I will back you, always. We will be fine. All will be forgotten come tomorrow."

The kitchen was in near silence that day, and that's just how I wanted it. I was distant from Kathryn and refused to entertain Andy with any contact. I removed myself from them all; returned to the sure comfort of my own embrace. During lunchtime service the wound from the branding I'd given myself in front of Max all those weeks ago began to itch. I had the word "King" seared in scar tissue on my arm and the temptation was to lock myself in the bathroom with a knife and slowly peel it off.

After the final diners had left the restaurant, I wandered back to my office. I sat there, alone, with my files and invoices and payslips and newspaper and magazine clippings from London and Paris and New York and Tokyo and Berlin and Helsinki and Toronto and Glasgow and Madrid and Washington and Lyon and Rome and Chicago and Dublin and Stockholm and Los Angeles, all of which said essentially the same thing – that

Glamis was serving some of the best food in the world and the reason was that I, Killian Lone, was a genius. I scooped them up and dropped them in the waste-paper bin beneath my desk. It was too small so I stamped them in, harder and harder, angling my heel in, crushing them down, and then it fell over and my foot accidentally came down on the side and it cracked but it felt good so I leaned on my desk for support and did it again and again and then I became aware of a face peering around the door. It was Kathryn.

"Are you going to talk to me about it? Or do you want me to go?"

I stepped back from the explosion of plastic and paper on the floor. She came into the room and held me.

"Why don't you come back to mine later?" she said. "Day off tomorrow. Come on, you've had a face like an Eskimo's bollock all day."

Of course – she didn't realise it, but she had a point. I didn't have to fetch any Earl's Leaf for the next service, because Glamis didn't open on Mondays. I breathed out and shoved the mess under my desk with the side of my foot.

"Sure," I said. "All right."

* * *

Forty minutes alone with Kathryn in Dorothy's old car and, already, I had begun to feel better. The moment I closed the hollow wooden door of her flat, we rose up into a magnificent kiss. Because we had been working so hard, we hadn't really had any time alone, in private. We felt the build-up of that tension like some sort of supernatural force. First against the wall, where I found the gap under her woollen jumper and the bare cold skin of her slender waist, my hands running smoothly and bumping tantalisingly over the odd mark and mole and the mounds of her spine and up to the clasp of her bra which, eventually, I manoeuvred open. She pushed deeper with her tongue as my fingers slipped around the sides of the lace fabric and touched the tender weight of her breast. She took my arm and led me to the sofa, where we lay on the stained cushions, which began slipping out from under us as we moved. Her fingers began exploring the scars on my torso, picking over them slowly, carefully, deliberately. When she found the raised mark from the occasion, one Christmas, on which I'd cut the skin at the side of my stomach with a broken Bailey's bottle, she let out a quiet moan. I popped open the button on her jeans and thrilled at the hem of her thin cotton knickers and how they lay flat over the skin of her narrow pelvis. I went for the dark gap in between, but she tugged at my wrist, pulled it away and then... what was that? The lock. Keys turning. *Andy.*

"Hello, Killian – blimey," he said, smiling. He closed the door and then stopped to observe us on the sofa, Kathryn with half her shirt buttons undone, me with my belt hanging from my buckle. "Sorry, ha ha. Didn't mean to interrupt. Wasn't expecting to see you here."

He sat down next to me on the arm of the chair. I felt the cold he'd brought in with him from the street and picked up the faint scent of the upstairs of buses.

"It's going great, isn't it?" he said, lighting a Marlboro Red. "You must be pleased. Big man, eh?"

He took a series of short drags from his cigarette. For some reason, I briefly thought I could smell menthol in the smoke.

"Yeah, it's good," I said, sitting forward. "Thanks to you."

He had his leg crossed over his knee, just like Max did on the television, and was wearing brand-new 501s and box-fresh, all-white, high-top Air Jordans. His shoulders were strong and square inside his pastel-blue blazer; his moustache dense and manly and perfectly trimmed. Kathryn was using the opportunity of his addressing me to surreptitiously fasten up the rest of her buttons. That was that, then.

"So how do you think Max is taking it?" I said, looking up at him. "I bet he can't stand it, eh? And what about that Russian tart he's shacked up with? Jesus!"

Andy exhaled gently on the tip of his cigarette. It glowed and crackled obediently under his command.

"Yeah," he said, smiling blandly. "You've done so well. It's great."

"It's going pretty well, yeah," I nodded.

He took another puff and then cocked his head at me in a slightly exaggerated fashion.

"Hey, listen, mate," he said. "I was thinking. We should talk about refreshing the menu sometime. I think it's important that we keep things evolving, keep things fresh. You know, we have some very wealthy customers who eat at Glamis regularly. They don't want to have to keep choosing from the same list."

I sensed Kathryn next to me, nodding thoughtfully. There he was, perched on the sofa on one side. There she was, agreeing with him on the other. I shuffled forward, suddenly feeling as if I didn't have enough room.

"Well, they keep coming, don't they?" I said. "If they didn't like my menu, they'd stop, and that wouldn't be a big deal because there's a million more people who want to eat my food."

He nodded earnestly.

"That's right," he said. He was still nodding. Up and down went his large head. Up and down, serious-like, solemn-like, grave-like. Up and down it went, agreeing absolutely with everything I was saying. "But what about the press?" he said. "And the reviewers? And you can't forget Ambrose. He eats off our menu every day. I'm not saying we should rearrange everything just for him, but take a bit of advice from someone who knows. It's always best to keep the boss sweet."

"Fuck Ambrose," I said. "I'm making Ambrose a millionaire."

He studied the end of his Marlboro again, as if trying to fathom what was wrong with it. His knee was practically in my face. 'Big man.' *Big man?* I stood up.

"You know, Andy, I don't know where you get off, telling me my menu's no good."

Finally, he stopped gazing at his cigarette. He pursed his rosy, chubby, cracked lips. "That's not what I said."

I picked my way over to the other side of the coffee table. The end of my belt was still sticking out of my trousers. It was on the highest notch on the buckle, and the rest of it was jutting from my crotch, all flaccid.

"I'll change the menu when I feel like it," I said. "It's *my* menu."

Kathryn moved closer to him. "Come on, Kill," she said. "Andy's allowed to have an opinion. He does run the kitchen for you." Her eyes darted towards my flapping belt.

"Anyone can run a fucking kitchen!" I said. "It just takes a bit of practice. There's nothing amazing about working the pass, you know. Christ, read the papers! It's me they're going to give a star to when the guide comes out."

With shaking fingers, I ran the cheap band of leather back through the hoops of my trousers. They watched me carefully. They weren't laughing. I was pretty sure they weren't laughing.

"Anyway," I said. "It's not about me, is it? I just want to prove that Max is over. He treated me like crap, he treated Kathryn like crap. He's not getting away with it. His food's ridiculous. Guinea-fowl and mango? Fuck off. It's an embarrassment. Ambrose will get it eventually. Max is a liability. If King has any chance of not becoming a laughing stock by 1990, he needs to get rid of the nutter." I glanced at Kathryn. "We should take over that place."

"I reckon we should ignore Max, don't you?" said Andy.

"Forget about him. It's not really about–"

But I spoke over him: "And now I've got enemies in my kitchen and I've got to deal with that." I drove my hands deep into the pockets of the flared corduroys that I'd had since I was fifteen. "I take it you saw that thing today? In the paper? I won't have enemies. I won't have disloyalty."

A silence crawled through the room. A breeze blew in from under the door. My too-short cords exposed my ankles and the cold air curled around them like the ghost of a cat. Andy hoisted a smile. "Such a good job you're doing with those sauces," he said, eventually. "They're amazing, really. Unbelievable."

The darning in my sock had gone and my toe was cold. It looked ridiculous, poking through the hole down there; staring out at the world, all bald and pink and naked.

"Are you trying to tell me something?" I said to him.

"No!" he said.

"There's no fucking secret ingredient if that's what you're saying."

Andy tapped the head of his Marlboro into the shallow metal ashtray. "All right, matey, I know that," he said. "You need to calm down."

I saw the thin blue vein running up the bony framework of my mother's ankle as she left me alone. I saw her face – pale, beautiful and fascinated – through the steam of boiling water.

"I'm not your fucking matey," I said. "I'm your boss."

Andy stood, pushed out his cigarette and chuckled to himself.

"Going to your head enough is it?" he said, leaving towards the kitchen.

"You better be careful," I shouted after him. "All those little journo mates you hang out with. If I find out it was you that leaked–"

He stopped, just short of the doorway.

"Don't even go there," he said, shaking his head, as if struggling to absorb what I'd just said. "No, hang on," he said. "How *dare* you?"

Kathryn looked in his direction with a fragile, uncertain expression. I pointed, right in the direction of his face, my King scar itching, my ugly teeth showing, a silver-grey fly buzzing over the ashtray.

"You're on a warning," I said. "One more leak and you're gone."

Kathryn turned to me, aghast. "Killian!" she said.

As I addressed her, tiny cartwheels of spit flew in her direction. "I'm going home."

I walked out in my socks, my shoes hanging from my fingers, slamming the door behind me. By the time I was halfway down the stairs, Kathryn had appeared at the top.

"Come on," she said. "Don't go."

"It's just Andy," I said. "I don't trust him. He's not loyal."

"Are you sure you're not being unfair?" she said, walking down to meet me. "I don't think it was him. It's just not the kind of thing Andy would do."

"I mean anyway," I said. "It's crazy, what they're saying. Drugging the food! What with? Pheromones? Please! It's a joke."

She gave a shallow nod. I don't know exactly what I wanted her to do, but her reaction felt incomplete, unsatisfying.

"I'm not doing it, Kathryn," I said.

"I know," she said, weakly. She crossed her arms and looked at her feet. "Let's just not talk about it."

I made a show of idly scratching the back of my head.

"It was you that said, whatever I get I deserve it. You know, it meant a lot when you said that."

"You do deserve it," she said. "Of course you do."

"I mean, just imagine where we'll be in a year's time if things continue like they are. You'll be earning enough to keep your mum safe, in the best home in London, maybe even getting better."

She smiled at that. Her hands pushed around my waist and she gazed at me with shining eyes.

"It's really, actually possible, isn't it?" she said.

"Totally," I said. "I've just got to keep fighting. I need your back-up, though. I can't do it without you."

"Well, you've got it," she said. "You need to do whatever you need to, Kill. Just go out there and bloody grab it." She rested her head on my chest. "Listen, if you can't cope with Andy tonight, why don't I come back to the cottage with you?"

I glanced towards the exit.

"Oh, there's no point," I said. "I'm still in a crappy mood, to be honest. I'll be rubbish company. Why don't I call you tomorrow?"

As I drove back to the cold, strange cottage, I tried very hard to think about something that wasn't Max or Kathryn or the secret that was beginning to feel like a bruise that was ripening and yellowing and spreading out over everything.

41

The *Restaurant Magazine* awards were held annually at the Café de Paris in the West End of London. It was the most glamorous fixture of the culinary year and, mainly due to the celebrity and minor royal guests, never failed to attract the attentions of the media – not to mention every working chef in the country. They all denied their interest, of course. It was fashionable in the kitchens of London to shrug at the mention of a nomination and, if you'd won anything in the past, to feign confusion, saying, "Did I? I'd forgotten all about it," perhaps adding, "For me, it's about the diners". The curious thing about that pose was how they would gossip about the event for months in advance. Contenders would hire the most expensive suits Moss Bros could supply and frequently react with such rage when the jury went the wrong way that walk-outs and even physical tussles were not uncommon.

Glamis wasn't nominated for any awards – we hadn't been open long enough – and that was fine with me. I was probably the only chef on the circuit who genuinely didn't want to attend. Whenever I was recognised – in the street or anywhere else – I experienced this shrinking, hunted feeling. So far, my refusal to make myself available to the media had had the opposite effect to that intended. The less I spoke, the more they somehow found to write. However, Ambrose had made it clear that it was important I attend this ceremony, for fear of alienating people he felt it essential to remain on good terms with. Besides, I thought, the greatest chefs in Britain and much of Europe would be there. I would meet my heroes.

The awards were held on a Monday, because that was the day most fine-dining restaurants tended to be closed. Ambrose sent a courier to Glamis with clothes for Kathryn and me. Modest as ever, Kathryn went to change in the locker room whilst I climbed into the suit in my office. I felt odd and stiff and fraudulent, like an ugly picture that had been placed in a beautiful frame. My shoes were tight and made of thin, hard leather that gripped the skin of my heels as I pushed my feet in.

"Don't laugh," came a voice.

I looked up to find nobody there.

"Kathryn?" I said, standing up tentatively. "You can come in. I'm dressed."

There was a silence.

"I don't want to."

"Why not?" I craned my neck a little. "Come in!"

"It isn't supposed to be a fancy-dress party is it?" she said.

"No...?"

"So please explain – why am I dressed as a Cornetto?"

I stepped towards the door and tried to peep out into the corridor, the rim of leather on the backs of my shoes constricting irritably.

"Oh God!" she said, on hearing my approach. "If you laugh, I swear, I'll turn your balls into nut roast."

With a rustle and a blush, she moved into the room. It was a cocktail dress, black and Merlot red, that finished just above the knee. The sleeves were high and ruched into the shape of huge roses; there was a low scoop that revealed more of her décolletage than I was expecting. It was all finished off by an enormous satin bow that ran vertically up her left side, pinned in at the waist. I was dazzled. Kathryn scratched her face and bent her knee, awkwardly, as if she was desperate for the loo.

"Why aren't you saying anything? Oh God, you're embarrassed for me."

"You look incredible."

"Oh shut up." She pulled at its low, diving neck with both hands. "Does it show too much boob?"

"No."

"I look like a freak."

"If you could climb into my head and feel what I'm feeling now," I told her, "I promise you'd never be shy again."

"I'm not shy," she said, sighing in the way that she sighed when she wanted a hug but was too shy to say so.

"Why don't you wear your hair up?" I asked, when I'd put her down.

I lifted it over her birthmark but, as I did so, her face dropped, an unhappy pressure gathering on her lips. I ran my fingers gently over it.

"It's beautiful, though," I said.

"I'm not putting my hair up."

"All right," I said, kissing the dark purple shadow on her cheek. "It's okay."

A distant thud interrupted us.

It was Ambrose, emerging from the corridor like a 1950s Bond, in a spectacular tuxedo, scarlet bow tie and shining spats, hair fragrantly Daxed and his ever-present, too-tight ruby ring stuck to his thumb like a boiled sweet that had been left too long in a trouser pocket.

"Come on, kids. It's time."

I winced.

"Be brave," said Kathryn. "I'll look after you if you promise to look after me."

I let her take my hand and we walked the short distance to

the venue in Coventry Street, my tight leather shoes scraping pain all over my heels. What made me more uncomfortable still was the man in the anorak who handed me a biro and an old Our Price receipt and asked for an autograph. Then the girl with the yellow exercise book. Then the woman with the diary. In the twenty minutes it took to walk from Glamis to the Café de Paris, I was stopped six times.

"Why do you look so shocked?" asked Ambrose as we rounded the corner, the celestial white glow of the venue's lights suddenly visible. "If you ever left that kitchen of yours, you might have noticed that you have become the most famous chef in Britain."

Then they saw us. It began with a single cry – "It's Lone!" – and it was as if someone had kicked a wasp nest full of glitter. There was an uproar of shouting and waving and flashing cameras. I stood, rooted in fright, on the red carpet that ran from the door like a tongue. I grabbed for Kathryn's hand as the mass of photographers, many of whom were on stepladders, called my name. I kept glancing back over my shoulder, not because I was looking for someone, but because I wanted to run away, down there, back down the alleyway, into the beautiful dark-ness. Ambrose placed his hand on my shoulder and squeezed, whilst a million tiny mosquitoes of light bombarded my face.

Eventually, we walked through the golden doors and managed to hustle a path through all the evening jackets and cocktail dresses and found a small space in the crowded lobby in which we could breathe. Ambrose said, "I really do appreciate your coming tonight. I know you're not comfortable with all this, but it's vital that you make the most of your celebrity – for Glamis and the Rookwood Group as well as yourself, of course. Max does a wonderful job of it, and it really does make an enor-mous difference."

I broke eye contact with him.

"Do we have to stay long?"

"Max is picking something up tonight. You should at least stay for that. We need some pictures of the two of you together, with Max holding his prize."

"It's just, I've not been sleeping too well…"

Ambrose turned to Kathryn, who was absent-mindedly chewing the inside of her lip.

"Kathryn, my dear, would you be kind enough to excuse us for just a moment?"

"Sure," she said, smiling emptily, visibly fazed by the restless thunder of hundreds of people trying to make themselves heard above each other.

"You wait here," he said. "We'll be back in a sniff."

Following in Ambrose's wake, I felt as if I was struggling through a narrow black corridor, with walls of dark pupils that clicked onto me a moment after I'd passed.

None of them wanted to be caught in the action of watching me, but I saw every one sliding in, blinking, crafty and quick. As we pushed towards a flight of stairs, a shameful urge grew in me. I wanted to grab hold of Ambrose's hand. I wanted him to look after me.

We went up a wide flight of empty stairs. There were golden statues of naked boys in dimly lit recesses and fake red flames flickering behind glass. We walked into a gent's bathroom. The walls were painted matt black and, by the sink, there were bottles of cologne and piles of perfectly folded handtowels made from fluffy cotton with "Café de Paris" stitched into them in golden thread.

"Are those real towels?" I said, amazed. "Aren't people just going to nick them?"

Ambrose disappeared into a toilet cubicle.

"Come on, then," he said, poking his head around the door.

"Ambrose, I don't really like things like this," I said, pulling the door closed behind me. "I don't want to stay too long."

He smiled broadly. One of his molars was made of metal.

"Well, let me help you enjoy yourself," he said. He removed a small silver case from his pocket, which had an elaborate engraving on its cover, and opened it with a click. There were a number of small paper parcels inside it, one of which he unwrapped carefully. It was powder, compacted so tightly that you could see the lines of the paper folds marked into its surface.

He slid a Platinum American Express card from a Burberry wallet and used it to push some of the powder onto the spotless black-tiled shelf above the cistern. I watched him arranging it into two lines of fine dust, his pushes and chops so practised he could have been a Michelin chef julienning a carrot.

He rolled up a grubby one-pound note and bent down to take his share, each particle of the stuff hesitating for a fraction of a second before rising up and disappearing high into his long nostrils.

"This will make you feel much better," he said, standing and sniffing repeatedly. He handed me the tubed note. "Well, go on, then."

I hesitated, then copied what he'd done. I was surprised how easy it was – for some reason, I had always imagined snorting drugs would take some sort of practice. It stung my sinuses and a plasticky, chemically taste made itself known, along with a gammy numbness that began to spread down the back of my throat and tongue.

"It is speed?" I said, standing up.

"Oh dear God, no," he said, laughing. I watched carefully to see if any detectable change had come over him. "Oh bless you. Speed! Here…" He dropped two wrapped packets into my palm. "You'll be needing these."

I looked at them doubtfully.

"Trust me," he said. "It's a long night. You'll be wanting to, er, what's the phrase they're all using these days? Re-record, not fade away."

"Don't you care about getting caught?" I said, my hand still open in front of him.

"Not a chance of it. Money may not buy you happiness, Killian, my fine boy, but it does buy you freedom. Reach a certain level, as no doubt you will discover, and you'll find that the tapestry of life becomes a good deal richer with possibilities, especially in the realm of things to do for fun."

I felt nothing at all as we strode back down the magnificent stairs, except for slightly enormous. But there was a clamminess on my forehead and my socks had sprung wet with sweat. As we turned the corner, I looked again upon the crush below – the thick, smoking stew of champagne, mouths and eyes. I took a breath and savoured the sensation of air filling my lungs, my body, my brain. I could do this.

"Hi, hi, hi," I said as we went. Each time I said it to a different face, I noticed a different reaction. It was like ringing bells. Delight, embarrassment, respect, defiance, quick nods that were rippled through with complex veins of envy, alarm and fear. I saw fat hands on slender glass stems, scarlet finger-nails lifting cigarettes to shining lips, spittle-flecked teeth in guffawing mouths, shirt collars pressed into scarlet, goosey throats and cocktail dresses with jewels that trapped rainbows and low-cut dresses that showed the skin, the smooth skin with the pearls and diamonds and the moles and the deep cleavage and the noses and the elbows and all the whispering words, all the hundreds of thousands of fluttering, skittering, whispering words, pointed at me: *there he is, there he goes, that's him, that's him, that's Killian Lone...*

"Where have you been?" said Kathryn when we found her.

"Just briefing Killian on protocol," said Ambrose, rising up on his toes with purring satisfaction. "Now – you two young things. Come with me."

I watched my feet as he guided us through the crowd, my shoes rubbing against my heel, my soles wet with sweat. They didn't suit me, those shoes. They weren't even mine. Hired for six pounds. Rented. Who else had walked in these shoes? Why were they wet?

"Killian!"

Ambrose's face was leering into mine.

"Allow me to introduce you to the editor of *Restaurant Magazine*. Craig Rolly, Killian Lone. Killian Lone, Craig Rolly."

"Fabulous to meet you at last, Chef Lone," he said, holding out his hand. "I've been following your career closely. Fascinating stuff. What a story. Meteoric, eh?"

I could see this Craig Rolly, with his triangular smiling mouth and his hair spiked high like the Russian out of *Rocky*. But I couldn't face him directly because I was transfixed by the man next to him. I was beginning to feel odd. There were stars running between my eyes and my brain. They were drying out my mouth.

"Hello, Max."

I looked at Max's shoes. They had buckles on them. *Buckles*. Look at the shoes, the shoes of Max Mann.

"I'm saying, it's amazing, the speed of your success," the editor repeated. "Max was just telling me..."

"You don't want to believe anything he tells you," I said.

Rolly glanced conspiratorially at Max, who responded with a snide, leonine smile. And there was a third man, in a loose suit of shiny grey, who snorted fatly at some private joke that had evidently been shared between them.

"And what's this one?" I demanded, pointing at him with my thumb.

"Bill," he said, holding out a hand like a boiled pork chop. "Bill Hastings, how do you do?"

"I know you," I said. "*News of the World.*"

I glared at Max, as the light from the chandeliers above fell softly on his shark-wide eyes and arboreal nose. "Mate of yours, is it?"

I turned back to Kathryn who was occupying herself staring up at the ceiling. "He's the one that wrote that shit about me crying."

"What?" she replied, irritably.

"That shit about my sauces being drugged. You know? It's him. Bill Hastings."

Rolly leaned in, his cow-eyes heavy with champagne smugness. "I can assure you, Chef Max has been regaling us all with tales of your fantastic rise."

Max took an oyster from a passing waiter, who was carrying a reef of seafood in a deep ice-filled silver dish with carved cupid handles. "Would you believe," he said, "that Killian could barely strip a bunch of basil when he started under me?"

He opened his mouth, pushed out the tip of his tongue and let the shining mollusc slip in.

"I spent six weeks with Max," I shouted to the editor. "That's all. Six weeks. My aunt taught me how to cook, not him."

There was another voice, from behind, trying to get in.

"Killian? Max?"

I turned to see Ambrose. A grease-sheen of sweat was visible over his forehead. Moisture sparkled from its creases. "Could I borrow you a moment, please?" He addressed the other two. "Sorry to interrupt, gentlemen. I'll have them back in a jiff."

The crowds parted once more as I followed the men, with Kathryn behind me, until we reached a clearing in a grubby corner by a fire exit. A white paper background had been erected, covered with the logos of Dom Perignon champagne, the company that had apparently sponsored the event. There was a white light that shone with such violence that it ached in the backs of my eyes. Just behind it was a cameraman, in an old blue polo shirt, loose jeans and sandals, and a woman in a wide shoulder-padded suit jacket in pastel blocks of yellow, green and red. I recognised her. She was from the television – Gillian something.

A crew member in fashionable brown oversized spectacles began clipping a microphone onto my lapel. I said to Kathryn, "That woman's from *Food and Drink*. My mum watches that."

"Your mum?" said the man, with a chummy smile.

"Yes," I said, a little embarrassed at his overhearing me. He began attaching a wire to Max, who was standing beside me, grinning in his condescending way. "I was just saying," I continued feebly, "my mum watches this."

And then, we were on.

"I am joined by two London chefs who are very much the stars of this glittering occasion, Max Mann of the celebrity restaurant King and his young protégé Killian Lone of the superlative Glamis, which is fast becoming one of the hottest gourmet tickets in the world." The presenter turned to Max. "Max, you must be proud?"

"Oh, enormously so," he said. "I have just been saying, when young Killian here began at King he couldn't even strip a bunch of basil. Hard to believe, I know. But I was an early supporter of Killian's, despite several of my colleagues expressing doubts. I could see something in him and I'm glad I had my way. He took up a good deal of my attention, I must say, but I think all my hard work has been worth it."

"Worth it indeed," she smiled. "Killian, it sounds like you have the so-called Gentleman Chef a lot to thank for?"

There was all that light and the black box pointed at my face and there, just about visible in it all, the woman I knew from the television. I pointed my mouth towards the tiny microphone on my suit.

"My aunt taught me to cook," I said, loudly and slowly so that nothing could be lost. "And now I'm the most famous chef in England."

I squinted back into the light and heard Max chuckle. My jaw ached. My tongue felt fat and dry, like something sitting dead in my mouth. Stuff. I needed some more of that stuff. I had to get out of there. I blinked irritably into the light and turned around to find Ambrose. Where was he? I could see Kathryn, her face all jagged with alarm. She was shaking her head, mouthing, "No!"

"Well, he's certainly got the confidence!" the presenter was saying brightly.

"And all this amusing nonsense about his adding secret ingredients," Max continued. "Well, he should just allow your crew in to film him cooking. That would silence the doubters. What do you say, Killian?"

The silhouette of the woman seemed to be looking at me.

"Any time," I said, into the blackness, which smoked and glowed. "Any time whatsoever."

"Thank you, Killian, maybe we'll take you up on that exciting offer," said the presenter. "And Chef Max, we certainly wish you the best at the awards tonight."

He gave a little bow. "Thank you."

I plucked the microphone from my lapel. "Come on," said Kathryn. "Let's get a drink."

I was about to address Max again but Kathryn pulled me so hard that I felt it in the muscle of my forearm. She led me, quickly into the hot mass. They were a vast army of murmurers squashed into the building, all in black and sparkles, their heads pink, jowly and painted and shooting out bursts of ugliness and beauty that hit me as I passed. Every one fascinating, grotesque, the women arranged with such startling prettiness that my heart would groan with joy and sorrow as I saw each one. So many faces. Each one firing eyes at me, spelling out the words with their wet and sliding drunken tongues: *there he is, there he goes, that's him, that's him, that's Killian Lone...*

Kathryn took me to a quiet corridor that led to the kitchen. We sat on the floor as the stern tray-carrying waiters came and went above us. I rubbed my eyes. Everything was so confusing.

"What's wrong with you?" she said, trying to pull her legs inside her dress. "How did you get so drunk?"

"I'm not drunk," I said.

I looked crossly at my shoes. My heels were sore; the leather was pinching my toes and the elastic in the socks was too tight.

"Well, what's going on then?" she said. "*'I'm the most famous chef in England'?* Come on, Kill, that's not like you."

I bent forward to untie my laces, surprised at how relaxed I was feeling about the whole thing. "Jesus, did you see those photographers? All saying my name. Shouting it! I'm going to take my shoes off. Shall we get some whisky?"

Kathryn's grump lifted into a smile. She gave a naughty, delighted laugh.

"What are you doing?" she said. "You can't go shoeless."

"Shoes aren't compulsory."

"They are in the Café de Paris."

"It's like Ambrose told me, money doesn't buy you happiness, but it does enable you to fuck around with no shoes on."

"Ambrose didn't say that," she giggled, making a half-hearted, flirtatious attempt to swipe at my fingers.

"He did."

I pulled one shoe off and then the other, before dipping a hand into my jacket pocket.

"Here," I opened my palm to reveal one of the little parcels. "Do you want some?"

"What is it?"

"Almost certainly not speed."

Her laughter vanished.

"Have you taken cocaine?"

"Don't worry. I don't think it's done anything."

Her eyes rose in stung disappointment.

"Why did you do it?"

"Because... why not?"

"Because it's just not the kind of thing you do. You said you were going to look after me."

"But it was Ambrose."

"God, Killian. Please don't turn into one of *them*."

Her eyes fell to her knees. Pushing myself up off the floor, I said, "Anyway, since when have you been Miss bloody Goody Two Shoes?"

"I'm not Miss Goody Two Shoes...".

A flash of dirty light glinted from her crucifix.

"Oh God," I said. "Of course. Kathryn the Christian."

I watched in prickly confusion as she sprang to her feet and marched back into the noise. After a minute spent trying to gather myself together, I followed in her general direction in my socks, ordering a triple Bells at the bar, before heading back to the bathroom to start on the next wrap of cocaine.

I could feel it as I walked back downstairs. This was it – the best night of my life. Kathryn would be all right. *Everything* would be all right. I was donating my jacket to an elderly man with a large golden medallion in the shape of a chop when, around the corner, came Max.

"On your way to the snort traps?" I said, following him back up the steps.

He glanced at my socks and smiled in a way that was almost friendly.

"Shouldn't you be going to bed?" he said.

He was wearing a velvet bow tie, his shirt collar baggy on his cadaverous neck, the legs beneath his trousers so bony that the material hung from his waist as if he was on stilts. Enjoying a sudden rush of wellbeing, I reached up and put my arm around his shoulder.

"Max," I said, grinning. "Come on, Max Mann, man. Let's stop all this. Let's be friends, eh? Hey, 'Max Mann' – is that a made-up name? Because if it is, it's not a very good one, is it?"

He looked, anxiously, over his shoulder.

"Come on, man, we're equals now," I said. "It's over. Let's just get on with making great food and forget all this rivalry. Why are we tearing strips off each other?"

He nudged backwards, so that my arm slipped loose.

"I really have no idea what you're talking – "

"Yes, you do," I said. "All this! Leaking bollocks to the press–"

His face tilted in, just a fraction, just enough to gather the best of the darkness that was hovering about the stairs. The shadows worked gratefully over his lines and pock-marks and deep grey bags.

"You better watch what you accuse me of. If I find out I'm being slandered, lied about, I shall have no choice but to notify my solicitor."

"Stop talking to me like that, Max. Why are you talking to me like that? I've proved myself to you. I can do it, Max. I can cook. I'm tough enough. I'm as tough as you." I raised my arms and announced proudly, "I am a turnspit dog!"

Max whispered, "You're poisoning your guests with some kind of *additive* and you'll get found out. People aren't as stupid as you think. There will be proof. And the instant that there is, you're finished. I'll make sure of it. So make the most of your stolen moment. It won't last."

"You're telling me I won't last? Do you have any idea what people say about your food? *Guinea-fowl and mango?* People are laughing at you, Max. Have you seen *Spitting Image* lately? They think you're hilarious. Take off your flared trousers, old man, and smell the future." I made a show of hungrily sniffing the air. "Hmmmm, smells like butter." I paused to feign the arrival of a sudden realisation. "Oh, but hang on, Max, you knew that didn't you? Do you think your mate Bill might be interested to hear how much of Echire's finest is used at King?"

He pushed me, with outstretched fingers, on the throat and I fell against the black painted wall behind me. Glancing quickly to check that we were alone, he spoke again, his voice in full whisper: "You have no idea how fragile your existence is. You have no idea how close you are to over."

"Tell me I'm talented."

"You're pathetic."

"Tell me I'm talented."

"You're ungrateful."

"Tell me I'm talented."

"You're needy. You're overrated. You're a fraud."

My head rang with it. My eyes began to swell.

"I'm not," I shouted. "I deserve it."

A couple passed by and Max stepped back. In the instant before he made his elegant way up the stairs and away from me, I saw his face lighten with victory.

Half an hour later I was back up there, forcing the remains of the first wrap up my nose. I leaned back on the wall and slid downwards, staring at the piss drips on the floor, waiting for the effect to hit. It didn't take long. I pushed myself to my feet and realised that I needed Kathryn.

I found her at the bar, looking more beautiful than I'd ever seen her, ignoring a young Italian man with an expensive watch who was trying to engage her.

"I've been looking everywhere for you," I said, above the sound of the editor of *Restaurant Magazine* giving out awards on the stage. "Why did you walk off?"

"You were being a cock," she said. "But luckily for you I've since realised this whole building is filled with drunken idiot cock chefs and the prospect of making small talk with them is a very slightly more hideous prospect than listening to you tell the BBC what an amazing genius you are." She paused and, before I had the chance to respond, said, "God, you look like shit."

Inside my head, a grand nation of cherubim ejaculated simultaneously.

"Don't worry," I whispered. "I think it's worn off."

All of a sudden, I felt rather chatty.

"What would your secret word be then?" I said.

"Secret word?"

"You know, what Andy was saying when we went out that night – about the S&M people. They have a word they say for when the pain gets too much."

"Oh!" she laughed. "Hmm... well, yes... Pippin. My word would be pippin."

"That's not very sexy," I said.

"No, but it's a lovely word, don't you think? Pippin. A lovely word and a lovely apple. My favourite kind of apple. What would yours be?"

"If yours is pippin, mine is windfall," I decided. "I always feel sorry for those windfall apples. They get blown off the tree and then stamped into the ground, with all the bruises and the maggots. But they're perfectly good apples that have just been ignored by everyone and that's why they die. So it's a good word for the pain getting too much, if you think about it. Windfall apples live a life of pain."

Kathryn nodded wryly. "You're very much the apple philosopher tonight."

I pushed my fingertip down inside my collar. I hated this starched, neck-tightening shirt. It was the shirt of a Victorian headmaster; the shirt of a corpse. I took off my tie and stuffed it into my trouser pocket.

"I have to sit down," I said. "Why is everyone looking at me?"

"They're not," said Kathryn.

I unfastened the first three buttons of my shirt.

"Is it because I'm famous?"

She patted my hand. "Yes, dear."

Finally, the barman delivered my drink. I gifted him my tie, opened my throat and poured down the whisky. A jellyfish of nausea wrapped its tentacles around my stomach. I sniffed heavily and gripped the bar.

"I think this cocaine's off," I said.

"Shall we go and sit down?"

A field of coloured prickles shimmered in front of my eyes. Then the sickness passed and a new surge of power charged up my spine like beams of light. That was better. There was no past, there were no problems. There was only me and Kathryn and our jewel of a restaurant and our perfect future. I had done it. I had become magnificent.

"Are you all right, Kill? Your face has gone a bit berserk. Come on, let's sit down."

"There's something I have to tell you," I said. "I love you. I love you so much. I want to spend the rest of my life with you and, the restaurant – I want to do it properly. I've always known I could be a decent chef, Kathryn. But I want to do it on my own terms. I'm going to do it properly."

She glanced anxiously at the drunken man beside her.

"Pipe down," she said. "No gooey talk in public. I love you too."

She kissed me quickly on the chin. I felt it again: the surge.

"I don't need those herbs to cook, you know," I said. "I won the Young Saucier. That proves I deserve it."

"Herbs?" she said, a blade of irritation evident in her tone. "God, what are you *on* about? Why don't you shush, hey? Do you want another drink?"

A wave. A slump. A dead wind. I gripped the bar again.

"I think we need to go home," said Kathryn. "All that cocaine has made you poorly."

"Hang on," I muttered.

I felt in my trouser pocket for the second wrap and held it towards her.

"Have some with me. Go on," I said. "Every fucker in this room is on it, having fun. But you walk around sometimes like fun is kind of *beneath* you; like joy is a toy you used to play with when you were a kid but now you're too grown up for. You shouldn't look down on happiness. You shouldn't condescend to it – that's just such an *English* thing to do. Happiness, fun, excitement, joy – why don't you deserve that? Why don't *we*?"

"It's just–"

My words were coming fast now, and from a place I hadn't accessed before.

"Trying new things. Being foolish. Risky. Fearless. Standing up to the pain and saying, 'I fucking love the fucking pain'. I mean, pain? What is it? Humans are built for it. We need it. It's like muscles need to tear so they can grow. Pain is nothing to be frightened of. You go into it, and it's a bit dark, it's a bit scary, but it's just a corridor. And at the other end of the corridor is happiness. It's *always* happiness. And that's life, isn't it? That's the *whole thing*."

For a second, I forgot what I was talking about. Remembering, I eagerly grabbed Kathryn's arms and gave her the full sell.

"It'll be fine. It'll be amazing. You know, all that stuff you were telling me about going out and taking what you can get? Well what about taking some *life*? What about doing it now? With me? We deserve it. Don't we?"

She didn't respond. I was close and I knew it.

"We'll look back on this, one day, when we're old, when we're at the end. We'll look back on tonight and it will be the most brilliant memory."

She hesitated. Then she downed her vodka, plucked the wrap from my fingers and returned fifteen minutes later, looking wary and crafty and thrilled.

"My tongue's gone numb," she whispered, her eyes alive with adventure. "It tastes disgusting."

"So does vodka," I said, handing her an icy tumbler. "And I've got you a triple of that."

Talking, talking, talking. Running through the crowd, with my hand in hers. Knocking elbows and collapsing in smiles, curled up in a dark corner, laughing until we ached in our stomachs and in our throats. More to drink. Another package from Ambrose. More to drink. To the toilets again. Up the stairs. Falling down. All looking at me. Talking. Turning around at the bar and Kathryn's lost.

Where did she go? And who is he? Why is he looking at me? Where are my socks? I like being sockless. I like how it feels on my feet. So many intricate sensations. Where is Max? So wrong, Max Mann. He shouldn't have doubted me. He shouldn't have hated me, he should have liked me, he should have loved me. I'll take them off, the shirt buttons, the rest, one, two, three, four, now you'll all see the scars from the ovens, the scars from the cuts, the scars from the kettle, the burns on my nipples and there, off with the fucking shirt, you can have that, don't mention it, sir, and now you can see the fresh cuts on my arms, and the cuts on my ribs, all skin and bone, all cuts and love –

A stage. The stage. Beautiful, bright. And there's that man, that man with the Rocky hair from the magazine about restaurants.

"Ladies and Gentlemen, please welcome to the stage the winner of the 1985 Restaurant Magazine Lifetime Achievement award – from the legendary London restaurant King, the Gentleman Chef himself, Max Mann."

It all goes black. A single spotlight, over the lectern, hard and brilliant and sharp. It's waiting for him and they're cheering. They're cheering for *him*. My night. Fuckers, look. I'll make the fuckers look. Step onto the stage, one, two, three, I'll make the fuckers look at my skin and my bone and my scars and my love. He should have loved me.

Inside the spotlight. You can't see anything here. Blinding white on my skin. Smoke in the air. The stage cold and sticky beneath my feet. The lectern. There's a little support in the lectern. Like a shelf. Like a step. Okay, so, I'll step on it then. One foot on the lectern. Then the other. All those people. I'm on the lectern. On top! *My* night. Look at the people, all in their hundreds. Look at them looking at me.

The lectern is shaking. It might fall, into the crowd. My arms out to balance. Now they can see what I am. Centre stage, high up here, the army of black murmurers staring silent, *tamed*. My arms straight out, the spotlight on me, my skin and my bones and my scars and my cuts and there he is, there's my own Max, at the side of the stage, and I shout to him, I scream to him, "You should have loved me", and the lectern falls and I fall.

Later. Outside. A man with his arm around my shoulder. Asking about me. Friendly but not friendly. Asking about secrets; about secret ingredients. A journalist.

Shouting. I punch him. I'm kicked. In the ribs. In the head. In the back. I curl into myself. I need to sleep. I can't. Stuff. I need some more of that stuff.

Alone. Cold.

And then someone reaching down. Pale hands. Shaking fingers. A face. *Her*. I lift my head from the concrete and all I want to say, as she takes me in her arms, is *windfall, windfall, windfall*.

42

I didn't sleep at all that night. I lay on Kathryn's sofa, empty of life. At around half past four in the morning I couldn't stand it any more. I tried to cry. I tried to force a break in the solidity that I had carried with me for years. But it wouldn't crack. I wanted tears. I wanted rupture. But I ended up just barking these ridiculous dry sobs that bottomed out into a thin, wounded cat whine.

I wanted to be clean again. I wanted purity for me and for Kathryn. This couldn't go on, this cheating. It was exactly what Aunt Dorothy had warned me about, and I'd failed her. Tomorrow, I would throw my pouch of Earl's Leaf away. As soon as I had the chance, I would burn the herb garden. And if that meant the end of Glamis, then that would be what it meant. Perhaps Kathryn would come with me to south-west France, where we would quietly continue our training. And we'd return to London in maybe five or six years and Ambrose could fund a new opening. Smaller than Glamis. Humble and simple and honest. I smiled as my plan unfolded itself. I felt a kernel of returning warmth in my chest.

I manoeuvred myself to a sitting position and thought about watching the television. The remote was nowhere to be seen and I didn't fancy the trek to the other side of the coffee table to switch it on. Besides, it would probably only be Ceefax or the

Open University at this time of the morning. There was a pile of magazines near my feet. They looked like issues of *Restaurant Magazine*. Urgh. Just beneath the latest edition, though, there seemed to be something else. I pulled it out. A brochure.

Ten Pines House. It looked like a beautiful place. A gloried country mansion in a world of green and blue. I stared at the picture. I wished I could wake up in Ten Pines House. I could tell, from the broken spine and the state of the paper, that the booklet had been read often. One of the pages had had its corner bent over. I opened it up to see a nurse in angelic white assisting a woman who was climbing out of a swimming pool. Another picture showed a huge vase of colourful flowers sitting in a sunlit window and, just visible in the corner, a precisely made-up bed. The pillows looked plumply inviting, the sheets gentle and new. There were some numbers on the page, drawn in biro. Kathryn had written: £2993 p.a. and underlined it.

For her mum. This must be where she wants to send her; her plan for when she earns enough money. You'd need to be the boss of somewhere, to afford that. *Chef de file*. The warmth in my chest vanished. I tried to stand but a wave of fizzing weakness struck me and I fell, helplessly, back onto the sofa. Once recovered, I crawled on my hands and knees into the bathroom.

Using the sink to pull myself up, I opened the medicine cabinet, found a pink razor and, gathering as much force as I could muster, crushed it on the floor with the heel of my hand. Picking the blade out from the shards, I swiped it into the side of my stomach and watched the long lips of skin open up and begin to dribble. I swiped again, the adrenaline and the endorphins making me feel comforted and powerful.

There were only a few sheets of toilet paper left on the roll. I groaned at the realisation that I had to somehow make it to the kitchen and back with a tea towel. Staggering, leaning, crawling, I finally managed it when I noticed the sickly dawn light slithering through the bathroom blind and up the dirty white walls. I wondered what Dorothy would say if she could see me now. I pictured her, here with me. *"Oh, Kill, my love, my darling, what's happened?"* and she would soothe me and she would understand.

There were footsteps coming from Kathryn's bedroom. I felt as if my heart was too strong for my body; as if the power of its beats might shatter the rest of me. The rattle of the door handle sounded unnaturally loud. The lock, I noticed, was broken. I managed to throw myself against it, just in time.

"Killian?" she said. "Is that you?"

"Don't come in."

"Are you on the floor? What are you doing on the floor?"

"Go to bed."

"Let me *in*."

She shoved the door, hard. The handle hit the back of my head and I cowed away. She was barefoot, the faint blue light from the window shining ghost-like off her plain white nightshirt.

"Oh my God, Killian! Is that blood?"

It looked black, instead of red, in the dawn's haze.

"I was going to clear it up."

She crouched down to look at my cuts.

"What have you done?"

"Sorry," I said. "I'm sorry. I was going to clean it up."

She reached out and tenderly touched my wounds. Fascinated by what she was seeing, she asked, "Does it hurt?" She wobbled, slightly, and I realised that she was still drunk. "You're crazy," she said, smiling. She picked the blade up from the floor and touched it with her thumb. Staring at it, she quoted me from earlier: "And at the end of the darkness, there's always happiness." And then, "I want to try it."

"No," I said. I tried to take the blade from her but she pulled it away.

"You're right about me," she said, with a smile of vaguely cruel defiance. "I need to be more fearless. Pain is nothing to be frightened of."

"Don't," I said.

The fastest struggle and then "Ach!" She'd done it. I clasped my hand tightly around her wrist.

"No, Kathryn," I said. "Please don't do that. Please don't *ever*–"

Dropping the blade, she touched the place where she'd used it. She looked intense and detached and fascinated. She brought her fingers back and studied the translucent red stain on their tips. Then she put her hands on my jaw and kissed me, lowering me gently onto the tiles and the blood that had pooled on them. Running her hands down the scars on my torso, she groaned gently and then lifted her nightshirt over her head. Her breasts pushed softly onto me; her perfection pressing in on my ruined skin. She rolled, slightly, deliberately, into the blood, so it was on her: on her arms; on her ribs; on her breasts. I breathed slowly; exhausted; weightless in the pleasure, as she kissed down my neck and stroked with her tongue and her fingers across my scars. Not a single blemish was left without her gentle attention; not even the fresh ones.

She moved down further and further still until, eventually, she slid my boxer shorts down to my knees. I stared towards the ceiling as her mouth worked between my legs, my eyes unfocused, my hands gripping and releasing in an attempt to modulate the bliss. When she was finished, she pulled her nightshirt on, her back to me to hide her toplessness, before walking with a drowsy, contented slouch towards the kitchen.

"Go to bed," she instructed. "I'll sort the bathroom out."

43

BAD BOY OF COOKING IN AWARDS UPROAR.

I moved the newspaper up to hide my face, grateful that I was in the hazy smoking carriage of the early-morning commuter train to London.

Fiery Protégé of Chef to the Stars Max Mann Steals ex-Boss's Big Moment.

My hands were shaking even more than they had been before I'd seen the huge picture of me on page 3 of the *Daily Mirror*. I looked deranged in the photo – topless, scarred, mouth half open, spotlit in the blackness of the Café de Paris stage and moments away from falling into the crowd from the lectern that I'd climbed, arms stretched out like some ghoulish, self-harming Jesus.

I'd spent the previous day in bed, back at the cottage. Earlier that morning, I'd forced myself to eat breakfast, following a long night in which I was still too strung out to sleep. I let myself in through the back door of Glamis and sat in my office for ten minutes with the light off, trying to turn all the noises and directions in my head into one firm and steady stream of awareness. When the phone rang, I jumped.

"Aha! The bad boy of cooking returns!" said Ambrose. "Bravo, Killian. Very well done. Excellent work. Bookings have gone wild. I know I told you to work the old image but, by golly, you have really excelled yourself."

"Thanks," I muttered, repetitively smoothing my eyebrow with my thumb.

"And the BBC have been on the phone. The *Food and Drink* people want to take you up on that offer. When can they come in to film? What shall I tell them?"

"I don't know."

"Fantastic opportunity. They're going to send Russell Harty. Good old Max for suggesting it. But, listen, I have to tell you – he is rather sore that you chose his moment for your little stunt. He'll get over it, but be kind to him, won't you? We're all on the same team, after all, and at the end of the day, you have a lot to thank him for."

The rage prickled down the back of my neck in fearful detail.

"Right," I said. "Okay."

As I was putting the phone down, the light turned on – a great scorching yellow burst of it like boiling water.

"Fuck," I said, squinting at the shadow in the doorway.

"Still suffering?"

It was Andy, leaning against the door frame with his arms folded, his fulsome lips bunched into a smirk, his heavy brows furrowed. I rested my forehead on a fisted hand in a way that I hoped he'd interpret as "fuck off".

"Bit of a shit service yesterday," he continued. "Bit of a shit two services, really."

I ignored him.

"Complaints," he said. "Food wasn't the same."

I couldn't work out what I hated the most: his nose, his eyes, his mouth or his hair.

"Well, what have you got to say for yourself?" I said.

"It's not my fault, Killian," he said, puffing himself up. "I didn't do anything wrong."

All of it. I hated all of it.

"You know, it's funny," he continued. "I followed the recipes in the blue book precisely."

"Well, you can relax," I said. "I'm back now."

I folded my arms, aware of the lump in my apron pocket where a fresh pouch of Earl's Leaf had been secreted. Andy moved in and perched on the edge of my desk, his large buttock bulging through his trousers, his voice softening into a condescending smear.

"Killian, mate. Level with me. How are you making those sauces? What's in them?"

"I'm not 'mate', mate," I said. "I'm 'chef'. And I'm sorry if your ego's hurting. Obviously I can never have another day off for the rest of my life. Obviously this place needs me more than you realised."

"Listen, mate," he said. "Don't give me that. I know how to make sauces. I've been learning this shit for years. Hours and hours, shift after shift, bollocking after bollocking, cuts, burns, aching bones, exhaustion so bad you can't sleep, years and years and years of it, so much work that your body moulds around it, like they could give you an autopsy and pick out your chopping muscle and your stirring muscle and your bent spine and your eroded fucking wrists and say, 'yeah, that's a chef, I guarantee it'. I know what I'm talking about. I've *earned* the right to be here, and I've earned the right to tell you what I know – and I know this for a *fact*. Those recipes are not as you've written them down. They aren't right."

A shadow moved in from the corridor. Kathryn. She entered with a cautious half-grin. "Remembered how your legs work, have you?"

Her smile faded as her comment clattered, unwelcome, to the floor.

"What's going on?" she said.

"I don't know," I said, standing. "I think Andy's accusing me of something."

"What are you putting in those sauces?" he said. "Just tell us."

"Talent," I shouted. "Fresh fucking talent. Why is it so hard for you to believe that I am a good cook? Don't you believe any of the reviews? Don't you believe our waiting list?"

There was no blood in the tips of my fingers. There was no blood in me at all.

"Disloyal cunt!" I shouted. "Get out! You're fired."

"You're doing a very unwise thing," he said.

"Don't flatter yourself," I said. "You're not irreplaceable."

As he rounded the doorway, he muttered, "That's not what I meant."

44

I sat down, slowly, behind my desk. Kathryn perched on its corner, where Andy had just been.

"You're not really going to sack him, are you?"

"If I can't get loyalty from my most senior chef, what's the point?"

She glanced at my pot of pens and said, "Loyalty isn't the answer to all your problems, Killian."

"It's the most important thing."

"But it's a lie, isn't it?" she said. "It's a compromise people make – people who are desperate to be loved. You're not like that, Killian. You don't need your arse kissed every day, like Max does. You don't need team players." She spoke the words as if they were fouling her tongue. "You need people who want to work hard for their own sake and who'll be brutally honest with you. And he was only being honest."

"What's wrong with being a team player?" I said.

"Team players?" Her face twisted. "Bland, middling, bulls-hitting, corporate kitchen politicians. You want lone rangers, people who do it for their own ego. Cooks who feel like knifing them*selves* in the heart if they make a mistake. That's Andy. You know, there's a reason communism doesn't work, Kill. Everybody has to work for the team, so nobody does any work at all."

She'd lost me, totally. "That's different," I said. "And, anyway, he was calling me a liar."

"He was asking about your sauces."

She met my eye and held it. My blood lurched. I refused to look away. There was a clatter, back in the kitchen. I was aware of the reflection of the light in her irises.

"There's nothing to ask about," I said.

She paused, and with a tentative look said, "Just talent."

"I mean, come on, what does he think? That man actually believes that I'm buying pheromones from a sex shop in Soho and dropping them in my food. Have you ever heard of anything as crazy as that? Think about it, though."

She looked down, apparently examining her thumbs.

"It does seem unlikely."

"He's delusional," I said. "I can't have someone with delusions working here. Imagine if he cracked completely and came for me with a fucking chopper," I laughed. "Imagine if he went for you?"

I tried to make her catch my smile, but she wouldn't.

"What's up?" I said.

"I just need reassuring, I think."

"Fucking..." I stood up. "Not you too?"

"Not about that," she said, quickly. "It's just, this is the right thing, isn't it?"

I wasn't sure what she meant.

"Of course it is," I said. "The way things are going, we'll have everything. Max is already halfway gone. I mean, the 'Lifetime Achievement' award – everyone knows what *that* means. He'll take his retirement, open up a monstrous pit in Las Vegas, cash his reputation in for good. And Ambrose will make me executive chef overseeing both restaurants and that means it's up to me to appoint the *chef de file* of King. And that will be you. By this time next year. I promise."

She glanced into the empty corner. We sat like that for a while.

"I spoke to my mum this morning," she said, eventually. "She said she's fallen again. Hit her face. I could tell that someone was listening in, though. I just don't know what to do. Last time I complained, she told me not to. She begged me not to make a fuss about it. I'm sure they got their own back on her somehow. Seeing your mother frightened like that, it does something to you. I'd do anything–"

I stood in front of her and placed my hands on her shoulders.

"You have to trust me. We'll get what we want. We have to grab it. Take what we want. And then just pray it all works out. Which, you know, it will. It *has* to."

Shortly afterwards, she left the office and an hour later, I gathered the brigade.

"Right, quick announcement," I said. "Andy's gone. He's not coming back. I'll be carrying on with sauces and I'll also be running the pass. And a word of warning to you all. I will not have disloyalty in my team. Not a whisper of it."

I scanned the men as they looked back at me, their limbs arranged in angular discomfort, their faces rounded out variously with alarm, defiance and fear.

"The last time I ran the pass you let me down. That won't happen today. I want you to remember: every plate that goes out there, every bite of every dish is a judgement on me. It's my name that's above the door. It's my name that everyone wants to fail. When you're working in my kitchen, you are no longer you. You don't exist. You're my hands, you're my eyes, you're my brain, you're my body. And be warned – I'm not the slightest bit afraid to punish myself, to draw blood, when I get things wrong."

I let them stand, for a moment, in the weirdness.

"We have made Glamis the greatest restaurant in the country; probably the world. We have a reputation to defend. Any mistakes and we lose it. There cannot be any mistakes. We must take perfection and better it. And if I hear any hint of d-disloyalty, you're going the same way as Andy. Okay? To work."

All day and all night, my anger radiated out through the room. At just after nine, I was about to dip my hand into my apron pocket when I was surprised by a presence that seemed to slide up to me, silently. It was our best apprentice, the shy boy from Leeds whose surname – something French or Italian – I could never remember. I only knew him as Marco.

"Don't fucking look at me," I told him.

Rather than shrinking back, as I had expected, he firmed up his shoulders and stepped towards me. Without thinking, I pushed him back, with both hands, and he fell against the steel unit behind him. He stood again, his face pinked, and balled his right fist. It was a blur; a mess; a panic; too quick for rational thought. Somehow, instinctively, I reached back for my paring knife. For a terrible moment, my fingertips touched the steel handle. I only realised what I was doing when I saw Marco's eyes widen. I pulled my arm back – as shocked as if I'd accidentally stuck it in the burner – then turned and announced to the kitchen, "No one fucking looks at me when I'm cooking. Do you understand? No one looks at me."

"Yes, Chef!"

That night was to be my finest service yet.

* * *

It was these days at Glamis that made me realise how badly my teacher, Mr Mayle, had been mistaken. Perhaps it said something about his failure as a chef that he believed the secret ingredient of unforgettable food was "humanity". My time at the restaurant also added depth and light to something I'd been thinking about for a while. It started after I'd seen a child psychologist on the *Nine O'Clock News* discussing the effects of spanking: "You must remember that every two-year-old, if they had the physical strength, would be a killer," she said. "They know they're dangerous – unconsciously, of course – and this can cause them great fear and distress. This is why all children need order and discipline. It's reassuring for them. Rules make them secure and therefore happy. And this doesn't really change as we grow into adults."

This made sense of so much for me. We are constantly in a state of internal war, our wants battling our needs. When we're young, our wants are so powerful that they terrify us. But if we're parented strictly and well, we learn that we're not alone in our fight against them. We have back-up. Our instincts for greed, selfishness and egotism will not be allowed to catch and ignite into murder, vandalism and chaos. To the most primitive part of our minds, there is nothing more reassuring than being told what to do. It may be unsatisfying in the moment to hear the word "no", but on a deeper plane, no music is more soothing.

I had realised that what separates humankind from the animals is an incendiary combination of imagination and obedience. These are the qualities that built civilisation. And the mortar that holds them together – the infrastructure, the pipes, the circuitry – is loyalty. It takes someone with imagination to lead the masses into disciplined self-sacrifice, and if those masses are sufficiently loyal to him, the end result is progress, genius, magic; the end result is everything good about the world.

A correctly functioning kitchen is the human struggle in microcosm; ideal society in excelsis. Every cook in there wants to be the *chef de cuisine*, the man with the imagination. They want to depose him. But at the same time they are violently devoted to him. Their fidelity is felt in the most primitive way. They are in the sphere of a strong, powerful leader, a man of vision and control, a man who they instinctively know could make a difference to humanity, and so billions of years of human evolution kick in and they slot into place. They bend their necks, raise their eyes and say, as one, "Yes, Chef".

And through this subservience they become incredible cooks. Through this loyalty, self-sacrifice and pain, through the force with which they battle their wants, one or two might eventually prove themselves hardy enough to become like their leader. This is how it operates: accomplishment through loyalty, happiness through struggle, freedom through work.

So now I knew where Mayle had got it wrong, with his happy proclamations about humanity. I had been taught a lesson I swore never to forget, the hidden truth of all the Michelin kitchens in the world. The secret ingredient of unforgettable food is suffering.

45

Driving home that night, I found myself taking risks I never had before. My foot taunted the accelerator pedal as I barrelled past junctions and lorries and around tight country corners. I was playing lightly with danger and it made me feel free. I would go faster and faster. I would take risks. And if the ground wasn't there to catch me, so be it. Notions of safety, of looking after yourself, of creeping through life constantly obsessing about arranging things just so that everything will always come out best for you – it all suddenly seemed so timid.

I pulled up outside Dor and walked through the tall, curling gates of the physic garden. The Earl's Leaf was surging forward in erect, willing clumps, and the other two herbs seemed to be doing better than ever, the snaking stamens of the Hindeling licking the air hungrily and the purple heads of the Cauter nodding in the wind. Flies zoomed madly here and there, a mathematical chaos of legs and wings and unfathomable purpose.

I harvested a fresh armful of Earl's Leaf and when I was back under the dull light of the kitchen, I noticed how much this room – the feeling of it – had changed. Whereas I used to remember the height and madness of the shelves and cupboards as tantalising and mysterious, now they seemed to loom in threat, casting great columns of darkness upon each other in some silent war of shadows. The jars and bottles lurked and plotted, spying down from their ceiling-bound eyrie; the mad contraptions had the air of torture devices. Perhaps the most dramatic shift of all, though, was in the disappearance of the warmth that had once seemed so unvanquishable. It was as if the chill that inhabited the stairs had leaked out and spread itself everywhere. The flies, at least, seemed to like it. They danced beneath the light, picked their way confidently over the table top and watched me with a jittery intensity from the cracks in the beams and in the mortar.

My task for the night was baking. I wanted to learn how to incorporate Earl's Leaf into a dessert. I knew, of course, that Dorothy's "Dotty Cakes" had softly bewitched the Herstmonceux villagers in the seventies, but I couldn't imagine how she'd done it because the way that Earl's Leaf worked with flavour seemed inherently savoury. There was a technical question too. It was one thing for the delicate plant to be added to a sauce right at the end of cooking, but dumping it in a dense, sticky dough and baking it in a hot oven? It would kill it off, surely.

I made twenty simple cupcakes, adding a little bit more of the herb into each. The first had a large crumb, about the size of a match-head, the last a dangerously powerful dose of five finely chopped leaves. After an impatient wait, I took Dorothy's old holly-patterned oven gloves, which were frayed and covered in scorched bruises, and pulled the trays out, allowing the fragrant steam to rise from the cracked, moist domes before breaking a nibble-sized chunk off the edge of the weakest cake. The taste was so incredible that I couldn't help but laugh. The Earl's Leaf had simultaneously lifted and darkened the complex vanilla, saffron and caramel flavours of the sponge. The plant also kept its aphrodisiac effect: I could tell that if I wanted to avoid problems, I should probably eat no more. It was amazing – the correct dose, it seemed, was just half a match-head.

I yawned so deeply that my jaw gave a painful click.

Conscious, suddenly, of something indistinct in the silence, I looked around. A fly took off from a crack in a beam. Then, I heard a noise.

Tap, tap, tap.

I stopped. I heard it again.

Tap, tap, tap. A voice. *"Killian?"*

It couldn't be.

"Kathryn?"

I paced through the darkness of the kitchen and the lounge and turned the key in the old door. And there she was – her head cast down, her shoulders raised defensively against the weight of serious night that she'd just made her way through. Strands of loose hair were picked out by the weak light of the hallway. Her nose was wrinkled in distress, her arms folded in her favourite ski jacket, its pink and pale-green triangles of colour looking jarringly modern against the gruff brick and mean ceiling of the cottage's dwarfish entrance.

"Sorry to come, but I really want to talk to you," she said.

I followed her into the kitchen and she sat at the table, looking carefully into the darkness – by chance, towards the exact spot that Dorothy used to stand and stir and treat me to her amazing lessons. I pulled out the chair beside her.

"What happened today, with Marco," she said. "I don't like it, Kill. I don't like what's happening. Not just to you – to both of us."

I stood up.

"I'm running my kitchen, that's all I'm doing," I said. "I'm controlling it. I'm doing a good job. I'm getting excellence out of those cooks. I'm doing it for you."

She didn't respond. She just sat there, staring at the void that Dorothy had left. And then, very quietly, she said, "You're becoming a bit like *him*."

"Him? What?"

"Like Max."

"How could you even say that? That's like, the complete reverse of the truth. *I'm the one who's standing up to Max.* I'm the only one who can serve justice on that bastard. What don't you understand about that? He's a bully and a fraud. He doesn't care about food. It's all about his stars. His fame. His celebrity. And I'm going to take them all off him, because that's what he deserves, and put you in his kitchen. That's what justice is. That's a *good* thing. And if you're not going to help me, if you're going to be so disloyal as to..."

Kathryn pulled back in irritation at the word, the leg of her chair letting out a little yelp as it scraped on the floor.

"Disloyal? It's not about loyalty, Killian, it's about doing the right thing."

"I am doing the right thing!"

"And you want me to turn a blind eye to whatever it is you're doing?"

"I'm not doing anything except cooking."

"You're putting something in the food, Killian."

"*What?*"

"I see you doing it all the time. From your apron! I've just not..." She closed her eyes and shook her head. "And then, the other night, you said you were going to give up herbs. Then I remembered, when I came to visit the last time. You said there was a herb garden. Is that what it is? Are you growing some sort of drug out there?"

"You're doing it now," I said. "You're questioning me. It's disloyalty. How can I be with someone like this? How can you have no *integrity*?"

The wind took a strike at the chimney and, behind the thick glass of the range's doors, the flames flared and bowed.

"Do you really think loyalty and integrity are the same thing?" said Kathryn. "Killian, they're not. They're opposites.

If you want to look for corruption, you've only got to look for loyalty. It's how powerful people get away with anything – businesses, the Church, governments, the bloody army. It's a con. Look at my dad. Loyalty made him believe that his life was worth sacrificing for his country. For his country! For Maggie bloody Thatcher! For some flag, some pattern on a cloth. It's the same all over Northern Ireland, loyalty to the Catholics, loyalty to the Protestants, loyalty to Britain, loyalty to the Republic. It's loyalty that means Americans are happy for their country to trigger a holocaust against the communists. It's the same in Leningrad and Moscow and Peking. Loyalty is a sin, Killian. It's corruption. It's a trick. It's evil."

"But you're supposed to be a Christian, aren't you?" I said. "You're loyal to your church."

"I don't go to church, Killian. Christ, what do you know about the Church anyway?" She took a moment to steady herself and said, more calmly, "I haven't been for years, if you must know. I don't agree with it. If you ask me, Adam eating the apple, that wasn't the original sin. The original sin was God demanding that the apple never be eaten in the first place, and then expecting that ridiculous order to be followed blindly, without question. That's your loyalty, Killian. It's cruel and pointless and bullying and it leads to evil, always. And please don't lecture me on God. I know more about it than you do."

I shook my head slowly in the difficult silence that followed.

"So you hate the Church and what God said in the Bible is evil? And you're telling me that you're some expert? I mean, you're forgetting – it's loyalty that makes such amazing food."

"Why aren't you *listening* to me? It's loyalty that makes evil, Killian. It's loyalty that stops all the chefs that work at King not going to the police and reporting him for ABH, GBH." She paused. "You know, was it virtuous when you defended Max after he beat up Greg? Is it virtuous when you defend your mum who is clearly some kind of monster?"

I shouted then, my voice hard against the stone walls and floor, smashing at the warm memories of boyhood that still, despite everything, clung to this room, "Don't talk about my mum!"

Her chair pulled back further and she looked towards her feet, a wet string of hair hitting her freckled cheek as defeat or regret or exhaustion calmed her a little.

"You can't expect me to be loyal to you and your ridiculous, pointless feud against Max. It's not fair."

"But I'm fighting him on behalf of everyone!"

"Yes, he's a bully. Yes, he's an arsehole. But I'm here because I'm trying to say..." She shook her head and collapsed, slightly. "*Please* don't turn into one, Killian. Please. I love you. I love you so much. I don't want you to—"

I moved behind her, my shadow falling over her pale form, and touched her head. I sensed her body soften and she turned, arms raised. I pulled her off her chair and she stood, her face lying in the crook of my neck, her hair in my eyes, the weight of her on me, and I could see the delicate pores in her skin and feel her chest as she breathed. It was as if her embrace was a door that shut out everything that wasn't her.

I pressed my lips into her and she lifted her head.

"All right," I said. "I'm going to tell you the truth now. I am keeping a secret ingredient in my pouch. I'm surprised Andy didn't tell you, really. It's no big deal. It's just pepper with a bit of ground clove in it. Not quite enough so's you'd notice. But just enough to add a kind of meaty richness. I'm allowed a little trick or two, aren't I?"

"Ground clove?" she said, with a slight scrunch of the brow. "And that's all? *Clove?*"

"What's more likely?" I laughed. "That or I'm drugging the food?"

Finally, she smiled. We kissed with a bite and fury that had no room for all that had just happened. I became lost in it. It was as if the limits of our bodies had become porous. She lay back on the table and I unbuttoned her blue checked shirt and pulled it off one arm and then the other. Then, lifting her gently by the small of her narrow back, I unhooked her bra and she pulled my shirt over my head and we kissed again, her breasts pushing into my chest and her fingers tending to my scars; luxuriating in them. Then her jeans. Top button, next button, then white cotton tight over pale skin and then her hand pulling at my wrist, pulling me away. "No, no, Kill. Sorry. That's enough."

I stood up, my face stinging hotly, and looked at her half-naked body that was laid out before me, the dim light forming rich shadows over her stomach and breasts and her stretched, almond belly button and it was the most beautiful thing I'd ever seen and it was turning, curling away from me.

"For fuck's sake. Fuck!"

Anything. I would have done anything. I perched on the edge of the table and ran my hand over the candy-pink King scar on my left arm. She sat up, blushing, and crossed her arms clumsily over her chest.

"I'm a virgin too, you know," I said, softly. "You don't have to worry. It'll be our first time together."

She picked up her shirt and used it to cover herself.

"I want to wait."

"Don't tell me until you're married?"

"That's not such a ridiculous thing."

"Come on, Kathryn, it's not 1955. This is 1985. It's the future."

"It's just what I want to do," she said. "You understand, Kill, I know you do. It's not never. It's just not now."

I could imagine what my mum would think if she could see me now. I pictured her laughing, rocking back with pleasure, that squawk that bottomed out into a witchy cackle: "Look at it! All skin and no boner."

I walked over to the rack on the kitchen table. I deserved this. That's what Kathryn had said. I deserved everything I could get.

"Sorry," I said. "I'm sorry. Here, cheer up. Have a cake."

I threw it at her and she caught it, a happy, weary grin raising itself on her face. I picked up the still-warm cake I'd cautiously nibbled at earlier and glanced, with a sense of excited, guilty trepidation, at the empty space on the baking tray where the five-leafed version had been seconds earlier. There was an instant, just before she took her first bite, that I wished I hadn't done it.

"Hmm, it's good," she said. "Oh, it's so – hmm. I didn't realise how starving I was."

Another bite and her cheeks began to redden.

"Good cake," she muttered – quietly this time, almost to herself, and with a slight self-conscious pull.

She ate in silence, groaning her appreciation every now and then, crossing her legs tightly as she took the final bite, pushing it greedily into her mouth with the side of her finger. She gazed at the floor for a moment, then swallowed. Her tongue swept over her bottom lip, which had become full and red and glistening wet. As her legs tightened around themselves even further, I smiled at her disorientation.

"I love you, Kathryn."

She pushed her hands down her thighs, as if to dry her palms, as another deep groan of pleasure came from her throat. "That was amazing," she said, staring at her knees. When she looked back up, through damp strands of dark hair and bleeding mascara, her eyes had taken on a look of pleading. I moved towards her and she lifted her arms to receive me, her shirt dropping from her chest, her legs uncrossing. She whispered hungrily, "Show us your scars then."

And she was there, where they found her on that night and where they'd continued to find her every night since. She was there, in the place that the cottage held her. To repeat, to attempt to heal.

Mary, weak and wordless up sixteen steps. The finder man says, "Take off her black thrumb'd hat because I cannot abide to look at her."

She turned from the men and looked at me.

"Why didn't you stop them barking?"

And the finder man turned towards me, his wide jaw and small eyes and high stubble all set in ugly English dread.

"Who's there?" he said.

He could sense me as I watched him.

"Foul spirit, show thyself."

And I was the dog that he wanted.

I was King of the Wastelands.

King of the Mischief.

King of the More.

I was the red and the yellow and the black.

And I would never stop them barking.

46

Sleep came, that night, in a thin layer. I kept breaking through its surface, disturbed by dreams and by joy and the unbelief: Kathryn – my Kathryn – was naked on the mattress beside me. I had decided to forgive what she'd said the night before. I loved her so much, how could I not? When she finally stirred, I was studying her ear, how it curled so perfectly, so tenderly, like young coral.

"What happened last night?" she murmured.

My arm, which I had draped over her chest just high enough that I could feel the kiss of her breasts on my skin, squeezed in. "Hmmmm," I replied, approvingly, and pushed my nose deeper into her neck so I could gorge once more on her dark and sweet pyjamary scent. She stiffened, her head lifting just a millimetre.

"What did you do to me?"

"What do you mean?"

She turned her head, dislodging me from the warm nest I'd made of her.

"Last night. What happened?"

"Last night was amazing, Kathryn. It was amazing."

She was looking down towards the sheet, her eyes disconnected.

"Do you think I'm an idiot?" she said "You must think I'm an idiot."

She stood, pulling the sheet up with her.

"I know what you did. You're a fucking nutcase," she said.

"No," I said. "Kathryn?"

She was a blur of frantic distress, picking up her clothes from the stone floor, whilst with an awkward, angular desperation, trying to keep the sheet covering her body.

"Don't look at me!"

I lay still, confused and aware of her pulling her knickers up.

"What is it, Killian?" she said as she buttoned her Wranglers. "What did you put in that cake? What are you putting in the food?" She turned towards the window. "It's out there, isn't it?"

Standing unsteadily, I made a foolish attempt at hugging her; trying to push all her moving parts back together.

"Get away from me," she screamed.

She ran outside and, in the daylight, she saw the gates to the physic garden for the first time, with the weather-worn gargoyles; their shallow eyes and ancient teeth, straining in their static howls, commanding the skies above them. The sight stopped her momentarily before she went inside, her feet heaving further into black earth. It was all there for her to see – the lush and the misty space, rammed with baying plants and droning with insects. She picked a head of Cauter and sniffed it.

"No!" I shouted. "Don't!" I grabbed it off her. "Not that one – it's poisonous."

"Is this what you gave me? Is that what you've been using at Glamis?"

I tried, once more, to hold her. She pushed me away.

"What's wrong?" I said. "This is ridiculous. Kathryn, you don't understand – I love you."

The cold dawn wind came through elms and spread itself cruelly about us. The cottage watched through the open gate as she collapsed onto the turf and sobbed.

"What did you do to me? What did you do to me?"

47

I arrived at Glamis late, and as soon as they saw me, every cook in the kitchen could tell how the day was going to pass. It amazed me, how I could manage the mood of my subordinates by controlling the look in my eye and the muscles in my face. The longer they searched in vain for some sign of my acceptance, the harder they worked to earn it. Throughout most of the service, none of them even had the courage to meet my gaze, and I remembered, with more bemusement than shame, how just a few weeks ago I had let this kitchen overwhelm me.

Everything was going perfectly. The diners were getting served promptly and, when I found mistakes, I had no trouble in letting the individual responsible know that such lapses were intolerable. Then, at the height of service, Drusilla the maître d' gave a nervous little bow and said, "Mr McClaren wishes to send his compliments to the chef."

Everything was *fine*. But for some reason, I reacted by punching a silver cloche off the shelf above the pass with the heel of my hand. It bounced off the back wall and clanged onto the tiles. With the disorientating feeling that my rage had become something sentient and separate from me, I found myself shouting at her, "No more compliments to the chef! No more! I *never* want to hear another compliment to the *fucking* chef."

She gave another fluttering little bow before retreating.

"Yes, Chef. Of course, Chef."

I watched Drusilla slip elegantly away and realised that I was panting. The backs of my hands were blotchy with red and white and I had a feeling of numbness and tightness over my temples and cheeks. I instructed Marco to take care of my duties, then went to the bathroom, locking the door of the toilet cubicle behind me and resting my head uncomfortably on the plastic pipe that led to the cistern. It wasn't long before I found myself picking, distractedly, at my scabs.

When I had imagined being in this position – when I had fantasised about being a world-renowned chef – I always seemed to conjure one particular image: me, at the pass, smilingly dressing a plate as friendly eyes looked on. I would be confident, at ease, popular with my brigade. But there was something wrong with my daydream; a disquieting flaw at its heart. That imaginary chef at that imaginary pass was not me. It could never be me. No matter how much I achieved in my career, I couldn't be that person. I wondered, as I sat there, if what I had thought had been a fantasy about success in the world had actually been a yearning for change in my soul.

I asked myself what Dorothy would have thought of everything I had done.

And that was it. That was enough.

* * *

During lunch service the next day, I watched the first few plates go out in a state of proud, paternal terror. I had prepared them honestly. I had not used any Earl's Leaf. And there they went, my true children, sent out into the world towards uncertain fortune. My confidence gathered as an hour and then another passed by, apparently without anyone noticing. At about one fifteen, Drusilla was back.

"I'm sorry, Chef," she said, clacking those long fingernails together nervously in front of her. "It's Mr Langeau. He's insisting it doesn't taste the same."

I put down the spoon I'd been holding and dried my hands slowly on my immaculate torchon. She clacked again.

"He's one of our regulars, Chef."

"Yes, I know that. What did he say?"

Her nostrils flared; her eyelids panicked.

"He says he won't pay fifteen pounds for five-pound food."

"Fucker," I said. "Okay. Don't worry, Drusilla. Give me a minute."

Just this once. To ease me in. I made Mr Langeau another entrecôte with sauce Glamis. I gave him a double dose of the leaf, to shut him up. But then another plate came back and then another. The fourth one, I smashed on the floor, the china and sauce flying towards Marco like shrapnel and napalm.

"You fucking useless prick," I shouted at him. "You're fucking all my food up."

"It's not me, Chef," he shrugged.

I looked at the congealing, returned plates that were piling up in front of me.

"Eat them," I said. "Take these plates, take them out into the restaurant, stand at the bar and eat what's on them."

"But, Chef!" he said.

"Drusilla!" I called the maitre d'. "Marco's hungry. Gather these plates up. Help him with them. He's going to have his lunch at the bar."

I watched Marco, looking paler than ever, place his tongs to the side and walk into the restaurant, his hips moving with a defiant lumber and roll. When he came back, I thought, for a moment, that he might physically attack me.

When service was over, I closed the door of my office and phoned Kathryn.

"Hello?"

It was her.

"Hello?"

Her voice. I loved her voice.

"Killian?"

I loved her.

"Killian, is that you?"

I put the phone down.

* * *

The following morning, I arrived at work before anyone else. I hung my coat on the mahogany hat stand that I'd purloined from the restaurant and checked my watch: 06:35. Damn. Too early. I sat behind my desk and looked at the telephone. Probably I should leave it until seven. I browsed through the order book, distractedly. I looked at the time again: 06:39. Fuck.

At 06:48, I dialled her number. I counted: it rang eleven times before she picked up.

"Killian?" she said. "If that's you, you have to stop calling."

I tried to hear every detail of what was happening in her world; to absorb her through the receiver. I didn't move at all as I took in her soft crying.

"Killian, if you do this again, I'll call the police. I don't want to, but I will."

The phone clicked off and gave me its heartless, electro-mechanic hum. I sat, in the room, and closed my eyes. Twelve minutes later, Ambrose called.

"I heard there were some issues yesterday?" he said. "With the food?"

I leaned forward as my stomach tightened painfully.

"Only a slight... Who told you?"

"Someone with your best interests at heart," he replied, a

note of *don't-start* defensiveness pushing in his voice. "So what happened?"

"My eye was off the ball," I said. "It was my fault. Me and Kathryn—"

"And that's all?" Silence. "There was no other problem? Nothing you want to tell me about? Nothing I might find out about by some other means? Nothing that might damage my business? Nothing at all?"

"That's right."

"What?"

"Nothing at all."

"I don't want everything to fall to pieces now that you've fired Andrew."

"It was the right decision."

"You'd do well to remember who owns Glamis, Killian."

I glanced at the pile of framed reviews that I'd had removed from the walls of the corridor and that still sat on my office floor, leaning against a filing cabinet. I was struck by the staggering height of the pile.

"You'd do well to remember who's made it world famous, Ambrose."

"Well, it's not going to stay that way for long on the basis of last night's food."

I noticed, too, how dusty the precarious stack had become. It was amazing, the speed with which dust could gather; how remorselessly life shed its dead material.

"That won't happen again," I said. "That's a promise."

"Look," said Ambrose. "I have no idea what's going on between you and Kathryn and, frankly, I'm not interested. You mustn't let all this personal idiocy get in the way of your success. You must remain focused on the positive things. We just can't have this. Especially not now. For God's sake, between you and Max, the situation is—"

"Max?"

"Oh, his blasted girlfriend has done a runner."

"Has she?"

"Of course she has!"

"But he didn't really give a crap about her, did he? He was just keeping up appearances. She was pregnant and everything."

"Oh, if only that were true, Killian. You couldn't be more wrong. Max adored her. He was besotted. Obsessed. The first girlfriend who wasn't a pushover, that's what I think."

"Where's she gone?"

"Who knows?" he sighed. "Back to Russia, more than likely. Max is crushed, bless him. Between you and me, he's barely capable of leading that kitchen and these are important days. Critical. That's what I'm calling about, actually. I've just heard – the monks of Michelin will be at King any day. *L'Inspecteur* from the Avenue de Breteuil. The last thing I need is for the place to fall apart. In fact, I might need you to do me a favour."

48

Ambrose's favour didn't come for another two weeks. During that time, I had to sack Drusilla. She kept *looking* at me. She was spying on me, of course she was – if not for Max, for Ambrose. If not for Ambrose, for the newspapers. Indeed, there was another Bill Hastings exclusive, clearly placed by Max. It excoriated the so-called "aggressive and terrifying" conditions of my kitchen whilst quoting a source "at the heart of Mann's operation" that described the heavenly conditions enjoyed by his brigade: "If only the young pretender had learned the lessons generously offered by the elder Gent: you don't have to be a bully to make good food."

Can there be anyone, in any trade, who has enough ambition to lead their field and yet who doesn't dance at the very edge of what's permissible? Ambition itself compels it; insists upon it. And so it was with me. All the pressures of the kitchen coalesced into a sharp beam of fury: *this* piece of veal; *this* fillet of cod; *this* sautéed carrot. When the weight of all the world is focused onto a single badly trimmed broad bean, the effect is indistinguishable from madness.

The fortnight passed in a smear of working and drinking and drugging. Despite what the newspapers implied, I wasn't having fun. I could sense the shadow of the wave on my back and a part of me wanted to drown.

In the elms, a small clearing. Mary, gagged, faint and soiled. Flames at her feet as the children sang, "Earl's heart and earl's leafs and earl's lusts abounding. Earl's fires and earl's grace and earl's witch is burning." The finder man called out his charges: "Witchcraft is the product of Carnal Lusts which is in Women Insatiable. Mary Dor did make for the Devil a work of Vile Bewitchment and destroyed the Soul of Full Grown Men by depriving them of Grace, inclining their Minds to inordinate Passions and delivering their Bodies up to the punishments for Sin..."

The silvery flesh flies crawled out from the cracks in the mortar and the cracks in the beams and the dark weight of the attic. They crawled over Mary's bed and her crucifix. They swarmed over the herbs that were piled on the kitchen table. They tizzed and crackled on the fire, dropping into the glowing coals, a stench like burning hair filling the cottage.

They broke in a great turning cloud above the garden. Flies amongst the elms. Flies over the men and women who had gathered in the forest to watch Mary Dor burn. Flies on their arms and cheeks and necks and covering their children. And as they screamed, flies in their mouths and down their throats and licking the sticky whites of their eyes.

And I saw it all.

And I knew that I was the red and the yellow and the black.

And that black is always death.

49

Before showering, I forced myself to study my face in the mirror. I touched the reddish-purple bags beneath my eyes, the areas of dry skin around my nostrils, the hair-thin network of cuts that extended from the sore edges where my lips met, some freshly descended crumbs from a cocaine nosebleed. I pulled back and took in the entirety of my reflection in all its hollow melancholy – the shaved head, the damaged eyelid, the wax and granite shades of exhaustion. Ninety minutes later, I was behind my desk, studying the news, hunting for references to Max when Ambrose called.

"This is it," he said, his voice confidential and excited. "I've just heard. Michelin. *L'Inspecteur*. He's coming to dinner at King tonight."

"How have you found that out?" I asked.

"I was wondering if you'd mind hopping over to Gresse Street to help out a little," he said, ignoring my question. "Just for the service."

I couldn't quite believe it.

"Oversee the sauces, perhaps," he continued, more cautiously now. "Just for an hour or two."

A blur of chefs in white tunics flitted past my open door, like nervous ghosts.

"Okay, so is Max going to come and give me a bit of help

when it's my turn?" I said.

"That's hardly the point, Killian. Things at King —"

I stood up at my desk, the twisted cable tugging from the receiver and lifting the corner of the telephone off it.

"What about Glamis? What about *my* Michelin stars? Do you think Max gives one rocky bollock about that?"

"And what about *me*?"

I sat, slowly, back in my chair, cowed by this rare show of fury.

"Where's your fucking *loyalty*, man? Where's your gratitude? If you want to fuck off and start your own place then be my guest and fuck off. No one's going to go bankrupt without you, least of all me. We'll all have simpler, more enjoyable lives without you. You are bringing a downmarket tone to my group as it is. I don't care what you think of Max. Your ridiculous falling-out is of no interest to me. But the man is not well at the moment and I am asking you to do a favour for me. Just for one service. Just one. For God's sake, man, do you realise what it'll do to him if he doesn't get his third star? After the year he's had? Have you even thought about that for one moment? And you know full well that if Glamis isn't awarded any stars whatsoever it will have no effect on the bottom line. We'll still be drowning in bookings. It won't make a scrap of difference to the money we're making."

"And the same goes for Max. He's booked up for months!"

There was a silence.

"Isn't he?" I said.

Ambrose cleared his throat.

"I think it would be fair to say the winds are, perhaps, shifting just a little."

"Well, I just can't believe you're asking me this."

"Killian, you're the best saucier in Europe. Easily. Why wouldn't I want to tactically deploy my finest employee for the good of the group? And you must realise, it does you no good to put King and its reputation at risk."

"It doesn't make any difference to me whatsoever."

"Killian, you're not thinking cleverly enough. You're too hot-headed. I mean Max..." His voice took on an arachnid thinness. "You need to think long term about this. About your future and where it might lead."

My eyes skittered guiltily about the empty room.

"Two thirty," he said. "I want you there. Just to support him. Help him along a little."

I licked my lips with a dry tongue, feeling each crease and blister of their cracked surfaces.

"Two thirty," I said. "Fine."

"Oh, and Killian. The *Food and Drink* people want to come in on Friday. They couldn't get hold of you, they said. No one at Glamis would return their calls. I told them fine. I take it that that will not be a problem for any reason?"

I could tell, from the way he said it, that the wrong answer now would be dangerous.

"Well–"

"Good. Goodbye."

I looked at the receiver in the moments after I put it down. I watched as it goaded me and then, not even trying to resist, I picked it back up and phoned Kathryn. She was weeping before she even said hello this time. I listened for a few seconds, then gently hung up.

I sat there, staring at the backs of my hands, my mind comfortably disengaged. I found myself presented with an idea. And I believed it was a good idea – the *right* idea – because of the silence. For months the noise in my head had been cease-less: the anxieties would fade in and out, weaving their way between the imagined scenes with Max, the agonising over the herbs, the running of the brigade, the wondering about Dor – all these lines of logic, words moving through wires, conversations held with different versions of myself that would go here and there and back here again and end up, frequently, with one half shouting at the other half and my resorting to rocking in my chair or using the paring knife that I had taken to carrying around in my pocket, with its split little plastic cover over the blade.

I had once read that wind is nature's restless attempt at filling voids in the atmosphere, and that was just what the noise in my head had come to feel like: great blusters of dissonance that blew around up there. They were my brain's continual attempts at finding a solution, at thinking its way back to silence. And that's what I heard, when this idea presented itself. Calm. Peace. Nothing at all.

I looked up as Marco walked past my door.

"Marco!"

He reversed, popping his head in, a strand of curly hair slipping down over his eyes.

"Chef?"

"Something's come up. Can you take over for the rest of the day?"

"Yes, Chef," he said. "Not a problem."

I pulled my coat on, ran to my car and drove back to Dor.

50

I walked past the crates of Perrier and over the discarded ring-pulls that were pressed into the cobbles and checked the inside of my apron pocket one more time. Yes, good. The three ancient gifts of Dor were still there. Then, with just one step, I was inside the music of King once again. In front of me was the line of fretful apprentices, their pink fingers on blue-grey steel surfaces, their blades flashing over basil and chervil and mango and tomato and raspberry and lime. I could sense the wave of thrilled alarm go through them as I passed and headed into that subterranean rectangle of smells and sounds and magic. There they were, all in place, the commis chefs, the first commis, the *demi chefs de partie*, the *chefs de partie*, working studiously, precisely, standing with their legs apart so they didn't have to bend so low over the counter, all of them in that peculiar state of concentrated determination that is so close to anger. The brigade looked so much a part of the kitchen, it was hard to believe that they all had different lives outside of it: different beds, different girlfriends, different histories in different towns.

None of them acknowledged my presence as I walked behind them, past the shelves stacked high with pans and dishes, the hissing stoves, the blue flames surging thickly through black-ened steel burners, the dented grill trays, the rows of hanging cleavers and ladles and copper saucepans and the oven with the door that didn't quite close. If I was to take over this place for Kathryn, I realised we'd probably have a battle with them. But that was okay. If I found that any of these chefs lacked the loyalty to follow their new leader, I knew I had the teeth, the breeding, to deal with them. And, tonight, I had something else. Two pouches of herbs from Dor. It was still unclear to me what their effects might be. All I knew was what the book in the attic had said: that the Hindeling caused a madness of the mind, whilst the Cauter somehow affected the body.

I walked through to the restaurant floor where Max was sitting in a corner, the Maître d' pouring him a drink from his pot of peppermint tea. He was staring out of the front window as the waiters moved about him ironing fresh tablecloths for the evening. Down by his lap, he was holding a menu, the corners of which were shaking, very slightly, in his hands.

"Chef?" I said. His trance broken, he looked at me for a second, his eyes tracking over me.

"Good morning," he said.

"Ambrose said –"

"Yes, yes, I know why you're here." He put the menu down. "Such confidence he has in me."

I thought about the charming, confident Gentleman Chef that appeared on Wogan two years ago; the one I'd watched again and again on the video.

"Well, it's an important night," I said, softly.

His eyes flickered down. He appeared injured, somehow. Humbled. As bad as I knew his depressed days could be, I'd never seen him like this.

"Chef, I just wanted to say, I know you don't need me here," I said. "I don't know why Ambrose has got it into his head that you do. But I suppose we might as well humour him."

His eyes tracked the menu. His top pocket, which usually held a brand new biro, hung empty.

"I'll go and make myself busy," I said. "I'm sure there's some prep I can help with. Tangerines or something."

"No pips," he said, without looking up.

"No pips," I replied with a smile.

For the next few hours, I was aware only of the squalls of murmur and laughter that were surely directed at me, gathering and then blowing themselves out as I passed by here and there. I was troubled more by the kitchen's haunted places: the stations at the cold pass where Kathryn and I had fallen in love; the freezer door where she had told me her name; even the corridor where I had first seen Max, feeling as if his presence was lit by rays that had escaped from heaven.

"Brigade," said Max when he emerged for service. He stood, leaning against the pass, the shadowless light falling greenish blue over his face. "Y-you all know how important tonight is for us."

He pointed his finger and panned it across the kitchen. I imagined that every one of his white-robed charges felt as I did – as if his cold, trembling digit had physically touched their skin.

"N-n-no mistakes. I don't care who you are, how long you've worked here. You will vanish. Out in the courtyard. G-gone."

"*Oui*, Chef."

His eyes flickered to each man in a pre-emptive strike of slithery accusation and I knew the fear they were feeling and I was desperate for them to know, despite their apparent contempt for me, that I was here to rescue them from this deathly man. He talked, his voice monotone and dry, and I saw his words as maths, as algebra, as lines of code – cold instructions from a dead machine, every one designed by a bloodless unit with only one function: to win and, by doing so, to make me fail.

When he was finished, I approached him. He seemed to have shut down, momentarily, and was just standing there alone, his limbs on hold, his gaze bland and unattached.

"I know you don't need any help on sauces, Chef," I said. "But I could just hang about in the general area, just in case."

I could feel my heart throb in the scabs on my arms. I knew: it all came down to now.

He glanced towards the cold pass, where the apprentices were working in anxious silence.

"You know, just the benefit of another set of eyes on a service like this. Can't do any harm."

He nodded, smally. A fly passed his eye-line. He batted after it rather feebly.

"Yes, fine," he said. "*Bon.*"

"Thank you, Chef," I said.

Then, behind me, a familiar voice: "Actually, I could really do with Killian in pastry tonight, Chef." It was Andy. I had heard he was back at King, but I was unprepared for the actual sight of him here, happily employed in Max's kitchen. I felt a jolt of ugly power. He was looking right past me – sleeves up, spatula in hand and a small thumb-smudge of icing sugar on his purposefully set jaw. Max returned Andy's request with an uncertain frown.

"Don't you think that would be a bit of a waste, Chef?" I said. "I'm best on sauces." I glared at Andy. I dared him to speak. "I mean, you know, sauces is what I'm best at. That's what I'm known for, isn't it?"

Max darkened, suddenly provoked. "*Non.*" He dismissed me with a small, limp wave. "Go with Andy."

* * *

I followed Andy into the pastry area, watching his bowed, slightly bouncy legs as they took me to the far end of the kitchen, around the corner from the sink where the fish was washed and de-scaled. I was effectively alone with him, amongst trays of empty pastry boats, a batch of freshly rinsed cumquats lined up on paper towels like miniature suns and, hanging from a shelf, tonight's special instructions – four birthdays and a golden wedding anniversary.

"So what do you want me to do?" I said.

He picked up his spatula from where he'd left it, next to the cumquats.

"Nothing at all. I want you here, out of harm's way."

It was having a strange effect on me, being back at King. My limbs felt gangly and awkward. My hands couldn't decide where to settle. Suddenly, I felt my age.

"How's Kathryn?" I said.

"I've not really seen her," he said. "I don't know what happened between you two, but she's barely spoken to anyone. She's with her mum today, I think."

I couldn't let myself be distracted by thoughts of Kathryn. I pictured those dogs, working the wheel.

"Ambrose has told me to help out on sauces tonight," I said, "so I might not be able to be in pastry for lo–"

He interrupted me. "You're staying here."

His environment had a magnifying effect on him. He appeared an absolute master of his workspace; as if the boundary between him and the kitchen was merely academic.

"Oh, you don't still believe those stories about me drugging people, do you?" I said. "It's like a conspiracy theory. Come on, mate," I smiled chummily. "You'll be accusing me of faking the moon landings next."

He didn't move. "If you try anything," he said, "I promise, I will make sure you regret it."

"Give over, Andy," I said. I put my hands on my hips. "Come off it, mate."

"With my contacts in the press," he said, "I could ruin your

346

reputation for ever. Don't forget that."

I gave him a small, dismissive laugh.

"That's funny, is it?" he said. "You saw that Bill Hastings piece? The *News of the World*?" He gave a satisfied nod before adding, almost reluctantly, "On Max's instructions, of course."

I rubbed my eyes, resignedly and said, simply, "Cunt." I thought for a moment, as Andy became distracted by the tumble of flies that had invaded the space over his station. "And I bet it was you that leaked about Max too, wasn't it?" I said, as he shooed them off. "When I was at King? You're on a little power trip with all your journo mates, that's what this is all about. I'm sure it's very helpful, having all those contacts. The problem with you is that you don't care about anything but your career."

He giggled as if lightly amused by some passing gibberish.

"How dare you think you can cheat your way to the top? Do you have any idea at all how hard I've worked to get here? How hard Max has worked? How hard we've *all* worked?"

I took a step closer and lowered my voice. I would have to be careful.

"It's about justice. Everyone thinks he's so nice, 'The Gentleman Chef', but he's evil."

"But haven't you noticed? No one's leaving. We all stay here, don't we? Do you know why? We're loyal to him. One hundred per cent. We might bitch about him. We might hate him at the end of a rough service. But the truth is, we'd fucking die for him."

Above and between our words could be heard the delicious music of the chefs of King. That they made it so perfectly without me felt like an insult. He was right, wasn't he? They loved him.

"They hate him," I said. "Every one of them. You don't give a shit about Max. You're not loyal to him; he's just your leg-up to the next kitchen. You told tales in the press about him, for Christ's sake! Nice little thrill, was it, seeing it in the paper?" I shook my head. "And anyway, all he's doing is training another army of psychos who will open their own kitchens and then bully anyone they don't like into giving up. He's despicable. He's a virus."

Andy leaned forward, his lip curling spitefully, exposing his yellowy teeth.

"You just don't get it, do you, Killian?" he said. "You're the bad guy. *You're the bad guy.*"

I walked past him slowly, feigning confusion, and began washing my hands at a small sink, letting the fine little bubbles of soft warm water run soothingly over my skin.

"This is ridiculous," I said. "You've got some weird things in your head, mate."

With that, we began working and continued in silence, preparing soufflés and baking meringues. At about twenty to eight that evening, there was a sudden drop as Max clapped three times.

"H-he's here. The inspector. Table 7."

Soon afterwards, I heard the unmistakable sound of Max at full hiss at the top of the kitchen. I peered around the corner. Poor Carlo. He was getting it again. There was a queue of four waiters bunched up at the pass, none of whom seemed sure which trays they should be taking, all of them too terrified to interrupt and ask. I said, to no response, "I've never seen it like this. It's a mess. Is this what's it's been like?" I had to do it now. Even if I had to physically fight Andy, I had to do it now.

"I need the toilet," I said. "You're not going to stop me going to the toilet." He didn't lift his head from where he was bending over his tray of kiwi marzipan petits fours.

"Two minutes, and I'm breaking down the door."

I paced around the corner, past the washing-up area where Danno the pots man was aiming the flexible steel hose at a stack of heat-warped baking trays, out of the door and into the room beneath the stairs where Max and Patrick had given me my palate test. In amongst the cleaning products and miscellaneous mops and traps there was, I remembered, a box of spare pepper grinders. I closed the door, switched on the light, and fumbled noisily about the shelves. The fat plastic packets and metal cans and cardboard boxes were seemingly frozen in disapproving silence as I hunted.

It took too long to find them – they'd been moved to a bottom shelf, next to an old split case of damp-damaged scourers. Cursing silently, I unscrewed the top of a grinder, my eyes continually darting to the shut door as I tipped a pile of Cauter seeds into my palm. In the book I'd found in the attic, it had said that these dark little balls – which looked exactly like half-sized peppercorns, bar a slight purple tint – were what caused a "madness of the body", whatever that was. There were nine or ten of the pellets within each of the herb's spiny flowers and I had no idea what they would do as I filled the grinder and slipped out of the cupboard. I wasn't even wondering: my rational mind was still in its perfectly silent state.

Corralling all lessons I'd ever learned about remaining unnoticed, I crept back into the kitchen. I could tell that it was approaching its point of maximum stress. Like a ship's hull at the height of a storm, you could almost hear the walls creaking and groaning with the pressures that were bearing down on it. Up at the meat station, Patrick was a porcine hunk of sweat, fat and acne leaning over his sauté pans. He looked barely more alive than the animals he was cooking, the straining little white-heads poking like poisonous mushrooms through the fine copper hairs of his half-grown moustache. As I approached him, I realised that there were a couple of silvery flies in the air about me. No, there were more than that. Four, *five* of them, at least. Ignoring the insects, I scoped the little pinch-pots of sea salt and freshly cracked pepper he kept nearby and carefully knocked them onto the floor with my elbow. He was in such a well of concentration that he could only find the space to mumble, "Twat."

I tutted showily at my apparent clumsiness and ran with the empty receptacles to the store where the spare salt and pepper were kept. I refilled his pots with salt and a half-pepper, half-Cauter mix and placed them gently back at his side, before doing a small tour of the kitchen, helpfully refilling the salt and pepper of all the chefs, being generous with my grinds of the Dor seeds. By the time I was finished, I knew that hardly a dish would now go out that didn't have at least a dusting of my ancestor's herb either on it or in it.

Before making my way to the exit, I palmed a couple of shredded Hindeling leaves and added them to a fresh brew of peppermint tea which I brought to Max. I placed the pot down on the pass and smiled at the sight of him sending his polar stare into the two guinea-fowl with caramel and mango that had just arrived in front of him.

"I've given Andy a help on pastry," I said, as he towelled a fingerprint off the side of a plate. "He was in trouble for a bit back there, believe it or not. Everything's motoring along perfectly now. And I've had a quick tour of the kitchen. You don't need my help at all. You've got an amazing team here." I began to untie my apron strings as he gave the dishes one final squinting examination. "You'll be fine, Max," I said. "With the Michelin guy, I mean. Easy."

I thought he was going to turn away, but he looked straight at me.

"You think?" he said. I felt myself automatically formulating a response that assumed he was being sarcastic. But something stopped me. "Yeah," I said, carefully. "Yes. For sure."

And then, watching the waitress pick up the tray, he wiped his hands against themselves and muttered, "Yes, well, good. Thanks."

"Sorry?"

He faced me, his rain-coloured eyes hopeful and open. The oxygen vanished from my throat.

"Thank you, Killian. For your help."

I had this insane urge to hold him, to push my head into his chest. I put my arm out to pick the teapot back up, but the maître d' swooped in first and grabbed it, intending to pour him a cup. My hand lingered over the spout for a moment, enjoying the pain of the steam. I left, as quickly as was possible, before I had to watch him drink.

51

I stalked out of the blue double doors, through the darkness of Stephen Mews and crossed Gresse Street with my head down. Hanging in the shadows by the post office over the road, a freezing wind blew around my face and, in it, I could smell cold concrete and the vague sweetly spiced waft of a distant cigarette, above the sickly yellow pong of fat and scorch that rose from my skin.

I had to wait, to watch. Above the silhouetted rectangular hedges I could see two oblongs of golden light – the windows into the dining room, the occasional shape of a beautiful waitress gliding with magnificent sex and ease around the tables, bending over the diners to serve. It was about half past eight when I became aware of the first strange noise. I crept forward, back over the road, so I could hear better. It was like a great, ribitting frog. I peered up at the window. An overweight man in a pinstripe suit and braces had begun hiccupping violently. An elderly woman at Table 3 looked on at him, making a great show of her shock at his apparent rudeness. Then, she let out a hiccup so powerful that it appeared to pull her a little way off her seat. Her narrow hand sprang to her mouth as her dining partner reached over to help her. It seemed that she was struggling for breath. I stepped back, nervously.

Shortly afterwards, a middle-aged diner in a tweed jacket and plum trousers stood up abruptly and walked, with all the haste that appearances would permit, towards the bathroom. Did he run the final few yards? Then a woman in a sequinned dress followed him. I watched as the initial intermittent hurry for the toilets became a small charge. A black vase fell on a tablecloth, spilling its water and partially ejecting a white orchid. A fork bounced onto the carpet. A chair tipped back.

Soon, the polite and sporadic disarray had deteriorated into general pandemonium. There were hiccups and dry heaving and demands for service and cries of outrage all merging together, discordant and confusing and muffled on the other side of the window. There were hands over mouths and torsos doubling up and then vomit – livid mauve-and-dun-coloured pulses of it – pouring between fat knuckles and delicate jewelled fingers, hitting crystal glasses and drenching cutlery. The waitresses reared in horror. Some began rushing around with towels, others crouched down by those who appeared especially help-less, but most just ran for the shelter of the kitchen. A woman in a peppermint-green skirt charged towards the bathroom in her heels, pushing a waitress out of the way, a light stain appearing on the back of her dress. All was hysteria. All was frenzy. All was terror. The air in the room had become hectic with hurtling insects. They appeared to be revelling in the bedlam, dancing above heads and settling greedily onto human fluids. I saw a man, dining alone, his face pale, his nose with an aristocratic bent, his suit ill-fitting old corduroy. He was at Table 7. The inspector! He looked about the room with mad alarm and then hunched forwards, as if struck powerfully on the neck, and exhaled a bright flume of bile. And then, a face in the back-ground, staring in ashen despair directly at him. Max.

I pulled myself back into the shadows and retreated across the road to the safety of the dark post office. The restaurant's front door opened. A woman in a short red skirt burst out as if kicked from behind. She pushed her head as far over the steel railing as she could and held the base of her neck as a long hose of vomit emerged from her stretched mouth. It came and it came and it came and she fell to her knees, curled up like a baby lamb, as the eruptions faltered and she began coughing up phlegmy gobs of thick slurry, each one accompanied by gross abdominal tremors. I watched with fascinated detachment as she retched and whimpered, too exhausted to cry, too distressed to care about her tall stiletto tumbling down the steps, her chin coated in a sticky beard of filth, her hand grabbing weakly at her bottom, which – judging by her movements – was also now expelling liquid in curious pumping little spurts. Her sobs came out in time with her breaths and only when she wasn't desperately heaving out more of the weird fudgy matter from her throat. Soon, she began making a mysterious and inhuman groaning sound. Flies landed on her face. She was too weak to brush them away.

Ten minutes later, a taxi pulled up and a photographer jumped out. There were sirens. An ambulance. Then another, their red and blue lights stroking the surface of Ambrose's upstairs office window and the walls of the Bricklayer's Arms and the craning faces of the curious drinkers that were now bubbling through its doors. I crept away in the orange-cloaked darkness, tiny in the vast city, its endless glowing web of streets crawling out around me in all directions, all over the country and all over the floating world, and me just a pale nothing, just a slip of skin and bone, alone in the anonymous quiet.

52

I arrived home to find Dor Cottage squatting in its square of night like a fat, satisfied toad, the moonlight reflecting in the dark eye of its attic window. It sat there and watched me, that great form of age and gathering mayhem, as I climbed out of the car and into the restless wind, the elms creaking around me. I stood there for a moment and tried to stare it down. I shouted, "Go on, then!" in its direction and paused nervously to see if anything would happen. It remained silent, scowling, insulted by the weather.

I let myself in and sat alone in the kitchen with an unscrewed bottle of Bell's whisky. The light laid itself over the contours of the glass and swam, as if panicking, inside the liquid. There was a thud from upstairs. I poured another large glass and drank it down. Nothing happened for a while. A repetitive knocking noise came from the lounge. It was the wind. It must be the wind. The sound abruptly stopped. I continued to drink. Feeling the whisky working its soft magic, I crawled on top of the table. I wouldn't take this. This was *my* house. I pulled myself to my feet and roared down at the space where she had stood.

"Aunty! Where are you? I can hear you." I paused. Nothing. "Please, Aunty! Aunty! I'm sorry. I'm *sorry*. I need you!"

A fly buzzed past and landed on my foot. Shaking it off, I climbed down from the table, lowering myself with unsteady legs. Another, different noise floated down from upstairs. Low, like the murmur of a faraway crowd.

I took a long draft of the whisky and waited, wondering what to do. I looked at the range, its dead black mass under the chimney, the holes where the spit used to be still visible in the fireplace walls. I looked at the surface of the old oaken table, the lines and notches that I'd known as a boy and that Dorothy must surely have known as a girl. I looked at the shelves and the jars and the prongs and the shredders and the pots and the small bale of drying Earl's Leaf on the sheets of newspaper that I'd gathered last week and hadn't managed to get through. I looked at everything in the room except the place that seemed to be inviting me; taunting me.

I stepped forward and peered into the darkness over the stairs. Another fly startled me, emerging from up there at speed and coming directly at me. I ducked to the side and followed its path as it disappeared towards the lounge. I wondered how many of them were in here, in this cottage? Studying me in their skittering way, from the beams and the cracks in the mortar? There was another noise from upstairs. It seemed to be coming from the attic.

I began climbing. When I finally reached the corridor, the murmuring had become even louder. It had a mechanistic quality about it. A sense of teeming. I came to a halt beneath the attic door.

It was creaking; groaning with a kind of weight. I looked up. Something came from the gap between the door and its frame. It popped out, darted through the air and went for the stairs. A fly. I squinted, looking closer. There were more of them: flies squeezing themselves out of the loft, their legs hauling their silvery bodies through and then, as they achieved their freedom, accelerating suddenly.

I retreated back to the lounge and tried to sleep in Dorothy's armchair, but ended up just drinking most of the whisky. I was roused from a bleary daze by the sound of the phone ringing, drunk enough that, momentarily, I didn't know what the noise was. I picked up the receiver.

"Kathryn?"

There was a sound amidst the static: a kind of swallowed gasp.

"Ambrose?"

"It's sad news, Killian," he said. "Terrible, awful news. I, er..."

I couldn't work out what was happening.

"Ambrose? Are you okay?"

"It's Max. He's dead."

There was a moment of blankness before my emotions caught up with what I had been told.

"But why? How?"

My mind scrabbled for sense. What had happened? The book had said three herbs taken at once would lead to death. Max had only had the Hindeling and that was supposed to do nothing more than cause some sort of "madness of the mind".

"It's not true," I said. "It can't be. It doesn't make sense."

"Oh, Killian, he hanged himself," said Ambrose. "There was the most horrific outbreak of food poisoning at King. Just unbelievable. Rivers of faeces and vomit. Beyond belief. Streams of it running across the floor. And flies – flies everywhere. I saw one old man, seventy years old at least, vomiting faeces. I can't imagine how it's happened." There was a pause. "I don't suppose you have any idea?"

"I left early," I said. "I just did a bit on pastry and left. I wasn't there for most of the night."

I heard static. I heard the wind. I heard my heartbeat.

"Your voice," said Ambrose, eventually. "Killian, you sound scared."

I heard that creaking noise again.

"Why are you scared, Killian?"

"It's, no – I'm sad."

"Patrick tells me you were tampering with the salt and pepper."

"I was refilling it."

"I'm going to have it tested."

"Why would you want to do that?"

"Your voice is shaking, Killian."

"I was helping Max," I said. "I was only trying to help."

"Killian Lone, you will listen to me now. I do not believe you weren't involved in this somehow. If this is true..." I stood there and listened breathlessly, as my silence made up his mind. "You have destroyed my business, you have destroyed my friend –"

Before Ambrose could finish, I put the phone down, then let the receiver hang. I dropped to the floor, where I let out a single, animal roar. I took my two largest knives from a kitchen drawer and walked outside, through the high gates and into the physic garden.

The old walls stretched on into the darkness, the elms rising behind them like a mob of sentinels, their straight trunks disappearing fearlessly up into the black heights. The plants, all arranged in their neat rows, bowed and whinnied under the pressure of the wind and looked as if they were joyously celebrating my arrival, each individual stem baying for attention. Through the crowding insects, I began swiping at their bases with my knives, grunting with each strike, the wind blowing them into my face, slices of leaf sticking to my wrists and arms and neck. My back ached and my hands complained at the pain of the cold as I pushed deeper and deeper in, cutting and pulling up roots, the smell of damp earth and chloroform steeping in the air.

Soon, my fingers were bleeding and my knives blunting. I

realised I had only cut down perhaps a sixth of the plantation. I ran back inside and found, in a box in the bathroom, two old hairspray aerosols. I pulled a rusting can of Castrol out of the shed and splashed what was left of it as far as I could over the plants. Lighting a match in front of the spray, I sent a plume of red fire straight into the garden and it was quickly engulfed in a breathing monster of strange violet flame.

It was the noise of the car pulling up that finally made me halt. I looked around, half expecting the blue lights of police cars. But it wasn't the police. Small and trembling in the feral madness of the countryside, it was Kathryn.

I braced myself for the onslaught of fury. She took in the sight of the fire and ran for me, throwing her arms around me.

"What did you do?" she said.

"Nothing!"

"You killed him, Killian. You *killed* him."

"I thought he was stronger," I said.

She looked at me, a huddle of shivers and tears and wild feeling.

"I don't know what happened, Kathryn," I said.

Slowly, she let me have more and more of her weight. "You made me love you," she said, eventually, into my arm. "You made me love you. And now look."

I couldn't take any more. I collapsed, pulling her to the floor. We sat there, sprawled in the mud as I pushed my thumbs into her cheeks.

"You're the only one I can be normal with, Kathryn. You make me normal." I grabbed her face hard and tipped it. I forced her to look at me. "I don't know how it works, Kathryn. I tried. I tried really hard but I always got it wrong. I don't understand how anything works. Without you I'm awful."

I squeezed harder, feeling the bones of her skull under my thumbs. She looked back at me, her eyes fractured red. A long tear worked its way towards the soft boundary of her jaw. I squashed it in its passage.

"Do you think I'm bad? Do you think I'm a bad man? Kathryn, I'm scared."

I let go of her face and began to sob.

"I don't think there are bad people. It's just – ordinary people sometimes think themselves into bad places. They look like good places but they're not."

"I tried to be good. I tried to always choose the *right* thing to do. But how do you know? How do you tell?"

She closed her eyes.

"Stay there," I said. "Wait. I have to get something."

I pushed myself to my feet and staggered towards the raging herb garden, to the far right corner where the stems, still unburned, groaned and waved in fear of the approaching heat. Carefully choosing one fat specimen each of Hindeling, Cauter and Earl's Leaf, I made no attempt to bat away the flies which were humming around my head; circling and swooping and playing.

I kneeled back down in the mud, my knees damp and cold, and, taking her hands, I made myself smile.

"Kathryn, it's going to be okay," I said.

"No, it's not," she said. "How can it ever be okay? Everything could have been so good. Killian, I don't have anyone. And then *you*... I thought I could be happy. And now you've done what you've done and I can't be with you any more. I can't... I'm *nothing* again. I'm invisible."

I pressed her palms and gathered my courage as the heat made a noisy and sudden advance.

"Stop now," I said, gently. "It's okay. You're going to be okay. You know, I filled in the will ages ago. Dor is going to be yours. And I'll never leave you. I will prove to you that loyalty can be good. I'll always be with you. I promise."

I lifted the three leaves and put them in my mouth. I wasn't aware of any flavour, just a feeling of prickling numbness as I bit into them. Kathryn's gaze sharpened.

"What are you doing?" she said.

A dead sensation hit my throat. It sank past my heart and into my stomach. I slumped a little. Over at the cottage, there was a rising rattling noise, as if it was being bombarded from the inside, and then a crack of something breaking and a low, deafening hum.

Kathryn's eyes grew huge at the sight, her fingers tensing as her neck craned up in horror. A black column of flies coursed into the filthy sky, moving and twisting up and up. It swarmed into the coming dawn like smoke and then came for us, spreading over the physic garden, a hundred thousand insects landing, silver and black and red, on stems and leaves and the stone faces of the gargoyles and into the fire where they fizzed and singed.

"It's okay, Kathryn," I said. "It's okay, my love. Don't be scared. You're going to be happy now. I've made everything okay."

She wailed at the final realisation of what I had done. The sight of her doing so overwhelmed me. I wasn't ready yet. I had to see her happy.

"Smile for me," I said. "Please smile for me, just once."

"No, no, no, no," she sobbed. "Not this, Kill. Not this, *please*."

"Just *smile*, Kathryn. Once more." I tried to look happy for her. "You can promise me something. You'll make son-in-law eggs."

Impossibly, her eyes lifted and shone for a moment. But they fell with the realisation that I had now become too weak to speak. I knew that her hand on my face would be the last thing I would feel of her. I rocked softly back as it all drained away.

Nine years of this pretence, this desperate game, this fantasy of strength – it left me as if it had never happened at all. I was eleven years old again. A boy, never a dog.

My breaths became forced, dragging at the back of my throat and catching in my chest. I attempted to keep my eyes open.

"We're fuck-ups, aren't we?" I whispered.

Kathryn, whimpering and shaking her head, stroked my face with her fingers. The tears running in trails down her cheeks and the flames glowing against her beautiful birthmark and chocolate-spray freckles, she forced a final smile. "Fuck-ups together," she said.

I fought, for as long as possible, to keep Kathryn in focus. I struggled to keep it all in view: her quick, smart mouth and her green- and gold-speckled irises and her rich brown hair all bunched in the rain. There she is, my wonderful girl. There she goes.

By the time Kathryn had gathered the courage to go into the house to call the ambulance, a gap in the dirt-coloured ceiling of cloud had opened up. When the sirens finally approached, a dart of dawn sun hit what remained of the top attic window. Two hours later, the herbs were reduced to sporadic blackened stems, the earth hot and black and giving out little eddies of smoke here and there. The morning's fresh light touched the stone gargoyles that guarded the physic garden. The elms fell silent.

On the day that Kathryn finally moved into the cottage, the kitchen seemed so warm and calm and beautiful, it felt as if its ancient walls were welcoming her arrival. Placing the first of her boxes on the table, she sat and wept a little. Then she climbed the stairs, gingerly opened the door of the front bedroom and closed the curtains against the tumult of light that was rushing in through the window and breaking against the walls. Laying herself on the bed, she sank into the deepest of sleeps. She dreamed of fire and knives and turnspit dogs; of boiling bones and blood under the fingernails of men.

Before the summer came to an end, she had a new wall built, higher than ever, to shutter in the gargoyles and barricade out the Earl's trees. The mischief became quiet. The old trouble slept. And Kathryn's life at Dor became one of stillness and *distance and memory.*

But our story never dimmed. It remained, ever present; waiting, watching; an unquiet frequency, a language of sighs that filled the rooms; an old tale remaining stubbornly unfinished.

And then, the long and wearying sickness; the same one that took her mother.

And now, her death. The walls of Dor Cottage breathing in.

An expectancy.

I can feel her coming now. I can feel our story finally coming to an end.

Acknowledgments

Many of the kitchen incidents in this book are based on real reported events. Sections of language and dialogue in the dream sequences were sourced from period material. I am hugely indebted to the great chefs Michel Roux Jnr and Guillaume Brahimi who granted me permission to work double shifts and interview chefs and apprentices at their restaurants Le Gavroche in London and Guillaume at Bennelong in Sydney. Needless to say, you won't find any of the gruesome events or characters that appear in these pages in their kitchens. Of all the books I read to research this novel, none was anywhere near as valuable as *The Perfectionist* by Rudolph Chelminski – a goldmine of insight as well as useful facts and observations. If you enjoyed the story of Killian Lone, then I urge you to track down his wonderful biography of the brilliant yet tormented chef Bernard Loiseau.

I am indebted to the array of talented writers who were kind enough to offer honest criticism throughout the four years that I worked on this manuscript. I owe thanks to Posie Graeme Evans and Lucy Dawson, undying gratitude to Rodge Glass and Edward Hogan and whatever it is that comes after that to my wonderful friend, Craig Pierce, who offered bracingly honest and insightful notes at no less than three separate stages – a truly heroic effort, and I have learned so much from it. Thank you.

Thanks also to Ann Eve, Jess Porter, Erin Kelly, Jonathan at The Bookseller Crow, John & Tam, Kirsten Galliott, Ross Jones, Emily Hayward Whitlock, Vanessa Beaumont, David Isaacs – one of the finest editors I've worked with – and all at Short Books in the UK and Allen & Unwin in Australia.

And very special thanks to my fantastic and fantastically patient agent Charlie Campbell, without whose wise counsel I would not have finished this book.

And bows, finally, to my beautiful and brilliant wife Farrah.

Will Storr is a longform journalist and novelist. His features have appeared in many magazines and broadsheet newspaper supplements in the UK and Australia, including the *Guardian Weekend*, the *Telegraph Magazine*, the *Observer Magazine*, *GQ* and the *Sydney Morning Herald (Good Weekend)*. He is a contributing editor at *Esquire* magazine. His radio documentaries have been broadcast on *BBC World*.

He has reported from the refugee camps of Africa, the war-torn departments of rural Colombia and the remote Aboriginal communities of Australia.

He has been named New Journalist of the Year and Feature Writer of the Year, and has won a National Press Club award for excellence. In 2010, his investigation into the kangaroo meat industry won the Australian Food Media award for Best Investigative Journalism and, in 2012, he was presented with the One World Press award and the Amnesty International award for his work for the *Observer* on sexual violence against men.

He is also a widely published photographer.